SWARM

swarm

a novel

LAUREN CARTER

Brindle & Glass Publishing Ltd.
brindleandglass.com

LIBRARY AND ARCHIVES CANADA CATALOGUING IN PUBLICATION
Carter, Lauren, 1972–
Swarm / Lauren Carter.

Issued also in electronic format.
ISBN 978-1-927366-20-2

I. Title.

P.S8605.A863S83 2013 C813'.6 C2013-902021-7

Editor: Lee Shedden
Proofreader: Heather Sangster, Strong Finish
Design: Pete Kohut
Cover illustration: Natalie Egnatchik, natalieimagines.com
Author photo: Jason Mills
Information on permissions for quoted material on page 281.

 Canadian Heritage Patrimoine canadien

Canada Council for the Arts Conseil des Arts du Canada

Brindle & Glass is pleased to acknowledge the financial support for its publishing program from the Government of Canada through the Canada Book Fund, Canada Council for the Arts, and the Province of British Columbia through the British Columbia Arts Council and the Book Publishing Tax Credit.

The interior pages of this book have been printed on 100% post-consumer recycled paper, processed chlorine free, and printed with vegetable-based inks.

1 2 3 4 5 17 16 15 14 13

PRINTED IN CANADA

For my mother.

The god of the bees is the future.
—Maurice Maeterlinck

Go, entrust your wound to a surgeon,
for flies will gather around the wound
until it can't be seen.
These are your selfish thoughts
and all you dream of owning.
The wound is your own dark hole.
—Rumi

1 Island

By the time I noticed you, Melissa, the supply ship was nine days late. Thomson had taken to rotating between resting spots—the couch, the chaise lounge, and, less often, his bed—while he grew sicker, waiting for the boat to deliver his pills. I was in the garden, tilling the soil, trying to encourage a larger bounty of tomatoes and collard greens, when I saw it. Your footprint. A dent in the earth as if a stone had been removed. Five toes, the heel no bigger than a head of garlic. A yellow zucchini flower curled over its crumbling edge. I stood and looked around—Thomson on his chaise lounge on the porch, Marvin invisible, out on the water, setting his nets. I lifted the thick green stalk half hiding your footprint and touched the hollow of your baby toe. So small. Quickly I buried the evidence: nudged the hole closed with the toe of my boot and went back to work. Tearing out the arugula that had gone to seed. Thinning the crowded beets.

Marvin acted unconcerned about the ship. "It's been late before," he said, reminding us of the time nearly three weeks passed before it sailed up to the town dock. It came from Midland, a larger city on the other side of the bay, loaded with donated rations and trade goods: luxuries like flour from the mills down south, sugar from Ohio beets, and a doctor who did his rounds, weighing babies on a battered chrome scale and delivering medicine like the prescriptions that shrank the shadows in Thomson's lungs.

Days earlier, I'd tipped the last of Thomson's pills into my palm and fed them to him with a ceramic cup of lake water. I hadn't wanted to tell him there weren't any left. But when I did, he only twisted his head to look toward our garden, the blue-shingled shed, the stand of pines and through the trees to the lake, which is always changing. The water moves from blue to turquoise-green to grey to no-colour, just a sheet of reflected sunlight like a large mirror you can lose yourself in. He didn't say a word.

Most summer days we eat the evening meal together. Like family, like normal. I lay out the tarnished cutlery the way my mother taught me—knives and spoons on the right, forks on the left. I enjoy it even though the plates are usually half empty—a dark slice of boiled beet, forest greens, a scrap of squirrel or fresh fish if Marvin's catch was big enough. In late fall and winter and early spring we don't do it like that. The table gets shoved into a corner and sits there, taunting. Last year I had to stop Marvin from breaking it apart and burning it and sent him instead to the mite-infested hives. A mistake.

In our L-shaped living room, off the kitchen, I laid three mismatched plates and straightened the hem of the ragged lace tablecloth. Tense, I tucked closed the gaps of its tears as Marvin talked about the last time we were worried about the missing supply ship. He sat in the plaid recliner, its fabric torn by a long-gone cat, and stripped his left sock from his foot. Cupped his fingers around his toes, white as fish fat.

"Anyway," he said. "I'm more worried about the hens." He glanced at me. "And you've been harvesting the carrots too early."

"I have not."

"Well, something is."

"I hear them," Thomson said from the couch. "They rattle the underbrush. They take things."

"Squirrels," Marvin muttered.

I set the last spoon. Not that we needed spoons. There wasn't any ice cream or crème brûlée.

"Nymphs," said Thomson. Greasy twists of grey hair hung in his face. His cheeks were sunken and waxy. Still, he was smiling.

"Trolls," I said.

"Fairies." His eyes glittered.

"Enough." Marvin nervously tugged the tangle of his ponytail. "This isn't a game."

Thomson exhaled roughly, an impatient sigh that started him coughing, and I went to him, pressing the back of my hand against his forehead. The heat of his skin made my knuckles burn. If the supply ship didn't arrive in a few days with Thomson's medicine, he wouldn't last more than a week. And then there would only be Marvin and me.

Our island is shaped like the leaf of an elm. The stem is the swing bridge to the mainland and the serrated edges are the limestone cliffs. The tip is occupied by the lighthouse. It had been dark for more than a year by the time we arrived and took shelter under its extinguished lamp. The farmhouse that's become our permanent home is a few miles east of the lighthouse, inland. Built by pioneers, there are cracks in the cement that covers its wooden structure. It's also unheated; like most houses on the island, we have no forced air furnace or electricity. The car that brought us here sits abandoned on the edge of the dirt driveway. Dark grey saplings grow through gaps in the engine block, weaving through the slackened belts.

According to Mr. Bobiwash, our nearest neighbour, the island has had many lives. Once, it was the bottom of a warm, tropical sea. Millions of years later, it became a sacred place for his father's people. He took Thomson and me to see the spot where his great-grandfather was buried, where the wigwamace once stood on the grave, a small house built of split cedar that held provisions for the journey to the afterlife: tobacco, dried corn, a bow and arrow, maple sugar cakes, a miniature canoe. That custom died out when white settlers came. Loggers cut down the giant pine forest and pushed the Natives onto reserves. They built busy wooden towns that were burned to the ground by fire. After the lumber was gone, most of the settlers left. Without the binding roots of trees, a lot of the topsoil blew away. Cedar grew in place of pine. Then white birch, black cherry, and beech, with its grey bark like elephant skin.

Mr. Bobiwash grew up on his white grandmother's farm. The western half of the island, where we live, is mostly limestone and sandy soil, but Mr. Bobiwash came years ago when the land was cheap. When he found us squatting in our house, nearly starving, he helped us, taught us to bolster the soil with fish guts, wood ash, organic waste. His first wife, Mona, had strapped their infant daughter, Abigail, to her body and helped me cut tall grasses to use as mulch. We learned to take water from the lake when the rain doesn't come, and when we get too much rain there's nothing we can do. Planting the gardens and wild harvesting are my jobs, and Marvin does the fishing, heaving his nets over the side of the boat, chunks of balsam bark tied to their edges as floats. In the afternoon, he drags the nets in again, silver fish flashing in the green weave. In the beginning, he had to be careful because we were on the run, but there's no danger since the government office shut and more and more unlicensed boats are out on the bay. *Too many*, Marvin says, always wary.

While we work, Thomson watches us. Early on, when his illness was still in remission, he helped with darning our socks, shelling peas, or scavenging in nearby houses for anything we could use. He even went to town with Mr. Bobiwash, to take fish and honey to the market and hear the news. Marvin asked him not to, but he said he'd learned not to be afraid in Czechoslovakia and Chiapas and he wasn't about to start now. "It's got nothing to do with that," Marvin said, and we both thought of it, the thing we were really afraid of, getting caught for what we'd left behind, but Thomson turned away and did what he wanted.

From him we got bits of information: fighting over good farmland, city streets powdered with soot. A woman once told him the central government had buckled, but nobody else could confirm it. There had been phones on the island, but they petered out when the cell towers fell, unmaintained, and the wire was stripped away. One day Thomson came home and said there'd been a meltdown at a nuclear power plant in China. For days we braced for impact, but nothing came of it. If fallout arrived it was invisible. And, as Marvin said, we no longer have the luxury of worrying about our health. Now, though, he is worried.

Leathery fish fillets disappear from the smokehouse. Tomatoes vanish. So do pods full of hard beans, vital to our winter supply. We aren't hungry right now, though. No more than usual. We have pickerel caught during the spring spawn, whitefish, the plants I learned to identify and harvest from books I looted from the library in town. Cattail roots, purslane, Labrador tea. But despite the summer's food, the white animal of winter is alive in Marvin's eyes. At night he stays up to watch for you, our garden thief, and I sit with him, hoping to distract him if you come into the yard. Maybe you slip into our plot when we are busy doing other things. Marvin peeing off the edge of the porch although I have asked him not to more than a hundred times. Me, in the kitchen, fetching us tea. I imagine you looking in: my face in the window, white like birch against the black rooms. *I know you*, I think. And I do. The divots of your footprints in the damp earth, your body's blur in the cedar trees. So quick you could be anything. An animal, an escaped thought. But what you are, I feel, is mine, and what I want is simple. For you to come inside. To wash you in a warm, soapy bath. Wrap a towel around your skinny frame. Braid your hair on picture day. Stand on the side of the road waiting for the yellow school bus. Play a cartoon on the computer, make popcorn in the microwave, and sit on the couch and laugh. That perfect life. The one we once aspired to that won't ever exist again.

2 City

My name is Cassandra Burch-Bailey. I'm thirty-seven years old. The winter I met Marvin, I had just turned twenty-one, not much more than a child. That isn't an excuse for what we did, but it is part of the reason why I went along with it.

For Marvin, those long-ago events are lodged in the past like a memory you sometimes think is a dream, but I know that they are real. For years I've been carrying the weight, with no one to talk to, no way to set it down and let the earth absorb the shock.

We did things, Melissa. Things that I can't bury.

Melissa means honeybee, Thomson has told me, reciting the story of the nymph who cared for Zeus. If he could have chosen my name, if I had been his daughter, that's what he would have called me. Melissa and Phoenix. Sisters. So that's what I'm calling you.

The morning I was laid off, the lights were flickering on the twenty-seventh floor. In the downtown offices of Parthenon Developers, nobody knew whether we'd have a blackout or not. An old song seeped through the ceiling speakers, dripping like water from a fractured pipe, and my co-worker Nadja sang along—*I want to be a billionaire, so freakin' bad* . . . She stopped when the company president began talking, telling us about the bankruptcy, about the end of all our jobs. A panicked rustle went through the crowd. There must have been fifty of us, and I swear I could smell fear, the sour odour of sweat as strong as it would have been on the over-packed, sticky subway in the middle of July. A man shouted from the back and Sissy shushed him, told him to listen. The president, whose name I can't recall—something like Jennifer or Jessica but different—crossed her arms and continued speaking, flanked on either side by security guards. She gave a deadpan speech about new opportunities, silver linings. It was late in the afternoon, a week into February, and a light snow tumbled into the cavern between the buildings. I remember looking out, south to the shimmering plate of the silver lake, not yet realizing I would never again see from such a height.

I know this is an old story. For my whole life I'd been hearing it: people talking about the coming crisis, the present crisis, the inevitable collapse. Some lucky people still had money, shopped at expensive clothing stores like the one where my roommate, Margo, worked or bought coffee at boutique food shops. But most people, people like us, lived hand to mouth, squabbling for the last boxes of tea on the shelves, cheap trays of animal organs, counting out our change at the till. There were rotating blackouts at least once a week, mob robberies, gas prices through the roof. Families couldn't afford to bury their dead so the morgues and funeral homes filled up with bodies. On the Internet I'd seen mountain lions lounging beside an algae-filled pool in an abandoned suburb down south. The loss of my parents' farm wasn't even unusual; it had happened to millions of people. I was used to that world and navigating through it, but I had still been raised to think that something special was in store for me. In the city, I thought my life was starting, that things were getting better, and I think that day was the first time I really realized that a happy ending wasn't guaranteed for me. My job might not have been the most lucrative, but it gave me enough money to buy cans of beans, bacon wrapped in butcher's paper, even the odd vodka martini out in a bar. It meant my own room in the small, second-floor apartment I had shared with Margo for nearly ten months. Without it, I would be one of them: the ranks my parents had already joined, lining up at the food bank for softening cellared apples and lone sleeves of saltine crackers.

After I lost my job, I thrashed. I didn't know what to do with myself. I slept in and didn't take showers and avoided the ping of Margo's computer when the power was on. I knew it was my mother, wanting to chat. My father had stayed in bed for days when we first lost the farm, my mother bringing him meals, the broth slopping over the side of the bowl, bleeding orange into the edge of the paper napkin. His face was pale from the drawn curtains, stubble on his cheeks like ash. I was afraid of being like him, of sinking, so I pushed myself to hit the pavement. Quickly I discovered that any store with a HELP WANTED sign already had fifty applicants. It was pretty much hopeless. I skim-read the forms, filled in what information I could, left only a few squares blank. In the evenings, Margo watched me. I felt her eyes on me as we sat in the living room, the windows wide open, wrapped in striped and patterned afghan blankets her aunt incessantly knit.

"What?" I'd ask her, but usually she'd change her mind about whatever she was going to say. It was a relief when she didn't speak because she was paying for everything—our food, the hydro bill—and I didn't want to field questions about what my plans were. Even the rent, due in a few weeks, would come entirely from her. She'd never lose her job. Her father had fought in the army with the man whose family owned the store where she worked. An upscale boutique. Limited clientele. Layoffs moved through, but Margo was always left standing, even though she occasionally stumbled into work acting weird after having been out all night. Once, when she got in around dawn, I found her clothes in the bathtub, soaking in soot-black water. When I asked her about it, all she said was, "I fell in the mud." Scratches over her knuckles, criss-crossed like a kind of script. Looking back I wonder why I didn't see it sooner, but those are the sorts of things you don't want to know, the hints you turn away from, hoping there's a harmless explanation.

It was Margo who took me to the bar.

Margo who introduced me to Marvin.

Margo who started it all.

That night, the fifth of my unemployment, when I was beginning to wonder if I could brave my parents and actually move back home, she took me to the Empire Tavern. It was housed in a shabby Victorian: huge, with rot like the shapes of continents spreading under the windows. War vets lived in the rooms on the second storey, Margo told me, before we went inside. The place smelled of damp ash and chemical aftershave, and I followed Margo as she marched forward with her arms at her sides and her chin tipped up. When we rounded the second corner of the square bar, I saw him. Sitting at a small round table, a backpack by his boots like a dog. The last spindle of a hand-rolled cigarette set in a glass ashtray, unwinding its smoke. A map was spread out in his hands like a quilt. When he looked up, his eyes were full of fragments of jade from the Christmas lights strung on the fake wood panelling.

Something moved in me right then, Melissa. Like a deadbolt worried in the dark, it fell into place with a clunk. I don't know why or if it was right or if, in hindsight, it wasn't just because of Marvin's good looks and the way he shook his black hair out of his face because when we got to the table, I realized pretty fast I wasn't welcome.

"You brought a guest," he said to Margo, frown lines dug into his cheeks like bits of flint. She slid into a wooden chair, the legs rocking against the floor tile's broken grout.

"I knew you wouldn't mind." She glanced around. "Where's Walter?"

Without answering, Marvin roughly folded his map and I heard the sharp tear of a seam giving way.

"Sit," Margo told me, but I stayed where I was. The men at a nearby table looked over, one wearing a parka with its hood half torn off, the other hunched forward, tugging a blue hoodie tight to his chest. He winked at me and I pulled my jacket zipper close to my throat. When I turned to go to the bar, I could tell Marvin was watching me. My ass in the tight jeans with glittering pockets that Margo had bought me back before my body was so scrawny. I strained to listen to them talking—their words a messy collage of hissing whispers—as I ordered us a pitcher of beer that Margo would pay for.

When I got back, Marvin was friendlier, or at least accepting of my presence. He finished rolling a cigarette, licking the edge of the paper to seal it shut. He offered it to me, but I shook my head. There was a weird silence between us, as if none of us knew what to say, and I tried to break it by asking Marvin what he did, if he'd grown up in the city, but he didn't seem to want to talk. The woman behind the bar turned on the television and a rumble started up, the picture sliding in and out of static. A litany of bad news—China banging war drums, forest fires out west, the crude bomb detonated a few months earlier at a gas station by a group called Jump Ship, the investigation ongoing. They hit randomly, that group. I remembered their first couple strikes, half a decade earlier, at a debit machine and a car dealership. How excited my father got when we watched the news coverage together, as if they were helping him take revenge. But then they seemed to go silent. Until a couple years ago, when they started up again—hitting the lobby of an oil company and then the gas station.

We all watched. No sound in the bar but the rattle of the TV until a voice—raspy, nearly a growl—sounded behind my back. "Nobody hurt," it said. "That's all they fucking care about." I turned and saw a man with the beginnings of a bald spot, hard blue eyes in a wide, pale face. His lips were chapped, a spot of blood on the bottom one. He reached his right hand out to greet me, the skin on his arm mottled pink and red, shiny and scarred.

"Walter," Margo said, and his palm was bone dry against mine. When he sat down, I watched as he reached for Marvin's tobacco pouch with his other hand, a metal claw that caught the colourful lights. Margo pulled out her own cigarettes, store-bought, and slid them over to him. I tried not to stare as he pulled one out, popped it between his lips, and snapped a match. The tip ignited, crumpled into orange. When his eyes met mine, I quickly looked away, settling on the nearly empty pitcher of beer. He smiled, his two front teeth speckled with bright white spots.

"More?" Marvin asked, standing, his body beside my face. That was before he wasted away, went skeletal, when he was lean and tall and good-looking and knew it. Blushing, I turned to Margo and her lips stretched into a narrow, mischievous smile. Something brewed in her—I could sense the simmer before full boil. "Why not?" she said. Margo's way was to plunge ahead, leap into frothy water; mine was to look for rocks.

"I don't know," I said.

"Come on. It's on me." She turned to Walter. "This girl got laid off."

"Shots," he bellowed, so loud I jumped in my seat.

"Got it," Marvin said and walked over to the bar.

"Margo," I said and turned to call out to Marvin to just get me some water. I hated spending her money. But she laid her hand on my arm, misunderstanding. "You're going to be fine. Everything happens for a reason."

Marvin carried back a clutch of treacly brown shots. He sat them down, and tiny rivulets ran down the sides, making the glasses sticky. We each reached for one, held them chest level, ready to drink, until Marvin said, "What will you do now?"

I shifted in my seat. "Find more work," I said and set the shot down, sucked the liquid off my finger. Sweet and sharp.

"A lot of people are in the same boat. What's unemployment at now?" The question hung there. It was weird because we were all waiting to drink. I looked at Walter, then Margo, but neither of them answered, both waiting for Marvin to finish. Walter pushed the moment forward, lifted his shot glass into the silence, and said, "Viva."

Margo and Walter drank. Marvin was still watching me, the tiny glass of alcohol ignored. He leaned forward, bent his head almost horizontal with the table. "It couldn't have been a surprise."

It's stupid, but I hadn't been expecting it. I thought the company might tremble around me but ultimately remain standing, my job intact. The early tremors had been there: phone calls from banks, meetings cancelled, our hours reduced. I'd told all that to my mother and she'd convinced me to give up my cellphone to save money. "Not at all," I told Marvin and threw the liquid into my mouth.

After that, we ordered more beer, and Marvin kept offering me cigarettes. Finally I took one and felt the brush of his fingers against mine. When he scratched a match to light it, the flame leapt between our faces and I felt a shiver of expectation move through me. But Walter wanted attention. With his claw he held out a tiny mechanical beetle, a delicate thing with legs of soldered steel and a carapace of hammered tin clipped from a soda can. Wires connected to a battery made up its innards. When he hit its "on" switch, it climbed over Marvin's tobacco pouch, Margo's wallet, even tried to mount my extended finger.

"Walter built that," Margo said, her voice firm with pride. He didn't look up. I felt sorry for him, for his disfigurement. But what did I know? A few weeks later, I would be several hours north in a stolen car fuelled by gasoline bought by Marvin, looking back through a blur of tears, Walter dead, my heart irreparably broken.

It wasn't very late when Margo and Walter stood up from the table. The lights were dim in the bar by then so I didn't see the look on Walter's face when his chair fell over and crashed against the hard floor. He grabbed at Margo, shoving his intact hand through the loop that her elbow made. Margo had her fingers over her mouth, suppressing a laugh, and she stumbled against him as he pulled on her. I thought they were going to dance, but Walter breathed some words in Margo's ear and pulled her toward a flight of stairs on one side of the room. They were together, I realized, and felt stupid that I hadn't seen it before. It didn't surprise me. Margo marched to a different drummer, as my mother used to say. She glanced over her shoulder at me and wiggled her fingers in the air to say goodbye and I knew I'd have to find my own way home.

Marvin split the foamy dregs of the beer between our glasses. We finished it quietly, beginning to build the silence that still lives between us. I was a bit drunk, my tongue thick in my mouth, so I didn't speak, afraid of how my words would slur. When his glass was empty, he packed his rolling papers and matches into a battered silver tin and slid that and his tobacco pouch into the top of his canvas backpack. He stood, so I did too.

The backpack bounced on his shoulders as we went outside. Writing was scrawled on the canvas and I squinted but couldn't make out the words. He zipped up his jacket and I looked south, in the direction of Margo's and my apartment, but didn't move. Instead, I waited, hoping that he'd offer to walk me home so I wouldn't be mugged for the handful of rattling change in my pocket, so I didn't have to be alone.

When he stepped down the stairs, I followed.

"Which way are you going?" I asked, the words big in my mouth. He nodded toward the intersection with the leaning streetlight, the echo of red lights all the way south to where I lived. "Me too," I said, inviting. Like a magic trick, he slid a cigarette out from behind one ear. "I have things to do," he told me. He sounded sober.

I thought he was trying to get rid of me so I nodded, ready to grit my teeth and get myself home. "See you later then," I said and started to walk away, but he spoke my name and when I looked back, he squinted through a plume of smoke.

"Do you want to come?"

Like a little kid, I giggled. It embarrassed me, but I couldn't help it. If I'd been forced to explain I would have told him that it was this sense of newness that I hadn't felt in a long time. Like a door had opened and I'd decided to plunge right through, moving in a direction other than the one I'd planned: lurching home on the sidewalk, fixating on my narrowing future, worrying myself to sleep.

"It's a long walk," he said. "And we'll end up at my place." He looked serious. I couldn't tell if he was hitting on me or just telling me the truth of what would happen. Either way, it was an adventure. Margo was always telling me to seize the day, so I decided to do that—or simply not resist.

"Okay," I said, and I'm sure we both knew right then what would happen. But not the extent of it. Not how we would change each other's lives.

Thomson often tells me that people most often make choices out of desire, but to be honest, Melissa, at that moment in my life I wasn't sure what I wanted or what I would be able to get. I knew what I didn't want—to have to move home, to go back to my parents' tiny apartment that felt like a prison, a place I couldn't leave even to go to the corner store without uncertainty shadowing my father's face. A year earlier I'd run away, bolted free, broken one of my grandmother's good china teacups in a rage when I'd come home from a date and my father tore my purse from my hands, emptied it out on the kitchen floor, looking for cigarettes or condoms, and finding only panty liners, pencils, my ID loose like playing cards. Eventually my mother calmed him, but in the morning, the birds singing when it was still dark out at 4:00 AM, I threw socks, underwear, extra pants and shirts into a cloth grocery bag and left with a hundred dollars in an envelope marked GROCERIES in my mother's boxy handwriting. From the city, several hours east, I called her, crying, and instead of telling me to come home as I'd expected, she gave me the phone number for her old friend Sissy, who worked HR at a housing developer. From those beginnings, I started building a bit of a life that was, that night, as Marvin and I walked east, through the downtown canyon I'd left earlier that month, about to become something entirely new.

3 Island

You might have noticed that Marvin stays home on Sundays. The boat by the shore is turned over, its tarred keel like a sea creature's spine. He says he needs a day of rest so he might as well follow the Christian tradition. But that morning he didn't sit idle. He tore out the waist-high pickets from around our garden and hauled cedar posts from the collapsed fence up the road into our yard. When I heard the shovel, I went outside and found him digging a hole in the corner of the garden plot.

"What are you doing?"

"Building a higher fence." His foot pushed the rusted blade deeper into the soil.

"Why?"

He didn't answer. While he dug, I tried to think of something to say, a way to defend your stealing without confessing that I knew where our food was going. But I could tell he wanted me to go inside, to leave him be. Over on the porch, I heard Thomson coughing, his lungs grinding, making a sound he used to call *the minutes*. He hasn't said that in a while, and I can't help but think it's because he knows his time is running out, that he's on the final rotation of the clock's hands.

"Sandy," Thomson called from the porch. I turned around and saw him fumbling to sit up.

"We aren't losing that much," I said.

Marvin stopped shovelling and stared at me. "We barely have enough. Last winter . . ."

I dropped my eyes. I tried not to think of those days, late February, early March, when we'd eaten the last of our fish, dug into rotten stumps for grubs to fry, made soup out of frozen roots and the inner bark from the yellow birch. The snow came and came. Usually Mr. Bobiwash brought us rabbit or deer that he'd managed to shoot, but he didn't show up for weeks. His wife, Shannon, was hugely pregnant, eating twice what she normally would. Angry at everyone, unwilling to share.

In bed, at night, my fingers compulsively found my ribs, running over them like a silent instrument, amazed. My mind moved from clarity to cottony dullness. And then the wild leeks sprouted and the sun shone and the soil loosened and the seeds went in and we were okay for another year.

This is different, I wanted to tell Marvin as he threw a shovelful of dirt onto the pile, but I couldn't. I didn't know if he would care that you were not an animal burrowing instinctually for buried food. Instead, I said, "We don't have cement for those posts."

"I'll bury them deep." Thomson shouted out my name again, a high-pitched urgency in his voice. I turned and ran to help him with whatever he wanted: to go to the outhouse, get a drink of water. Something simple that he couldn't do on his own anymore.

While Marvin worked, burying the posts and stringing old chicken wire, I sat beside Thomson on the porch. I read to him from a book we'd found weeks earlier, a mystery novel with pages torn out to start fires so we had to make up bits to link the plot.

In his thin, gruff voice, Thomson placed the detective in an underworld the author hadn't even hinted at. Somehow the change made sense. "You should write the books," I told him, and he smiled. I often told him that. Whenever the Bobiwash kids came by, their brown eyes fixed on his face as he spoke about the places he'd been. Israel, Greece. They listened, popping blackberries into their mouths, under the scarves we made them wear to visit Thomson when his sickness re-emerged. Their faces filled me with yearning.

I tried to have children. Our third spring on the island, I started watching my cycle like Phoenix had taught me. Writing dates down on the bumpy plaster of our closet wall. Whenever I attempted to talk to Marvin about it, he refused, his voice hammering out those solid words: "No. There isn't enough." So I didn't tell him. Still, nothing happened. Every month, my imagined baby melted away in a stain of slippery red on my fingertips and finally, after years of that, more than a decade, I gave up.

And now you've come.

As I sat with Thomson, I stared into the woods, at the trail lined with goldenrod that leads to our single beehive. Past Marvin's head, to the backdrop of wide water like an extension of the sky. I knew you were out there, listening to the story through the strikes of the hammer on the fence posts. *Come closer*, I said in my mind.

After his nap, Thomson shuffled up to lean against the couch cushions on the chaise lounge. His baggy shirt twisted around his waist. I lay the book open on the floor of the porch and helped him tug the shirt out from under his skinny buttocks. The pants were belted with a blue computer cable. When he was settled, he stared across the yard at Marvin, who was plucking rusty nails from his mouth and hammering the wire against the wood.

"I'm not happy about this," I said, following Thomson's gaze.

"Why not?"

I shrugged, nervous about telling Thomson the truth. He had enough to deal with without thinking about another mouth.

"Things have changed, Sandy."

"I know."

"They were easier back then."

I glanced at him, his hands in his lap, one knotted around the other. In earlier days, he'd lived with the poor, helped overthrow a regime, monitored a fledgling revolution in Mexico, finally moved down to the dark zone with Phoenix to start a soup kitchen. Lost people he loved. How was that easier?

"Marvin is doing what he thinks is right," he said. I stared at him. How was that a good thing? It certainly hadn't been back in the city. But Thomson was recalling our new lives, how Marvin had settled us here, working in a kind of trance to patch over the holes in the roof and reframe the broken areas of the house with Mr. Bobiwash's help. He'd surprised me; I'd expected him to start talking, soon after we arrived on the island, of going home, getting back to the city, planning a way around our fugitive status. But he rooted down, we all did, sending shoots into the rocky terrain turned organic from the memory of the bodies we'd left behind. Those first few years we hid in our work, moving in a manic effort to simply stay alive. Often I thought of Phoenix, how she would have thrived. It was hard to get her out of my head. Maybe we all felt that because we never spoke of her. Time tried to bury her, like skin growing over shrapnel.

"We can't feed every small thing," Thomson said.

Was that what you were? A small thing?

It was time for Thomson's walk so I helped him as he swung his legs into a sitting position. I took his bony elbow and pulled him to standing. We climbed down the steps, his feet in a pair of torn boat shoes. Marvin touched the head of the hammer to his forehead in a kind of salute. Thomson turned right, toward the clearing in the pines occupied by the last of our honeybees. Mites or sudden, strange vanishings had killed most of them. We had one hive left, full and functioning but neglected.

"Let's go to the lake," I said, turning him around. When Thomson had been well, he had visited the hives every day. Inspecting. Pulling out the brood frames to check for those tiny black specks, the earliest sign of catastrophe. Mites. But Marvin and I hadn't been looking after the hive. A losing proposition, Marvin called it. Too much work for too little return. "We need protein, not sugar," he said. Despite my desire to care for them, to continue Thomson's legacy, I found myself drifting away, willing to accept Marvin's reasoning if it meant less work. The gardens exhausted me: the canning, the cooking, the effort to make our way into town at least once a month and trade what we could. Wild mushrooms with their fleshy, white fins, fish, greens gathered in the woods. *A million people make honey*, Marvin says, and I don't argue although I know how Thomson would respond: *The people don't make it, the bees do.*

"The lake's a long way," Thomson said, stopping before we reached the trailhead.

MELISSA - IMAGINARY CHILD/HONEY BEE

THOMSON + CANCER. (9) 12

MARVIN - YOUNGER.

IMAGINARY/FICTIOUS TOWNS, CITIES

"It came from Midland...." 3

"....from the mills down south" 3

MR. BOBIWASH

CASSANDRA Burch Bailey 37 yrs old 8

SHE WAS 21 yrs old when SHE MET MARVIN

$$\begin{array}{r} 37 \\ -21 \\ \hline 16 \end{array}$$

MARGO - roommate

WALTER @ THE EMPIRE TAVERN METALCLAW OR

HE KNOWS THAT LIFE is CHEAP. 8.20.14.

WALTER 14

PHOENIX? 19, 20

AND SEES the SENSLESSNESS in it All,

while PEOPLE indulge THEMSELVES so

IN DENIAL - IGNORING the INEVITABLE.

LE: 12,000 dreams interpreted : a new edition ... 21st c
AUTHOR: Miller, Gustavus Hindman, L

CALL 241 Brestin 2012 ITEM TYPE: null
TITLE: Idol lies : facing the truth about our deepest desires
AUTHOR: Brestin, Dee, L

CALL 242 Niequist 2010 ITEM TYPE: null
TITLE: Cold tangerines : celebrating the extraordinary nature o
AUTHOR: Niequist, Shauna. L

CALL 248.4 Macomber ITEM TYPE: null
TITLE: God's guest list : welcoming those who influence our liv
AUTHOR: Macomber, Debbie. L

CALL 296.4 Klagsbru ITEM TYPE: null
TITLE: Jewish days : a book of Jewish life and culture around th
AUTHOR: Klagsbrun, Francine. L

CALL 306.7 Steffans ITEM TYPE: null
TITLE: The vixen manual : how to find, seduce, & keep the ma
AUTHOR: Steffans, Karrine,

CALL 345.02523 Goldberg ITEM TYPE: null
TITLE: The prosecution responds : an O.J. Simpson trial prose
AUTHOR: Goldberg, Hank M.

CALL 385.09 Burns ITEM TYPE: null
TITLE: Iron trails of North America : 1978-2008
AUTHOR: Burns, Robert W.

"Tell me if you get tired." He needed the air, the exercise.

We didn't fit side by side on the trail so I walked behind him. I found a stick in the woods because we'd forgotten his cane. The bugs were out and strangely thick for late summer. We paused so Thomson could roll his sleeves down and button the cuffs. I tucked his pant legs into his socks. I was still wearing the thin cotton pants of my pyjamas, which the mosquitoes bit through. I longed to run, to break into a sprint and burst through the trail opening, into the wind off the lake, but Thomson inched forward, nudging his shoulder up to his neck to push the bugs away. I waved my hands around his head until he told me to stop. And then we were stepping carefully onto the sand near the boat and in front of us were three delicate footprints. Thin slivers, moonlike, as if you barely touch the ground. Thomson stopped and stared at them, leaning on my arm.

"What's that?" he said, poking the imprints of your toes with his stick. I held my breath. His eyes lifted to find my face and I saw the old shine in them.

In June, Thomson had been well enough for us to bring two passengers home after the last supply ship had docked. We gave them a meal and a place to stay for the night before the boat left in the morning, heading farther up the coast into deeper wilderness in the north. They had come from a squat in a suburb on the edge of the city we used to live in. At night, they told us, they'd barricaded themselves in and waited for morning when a Baptist Church group sometimes delivered food and water. Once, they opened the door when they shouldn't have. Men with guns took three young children and a woman. "Probably to be sold," Marvin said.

"Maybe that's what she ran from," I suggested to Thomson as we walked back to the house.

Things like that happened. At times I was relieved that we'd escaped early enough, left the city before all the lights went out, or most of them. The majority of the population toiled now in the dark where violence flourished like a night plant. Our island was calmer, quieter, hidden away.

Thomson pushed along the trail, wobbling over fat ridges of cedar roots.

"Maybe she was taken and then she escaped from the boat," I said. He stopped and put out a hand, curving it around the wrinkled trunk of a beech. I fidgeted, dancing inside the cloud of bugs while Thomson leaned his shoulder against the tree, breathing heavily.

"She?"

Why had I said that? Because I know you by the slim indentations of your footprints. By your thieving sleight of hand. Lighter, more delicate than a boy.

"I think."

"She is the one taking our food?"

I nodded.

"An orphan?" Thomson said. A shimmer moved across his face, like glee.

"Maybe."

"Does Marvin know?"

I shook my head hard. That wasn't what I wanted. "He'll take her," I said. I hoped to keep going: plan how we would catch you, talk about bringing you home, but Thomson interrupted me.

"Where?"

I couldn't answer that. "He doesn't want her here," I said, but my words were cut off as he sputtered, the ever-present cough ending our discussion. I wrapped my arm around his shoulders, relieved because I'd heard judgment in his voice, like he didn't really believe me. "It's not far now," I said and led him along the last stretch of the trail.

Thomson had taken to sleeping downstairs, saying his room was too cold at night. I brought him to the couch and slid his shoes off and tucked him in with a beige wool blanket that the supply ship had delivered last autumn.

"How is he?" Marvin asked when I entered the kitchen.

"Up and down. Now he just needs to sleep."

A pile of cedar roots sat on the counter. Their thin red skin chipped by the shovel. I picked them up and draped them over a nail pounded into the wall.

"Did you finish the fence?" I asked, playing with the dangling roots as if they were hair.

Marvin nodded.

"I'm glad nobody barricaded us out."

"Come on. That's different."

How? I wondered.

Marvin moved over to the sink as I pulled two beets from their bin of dirt in the cupboard. I turned away from him, thinking of the things I would have to teach you. Wild harvesting. How we use cedar for so many things. String for shoes and tying together stalks of herbs for drying. We make a tea from its foliage for vitamin C. Without that your teeth will fall out and your skin will turn black. Thomson taught me about Jacques Cartier, the early explorer. How he'd watched his crew drop dead from scurvy before the Aboriginal people showed him how to make cedar tea. That was in the 1500s. Back when people lived a lot like we live now except that they didn't know any differently. Sumac is also good. Soak the red berries and drink the liquid. It's tangy, like a juice.

"If you went to the lake you should have brought back water," Marvin said, interrupting my thoughts. He washed his hands in a basin of grey water in the sink. I cut up the beets as he slid a bar of soap between his hands and placed it, coated in brown grime, by the hot water tap that doesn't work. The silence between us was tense, and it reminded me of our last night in the dark zone, lying together in the cold attic room, after he'd told me most of the truth, trying to think of a way out. He'd wanted to run, I remembered. The easy way out.

I kept my back to him, relieved when he laid the towel on a stool under the useless wall telephone and left the room.

By the time I served supper, Thomson was deeply asleep. Mouth open, he lay awkwardly, his shoulders twisted toward the back of the couch. Normally I would have let him sleep, but that night

I shook him awake while Marvin watched. I wanted him to eat something, to fill his stomach with nutrients.

"Lascaux," he said, his eyes fluttering open, the whites tinted yellow. "Lucy."

"Where's he gone to?" Marvin asked.

"I don't know." His delirium scared me. Bringing him to the lake, out into the evening wind, seemed like a mistake. I should have let him rest or bathed him and sat him by the fire. He was overdue and starting to smell. Night was settling. Marvin went out onto the porch as I helped Thomson swallow a few sips of thyme and mullein tea and then let him slide back into sleep.

Dusk filled the house while Marvin and I ate supper.

"We need to check the bees tomorrow," I said and told Marvin how Thomson had wanted to go there. Marvin shovelled a forkful of greens into his mouth.

"The mites are just going to get them," he said as he chewed.

"That's optimistic," I mumbled.

"It's true."

"Do it for Thomson." I pushed my beets around on the plate, watched their juice stain the fish pink. I was sick of them. On the other side of the large room, Thomson choked in his sleep. Marvin pushed his chair back and went to the couch, holding him upright as Thomson spat into the torn square of a sheet. I shaded my eyes with my hand and stared down at my plate. Before Marvin was through with Thomson, I took my food to the kitchen. From the cupboard, I pulled a package of red paper plates and filled one with my leftover beet slices and a large chunk of whitefish. I took it out the back door and put it on the porch for you. As if you were one of the stray cats that wandered the island before they were all hunted out. Skin and bones, on your way to going wild. When I stood and turned around, Marvin was standing in the doorway.

"What are you doing?"

"If she's going to steal," I started to say.

"She?"

And I told him. Thomson would have, sooner or later, even if it just slipped out.

Through my life, I've imagined certain moments. My wedding, the way I would tell my husband that I was going to have his baby, how I would deal with my mother's death. But that evening, I stood on the porch, the crickets in the background, a distant owl screeching its strange whinnying cry, and what I told Marvin was that I'd seen your footprints in our garden. Evidence of a new beginning. A child that could be ours.

"They're tiny," I said. "She's a little—"

"That's a third of our food," he said, gesturing at the plate. A bright red polka dot on the weathered boards. It was August, no longer the beginning of summer, and we'd been salting fish for three months. There were beans and carrots and jams to can. Wild apples to dry. I looked down at your fish and beets. I'd covered your food with torn shards of plastic wrap from the ancient roll I'd found with the plates in the cupboard of a church.

"Without the ship . . ." Marvin said.

"The ship will come."

"Sandy. We can't do this. We won't survive this way."

"If she was our child . . ."

Marvin paused. "Maybe we'd eat her," he said, his voice harder than I'd ever heard it before, and he went back into the house.

I stared at the slammed door. When I heard the bush rustle behind me, I turned toward the sound, but the night was dark. The moon a waxing crescent. I wanted to call out to you—*Melissa*—shout your name like my mother did during summer twilight, the sun setting fire to the corn stalks. But I kept silent. All I could do was hope you'd come before the animals.

4 City

Marvin's eyes scanned the dark cross-hatch of intersections, assessed figures that slipped out of doorways. Most kept moving but when a few remained, standing in a lopsided triangle on a low stone step, he turned abruptly to cross the street, corralling me with his body. Around us, the buildings grew taller. In the wealthiest area, near where I used to work, the sidewalk was littered with dead birds that had flown into the skyscrapers so we moved into the gutter to avoid the crunch of their little bones. I pointed out the Parthenon offices and watched as Marvin's gaze climbed the glass exterior and fell back to the front doorway, its glass smashed in. A closed-circuit camera lay in the entranceway, red and green wires pulled out like entrails, and I thought of the mice our barn cats sometimes left at the back door. "Impressive," Marvin said as we continued past a row of cut-open streetlights, all the copper stripped, into a poorer part of the city where prostitutes lingered, their eyes dismissing us, and as I began to sober up, I started second-guessing myself, thinking that this was likely a mistake, taking an unknown journey with a strange man I'd just met.

In our lives now, on this island, there is little room for self-doubt, probably because our well-being doesn't depend so much on our own decisions, the directions we choose, but on other forces like the weather, the people around us, our capacity to work. That night, though, I'd made a choice and realized too late I might regret it.

"How did you meet Margo?" I asked, trying to lighten the heavy silence.

"She told me about you," he said, his voice a low whisper like we were moving through a giant's house, trying to avoid waking it up. "But you aren't what I expected."

"What were you expecting?"

He shrugged, but I thought I knew: someone tougher, more like Margo. What he said, though, surprised me. "She didn't say you'd be so pretty." I glanced into the street and blushed.

"You can't take a compliment?"

"Sure," I said, and we were silent. We walked a ways before Marvin turned suddenly into an alley. I hesitated at the open mouth. "Come on," he coaxed. Beside me, the steel door of a strip club swung open and a man tumbled out, his watery red eyes fastening to mine. Our gaze held for a split second before I moved, following Marvin down the greasy tunnel that smelled putrid and dusky, like urine and rotten garbage.

The alley was a shortcut that Marvin took to forage for bottles and anything else that might make him money—or so he said. He dug a couple of green glass bottles out of an aluminum garbage can and turned his back to me so I could slip them in his pack. After that, we headed south, and as we walked, he scuffed the soles of his shoes against the sidewalk, sending chunks of ice and grit into the gutter. We passed a sugar factory with silent smokestacks, windows clear of glass. In the distance I saw the closed highway overpass, chunks of rubble around its footings. I slipped a hand into my coat pocket, wishing for a cellphone. Stores with iron gates over their windows lined the street.

"Your friends are down here?" I asked. Up ahead, I saw a crowd of people gathered.

"You could call them that."

"What do they do?"

"They apply bandages."

"Like first aid?"

He laughed. He pointed ahead. "Ten minutes." Soon we would run into the lake and I wondered what was between here and there, apart from the clutch of people who stood in a knot on the sidewalk.

"What happened to Walter?" I asked.

I expected Marvin to tell me that Walter had escaped being redeployed to the Middle East or something, because Margo had said that those were the people who lived at the Tavern. But it turned out that he was from a city close to where my parents lived and that he'd blown his hand off making crystal meth. Marvin told me this in a deadpan voice, matter-of-fact. I wondered why they were friends.

"They're together? He and Margo?"

"You don't know?"

"She doesn't tell me everything."

I tried another question: "Did you meet Margo through Walter?"

"My turn," he said. "What'll you do if you don't find a job?" I shrugged, and he said, "Go home to Mommy and Daddy?"

"It isn't like that," I said, annoyed. "There's not much of a home to go to."

"No?"

I told him what had happened, how my father had found oil on our land. He stopped walking, his lips rounding around the word: "Oil?"

I was glad to have his full attention so I told him the rest, how I grew up in a cornfield, the horizon yellow and blue, a wide, white field in winter. I spent a lot of time staring out at that expanse, thinking about my future, and I guess my mother did too because she developed a lot of ideas about what I would do with my life. Most of them coincided with the summer a tornado came through and dug a deep trench that grew a slimy black snake of oil. Four men came, their glossy shoes making small explosions of dust as my father led them into the corn. An hour later, my father came inside. "They'll let us know," he said, and I saw a light in his eyes, and that's when the planning began.

"For what?" Marvin asked.

"University, renovations, even a brand-new house." Every Sunday they sat at the picnic table behind the house. Chunks of broken bricks from our half-collapsed chimney holding down unpaid bills and hand-scrawled budgets. The corn stalks bent like foreign letters spelling out a secret way. Over and over again, they asked me, *What do you want to be? Where do you see yourself in ten years?* As if I could possibly know.

I told Marvin the rest: how we'd lost the property, how the bank came in and took it all away, how my father fought them and how it was the beginning of the end for him.

Up the street, the gathered men seemed to be watching, waiting for us to move. The smoke from their cigarettes lifted like a mist off cold water.

"Do you have a job?" I asked, trying to move the conversation along.

Marvin shook his head.

"How do you get money?" I thought about having to eat, not knowing at all where next week's food would come from or even how I would pay my share of the rent. I waited for him to tell me how he could live without that, what his secret was, but he reached out and grabbed my upper arm. I thought he was going to kiss me.

Instead, he waved his free hand, taking in the collapse around us, and said, "None of this is going to last." I thought he was talking about us, whatever we were, and I started to say something rehearsed, a phrase I was used to speaking like, *I'm not looking for a relationship*, even though that wasn't true, but Marvin interrupted me. And that was when he gave it to me. Right then, standing across the road from a broken white rectangle of a pawn shop sign, beside the faded posters of the Eiffel Tower in Paris and palm-treed beaches posted in the window of a travel agency.

Face flushed, fingertips pressing purple dots into my arm, he said, "It's all coming down. It has to." I winced and tugged at my arm. His fingers opened and I stepped back. His hand hung in the air as if he was a businessman, asking me to shake it, waiting to seal the deal.

"There's no going back."

I thought he meant me. I glanced at the street we'd walked down, the pocket of men waiting up ahead.

"Us," he said. I waited, and his voice hammered each syllable as if he was talking to an idiot: "Our society. We're like the Roman Empire. A glorified era that ended in the Dark Ages. From there they could have gone anywhere. And what happened?"

I didn't know history. My father was the scholar in our family, but my mother always waved away his commentary, accusing him of ranting. Probably I could have learned something, if I'd listened instead of seeing only his dark side.

"The Renaissance."

Quickly he twisted and grabbed a bottle out of his bag and before I knew what was happening he pulled back and whipped it against the travel agency window. The bottle smashed, the glass cracked across the name: Phantasy Travel. In the sudden silence, we stared at each other.

"Marvin," I said, the first time I'd ever spoken his name, and then the men cheered, and he grabbed my hand and we ran.

South, near the edge of the lake, Marvin led me into an empty lot.

"Hold on," I said, panting. I leaned over, hands on my knees, trying to draw enough air into my burning lungs. When I stood, his back was to me, his head swivelling right and left like he was on patrol. I turned to look at the road behind us, all the streetlights off or broken open, and thought about walking away, but I knew that it would be a long, scary journey back to my place. I likely wouldn't make it without being hassled or mugged or worse. There was no transportation. The subway and streetcars had already stopped for the night and the only cabs left doing business would be trawling through the wealthier neighbourhoods up north. "Shit," I murmured. I felt stupid, trapped, like I'd been tricked. I wondered why he'd invited me along.

"You ready?" Marvin said from behind me, and I turned around to face him.

"What the hell was that?"

"Humanity is renewed through violence."

I gestured back, to the building a couple blocks away, to the moment that had passed. "How is that renewing anything?"

"It evens out the playing field. You don't think it's violent: some motherfucker using up the last of our resources so he can go to Maui for a week?"

"So it's revenge?"

"You've never wanted to do something like that?"

"No!" I shouted, but I remembered my mother picking up the shards of Grandma's cup, saving a piece with half a red rose's bloom. My own rage.

"Come on, Sandy," he said and stepped toward me. The way he held himself, shoulders squared, chin lifted, made my anger waver. Maybe it wasn't such a big deal. His green eyes gazed at me, and when he turned, I simply followed, moving carefully because the ground was frozen in bumps and ruts and I didn't want to twist an ankle. Marvin stopped at a chain-link fence with barbed wire spiralled on top. He pulled out a penlight and illuminated a large sign. ECOGRID, it read. NO TRESPASSING. Orange graffiti was scrawled over top: ILLEGAL SEIZURE. I smelled smoke and saw it rising, a fat grey plume, imprinted against the night, on the other side of the fence. Voices shouted; there was the regular beat of a hammer. More and more, I worried about where we were going, what his intentions were, but I see now, Melissa, that the life I had before that night, before I was laid off, the easy one, the one that seemed safe, was actually a more strange reality.

Farther along we came across two men, one sitting on an overturned kitchen sink and another wearing a parka with a gash in its dirt-smeared sleeve. The chain-link rattled when he pushed away from the fence. Tiny feathers drifted out of a tear in his puffy coat. Marvin handed out cigarettes, and they both lit them on a fire burning in a rusty barrel. I crossed my arms, wanting to step closer to the heat, but uneasy. One of the men kicked his foot against the barrel and I heard the shattering sound of charred wood shifting. Marvin held his hands above the dull orange glow.

"Cops come by?"

The man who'd been sitting on the sink pointed the ember of his cigarette toward the road. "Drive by, no stopping."

Marvin nodded.

"You get something to eat? Soup's on," the other man told him.

"Good," said Marvin. I was standing so close to him that his body was sheltering me, and when he stepped back, I felt the cold wind off the lake. The feathers from the parka glowed bright white on the earth. Marvin nudged me in the back, pushing me toward the men. I held my ground. I didn't know what he wanted, but then the two of them stepped aside and revealed a gap in the chain-link. There was nowhere to go but forward. Hunched down, knees lifted, I slipped through the hole.

They called it the dark zone. I'd read some articles and heard people talk about how the city had claimed the area for a solar farm and relocated the residents. EcoGrid had been granted the contract, but then a protestor lost her eye from a rubber bullet and the company went bankrupt. I didn't know the whole story, just enough to know I shouldn't be there.

We walked past brick row houses with their doors smashed in. Spindles and bits of gingerbread trim hung like loose teeth. By now everyone knows about how quickly things can fall apart, but that was my first real glimpse of the unravelling. I waited for Marvin to lead me into one of the houses, but we kept walking, turning left and then right onto a wide street lined with empty storefronts. I heard a noise and looked behind us. The road was marked with hollow doorways, like burrows where any kind of creature could hide. They were back there, watching us. Squatters and homeless people: a population that made its own rules. Marvin didn't seem to mind. He walked with confidence and I stayed close to him. We passed a green-and-white awning torn in half, one side collapsed against the storefront. Two wooden chairs lay in the middle of the street, blackened by fire. The upper torso of a mannequin leaned out of a shattered window, naked, one arm reaching out as if to flag down a passerby for help.

"This is Alice," said Marvin, brushing its fake fingers with his own. I said nothing. The place was an image of apocalypse and I didn't feel like joking. I wanted to ask him if this was what he'd meant before he broke the window at the travel agency, about how things were caving in and there was no way back, but before I could speak he pointed to a glowing window half covered with plywood.

"Brass Tacks Bar and Grill," he announced. A lineup snaked to the doorway. A woman sorted through a boy's blond locks, examining his scalp with a penlight, looking for lice. The men ignored me or stared with indifference. We moved through to the front door and I smelled a strange mixture of sweat and beef. My empty stomach rumbled. A fat man stood at the door, his pale face bracketed in greasy black locks of hair. He lifted two fingers in a salute to Marvin and pulled the door open for us.

Bells jingled as we walked in, but no one looked our way. It was too loud, with everyone talking at once and dishes clanging and the occasional outburst of rattling laughter from deep in the back. Like an animal call, I thought. Those people were close to the earth, as close as we are now, with their faces and hands dirty with soot from homemade fires. Hair matted or twisted into dreadlocks, worn-out clothing stained or too large. I didn't know her name yet, but Phoenix stood out right away, in position behind the counter, wearing a puffy down jacket, unzipped, her head wrapped in a red scarf printed with black skulls and cobwebs. Black stubble showed at the scarf's edge. She ladled soup into a dull grey aluminum bowl held by a man with dirt pressed into the creases around his eyes.

"One," she said sharply. He pulled his hand out of a large plastic bowl, his fingers clutching several round pieces of bread.

"Fuck you," he said and pocketed it all.

She leaned forward. Pressing the ladle against his arm, she snarled at him: "Do you ever want to come back?" Her black eyes hard as she held his gaze. I flinched, afraid of what his reaction would be, of how the tension would break, but the man gave in, his hand returning to the bread bowl to drop the small pieces of hard crust. *Who would fight for that?* I wondered, but I know now, anybody would who was hungry enough. In winter I remember that hard bread and drool.

When I shifted my eyes, I found Phoenix looking at me and

something moved between us. Like seals passing underwater, aware of each other's forms.

"This way," Marvin said, and my gaze broke away from hers as he pulled me farther into the restaurant.

Thomson was at the back, although he was still a stranger to me then. His hair was grey, pushed back off his bald spot, and his hands looked old. He sat in a booth, cutting slices of bread off a long French roll. Mouldy scraps made a pile where the salt and pepper and chrome napkin holder once would have stood. As we approached, he looked up at Marvin and said, "Where've you been?"

Marvin tossed his backpack onto the seat. "Calm down."

"Don't talk to me like that. I'm not an old fool."

"I know."

"These times call for smart people, but they don't seem to exist anymore. They've all lost their brains. It's like the Roman fucking Empire." He looked up at me, his eyes angled as if he was peering over invisible glasses. "Are you smarter than him?"

I thought of the wild swing of Marvin's arm, the window shattering. "I just met him," I said, as if that were an answer.

Marvin waved his hand at me. "Sandy, meet Thomson."

But Thomson went back to cutting bread. He was using a hacksaw. The hard crust shattered as he dug the serrated blade in to start a new slice. Marvin slid into the booth and opened his backpack. He pulled out a fat envelope and laid it on the table. The saw stopped. Thomson sat there, staring at the bricklike bulk, an address scratched out in pencil.

Marvin jabbed a thumb over his shoulder, toward the front of the restaurant, and said, "Why don't you see if you can help." It wasn't a question. I did as he said. Turned and walked away from them, back into the crowd of dirty bodies, demanding in their hunger, their need for food.

Phoenix didn't speak to me when I joined her at the counter. Another woman faced the back wall, cutting carrots on the countertop. Phoenix continued ladling soup as the line moved, as the mugs were held out to her. "Marvin told me to help," I said, glancing around to see what I could do. There was a tea towel tossed over a cutting board and I picked it up, twisted it in my hands.

"Marvin did?"

"Yeah."

A woman on the other side of the counter pulled back her steaming mug. "Thanks, Phoenix," she said as she shuffled closer to me. A single tooth stuck out crookedly under her top lip and I suppressed a shudder. She was wearing a sweater that gaped open, revealing a tattoo of a purple dragonfly, criss-crossed with wrinkles that ran into her cleavage. "Bread," Phoenix said loudly, jolting me out of my thoughts. She pointed at the bowl on the counter, pulled out of reach after the man had tried to take more than his share. I handed the woman a slice, noticing delicate seams of dirt under her fingernails. It was shameful how I judged her, not realizing how hard it can be to get clean, how much effort it takes to get water, warm it, undress in the cold. When she thanked me, I nodded at her, and she was replaced by a teenager with brown frizzy hair, a vacant look in his eyes. He sucked on his spoon.

We worked like that for a while and I saw all kinds of people—some as dirty as that woman, with greasy hair and weltlike scars on their skin, others dressed well, with teeth that were still white. But they were all needy, and even though I heard the noisy protests of my own stomach and kept wondering if I could ever end up like that, if my mother already had, I remember feeling like I was somehow better than them. My voice came out high-pitched and patronizing, as if I was talking to children. I moved through that night strangely, thinking I knew where my feet were landing although in retrospect I really didn't know at all.

"You work hard," Phoenix said when we were finished. It had been more than an hour, one person after another until we'd nearly run out of soup. The other volunteers—a woman and the fat man who let people in, Zane—carried bowls of soup over to a booth as Phoenix turned the deadbolt on the front door.

"I guess so," I said, shy from the praise. I finished wiping off the counter, brushing crumbs into the palm of my hand. As I threw them into a bin, I looked over and caught Marvin watching me from where he was sitting with Thomson, his lips leaking smoke. I prickled, anticipating the rest of the evening, where we might end up, if he lived there, if we'd go to his room.

"No guessing. You do." Behind her the door rattled and she pulled aside the blind. "Closed," she shouted. Something hard slammed against the door frame, the flat of a hand or a fist, and she jumped back. From her seat in a booth, the other woman twisted to look. Marvin stood up, stared the length of the diner. Phoenix walked back as if nothing had happened. "Desperation," she said. "That's all."

"And you think you can keep feeding that?" Marvin asked.

"Somebody has to," Phoenix snapped as she moved behind the counter. She poured a bit of water into the soup pot, stirred it, and let it warm. When it frothed, nearly boiled, she ladled out four mugs, setting each one down in front of me, on the counter between us. "Are you Marvin's new recruit?"

I didn't know what she meant. I was about to disagree, to tell her I hardly knew him, when he appeared behind me.

"It's time to go."

"Speak of the devil," said Phoenix. "The rebel without a cause."

"I have a cause," said Marvin, and his hand slid onto the small of my back, surprising me. His fingers pressed against my vertebrae, following them downward, and I sucked in my breath. When I glanced back, I saw he was still staring at Phoenix.

Phoenix unplugged the hot plate from its battery pack. "Do what thou wilt shall be the whole of the law?" I recognized the quote scrawled in black marker on his backpack.

"You remember," Marvin said.

"That works if people aren't motivated by their lowest desires."

"You don't have much faith in people."

"I don't have faith in the system that produced them."

Marvin took his hand off my back. He gripped the edge of the counter and leaned toward her. "We're so close. We're a rallying cry."

"You're a dispersive force."

"Children!" Thomson shouted from the last booth in the diner, and I was glad he stopped them because I didn't have a clue what they were talking about. Phoenix slid two mugs of soup over to Marvin and me. He was already carrying his backpack, wanting to leave, but I told him I was hungry.

"She's been working hard," said Zane, standing with another volunteer, their soup finished, dirty aluminum bowls left on the counter. Phoenix handed them each a clutch of paper, a few floppy squares of newsprint, before they slipped out the front, headed for their squat down the street.

"What's that?" I asked as Marvin and I sat across from Thomson.

"Our currency," Thomson said, pulling a bill out of his breast pocket, a torn strip of newspaper stamped with the complex design of a Celtic knot. "Dark dollars. We give soup in exchange for this and we give this in exchange for work." I took it from him. It was flimsy, easily torn.

"What about counterfeit? Don't people cheat you?"

"People do what they need to in order to survive," said Phoenix, walking back to us. She'd let the others out and locked the door again. "Wouldn't you?"

"Of course," I said, remembering my mother talking about the food bank. How she'd had to fit into the crowd in the tiny waiting room that stank of cat litter and sour, old smoke and wait for her number to be called.

"The important thing is organization," said Thomson. "You give me a promise to wash dishes or help with the hives and I'll give you these." He wiggled the bill. "Marvin calls our activities stop-gap, but we do what we're able. We keep bees. We garden. We organize."

Marvin smiled, lowering the mug from his mouth. He had guzzled it down.

"Why do you run it so late?" I asked, tasting the soup. It was delicious: salty, with flavours of licorice and cumin and carrot.

"People are hungrier at night," said Thomson. He pushed his own soup aside, half eaten.

"At night, we're less bothered," Phoenix said.

"By the police?"

"Among others." Her eyes shifted warily to the front door. No one was there. The door shut and locked. A striped brown sheet turned into a curtain covered the few surviving panes of glass in the front window.

I asked them other things: where they got water, if there was ever violence, how long they planned to stay. It was mostly Phoenix who talked, telling me about the grocery store outside the dark zone that donated withered mushrooms and soft hothouse tomatoes and garlic sprouting green shoots. "The beef and fish bones come from Chinatown," she said, her eyes on mine. They were the blackest I'd ever seen. I thought of the ocean—the deepest places where things get lost. Ships, skeletons. The broken steel bodies of oil rigs. I looked away. It was cold in the restaurant, a seeping chill that felt like liquid.

"And you keep bees," I said to Thomson. He nodded. "Can I see them?"

"Nothing to see. They're snug in the hives, living off the fruits of their labour." Thomson must have seen the disappointment on my face. "Another time," he added.

"Do you know about bees?" Phoenix asked. I shook my head. I wondered how she wasn't cold. All she was wearing was a long-sleeved red T-shirt, the cuffs spotted pink from bleach. Her jacket tossed aside on a chair. "Each bee has a duty. Forager bees collect the nectar. Undertaker bees remove corpses from the hive. They work collectively for the sake of the colony."

"Like communism," Marvin said.

Thomson laughed, a dry snort. "Not quite. Nobody instructs them. No one suppresses their free will."

"What would you call it?"

"Nature."

"And what's happening now?"

"In the hive?" Thomson asked, confused.

"No," said Marvin. "In the city. They claim private property for the supposed good of all and they continue, with whatever laws they can muster, with a police force they can barely fucking pay, to crack down harder and harder—"

"Yes," Phoenix said, interrupting. "And you're making it worse."

Marvin started to speak, but Thomson held a hand up, stopping him. "In 1989, our dissidents would have been entitled to plant bombs, blow things up, fight violently for what was ours, but we chose not to." His finger jabbed the air. "Not one window was smashed."

"That isn't what we're doing," Marvin nearly shouted. Tentatively I touched his knee, trying to calm him, but he pulled away from me with a jerking motion. "The whole system is struggling to keep this fucking boat afloat with only the wealthiest still breathing. Everyone in steerage has already drowned."

His last word echoed in the quiet night air of the diner. Thomson and Phoenix stared at him. I could feel my heart beating, the steady thump of it, driven harder by his anger. His hair had fallen into his eyes and he brushed it away with the palm of his hand. Abruptly he sat back and dug into his tobacco pouch and soon his fingers were busy, moving like wind in the underbrush, scattering tobacco, rolling cigarettes, folding tiny strips of cardboard into filters. Under the table, I pressed my fingers against his legs, but he didn't respond.

I would have left with Marvin right then, but Thomson started speaking. "When the people here lost their homes, it was state control." Marvin looked up. "It reminded me of my grandparents' stories about the coup in 1948 when nothing they'd worked for mattered anymore."

I ran my thumb along the chrome edge of the table. Rust spots showed around the tiny bolts. I was still living at my parents' apartment when the city cleared the way for EcoGrid to build their solar farm, triggering one protest after another. I remembered the news: how some of the evicted residents set up an encampment on the lawn of a community centre in a wealthy neighbourhood.

The media reported plenty of complaints from the homeowners. The protestors crushed the tulips and cleaned themselves in public washrooms. A little girl was startled by a couple having sex under the swings. That's what the news reported. And one night, the police went in and arrested them all.

"After that, a lot of us started squatting down here," Thomson told me, reaching for one of Marvin's cigarettes. "And the company gave up because they knew it was too late."

"Too late for what?" I asked as Thomson leaned into the flame from Marvin's match. He inhaled, and when the smoke streamed out of his mouth, he coughed, bending forward, his fingers gripping the edge of the table. He was coughing too hard to answer. Phoenix took the cigarette and dropped it into her mug. I heard the hiss of the ember against the remaining dampness. She filled my empty cup with water from a jug on the counter.

Marvin nudged his shoulder against mine. "Solar," he grunted.

"What?"

Thomson drank, finishing the water, handing the cup to Phoenix for more. He wiped his mouth with the back of his hand. "It's too late for solar," he said, and when Phoenix set the mug down he ignored it. Instead, he returned to his soup, sloppily shoving the spoon into his mouth like he was all of a sudden starving. I heard the metal clang against his teeth. Drops of broth fell on his chest and I noticed the holes in the weave of his sweater. His grey hair hung down to his collar. There was a smudge of black dirt on his bald spot. Late fifties or early sixties, I thought.

Marvin slid his tin of cigarettes into the top of his pack. He was getting ready to leave. Suddenly I felt tired. All I really wanted was to go home, to sleep. I had no means of making money, feeding myself, paying the rent. I realized this as if the fact was only just coming true. I thought of telling them about my situation, but our conversation had taken a long time. It was after 1:00 AM.

Thomson wiped his mouth with a towel Phoenix had brought over. The red broth smeared onto the fabric from his lips and facial hair. "What do you think of this?" he asked me. "Our project."

"It's great," I mumbled.

"We should go," said Marvin, standing. I nodded and pressed my hand against the torn vinyl and slid to the edge of the bench, but Thomson persisted.

"What do you like about it?" I thought about it. My mother always used to say a change is as good as a rest and that's what I liked. Going down there was different, entirely new, a foreign landscape. It had helped me stop focusing on my own miseries. But I knew I couldn't say that. I dug around for another reason. And when I said it—"You're doing something meaningful, you're making a difference"—I realized I meant it.

"Marvin's found a nice girl," Phoenix said. She sounded sarcastic. My face grew hot. It was like she could see through me, to my soft life, the frailness of my reasoning. When we said goodbye they hardly even looked at me. Phoenix had turned her back to finish the last of the dishes and Thomson was counting his dark dollars, licking his finger to move through the stack.

When we walked away I considered all the things I could have said to impress them. The things I knew how to do, the skills I had. How to force rhubarb. How to save the best of the crop for seeds. Canning. Even making butter.

Maybe I could help them.

But Marvin broke into my thoughts. "They think you're simple, but I know you're not." And he took my hand. Not like a lover but like a brother. Fingers folded over mine as he led me deeper into the dark zone.

Along the street, nearly every neon store sign had been smashed, their letters broken into brightly coloured pieces that crunched as we walked. Nobody else was out. Up the way, I saw a dog and then another, working their noses in gaps under separate doors before coming back together. I pressed closer to Marvin, wanting him to take my hand again, to slide his fingers between mine, but his hands were shoved into his pockets. In a quiet voice, he filled me in on the neighbourhood's history.

"After the city cut power to the neighbourhood, most of the stores and houses were looted. I came down a few months later."

"How do you know them?" We'd moved into the middle of the street, crossing to head south. Frozen tufts of pink insulation skidded past.

"He's my uncle. In a way."

Thomson had come from the Czech Republic, Marvin told me. "Czechoslovakia then. He was a dissident. He and his friends fought for the revolution. They rallied in the city squares with Vaclav Havel until communism fell."

"Who's that? Havel."

"Playwright, dissident, first president of the Czech Republic."

"Oh," I said, and he continued.

"They were happy. Thomson and his friends. Those who wanted the change, who wanted freedom. But then capitalism moved in and he saw Operation Desert Storm T-shirts fill the shop windows. McDonald's. KFC. Then he heard about his cousin Katja. Her husband had died in a labour camp before the revolution and she needed money so she did what women can do—she went to the German border wearing sexy clothes. Germans crossed over, probably still do, and picked them up and fucked them behind the border patrol buildings where the guards used to stand and shoot you if you tried to run across."

He glanced at me. I didn't know what to say.

"People needed money," Marvin said, as if defending her. "They need to eat."

As if I didn't know that.

We turned the next corner. My eyes moved from one window to another, most of them empty pits, a few glowing with a dim internal light.

"So Thomson decided to travel," Marvin continued. "He ended up here as a student. He met my mother at school and she sponsored him to stay."

"Why was he so mad at you?"

Marvin shrugged. It was clear he wouldn't tell me.

"And Phoenix?"

Marvin stopped to straighten a bent cigarette. "She's just a bitch."

"I didn't think so."

"No?"

"No. Who is she?"

Marvin stuck the smoke in his mouth and mumbled around it. "His one and only. The apple of his eye."

"His daughter?"

"Stepdaughter. Born in Chiapas. Her parents were activists. Well, everyone was, unless you were military or a landowner."

I didn't know where Chiapas was, but Marvin didn't give me time to ask. "You know you don't have to prove anything to her," he said, stopping at the last in a line of row houses. "You don't even have to see her again." I followed him up the path and through the front door, already aware that was the opposite of what I wanted.

People don't always have reasons for what they do, Melissa. I left the diner knowing I would sleep with Marvin that night. Partly because I liked the feeling of his hand on my back and the heat of his confidence but also because the evening demanded it. I had never slept with a guy so quickly before, but Margo did it all the time and constantly told me to loosen up, be more spontaneous. Maybe it was out of character for me but since everything else had changed, I thought that could too. The box that had been my life—job, home, regular routine—had caved in, and going back to Marvin's squat was just the breaking of one of the seams.

The house was freezing cold and smelled musty. Marvin dumped his backpack on the floor. I heard the snapping of a match as he lit a candle lantern and the flames stretched every shape into large shadows. I saw a table with five chairs. Three books piled next to a typewriter. A black sleeping bag coiled on a mattress on the floor. The walls were covered with newspaper, cardboard, a blue tarp, and strangely shaped patches of plywood. In the mix a map was pinned up. Shiny red, silver, and gold stars formed a circle on streets north of the dark zone and the empty spot that was the lake. They glittered in the jumping light. They caught my eye, and I started walking over to look but Marvin said, "Come over here." When we met in the centre of the room, he put his cold hand on my neck and a tremor went through me. He leaned his face toward mine and when he kissed me, it was like the opening of a black hole, hot and magnetic, sucking me in.

5 Island

After Marvin rowed the boat into the bay at dawn, I went outside. A few of your footprints were on the far side of the garden fence. You wouldn't have been able to climb it and I ached for you, your hunger, your helplessness, but the plate was also gone from the porch. I hoped that was enough. Like the fish, beets are good for iron. Greens are plentiful in the fields. Dandelion leaves, although the flowers have gone to seed so they taste bitter. Still, they're better than nothing. If you don't know what to look for I will leave a little bit out and you can learn.

Mr. Bobiwash came when I was peeling the thin skins off the Roma tomatoes and sterilizing the jars. Mid-morning. Marvin back home and in the shed. Thomson made a sound like a woman starting to sob but fell silent when the knock came. Red pulp smeared on my apron, I opened the door. Mr. Bobiwash and his eldest son, Samuel, stood with guns balanced on their shoulders like sticks. They looked like hobos seeking work during the long-ago Great Depression I'd read about in newspapers in the dark zone.

"The cranes are back," Samuel told me, excited. They come every year, at the beginning and end of summer. Hundreds land by the stone foundation of an old barn up the road. They move on their stick-thin legs, their brown bodies hovering above the milkweed pods and rust-coloured grass. I'd already heard them. They were calling the day before when I was in the kitchen, cleaning last year's jars. Their strange, prehistoric warble. Thomson was too sick to walk up the road to see them so I laid down my barbecue tongs and went into the living room and opened the door.

"Listen."

"The dinosaurs," he said and closed his eyes. Gently, I wiped a bubble of spit from the corner of his mouth. He twisted away from me.

Have you heard them, Melissa? They are on their way to the Gulf of Mexico, a thousand miles south. Once upon a time we would have thought nothing of travelling such a distance. Now it's hard to imagine going such a long way away or even what it's like there, the mazes of salt marshes still tarry with oil from the spill that happened when I was just a girl, probably no bigger than you.

"How's Thomson?" Samuel asked. He put a hand on his father's arm and bent sideways to look around me. I stepped aside so he could see. The bald top of Thomson's head. Liver spots and wispy white hairs.

"Not so good." I wiped the sweat from my face with a clean corner of my apron. "We're waiting for the ship."

Mr. Bobiwash walked around the easy chair so he was facing Thomson.

"Jack," said Thomson, lifting an arm, his fingers crooked.

Mr. Bobiwash squeezed Thomson's hand. "You're a lazy son of a bitch."

Thomson laughed, a weak chortle. Samuel stood in the doorway, watching.

I heard the hiss of the water as it boiled over onto the hot top of the cook stove. My jars rattled violently against the sides of the aluminum pot. "Marvin's in the shed," I told them, but they followed me into the kitchen. I held a spoonful of sugar out for Samuel although we didn't have much left. He grinned but shook his head and I realized how old he was getting. Almost sixteen, nearly a man. Mr. Bobiwash gestured to the kitchen door, the garden outside. "That's a big fence."

"Deer," I lied, scooping boiling tomatoes into the hot jars. Samuel screwed on the lids.

"Don't burn yourself." I glanced at Mr. Bobiwash. "How is Shannon?" I wanted to change the subject. Only a few weeks ago, his wife had squatted between two poplars, her hands holding their narrow trunks, and delivered her baby. The small head crowned as blood gushed onto a carpet of pine needles. I helped Sarah, the midwife, by pulling the sharp knife from her leather satchel and boiling it clean so she could cut the cord. We talked about how hospitals used to be. All that shiny, functional steel. Clean green uniforms. Masks and disposable latex gloves. Babies died now. More than before.

Afterwards, with the tiny, purple infant in my arms, I thought about my mother. How she would have been proud. Not a flinch in me. Just this eager humming. The sound in your ears when you're running hard but happy. She was proud of me when I lived in the city. Proud that I worked for Parthenon. But that was before I was let go, before the dark zone and Walter and Phoenix. Before I irrevocably faded from their lives. I didn't even know if they were still alive. I tried not to think about that.

"The baby's got that red stain," Mr. Bobiwash said, gesturing as if removing a mask.

"It's just a birthmark."

"It's dry. I think it's itchy."

"The salve isn't helping?" I wiped spilled tomatoes off the counter.

He shook his head. He stared at the jars that filled the counter, which would sit until their lids popped. "She isn't feeding either."

"Can Sarah help with that?"

Mr. Bobiwash wobbled his head, staring down at the ground. I didn't want to pry so I stopped asking questions. I knew Shannon—her suspicions, how she called Sarah "the witch doctor." She'd tried to get the doctor from the supply ship to do a Caesarean rather than rely on Sarah's help. "Too dangerous," he'd said. "Inadequate facilities." The hospital in town operated with no power, all those bulky machines heaped up in a kind of scrapyard that overtook the parking lot.

Marvin came out of his shed. Through the window we watched as he clicked the padlock closed. I put the pot in the sink and we went outside, wandering over to the garden where the last of the lettuce had gone to seed. I picked at bits of tomato skin stuck to my fingers. Thomson's blood-stained handkerchiefs flapped on the line like prayer flags.

"I'm going into town," Mr. Bobiwash said as Marvin approached.

"No wagon?"

He shook his head. "Walking. We'll see more."

Town was five miles away. A community of about two hundred. A church we never went to, sticking instead to the market, the occasional dance. For years we'd hidden on its edges, but as things unravelled we grew braver, not so afraid of being caught.

"I'm going to meet the boat. Find the doctor."

"It's here?" I asked, eager.

"Every day," said Mr. Bobiwash. "I go every day."

"It's been late before," said Marvin. Mr. Bobiwash picked up the gun, balanced the stock on his shoulder. Marvin was right, but those times we had known where it was, could follow its progress. The only shortwave radio on the island had melted in a fire during a cold snap last January.

Samuel walked up one side of the garden, dragging his foot in the dirt, making a line. The chickens crowded behind him, pecking at the exposed bugs.

Mr. Bobiwash turned to me. "Eric picked a load of bulrushes yesterday," he said, referring to his middle son. "There's lots."

I knew this was Mr. Bobiwash's way of asking me to stop by his house, to check on Shannon. He closed his free hand around the fencepost and turned to Marvin. "I'm stopping at the Sharmas' place." His hand pulled on the wooden stock of the gun so the barrel gazed up at the sky. "Something's been eating out of their garden."

A crow called, landing on the peaked tin roof of Marvin's shed. "It's just deer," I said, but Mr. Bobiwash ignored me.

"Carrots pulled out. Eggs gone. The Sharmas shot a mess of ducks and offered me one."

Marvin was already nodding as he spoke. "To look for whatever it is."

"It's a deer," I repeated, as if Mr. Bobiwash would believe me.

I pushed Marvin's arm, trying to get him to agree with me, to tell Mr. Bobiwash the same thing.

"They've set traps."

"Traps?" said Marvin.

"Box traps."

None of us spoke. The wind moved around us. A blue jay scolded from its perch on a jack pine.

"The Sharmas are old people," said Mr. Bobiwash. "They don't have a lot. Their son probably needs most of their food. He works hard."

"You can't kill it," I blurted.

Mr. Bobiwash settled his brown eyes on mine but didn't say anything.

"All right," Marvin said. "I'll go."

"I'll come with you," I told them.

Marvin turned to me. "You have to stay with Thomson."

"He's sleeping."

"Sandy . . ."

I walked away, opened the plastic ice cream pail of corn and crushed clam shells and saw that it was almost empty. The crow cawed into the heavy air. It was humid, rain hanging in the sky. Another bird answered. Waking you from your daytime sleep in the dark rock hollows, telling you to watch out.

In our bedroom, I sat on the mattress while Marvin changed from shorts to a pair of corduroy pants. *Stop him from hunting her*, I wanted to say, but he glanced at me and said, "Don't."

"What?"

"You signed up for this."

"Who would sign up for this?" Our rumpled bed, the hardwood floor rotting where it meets the walls.

"All I'm doing is trying to protect what's mine. I'm a man. It's what men do."

"And what will you do if you find her?"

"She's a thief."

"And we were terrorists."

His jaw went hard.

"Promise me you won't tell him. Just for a few days."

He didn't say anything as he walked away. I heard his boots pound down the stairs and Thomson speaking to him in the living room. Marvin responded, but I couldn't make out what they said. The words were quiet enough that I could imagine whatever I wanted. Thomson asking him to protect her and Marvin simply agreeing, out loud. A scenario that would never be. The front door slammed. Through the window, I watched them go. The two men and the boy, ambling up the driveway like a family, like they were all related. Far above, three turkey vultures circled, tipping toward the west.

6 City

I woke on a cold mattress, not knowing where I was. Slowly the strange puzzle of the walls came clear. The windows on either side of the fireplace sparkled with frost and I shivered from the chill. Marvin's shoulder blades pressed against my breasts and that was the only part of me that was warm. Still, I pulled back, unlooping my arm from around his chest as I remembered the night before. I hadn't slept with him. I'd chickened out. After we'd climbed into bed and taken each other's clothes off, I'd stopped him, alarmed by how quickly things were moving. We'd gotten dressed and gone silently to sleep, gradually embracing each other in order to stay warm.

Marvin rolled over. "Morning," he said, his eyes still shut. He sounded friendly when I'd expected him to be brusque, to get up quickly, dismiss me or lead me back to the fence and point me toward the greater city and my home with Margo. I thought the night was its own island that I would swim away from, ashamed, and never look back. "Morning," I repeated, lying on my back with my arms crossed over my stomach. He snaked his arm around my waist.

"Last night," I said, starting to explain. I wanted to tell him about the kind of girl I was, although it seemed I didn't really know her, except that she wasn't Margo.

His hand slid under the hem of my shirt. The tips of his fingers ran over my skin and I realized he wasn't listening, that it might not even matter. I stopped talking, closed my eyes. Above us, on the second storey, pigeons warbled, their feet scattering around on the floor. I heard them as his hand moved to my breast and slipped under the left cup of my bra, stroking the hardened nipple. I groaned, giving in to my body's ache. I curved into him. As close as we could get. And that was how it happened. Our first time.

Afterwards, we pulled our clothes back on and Marvin lit a cigarette as we lay in bed. "Do you want coffee?"

"Coffee?"

"Yeah."

"Fake?"

"Real," he said. Surprised, I pushed myself up on one elbow and stared down into his face. "I have a friend who works security in a boutique food shop," he said. "It's swept off the floor, but it's the real thing." Coffee was so expensive, I hadn't had it in months.

He threw the covers off. He wore a suit of black long underwear. "Can you start a fire?" he asked, dragging the heap of his shirt toward him.

"Okay."

"Stuff's in there." He gestured at a box containing a few paperback novels and kindling chopped from abandoned items of furniture. A yellow lighter lay on the floor, SECURE YOUR FUTURE and a phone number printed in red text on its side. Trailing cigarette smoke, he left the room. I watched his body move away, the long, hard muscles in his legs, and felt suddenly ravenous, like I could never get enough to eat.

The books were swollen from being soaked and dried, dropped in a bath or left out in the elements. I pulled out one called *Pirate Nights*, an old library code still stuck to the spine. The pages smelled musty as I crumpled them and lay them in the hearth. When I had enough paper I put a couple pieces of kindling on top but I couldn't keep it burning. The pages blackened and went out, over and over again, their edges curling into ineffective ash. Frustrated, I looked toward the door that Marvin had gone through and then at the wall where the map was posted, the one I'd noticed before Marvin had kissed me the night before. The stars had stopped glittering. I gave up on the fire and went to look at it, arms wrapped tightly around me to try to keep warm. One star was stuck to the place we'd been the night before, where Marvin had broken the window of the travel agency. When he came back in the room, carrying two mugs, I pointed at the map and asked, "What is this?"

"What happened with the fire?"

"I couldn't get it going."

From the way he looked, I could tell he was judging me, that I hadn't lived up to his expectations. He set the coffee down on the mantle and pulled his jeans, the knees torn and patched, over his long underwear. "Let me show you," he said, and I walked over. I reached for the coffee. "Not yet," Marvin said, from his crouch on the ground. "Watch."

He built a thick tepee of sticks around the balls of paper. The fire caught quickly and we sat watching the flames. Gradually, as he added wood, my body began to grow warm and the strong, black coffee tasted like a long-ago treat from childhood: chocolate or sugary soda pop. Marvin lit a cigarette and I reached for a drag.

"Don't blame me when you get hooked."

I smiled, sucking in the velvety smoke. I thought of asking him about the map again, but I didn't. Probably I didn't really want to know. "Where's Chiapas?" I asked instead.

Marvin reached for the side of a picture frame and snapped it over his knee. He fed it to the fire, one part at a time. When I handed him back his cigarette, he laid it on a mortared groove between the bricks of the hearth and broke up more kindling. "Why?"

"I'm curious."

But he didn't tell me. He nodded toward the map. "Jump Ship. That's where they've hit." My back was turned to the wall where it was posted. I cupped my hands around the warm mug. He shoved a sharp piece of wood into the flames. I didn't know what to say. I felt uneasy, a burn in my throat forming from the acidic drink. "You follow them?" I finally asked. My mind scrambled around the details I knew, their few targets: a gas station, a bank machine, a car dealership. They were small bombs, minimal damage, no victims, the reasons never given. At least not through the media.

Marvin's hand flicked toward my coffee. "More?"

"No, thank you."

He scowled slightly and I again noticed the lines around his mouth. "There isn't much left," he muttered. When he spoke again, his voice came out flat, without inflection. "Chiapas is a state in Mexico," he said, his eyes following the motions of his hand: twirling the end of his cigarette against the brick, carving off the brittle edge of the ember. "Phoenix's mother was part of a non-violent revolutionary group called Las Abejas. Thomson went there as a human rights observer. He met Phoenix's mom. They got married."

"How old was Phoenix?"

"Six, I think. Seven. I was also just a kid."

"Were you there?"

Marvin shook his head.

"What about her dad?"

"He was a casualty," he said, as if that was something normal, a usual occurrence, like saying he'd run off with another woman. I wanted the whole story, all the details. It seemed like something far off, long ago, barely real. Like a legend, an epic novel.

"What do you mean?"

"The paramilitary took him a few years after she was born. He 'disappeared,'" he said, forming quotation marks with his fingers around the word.

"Oh."

"A couple years later the army came in. There was a standoff. People hid in a church." Marvin nudged the fire with a piece of wood that looked like a painted chair leg. The words from the book vanished into black carbon.

"Phoenix was there with her mother. A paramilitary group went in and when the guns went off, she was buried in all the bodies."

Marvin waited for me to say something, to react in some way, but I didn't know what words to use so I stayed silent, listening.

"Thomson was away in Mexico City, at the embassy, he said. Phoenix lay there until help came and then crawled out and Thomson brought her home as soon as he could arrange it."

"Home?"

"Here," Marvin said. I nodded and he continued. "They supported the Zapatistas. Indigenous rebels who wanted equity, control over local resources." His voice grew louder, as if he was speaking to an audience. "The state was rich, but the people were poor. Our battles are similar, although that was a long time ago and a long way away."

He swallowed the last of his coffee and the mug hit the floor with a crack.

What are our battles? I could have asked, but I didn't. I thought I already knew. Survival, putting food on the table. "They've been through a lot," I said, but Marvin talked over me: "I'm not that into making soup." He stood and walked over and pointed at a green square in the centre of the circle of stars. "I want to take you here."

Half an hour later, we left through the back door of the row house. I used the outhouse and then we walked through a clearing, past a huge billboard that showed a man and woman, faces corroded by weather, under the words THE LUXURY YOU DESERVE. Marvin tossed his apple core aside and I followed its trajectory to a red brick building whose window frames had weathered into silver wood. "The lamp factory," he said. "It was supposed to be turned into lofts." Outside the building's front door, a woman stirred a smouldering fire, her hair dirty and tangled, her face burned red by the wind. I didn't know then, and wouldn't have wanted to know, that would be me in fifteen years. As we walked toward the edge of the dark zone, I kept eating my apple, its flesh grainy, overly dry from the many months it had been off the tree.

"Here" was a botanical garden north of the travel agency Marvin had vandalized the night before. It was in the middle of a park where an encampment was set up. Several tents stood between a grove of birch trees and the street, by a sign that read, ABSOLUTELY NO LOITERING. A bike lay on its side near a firepit scratched out of the lawn. Marvin waved at a guy in a lumberjack jacket who was tying a line to a tree branch to lift the peak of his collapsed tent. The smell of food drifted out of the doorway of a round yurt. On its side, a large sign read, HOUSING IS A HUMAN RIGHT. A woman ate out of a plastic bowl, sitting on the edge of a large marble fountain that was empty of water. Marvin told me it had been drained when people started using it to wash themselves, their dishes and clothes. At one end of the park, the garden buildings gleamed like a palace. They were made entirely of glass—a huge central dome with two smaller ones on either side and rectangular greenhouses jutting out the back. Marvin pointed at a bright sign over the front door that blared the name of one of the big banks. "Privatized now," he said. "The city used to own it. It was built by citizens in the 1800s."

We had to pay to get in. Marvin pulled a fold of crumpled bills out of his pocket and handed one of them to the attendant. She took it and gave me a brochure, her smile disappearing as Marvin said, "It used to be free." A security guard watched us as we went inside, his radio stuttering static.

Under the curved roof, my eyes crawled up a skinny grey trunk to green fronds sprouting from its top. A palm tree. Plants with wide, ruby leaves grew around its base. Angular orange blooms jabbed out of the foliage. *Birds of Paradise*, the brochure said. In the sudden humidity I uncoiled the wool scarf from around my neck and shrugged out of my winter coat. It was another season in there. Summer. In the deep, cold hollow of winter, I still think about those gardens. A flickering memory I turn away from as quick as I can.

"You like it?" Marvin asked.

"Love it," I breathed.

He gestured toward a plant with a fat stem amid its wide, flat leaves. A deep purple bloom that looked shiny like it had been greased. "Banana tree."

I stared at him, surprised. The tropical plants made a foreign wilderness, entirely unfamiliar. I fingered the edge of a huge waxy leaf, then a red one veined with lime green.

"It's beautiful."

"Yeah. But it's fantasy."

The smell of humus and floral perfume reminded me of the farm in early summer. It seemed very real to me. I let go of a white trumpet-shaped blossom and wandered past the poinsettias. In a room for desert plants, a woman was sketching a barrel cactus. With a charcoal pencil, she tapped out the dark thorns. When Marvin started to speak, she looked up. "The only jungle we ever had was white pine," he said to me. I turned down a trail crowded with yellow hibiscus, pink Allamanda, smoothly barked branches draped with Spanish moss. Fleshy leaves dangled from a hanging succulent, and I squeezed one like an earlobe. Marvin followed closely, whispering, his voice a hiss as his lecture continued. I felt overwhelmed, attached to him, as if every time I moved away whatever was tied between us tugged him along behind me. "Old-growth forests demolished by settlers to make fields for wheat farms that are now suburbs and housing developments like Parthenon's. We've lost hundreds of farms by now, but long before that we had all these huge white pines." He stretched his arms out to illustrate their girth, but I doubted him. The part of the world that I was from had farm fields all the way to the horizon.

The outer walls were monochrome, dimmed by winter on the other side. A woman in a red coat stood like a large flower against the grey glass. Gold gleamed around her wrist and her slacks were neatly pressed. She looked up as we went past, Marvin's voice crackling, and I felt self-conscious, wearing wrinkled, grimy clothes, smelling of sex, sweat, and wood smoke. I looked away, my eyes moving up to the curved panes of the glass dome held together with iron spokes, and I thought about Margo, wondering if I'd see her when I got home, if I'd be able to talk to her about my strange night or if she'd already gone off to work.

Marvin kept talking, but I wasn't listening anymore. Irritated, I interrupted him. "I'm hungry," I said.

He stopped mid-sentence and stared at me, his mouth slightly open. His arm swung forward, pointing. "There's another wing." I hesitated. He stepped closer. "You don't like it," he said, reaching for my hand.

"No, I do," I said as his thumb slid over my palm and the memory of that morning resurfaced. I let him lead me through the next doorway into a room full of humid jungle.

“Imagine this place back then,” I said. “You’re living in this inescapable season and suddenly somebody makes this place and you can come here, be warm, be around all these plants from places you can’t ever hope to see. The desert, the Amazon jungle. I mean, even for me . . . I’ve never been anywhere.”

My mother had travelled. Using the inheritance from her grandmother, she went to Latin America, Europe, even Japan. I wanted to tell him about that, about her, but his voice grew sharp-edged in exasperation, like I’d done something wrong. “That isn’t the point,” he said at the same moment as a security guard rounded the corner, and as if he was changing costumes, Marvin softened and quickly turned to a glassed-in case of orchids and started telling me about them. The guard brushed by us, moving slowly, like a stalking cat. Marvin twisted his face away, like he was hiding.

“They live on air,” I repeated, to show that I’d been paying attention, although I hadn’t. I’d been wondering what he was originally going to say, where I’d gone wrong.

“The water in the air,” Marvin corrected. The security guard hovered at the entrance to the far room. I looked in at one of the orchids, its white petals like a bird’s lifted wing. Thick roots dangled out of the pot, absorbing invisible nourishment. Marvin moved closer to me, his breath warm against my neck. I wanted him to take my hand, slide his fingers up the back of my sweater. Seduce me again. Instead, he only whispered in my ear: “Back then our horizons were expanding. Now they’re narrowing.”

“I still like it.”

“Of course,” he said, as if that was never in question. I didn’t know what he wanted. My head felt foggy from lack of sleep and food as we walked onto a humped wooden bridge. Orange carp swam under the reflection of the rounded glass and the weak, watery sun far above.

“But it’s a bubble,” he said as we stared down at the copper pennies on the bottom of the pond. “And bubbles have to burst.”

By then, Melissa, I wanted to go home. So much had happened in such a short time and I needed to process it all. Outside, a cold wind stabbed through the thin fabric of my jeans, which were smeared with soot. I was about to ask Marvin when I would see him again, but his pager buzzed. He tipped the small screen to his face and said, "It isn't personal, Sandy. I mean, don't get too attached." His gaze slid across the shiny glass buildings of the gardens before he kissed me, his lips pressing warmly against mine. His hand lingered on my waist before he pulled back and walked away, headed for one of few pay phones in the city, the location of which he had mapped out in his head. I was left alone. I followed the rutted pathway through the park to the road. Perplexed, slightly humiliated.

Right then what I wanted was to go back to my old life, to the things I knew and was used to. My apartment, work, laundry on the weekends. Promising my mother I'd get home for a visit and never going. But I couldn't do that, and panic bubbled up inside me as I walked quickly west. When I was small, I'd been accustomed to the idea that there were many choices open to me, that I could do or be anything I wanted. There had been so many options. All the brands lined up, their hundred advantages stamped on brightly coloured packaging. But that wasn't the way things were anymore. In truth, it hadn't been like that for a long time. Maybe it was a trick, the notion that they ever were, that a fantasy like that was sustainable. Perhaps Marvin was right—nothing lasts, not even the Coliseum, that grand stone structure that could hold fifty thousand spectators where cows were grazing a few hundred years later. I wondered what it all meant, that long strange night, so out of character for me. A smile pushed at my lips as I thought of telling Margo what I'd been up to, how surprised she'd be, perhaps even jealous. A streetcar rumbled by but I watched it go, not wanting to spend the last bit of change rattling in my coat pocket.

There was hardly anything to eat at home. The refrigerator was empty. I opened the cupboard, but there weren't any canned beans or macaroni and cheese left from the last time Margo's mom had come to visit. She always brought us food, pilfered from the dollar store where she worked. I lifted one of the last two eggs out of a bowl on the counter. When I turned the burner on, Margo appeared in the doorway. She watched without speaking as I cracked the egg into a frying pan and stared down at the unmoving yellow yolk.

"Power's off," she said.

The city was divided into zones and our power-down night was usually Wednesday. That way people could be prepared—fill their bathtubs, cook food ahead of time.

"It's not our night." I slid the pan into the slight chill of the dark fridge.

"Yeah. I don't know."

I found an old package of wasabi peas in a drawer and followed her down to the front porch where we sat on rickety wooden chairs. She studied me, looked at my hands, black under the fingernails from helping with the fire at Marvin's. I wiped them on my pants and thought of the guards at the gardens, watching us.

"What the hell happened to you?"

"Marvin," I said, smiling but trying not to.

Her eyes slid away. "That dirty squat." She tossed the blackened twist of a match over the porch railing.

The peas were too hot for me so I put them aside and pulled a lock of hair across my face. It smelled of wood smoke.

"Have you met them?"

"Them?"

"The soup kitchen people?"

"The good Samaritans? That smelly old man and his concubine."

"She's his daughter," I blurted, but Margo gave a rough little bark that sputtered smoke.

"Is that what they're calling it these days?"

I fell silent. I couldn't share much with Margo. She was jealous of anyone else's successes. When I first got my job she would show up, entice me out for smoke breaks, as if attempting to get me fired. So what I felt then was off-limits to her. It was big. It was like I'd discovered a secret tunnel inside myself and shone a light on the slick, dark walls to find a mineral glitter.

"Well, I had a great night," she said, as if we were competing. I didn't ask the obvious: what it was like, those steel pincers against her bare skin, even though I knew she was waiting for the question. Instead Margo told me how Walter had lost his hand—a bomb in Afghanistan, a checkpoint, insurgents arrested.

"Walter told you that?"

"Who else?"

He was lying, at least according to what Marvin had said, but I didn't say anything. "Are you guys a thing?" I asked.

"There's a story unfolding," she said in her overdramatic way. Margo tended to choose boyfriends like an actress decided on parts—looking for the best drama. She fell silent, staring out at the soggy front yard, the chain-link fence between us and the street.

I tried again, attempting to sound casual: "Marvin's a good kisser."

"I'm surprised he went for you."

I shut up, stung by her nastiness, but also because I didn't want to know what she meant. Now I realize he needed help, recruits as Phoenix had said, workers for his agenda, but right then Marvin had drawn me in like a game, like one of those Russian dolls that split open at the belly and inside each is a smaller one. You keep pulling them apart until you find the smallest, the baby, the size of a beetle. I couldn't imagine seeing that far inside Marvin. One doll deep, maybe. That's how far I'd be able to delve.

I can't remember what else I did that day, except for one thing. A trip out for groceries that Margo made me take, handing me her debit card. I was in line at the Portuguese butcher, ready to ask for a half-pound of gizzards, when the woman in front of me started fishing out money to pay for a pound of bologna and a jug of milk. Her change clattered on the counter, lay there like tiny silver ponds, and the bills made a rustling sound like leaves. Her hair was pulled back off her face and a bruise, yellow and blue on her dark skin, circled her eye. She didn't have enough. I was the only other customer in the store, but I kept my eyes on the half-empty tub of ground beef in the glass case, its bloodiness turned brown, as she lifted her head and looked around and said her mother was sick, that they needed food. I doubt either of us believed her—the butcher behind the counter or me—and so as he drew out his sharp knife and chopped a quarter-pound off the meat, I just stood there, feeling Margo's card, flint-hard, in my back pocket. It wasn't until after she left that I saw Phoenix's face in my head, her black eyes on me, and I felt shame that not even the butcher could alleviate when he said, "Tough times all over," and gave me a couple extra gizzards after he'd weighed them on the scale.

Days passed. Nearly a week. I didn't hear from Marvin. I thought that whatever had happened between us could be chalked up to a strange, single adventure. Lying in bed at night, I recounted the details of that night, but part of me was relieved that it had ended. I knew I'd wind up going home, living with my parents, listening to my mother's travel stories and all her old regrets. Trying to dodge my father's depression. That's what should have happened. Over the years, I've thought many times about how things would have been different if I'd simply made that decision instead of waiting for an escape hatch, an alternative path. My parents could have helped me. Ultimately, although they were far from perfect, I think what they wanted for me was what I want for you, Melissa: a better life. And what did I want for them? That thought didn't even occur to me.

I applied for a couple dozen jobs but heard nothing. The white digits on the ATM screen ticked down as my panic rose. Finally, when I hit zero and plunged into overdraft—money I never paid back—I pulled my suitcase out of the closet with a deep sense of dread and started considering what I could keep and what I would give to Margo. That was the day she came home from work and stuck her head in my room.

"Going on a trip?" she asked, pulling off a red leather ballet flat to rub her heel. I didn't answer. She knew as well as I did how narrow my options were. The shoes dangled from two of her fingers. "By the way," she said, as if in afterthought, "I saw Marvin today."

My heart lurched but I was careful. I didn't look up from the clothes, sorted into piles on my bed. "Yeah?"

"At the store."

"Was he picking up a designer outfit?" She turned away and half disappeared. I took two steps toward the door and spoke to her back as she retreated down the hall. I couldn't stop myself. "Did he ask about me?"

She spun around, unbuttoning the shiny purple blouse she had on.

I saw the edge of her black bra and looked away. "He asked if you had another job."

"That's it?"

"Sorry," she said. "Dinner?"

Since she paid for mostly everything, we'd agreed that I would cook. "It's on the stove. Gizzards, peas, and rice. Nothing exciting."

"Well, I was expecting steak."

I couldn't tell if she was joking.

I wanted to ask more about Marvin but was wary of being mocked. Sometimes she took the things that you were vulnerable about and turned them into weapons. We ate at the table, and when she had finished she pushed her plate into the centre, knocking over a salt shaker, which I righted.

"I don't want you to go home," she said, opening the window. There was no screen and the small, potted jade plant on the sill rocked, nearly fell over. A cold breeze billowed into the kitchen and Margo slid the glass pane halfway shut. She lit her cigarette, a hand-rolled one, like Marvin smoked. "What am I supposed to do?"

I raised my eyebrows. "I have eight dollars, Margo. Rent's due on Friday. You can't keep paying for everything."

"You can pay me back."

Her face looked stern in the low light. Until then, I'd had no idea she thought that way, that she wasn't just being generous. If a bill was slowly being rung up, I already owed her hundreds in the extras she'd purchased: drinks out, everyday food, the huge hydro bill. Panic fluttered in my throat.

"Can't you borrow?" she asked.

"Who from?"

"Your parents?" When I didn't answer, she said, "A rich aunt?"

I mashed the peas with my fork, then scraped them up. "There are no jobs," I said.

"You'll find one. Or there's always prostitution." She laughed, but I thought of Thomson's cousin at the German border. Stabbing her smoke out in a tiny nest of undercooked rice, she said, "You didn't tell me you slept with Marvin."

I swallowed the food in my mouth. "He told you?"

"He's good, isn't he?" A heavy swell entered my stomach, like a ship taking on water. She smiled into the shock on my face and tsked her tongue at me. "Don't be like that, Sandy. It was a long time ago."

With the side of my fork, I sliced through a gizzard. "How long?"

She shrugged. "Six months."

"Once?"

She smiled, sneakily, the secret hidden on her tongue.

I told myself it was not a big deal. Most girls my age—just turned twenty-one, barely out of my teens—slept around, had Internet sex, posed for porn without a second thought. It didn't matter at all. Except it did. The image of Margo and Marvin talking about me, probably laughing at me, wouldn't leave my head. I wondered how I could possibly be as good in bed as she must have been: an animal that immediately devoured him. No hesitation. No holding back. I put down my fork and reached for her matches, lit one after another, calmed by the tiny explosions, the dead black curls dropping onto my plate.

"Whoa, there," Margo said and took them away. But then she lit another, pulled it up to the cigarette in her mouth, and said, "He can be pretty intense."

Images flickered through my mind: the gardens, the Jump Ship map, the diner. They were things I might have asked her about, but not now, not now that I had the image of them fucking on his cold, dirty mattress and Marvin comparing her to me. "Yeah," I said. "Got that." And then: "You mean compared to Walter? Walter the one-handed wonder." I laughed. Margo rubbed her free hand against the edge of the table like she was wiping away something gross. She narrowed her eyes.

"Maybe you won't care then that he says he has a job you might want in on."

"Marvin?"

"Walter."

She handed me her cigarette and I hesitated before taking it and sucking some of the hot smoke into my lungs. I knew she was making nice, with the shared cigarette and a job offer, but I didn't want to accept, didn't want to let her off so easily for shoving my face in the fact that she'd already had what I found I wanted. But I had to. If there was money involved, I didn't have a choice. Cold air pressed through the window. "What kind of a job?"

"Salvage," Margo said. "Up in the suburbs."

"Illegal?"

"It pays well."

When I didn't answer right away, Margo took the cigarette back. She inhaled the last of it before tossing the butt out the window into the jungly garden where we'd tried to grow tomatoes and broccoli the summer before but only managed a meagre yield. The moon had come up, a sharp, silver hook in the sky, and out of the blue she posed a question we often returned to because we were still young and still asked each other things like this: "What's your greatest fear?"

"Drowning," I said, without thinking. It's what I always said.

Insignificance was her usual answer and that's what I expected, but this time she said, "Death."

I hadn't thought much about death. Not in a personal way. Not yet. Now it's always present. Thomson, so sick, headed down a road with a single destination. *But the same is true for all of us*, he would say. I know that now. Every winter I know that threat of being extinguished. I didn't know it then and that's why I did what I did.

That night I called my mother. Margo was paying the wireless bill so we could still connect to the Internet, as long as the power was on. When she answered, her figure blurred in the screen, then settled. In the background, I saw my father in the lit rectangle of the kitchen door. He disappeared and reappeared and I realized he was pacing.

"I've been trying to get you," my mother said, her voice tinny, the words slightly detached from the movement of her mouth. "You never answer your cell."

"I gave it up. Remember?"

My father's voice rumbled in the background like the early warning of an avalanche. I knew that sound and I felt my body brace. "Everything okay?" I quietly asked her, although I didn't want to. I wished I hadn't called.

"Fine." Her eyes widened with a brief bright flare. "Just checking up on you."

"What's Dad up to?"

She shook her head, as if it wasn't anything, that telltale restlessness. Her hand waved dismissively, a streak across the screen. "He can't sleep."

"Is he taking his meds?"

"Yep," she said, but by the hard jab of her voice I knew she wasn't telling the truth. The pills cost two hundred and thirty-seven dollars a month. My mother rushed into the next question, securing the lie. "How are you? How's work?"

"Fine," I said, and then, just to see, I said, "I've been thinking about coming home."

"Oh," she said, startled. She looked down at the keyboard like there was an answer in that jumble of letters and she just had to figure it out. It was probably the moment that secured my fate, that subtle rejection, something I'd never do to you.

"You know," I lied, "a visit."

"That would be great, Sass," she said, using my old nickname. "But we'd have to—"

My father appeared, cutting her off, his face looming into the screen. A tear track stained his cheek like the trail of a slug. "Sass?"

My stomach clenched. I forced my voice to sound lighter than I felt. "Hi, Dad."

"Come on home. As long as you like. Forever. You can help me with our legal battles. I haven't given up on the farm. Sorting paper, research, that sort of thing. Of course, I'll pay you."

My father's eyes were wobbly and big and I smiled into them, not sure what to say. Of course, he couldn't pay me anything. My mother's arms reached out from behind my father, and for a moment it looked like they were growing out of his waist, and then she pushed him aside and they split and I realized I was the thing that had come out of the middle. I almost started to cry, but I pulled it all back, hardened myself. My father left the screen.

"It's not for sure," I started to say, but my mother leaned forward, eyes squinting. Concern emerging in her expression.

"You're bleeding," she said and touched her own nose. I felt the hot trickle running out of my nostril and excused myself. In the bathroom mirror, my face seemed sharper, more real, compared with hers on the computer. The blood a bright spot of colour on the white, white toilet paper. That other room, seen through the screen, a grainy, muted blur, as if it was already vanishing.

7 Island

I don't really like Shannon. She's bitter. She complains a lot, talking often about her old life on the mainland, all the tips she made waitressing as a teenager. The way she says things you'd think Mr. Bobiwash kidnapped her, that she didn't have a choice in how her life ended up. She answered the ad that Mr. Bobiwash ran, looking for a new wife. He put it in the newspaper Thomson and Albert, the former museum curator, started eight or nine years ago. But then the antique printing press broke and that was the end of that.

Once, I asked Shannon how she felt about what had happened to Mr. Bobiwash's first wife, Mona, disappearing like she did with his youngest. Shannon just looked at me vacantly, as if she couldn't hear, as if she was preoccupied, sort of like my father whenever I offered counter-arguments. Now I don't speak much. If she offers me tea, I sip the hot, watery liquid and listen to the kids playing outside, the baby's strange hush, allowing her whatever complaint she wants to make. But I also feel pity. I watched her give birth in the woods with only a stained blanket over her shoulders. She screamed and wept as if caught in a trap and I remembered my mother saying, *Childbirth is natural*. But, Melissa, death is too.

There are times I miss Mona—especially when I see the two women in contrast. Shannon doesn't know what to do with the boys, that wild trio, and she treats them with indifference, barely ever touching them, while Mona was so affectionate. A heavy, fleshy woman, she made feasts for all of us out of the turtles and fish we'd bring over or the deer Mr. Bobiwash shot. He was happy, especially when his daughter was born. Abigail, Abby, her eyes bright blue but soon bloodshot with sickness. They decided Mona should take her south, to her parents, her father a doctor. I thought about going with her. For days I toyed with the idea of leaving the seedlings unplanted, the garden to grow over with weeds. But in six months it would have been winter and all I could imagine was Thomson wasting away and me lost again down south, hiding out in another dirty squat. It was too late. Despite whatever I'd once wanted out of life, I had made my reality. Mona left and didn't return. She waved from the deck when the boat took her, the baby held in one crooked arm.

Why he ran the ad, I don't know. We all could have moved in together, like we'd tried to do in the dark zone. A community.

Before I went to the Bobiwashes', I left Thomson on the porch as he'd asked.

"I won't be long," I told him. The sun hung over the garden, muted by watery clouds. Halfway up the drive, I looked back and saw that he hadn't moved.

At the Bobiwash house, flies buzzed around a heap of wet diapers in a hamper. While I waited for Shannon to open the door, I felt Mr. Bobiwash's other two boys watching me, staring from their hiding spots. An incomprehensible shout blasted out of the bushes from Graham, the mentally challenged one, who had been five when their mother left. I knocked again.

"Shannon?" I tried the doorknob. It seemed stuck.

"I've got it," Shannon said, and when I let go, she pulled the door open. The daylight hit her green eyes and lit them. They looked a lot like Marvin's. Her forehead gleamed. The front of her plaid shirt was dark in spots, soaked. A rag hung from her hand, dripping. It was like she'd swum up from underwater, broken through the surface of the lake. She waited for me to speak. I held out a tattered plastic bag containing bunches of herbs—raspberry leaf and wild mint. She took it, stepped back into the house.

"The floor's wet," she said as I followed her. I stopped in the kitchen doorway and saw the prints from her bare feet appear across the linoleum and quickly fade away. Kneeling beside an aluminum bucket, she scrubbed at the tile with a bunched-up rag. Elastics around her forearms held her shirtsleeves up. One arm stretched across her breasts, holding them in place. Tendrils of black hair curled around her face, drawn in concentration.

"You're busy."

"The house is filthy. It's always filthy."

I stepped back into the hallway. "Where's the baby?" She didn't answer so I walked from room to room, looking.

Stretched across the baby's cheek, the red mark looked like a wing. Her eyes fluttered open and closed and she smacked her lips, the bottom one marked by a white worm of skin where it was chapped. Carefully, I lifted her small, warm body off the quilt pushed into a blue recycling box and carried her to the kitchen, her tiny, hard head cupped in one palm. Her left arm pinwheeled and she released a puff of air. Standing at the counter, Shannon filled the kettle from a plastic jug and brought it to the electric stove, fuelled by power from their solar panels although the battery banks are beginning to corrode. Still, I'm jealous because all I have is fire. Dirty, slow to heat up. I cooed to the baby, brought her face closer to mine.

"Don't wake her," Shannon said as she spooned a powder of roasted dandelion root into a mug. A green cabbage, small, not even ripe, sat on the counter.

"Yours are ready?" I asked, although I knew they weren't, that she'd harvested it early.

"That's what Sarah told me to do," Shannon said, turning to face me. She pulled open her shirt to show the wrinkled edge of a cabbage leaf sticking out of her yellowed bra. The skin on her chest was flushed red. "It isn't working. Big surprise."

"Maybe it takes time."

I cooed at the sleepy baby and she said again, her voice edged with warning: "Don't wake her."

Light shone through the clean windowpanes. The bulrushes that Eric had cut were in a bunch on the counter, their tops lopped off and the outer green peeled away. The white had started turning brown. I didn't want to ask for them, despite Mr. Bobiwash's offer.

Steam lifted around Shannon's head as she filled a mug. From outside I heard Eric and Graham calling to each other through the fields. The sounds of a game, a pretend battle, or negotiations over a job they had to do. As she carried the imitation coffee to the table I thought of telling her about you, but her face was grim, deep lines bracketing her mouth. I stayed quiet, leaning against the door frame, the baby a weight in my arms. She sat down and I realized she hadn't made a drink for me.

"What else did Sarah say?"

"Nothing," Shannon said and blew on the surface of her drink. She stared into the corner at a crate of empty jars, ready for autumn preserves, their glass walls dusty from storage. "Jack thinks it's just a rash. Just a temporary thing." Her gaze slid over to me and stopped on the baby. "But it's so fucking red it's like a bull's-eye."

"He's worried about you." In my voice, I heard the argument, the pitch of imploring, and I thought of my dad—trying, over and over again, to convince him it would be all right, that we'd be okay without the farm, and how nothing I said ever seemed to help him. He was sunk inside himself, imprisoned. I couldn't help him and I couldn't help Shannon either. Suddenly I felt very tired and refocused on the baby, that child, you, all our new beginnings. They needed such care, such cautious attention, lest we poison them with our old diseases. I thought of leaving, backing out the doorway with the baby in my arms, running up the road, and I wondered if Shannon would bother to follow or if she'd be relieved.

"He went to find the doctor," I told her. She sipped the drink without acknowledging me, like I wasn't even there. I tried again. "We'll find him," I said, the sort of false reassurance I'd learned to offer to women. A lie. Shannon pursed her lips. "We have to," I added.

"We? What problems do you have?"

"Thomson," I said, too loud. The baby woke, her lips sputtering as she started to cry. Shannon pressed her fingers against her forehead. When she took her hand away I saw tiny crescent moons pushed into her pale skin.

"I forgot. I forget things all the time." She glanced at me as I jiggled the baby, trying to calm her. "But those boys. They devour everything." The baby's cries rose to a high-pitched panicked scream. I rocked her back and forth, unable to soothe her with a name because she didn't have one. Shannon sighed but didn't move from her chair even as the wrinkled face grew furious and hot.

I don't know what it's like to have an infant. I was an only child, born years after my parents deliberated over whether to have kids or not. My cousin Emily, ten years older than me, happily became a mother, making jokes about how exhausted she was, sleeping when she could, tending easily to her newborn son. Shannon was different; she scared me. The baby wailed, arched her back like a cat intent on getting away. She wrinkled and squirmed. My hand felt wet. A bad smell rose from the small body.

"She does this," Shannon said, looking over at us with narrowed eyes. "She does this to me."

"Where are the diapers?" I asked, my stomach in a knot, but Shannon didn't answer. Calmly, she set down her mug and stared at the window above the sink.

"Shannon," I snapped, but she wouldn't speak. Entranced by something I couldn't see.

They weren't by the makeshift crib in the living room. I couldn't find them. Outside, the boys were in the yard, Graham kicking his legs out and circling in a strange dance and Eric, the youngest, squatting on the ground, untangling a trapline. He led me upstairs to his parents' room and took the baby from me. He laid her on the bed, undid the safety pins, and changed her by himself. Methodical, effortless, as if he had been doing it for years.

"Is your stepmother okay?" I asked him in a whisper, but he didn't answer me either.

Downstairs, I carried the baby back into the kitchen. I expected Eric to follow, but the front door opened and closed and I heard the sound of his footsteps crossing the porch, racing away. "Eric changed her all by—" I started to say, but stopped when I saw Shannon, leaning against the counter with her shirt open. Her left breast exposed. The wide nipple chapped and bleeding. A drop of milk like a strange tear, turned pink.

"I wanted you to see." The baby screamed again, writhing in my arms, as if she sensed the proximity of her mother's milk. What I wanted was to put her down, anywhere, in the sink even, and leave. But I felt her agony. The small cage of her ribs, wrapped around her hollow stomach. I took a breath and walked over to Shannon.

Together we fed her. Slowly, painfully, Shannon's fingers gripping the edge of the table as the small mouth suckled. A hot cloth to bathe the nipple.

"Are you okay?" I asked over and over. Not once did she answer. Her eyes were stuck on my necklace, the heart-shaped locket that dangled over the baby's head. Coveting, I could tell, and I slipped it under my shirt. She had a tattoo, a small black and orange snake wiggling at the top of her breast. Warped from the swelling, its belly looked distended, like it had swallowed a rat. I touched it with my finger. "When'd you get that?"

Shannon shrugged. "A long time ago. My sister. Her biker boyfriend." With the back of one hand she pushed wisps of hair off her sticky forehead and we switched breasts. As the baby latched on, Shannon sucked her breath between her teeth.

Keeping my voice light, I asked, "Have you thought any more about names?"

Shannon laughed derisively. "He wants to name her Crow. What kind of a name is that?"

I liked it but didn't tell her so.

When we were done, I carried the baby into the living room. She was smiling, a slight new flush in her sunken cheeks. One fist closed around my locket and tugged until I forced each finger open, pulled her hand away. I talked to her, the small, sad body, as her eyes drifted over my face, the whites slightly yellow. I wanted to carry her away, bring her home, but I knew that even if Shannon didn't fight me, Mr. Bobiwash would, the boys. A girl was an asset—any child was—and she wasn't mine to take. I put her on the couch and stood while Shannon sat beside her and laid her hand on the child's belly. She stared at the mantle over the fireplace and I turned and saw old family photos. Children I didn't recognize. A young, chubby girl, standing beside a motorcycle with a man. He wore a cowboy hat and the two of them were laughing. "Is this you?" I asked Shannon.

"Mona. The love of his life."

"I'm sure that's not true," I said.

"But he especially loved Abby. He'd trade me for her like that." She snapped her fingers and the baby stirred under her hand. I sat on the edge of one of the chairs, wondering when I could leave. Her shirt gaped open; her hair lay matted against her skull. She smelled sour. I knew I could never tell her about you. I wondered how she'd even survive.

"You know I didn't ask for any of this," Shannon said, her eyes bumping over the mantle and moving through the room like a snake over a rock face. Branches of light came through the crack in the drawn curtains. Dust sparkled in the air. "Like my granny. She lived in Newfoundland. Wife of a fisherman who went down with his ship." I winced, but Shannon didn't even see. Her gaze had slumped to the floorboards, stuck there as she spoke. "We went there once. Beautiful place. Like Ireland, I guess. The same continent cut in half. That was our last vacation. We even flew." When she said that, her chin lifted, something to be proud of. I smiled slightly, a small offering.

The baby squirmed. Shannon's hand fell away weakly when I picked her up to lay her in the recycling box. I pulled back the curtain and saw that a light rain had started, the first drops marking the dirt in the yard like a tally. The boys were gone.

"Granny told me about fairies," Shannon said suddenly, surprising me. When I turned, her eyes darted up to meet mine. "Little fucking thieves." She held my gaze and I stared back at her, a twitch flickering around her scowling lips. Did she mean you? It seemed you needed protection from everyone except me. I waited for more. None came. Shannon groaned and stretched out on the couch, turning toward the back cushions. In the corner of my eye, the boys moved and I saw where they were, crouched in the garden, down the long rows of corn, weeding.

Relieved, I left that house. Worried that they'd caught you, I walked home fast. In my mind I saw Mr. Bobiwash, waiting on the wharf for the doctor, a duck held out in offering, its bloody feathers gleaming green-gold, Marvin by his side.

8 City

At first I was a thief. The three of us were: Walter, Margo, and me.

It was dark out when Margo woke me. I groaned, snapped the light on. It didn't illuminate.

"What time is it?"

"After five," she said. "He'll be here soon."

She shut the door before I could answer, and I think that was because she knew I was having doubts. I lay there, watching the slow crawl of dawn through the corners of my room: across the poster of a mermaid stretched out on a seaweed-draped rock, the plywood shelf on steel brackets my dad put up when they'd visited in the fall that one and only time. They slept on the futon in our living room. My father had dropped the shiny hooks of his depression throughout the visit and I'd refused to be snagged. When they left, he gripped my upper arm and asked me to come home and all I could do was turn cold—a technique I sometimes try with Marvin, although he is not needy, only indifferent.

"Hurry up," Margo called through my door, and I had no choice but to drag myself out of bed. As I pulled on my jeans, I wondered where Marvin was, if I'd see him that day, what was happening down at the soup kitchen. Those prescribed duties had been a relief—do this, do that, do this. Like a job.

Walter was late. By the time he arrived—bumping onto the sidewalk in a borrowed red car, one tire nearly flat, the radio antenna snapped off at the base—we'd lost the advantage of darkness. Margo flipped the front seat up so I could climb in and Walter grunted at me, a sound that could have been hello. His odour was strong, like a weird spice.

We drove for twenty minutes or so, headed north, the city shifting from tightly packed downtown houses to industrial parks to a sprawl of huge homes, lined up like a planted pine forest. A pillar of smoke stood in the distance where somebody was burning garbage or a building had been set on fire. Over the years, the suburbs had pretty much emptied out. Families had walked away from their 3D TVs and cheap composite furniture. But Walter said we weren't there for that stuff. We would strip out the central arteries, the copper wiring and pipe. "There are still shops that'll pay," he told me. "Cash or trade, canned food, clothes, bits of silver and gold. There aren't a lot of places left, but if you dig around you can find them." He nodded as he talked, moving his whole upper body. I wondered if he was high. "A buddy of mine does this in New York," he said, his eyes flicking over my face in the rear-view. "He's got a unit too. A team. You should see if Marvin's interested."

I said nothing. Margo knocked her cigarette against the ridge of the open window.

It was fully daylight by the time we entered the subdivision's winding streets. Walter slowed to the speed of a restless pace. My stomach growled into the quiet and he hooked a plastic bag on to his claw and swung it back to me. I pulled out a strip of jerky. The meat was spicy and warm.

We pulled into the driveway of a house with yellow grass poking through the dirty snow. Inside, the walls had already been sliced open, wiring and piping removed. Walter climbed under the kitchen sink and quickly slid out again. "Fucking plastic." His hand on the floor made a clattering sound.

At first the plan was to go back into the city and find an older house, but when we went outside, Walter's gaze swung left. In the neighbour's front yard, a toppled real estate sign was half covered by a fading pink sticker that read, REDUCED!

"Is this safe?" I murmured to Margo as Walter slipped a folded strip of aluminum cut from a soda can into the lock and opened the side door. A baby cried somewhere close by.

The house was still furnished. Two glasses stained with the red powder of dried-out wine stood on the granite countertop. A bowl half full of yellowed milk sludge and mouldy cereal Os sat on the table. I wondered what had happened.

"Jackpot," Walter said as he pulled a stereo out of a wooden hutch in the great room and handed it to me. "If anyone asks, you work for Walter's Trash-Out," he told me as I carried the machine out the front door. Lots of stuff went into the car—a Spiderman alarm clock, a set of stainless steel pots. Walter was elated. He jumped around, his one-piece green mechanic's suit billowing with air. In the basement, he had to turn the power off before he started slicing open walls to unthread the wires.

Nobody showed up to ask us any questions, and after a while I started to relax. Every room we went into was like a treasure chest. In the bedroom, I opened the top dresser drawer and found a blue velvet pouch full of jewellery. I pulled out a locket, heart-shaped, engraved with a winding pattern of vines. Inside were tiny black and white pictures of old people—a man with a handlebar moustache, a woman with her hair done up, smiling without showing her teeth. "Gold," Margo said, coming up beside me. She opened the blue bag for me to drop the locket back in, but I closed my fist around it. "Just this," I said because I knew what would happen to it—the miniature heart would be melted down, the pictures burned off, somebody's past disappeared. Margo shook her head. She took it from me, pulling the threadlike chain through my fingers. "Stop being sentimental."

On the way home, Walter wanted to stop right away to swap the gold for cash, but I asked him to drop me off first. Margo offered us granola bars that she'd taken from the house. "No, thanks," I said.

She turned to Walter. "Sandy's grown a conscience."

"Must be nice," he said, his eyes hanging on to me, bloodshot and blue, moving to the road and back again. We drove in silence for a little while, passing a group of kids pushing their bicycles along the side of the road. Up ahead, the turquoise ring of a roller coaster twisted high above the buildings. "What did you and Marvin get up to the other night?" Walter asked.

Margo slid one finger into the closed fist of her other hand and giggled.

"Margo," I snapped, annoyed.

"Down there in the dark zone?" Walter said, not letting up.

I didn't answer. All I wanted was out of the cramped, claustrophobic car, but Walter kept talking. I watched his mouth moving in the mirror as he told me things I didn't know.

"You know Marvin lives down in that filthy squat when his mother is loaded," he said, his eyes meeting mine in the rear-view mirror. "That asshole doesn't know what he wants." He opened and closed his remaining fingers on the steering wheel. "And Phoenix," he snarled. "Fickle bitch."

Margo stared into her lap, smiling, as Walter dragged his gaze over the landscape: an ocean of rooftops and the tall spirals of wood smoke climbing into the overcast sky. He pressed his lips tight together and all the light went out of his eyes. Momentarily, but I saw. When he turned back to Margo, a manic glow had relit itself in his face.

"They should be overthrown," he said, as if we were talking about royalty.

By the time we got back home, I had a headache. Pressing a finger against my left temple, I leaned into the front of the car and asked Margo how much my share of the money would be.

"Nothing now," she said.

"A couple weeks," Walter told me, and Margo got out to let me onto the sidewalk. As I watched them drive away, I wondered where I would be by then.

On that day I hatched another plan. It was all mine; none of the others had a part in it. Not the bum, as my mother would have called Marvin, if I'd ever told her about him, or Walter the disfigured, drug-addled lunatic, or the drama queen roommate I'd randomly met eleven months earlier. Instead, it involved Phoenix and Thomson. I liked them. With them I could have a chance at a good life, one my parents would be proud of. Not breaking windows or stealing. Down there, dishing out food to hungry people, I had felt useful, like I was contributing something, patching over small holes in the shambles all around us. Would they take me in? Was I brave enough to ask?

When Margo came home the next morning, I told her we needed groceries and I'd get them if she gave me fifty dollars. She hesitated. "What are you getting? Sirloin?"

"We're out of a lot of stuff," I said, but she still only gave me thirty dollars.

Just before dusk, I set out. I bought a small bottle of whisky and took a taxi down to the dark zone. The driver dropped me off on the edge of the same pitted field I'd crossed with Marvin several days earlier. I slipped money through the slot in the thick plastic shield and he took it, turning to face me. His brown eyes soft with concern.

"Miss, are you sure?" I nodded and smiled, showing him I was where I was supposed to be. That time I looked the men at the gate full in the face before crouching to step through the hole in the fence. They didn't speak to me, but I felt their eyes on my back. My heartbeat drummed hard at the base of my throat. I couldn't help wondering what they would tell Marvin. He was still in my system. In my mind, I had already moved down to the diner. I had my own room, but I wasn't sure who'd be visiting me—Marvin with his secrets and his sex appeal, or Phoenix, keeping her own counsel, like a flower tightly shut until dawn.

The restaurant was quiet, the door locked. I knocked, but no one came. The late-afternoon shadows were deepening so I went around the back looking for another way in. I saw the hives, capped in a crust of soot-speckled snow. A strange sound—a high-pitched vibration that I could feel in my skin—came through the glass door. The room was blurry like a soap opera flashback because the door was covered over in plastic, but I saw a candle glowing, Thomson reading and Phoenix with her mouth on the end of a long tube, its base on the floor. When I knocked, Thomson jumped. The music stopped. Phoenix straightened away from her instrument. She stood, uncertain, and when I knocked again, she walked over and peered through the blur at my face.

"Go to the front," she said, her voice muffled as if time had slowed.

"Sorry," I said over the jingling bells of the restaurant door. I stayed on the threshold, not moving until she reached out and tugged on the sleeve of my jacket, pulling me inside.

"Are you alone?"

"Yes."

I thought she would invite me in, lead me to the back room where she and Thomson had settled in for the night, like a pioneer family around the small, hot stove. Instead, she stared at me. "What are you doing here?"

I held out the whisky bottle, but she didn't take it. I told her. Not the whole truth. Not about Marvin and me or my morning with Walter and Margo. Not that I had no money and no job and didn't know what to do. Only that I wanted to help. Down there, with them. "I felt like I was making a difference," I said. "The other night," I added, in case she didn't remember.

Her face was stern—the way she looked when she was evaluating, assessing, as if playing a complicated game. Her scarf was off, and I noticed the short dark brown stubble that covered her head, white scars standing out like a small galaxy of stars.

"Come to the back." I remember her smiling, but did she? Probably not. If I had been her I wouldn't have. I would have wondered what this woman—this girl—was angling at, with Marvin one night and the next appealing to her. It must have been obvious that I didn't know what I wanted, that I was stumbling between options. Phoenix walked the length of the diner. Her chin up, her body straight, she moved like some sort of storybook princess, and I followed as if under her command.

In the back room, Thomson was sitting on the couch. He laid down a blue paperback novel titled *Black Robe* when we walked through the door. "Marvin's not with you," he said, looking behind me.

"No."

"You startled us."

"Sorry," I said for the second time, sitting in a leather chair patched with duct tape, moving aside the strange tube. It was hollow, painted with squiggly red and blue lines and yellow dots, the mouth thickened with what looked like wax. "What is this?"

"Didgeredoo," said Phoenix. I waited for her to tell me more but she didn't. I offered the bottle to Thomson. He held it at arm's length so he could read the label, as if it was something special. Phoenix stuffed a broken picture frame into a tiny pot-bellied stove and pulled the side off a dresser drawer.

"This is made out east. By monks," Thomson said, holding up the whisky. "Shall we try?"

"Sure," I said.

Phoenix was busy with the fire so Thomson looked at me. I stuck a thumb back, toward the door into the restaurant. "Do you want me to . . . ?"

"You know where the glasses are."

In the cold dark of the kitchen, the air smelled of onions, garlic, and a spice I couldn't name, buttery and strong. A row of mismatched glasses and mugs sat at the back of the chrome counter. I selected two—one fake crystal and another embossed with a black pattern of a twisting fish—and paused before grabbing another, a mug with MARSON'S PLUMBING on it above a phone number. It was a relief to step back from the cold into the close, comfortable heat. I set down the glasses. Thomson shimmied forward to the edge of the couch and opened the bottle. The cap made a cracking sound.

"None for me," Phoenix said as he dribbled the gold liquid into the cups, but he ignored her.

The firelight lit the whisky like maple syrup before Phoenix closed the doors of the woodstove and it dulled into hardened amber. I sipped. My tongue stung. Thomson lifted his glass.

"*Na zdravi*." He looked into my eyes before downing the shot. "Have a toast with us," he said to Phoenix, but she shook her head and stood, sliding her hands into the deep pockets of her cargo pants, warming her back on the stove.

"More for us," Thomson said, but he didn't touch her mug. It sat there, actually, for days, trapping dust and even a couple of fruit flies as the winter warmed to early spring.

We drank in silence. The liquor buzzed in my mouth. Finally, to fill the quiet, I pointed at the book. "Is that good?"

"Very," Thomson said and picked it up. He read aloud to me, but all I heard was something about not trying to walk out blindly when you're lost in the woods, a rule I already knew. As he continued, I scanned the spines of other books lined up on a shelf built out of lumber and crumbling red bricks. *Small Engine Repair*, the *Tao Te Ching*, *Fifty Years Among the Bees*. I wasn't listening. In one corner of the room a low table held a dusty brown candle shaped like a fat Buddha and a brass bowl full of rocks. Beside it sat a television set, a Star of David drawn in the dust that coated the screen. On top was a glass box filled with foliage. A terrarium. I peered toward it, curious about what was inside, but I didn't want to break the spell of the cozy room. I was glad that I had come. I almost expected Phoenix to ask me for help with a chore, some sewing or breaking furniture into burnable wood, or for her to start playing again, filling the air with that odd droning sound. I thought it would be that easy for me to move into their world, that there wouldn't be any questions, that my assistance would be unconditionally welcomed, that I would simply make myself at home.

Instead, Thomson laid his book down, leaned back, and I watched the candlelight reflect off the buttons on his sweater as he spoke: "Marvin said you lost your job." I flinched. I wondered what else he had said. Did they know we had slept together? They both listened as I told them the basics: about Parthenon, about being laid off, about not being sure what my future held. I considered telling them about what I'd done that day but I didn't.

"So that's why you're here," said Thomson.

I nodded and stared into the smooth central hollow of my drink.

"Why here?" Phoenix said, sitting down. She sounded impatient, tired. I felt as if I was one of a long line of applicants interviewing for the same job. "I mean, what do you imagine?"

"Living here, I guess. Working. You know I'm a hard worker."

She nodded. "I also think you have a fantasy that's far from the reality."

"I don't have a fantasy."

She stayed silent. Of course she was right.

"There's a quote," Thomson said. "'Flies collect on a wound.' That's Rumi."

"Are you Buddhist?" I asked.

"Rumi was a Sufi."

"Oh." I felt stupid. I looked down at the floor, at the carpet marked with black burns from fires that had come uncontained. I didn't understand.

Thomson leaned back and for the first time I noticed how skinny he was. Veins bulged in his forearms like blue roots. "This is a hard path. Why this path instead of another?"

"I don't know," I said and then decided to tell them the truth. "I don't really have anywhere else to go."

"Not with Marvin?" He watched me. Phoenix drifted one hand through a basket beside her, pulling out a sewing kit and a sock. I shifted in my chair, set my empty cup on the floor by my feet.

"I guess I'm with him," I said because they'd probably heard. They probably already knew. My face grew hot. "If that's what he wants."

"What he wants?" Phoenix asked.

Thomson sipped his drink.

"Why don't you like him?" I blurted.

They glanced at each other. "That's far from true," said Phoenix. "But he's in a hurry, and impatience is dangerous."

"Isn't it dangerous here?"

"It can be," she said.

"Why do you do it?"

"Our project is totally different from what Marvin—"

"And I'm choosing it," I said. Thomson smiled. I felt good, strong. Like I was standing up for myself.

"Yes," he said. "Make effort for the positive. It always comes back to that. These days. For us."

Thomson and I both looked at Phoenix. She was peering into her task, prodding the needle into bright red wool. "We get up early," she said. "And we work hard." I nodded. I wanted another drink but knew I shouldn't ask for it, since it was a gift I'd brought. Dusk had come and gone and the plastic over the sliding glass door was a blurry black. The candle started to gutter and after a little while, not long, what felt like only a few minutes, Phoenix stood and replaced it. She tugged a puffy orange sleeping bag from behind the couch and that was how I knew that I'd succeeded. I could stay there, at least spend the night. It was weird, why I didn't think of that, that if successful I'd be living down there. Surprising, like when you go on a trip and the arrival is still a bit of a shock. A little drunk, I felt in my pockets for the things I'd brought, but I hadn't brought anything.

I scanned the coffee table, examined the wide arm of the couch where Thomson had laid down his book, wondering if they had a phone. Margo needed to know where I was in case my mother called or Marvin went looking for me, but there were no screens glowing in the dim candlelight. I resolved to walk back home the next day, even though it would take a while, to collect a few clothes and other stuff and tell Margo what was happening.

The skin of the sleeping bag was cold against my neck when I wrapped it around my shoulders like a shawl.

"Where do I sleep?"

She tossed a thin air mattress onto the floor. "Here. This isn't Buckingham Palace."

"Where do you . . ."

"Here. The couch is a bed. Thomson and I sleep there. When there's a blizzard and all you have is this stove, you have to keep each other warm."

Thomson leaned forward and poured another finger of scotch.

He lifted the bottle toward me and I pushed my glass under the spout. It didn't make sense to me then, that lack of boundaries. It was why I'd run to the city—to escape my parents' place, where my bed was in the centre of the apartment, on the couch.

Phoenix went back to mending her sock. Thomson picked up his book, and the two of them settled in like that, more or less as they were except with me in the chair across from them, as if I was watching a play. I didn't know what to do. It seems so simple to me now—get up, choose a book, find a shirt that needs new buttons, sit back down—but at that time I wasn't used to silence, slow time. It reminded me of when I'd first let my phone go. How I rode the overcrowded buses or walked down the street, suddenly seeing the world outside of the screen I'd been anchored in since I was fourteen. I saw others like me—that shocked look on their faces, holding the collars of their jackets closed as they covered the distance between now and then with only their brains to keep them occupied. I'd felt a piercing vulnerability, exactly the same as that night down in the dark zone, entirely at the mercy of what was happening around me, with no mediation to dull the discomfort. I walked over to the sliding glass door and pushed my face against the plastic. The hives glowed white.

"Read whatever you like," Thomson said, and I went to the bookshelf, touched the tarnished gilt on a book's spine. It had been a long time since I'd read a book. I'd loved them as a child, reading with my mother or in the early years of school.

Phoenix was already annoyed by my wandering. The sock draped over her knee like a dog's tongue. "You'll have to find ways to entertain yourself," she said, and I began to feel panicky, already wondering whether I'd made the right choice.

"Is there a bathroom?"

"I'll take you."

"That's okay."

But she'd already gotten out of her chair. I followed her into the hallway and past a flight of stairs. She stepped through a hole smashed in the wall. "Our escape route," she said as I lifted my legs over the ledge of crumbling plaster and brick. I didn't ask from what. We were in the back of the neighbouring unit. At a heavy wooden door, she twisted open two brass locks and pointed into the night at an outhouse in the far corner of the tiny backyard.

"You can find your way back?"

I nodded. Stepping outside, my feet sank into mushy grass and mud. I had two soakers by the time I swung open the door of the stinky, small room and sat on the hole in the crude bench to empty my bladder. I remember that rush of hot urine, the pungent smell of waste far below. How foreign it all seemed. And how scared I suddenly was: scared at what I was doing. The loose reins in my hands, attached to wild forces.

"No problems?" Thomson said when I returned. I shook my head. I had decided to occupy myself as best I could until it was time to go to sleep and decide in the morning whether or not to stay. Grasshoppers were in the terrarium and I watched them leaping, knocking against the glass walls and tumbling back down. There was a mass of them, maybe a hundred. "Are these pets?" I asked.

"They're lunch," Thomson said, his voice thick. I looked at the bottle. It was almost empty.

"They're good protein," said Phoenix.

"Really?"

She shrugged. "It's something I'm trying. In most places in the world they eat bugs." She set her sewing down carefully, the needle pinched in the fabric, and walked over to where I was. "Want one?"

It was like a dream, or maybe the extension of one that had started the night I'd been laid off. A series of dreams.

"No, thanks."

But Phoenix didn't notice the tremor of disgust in my voice. She opened the lid of the terrarium, reached in, and pinched one between two fingers. "They aren't so bad." The squirming insect emerged, futilely rubbing its wings. "We ate them in Mexico." She popped it into her mouth. I heard the crunch of its body between her teeth.

Behind me, Thomson started laughing, a hooting bark that

grew loud enough to make me smile. Phoenix pulled out another and held it between our faces. Its angular yellow body, its black specks of eyes, reminded me of lying in the long grass as a kid, watching the locusts fly across the sky. How my father hated them. How they decimated crops. But I realized I was hungry. Around four I'd had a small bag of stale potato chips and nothing since. Phoenix and I stared at each other. I closed my eyes, giving in. Her fingers nudged my lips and let go, and I bit down on the delicate exoskeleton, crushing the legs and wings. It tasted a bit like fish.

9 Island

When I got back from Shannon's, Thomson wasn't on the porch. The chaise lounge stood empty, the blanket a dull beige heap. In the house, I called his name, my voice loud in the empty rooms. I thought of Shannon's story about the fairies. Had she seen you? Were you also stealing from them? Perhaps you were part of a pack, a secret colony. I rushed outside. Marvin's shack was still locked. The outhouse door open, knocking quietly in the breeze. The air was full of the mineral smell of water hitting hot earth, the sharp scent of wet tomato vines. Thomson wasn't at the beach. Looking out at the water, speckled with rain, I remembered our walk the day before and raced back up the trail and around the house to the clearing where the bees lived, circled by tall pines that creaked in the wind. Thomson was bending over the open hive, staring through a mesh veil attached to his hat. Raindrops speckled the black fabric of the kimono-style robe he wore. A tarnished metal smoker for calming the bees hung from his hand, leaking grey coils of smoke.

"Thomson," I called, scolding him as I ran into the crowd of insects. I took the smoker and squeezed the accordion-like handle like he'd first taught me, releasing acrid puffs. But it didn't stop them entirely. One stung my arm and I jumped back, brushing one hand over my body to clear away any others. Another stung me on the neck. Despite the calming effects of the smoke, how it made them stuff themselves with honey and less likely to sting, they still seemed angry. Impulsively, I dropped the smoker and ran to the edge of the clearing, into the skinny black tree trunks that Mr. Bobiwash once called the bone forest.

"You shouldn't be out here," I shouted, swatting at the bees that had followed.

"Why are you so chicken?" Thomson called, leaning on his stick. Bending over, his fingers fished around on the ground. His naked arm extended through the wide sleeve of his robe. When he'd fastened onto the smoker, he straightened with effort. The bees clustered on him—his sinewy wrist, the rough red patch of his elbow. If they were stinging, he didn't seem to notice, and I wondered if I'd have to help him later, dab the spots with a cooling cream made from yellow calendula. Thomson blasted his body with smoke so he looked regal, a strange god emerging out of a cloud. When he turned to face me, a few feet away, the smoke still drifted around him and I could see how angry he was.

"You and Marvin haven't been taking care of things."

I crossed my arms. "There's a lot to do."

"I don't care about that."

I stepped forward into the bramble that was the bees. On my fingers, I counted off our tasks: planting, weeding, harvesting, canning, setting the nets, hauling them in, gathering water, making fires, cutting wood, making salves, collecting herbs and mushrooms from out in the woods. "Even that fence," I said, using Marvin's barricade against you as an excuse.

"I don't care," Thomson repeated, his hand closing in a fist. He sounded like a child. "Look," he shouted. A dense thicket of bees was crowding out of the dark opening at the bottom of the hive. They made one writhing body. A rumble of thunder sounded from up the coast, over the lake where the sky was darkest. I counted until the next one. The storm was far away, passing quickly. Thomson's free hand fumbled for mine and he pulled me, hard, toward the hive, puffing madly, making grey clouds. He handed me the smoker and used both hands to pull a brood frame out so I could see what he wanted me to: a row of cells, plugged with yellow wax, shaped like small peanuts. "Queens. Eight of them. Maybe more."

Patiently, he waited for me to get it, to remember what I'd learned. I focused and the thought crystallized, emerging from past lessons. "A swarm," I said.

Thomson nodded. "A secession is underway."

Wet darts of rain bit through my shirt and I shivered. The

temperature was dropping as the day came to an end. I took hold of Thomson's arm. "You need to come inside," I coaxed, working around his stubbornness, but he pulled away. The frame in his hands clattered against the corner of the hive. The sluggish bees buzzed closer.

"This colony is all we have left," Thomson said, his voice loud in the empty clearing. The ground still imprinted with the square shapes of our old hives, some stolen last autumn, others, the empty ones, burned when we ran out of wood. In the midst of January, our skin aching with cold, the thought of rebuilding our bee stocks had seemed impossible. "Now half this hive is going to leave."

It was Phoenix who had taught me first about swarms. In the city. Over the years, I'd seen it again and again, learned the complexities of the hives, the knowledge rising and falling as needed.

Swarms happen when the colony is disrupted, I knew, when it becomes too crowded, when another queen is ready to emerge. Half the bees stuff themselves with their stores and empty out of the hive. Clinging together, wrapped tightly around their queen, they settle close by. Scout bees search for another place to build. When they find one, they come back and dance out the directions. And then they disappear to a new home—a hollow tree, a crack in the rocks. But it was late in the season for a swarm. Neither colony—the one left behind or the new pioneers—would likely survive the winter. There was very little hope.

I wondered where you were. If you'd found shelter from the rain, lit a small fire, sat close to its warmth. My fingers found Thomson's arm again. Gently, gently, I said his name, cupped his sharp elbow, but he ignored me. He lifted the brood frame close to his face and spoke, as if to them. "We have to kill the larval queens."

I dropped my hand to my side. He looked at me.

"It's the only way."

They were alive in there, those new creatures, fattened on royal jelly, bound for special lives. I didn't want to kill them. As he reinserted the frame, the long robe swayed around his bony legs and he stumbled. I reached out and grabbed his elbow. When he'd found his balance, I pulled the lid off the plastic bin a few feet from the hive and reached in for my gloves. He wouldn't go back home until we solved the problem, stopped the impending split. I slipped my hands into the gloves, the palms yellow, the backs printed with blue tulips.

"Tell me what to do," I said.

"**Thomson** talked me through it," I told Marvin later, at supper. He'd brought home a mallard and butchered it for supper in the yard. I'd noticed the pool of blood, kicked over with a lace of dirt, on our way home. What had he done to get it? It worried me, but as I helped Thomson into the house, the smell of frying meat made my stomach growl. A sudden emptiness inside me, like a floor fallen away. Thomson's belly also rumbled, but when I asked if he was hungry he said no. Right away he asked Marvin about the boat. Marvin shook his head. "No sign of it." Thomson's eyes drifted downward, as if he'd lost an argument.

"What happened?" I asked Marvin as Thomson lay down. I pushed the blanket between the arm of the couch and Thomson's bare toes, calloused from years of wearing scavenged shoes that didn't quite fit. The plates landed on the table with a clunking sound. There were three servings, steaming, but Thomson was already asleep. Marvin roughly cut the third chunk of meat in two and gave each of us another piece. He divided the dandelion greens, giving more to me. "We should save some for later," I said, thinking already about the plate I'd make up—not for Thomson, but for you.

"Why'd you even take him there?" Marvin asked.

"I didn't. He went by himself."

"Where were you?"

"At Shannon's," I said, annoyed.

Marvin chewed a large piece of meat, his cheeks rounding out like a squirrel's. The greens were bitter, too old, the leaves too big for harvest. I ate them anyway, first off, to get them over with. From the couch, Thomson spoke, surprising us.

"We wouldn't have had to do anything if you'd been paying attention."

I wasn't sure what to say. My shoulders sloped over my plate, the food a central point, the meat succulent and rich, sinking inside me. It put me in a kind of trance broken harshly when my teeth came down painfully on a grain of shot. I pinched the lead nugget off my tongue and ate more carefully, pulling the meat apart with my knife and fork, afraid of chipping a tooth.

Finally, Marvin spoke, his words muffled, pushed out around his food: "Isn't it enough to be a fisherman? Do I have to be a beekeeper too?"

"You think you have a choice?" Thomson pulled himself up to look over the back of the couch. "You used to know better than that," he said, but his voice faded away as he watched us eating, the duck fat smeared across our mouths.

"Give me some of that," he said, and I carried my plate over and sat beside him, fed him. He didn't want much, only a few mouthfuls. The chewing tired him out. When he sank back on the pillow, uncased, one end speckled with old mould, I dabbed at the grease on his face and beard with the cuff of my shirt. "I'm not a goddamn kid," he growled, and I pulled back. Some food had fallen to the floor. I picked it up and brought the rest of his meal back to the table. The leftovers I scraped onto Marvin's plate and I went back to my own supper. Marvin started to speak, but I shook my head.

"Leave it." Thomson had stretched out on the couch, his breath deepening. Marvin finished his food, licked the residue off his plate.

It took a lot of effort to save the rest of my meal, but I did. In the kitchen, I scraped my leftovers onto one of the red paper plates, covered the food with several shredded strips of the old plastic wrap and left the meal on the porch. I'd already decided to assume the best. You were still out there, still needing me, on your own and hungry.

Marvin said nothing when I came back inside. I gathered the dishes as he rolled an herb cigarette in an old slip of blank paper torn from some book. On the couch, I pulled Thomson's feet onto my lap, wound the bottom hem of the blanket tight around his cold toes, swaddling them, picking at a hole in his sock that I'd have to mend soon. Marvin pushed the front door open and went outside.

The smoke from the burning catnip and mullein drifted through the screen door. Thomson tugged the blanket over his face, unravelling it from his feet, and turned toward the back of the couch. I felt his forehead. Fevered. Damp with sweat even though he was trembling. He muttered something. I stood to close the door.

"I've been watching that useless hive all summer," Marvin said, tapping ash onto the floorboards. "You couldn't have defended me?"

"You have not."

He exhaled: a drift of smoke tamped down by the dampness. "How do you know?"

I stepped outside. I didn't want to fight. At the far end of the porch, your plate sat, hidden by the coming dark.

Marvin pulled the spindly cigarette to his mouth. It hung from his bottom lip as he dug a hand into his pocket and pulled out a small swatch of fabric. White with a tiny red rose, half the bloom lopped off.

"That's all we found," he said, and I held the scrap with my fingertips. Its weave was loose; the edges frayed. "Caught on the edge of the Sharmas' garden fence," said Marvin.

That hint made you real. I looked over at him, ready to talk about everything that I thought we could have. A family. But he ran through the rain to his shed. "My mind hasn't changed," he called back as he opened the padlock, its metal scraping. A candle came on: four squares of yellow light in the window. I slid the small bit of material into my pocket and went in the house to Thomson, who was sitting up, coughing, spots of blood in the cup of his hand. I held his head and rocked him, tried to ease the panic in his eyes.

"It's okay," I whispered, followed by all the placating, soothing words I could think of that he said he hated when he was well. Eventually he went back to sleep, sinking into exhaustion. Marvin was still in his shed, illuminated, his face bent over some task. Untangling a net or straightening nails. He rubbed his jaw, the rough brindle of his beard, turned salt and pepper in spots. I went to the outhouse. On my way back in, I saw that you'd taken the plate.

Marvin needed my help the next morning so I went with him. I didn't want to leave Thomson, but the truth was that I needed a break. We left him dozing on the couch, a jug beside him, full of strong tea. Coltsfoot, I'd told him, because that's best for the lungs. Really, we'd run out and it was a brew of raspberry leaf and mullein. I worried out loud that he wouldn't drink it, that the jug was too heavy to lift, but he waved me away, impatient, and then called me back to ask me to bring him his book.

It was sunny and warm as we walked through the woods. The leaves had that ragged late-summer look, like they've been busy cleaning spills. Branches broke underfoot, cracking loudly. I looked around, peering eagerly into all the small rooms of the forest. One glimpse of you was all I needed, one set of eyes staring back at me. But there were none. Only the forest's usual emptiness that had made me claustrophobic when we first arrived, all that silence leaning into me that I've become used to by now.

My fingers twisted and tumbled the slip of fabric in my pocket as I followed Marvin, wondering why I wasn't in front. He clambered loudly through the woods while I walked quietly. We kept going like that, not speaking to each other, both of us worried about Thomson and the ship and opposed over what to do about you, about anything. I knew that Marvin was capable of changing his mind. I'd witnessed that once. I turned that memory over in my mind, like wiggling a stone loose, and quickly hid the worms beneath it, before saying loudly, "We could look for her ourselves."

His back rippled with tension, shoulders rising under his plaid shirt. "We don't know anything about her, him, whoever."

"She's taking the meals."

"How do you know it isn't Eric or Graham?"

"The boys wouldn't do that."

"Wouldn't do what? Steal from us? Take our food?" The words steamed out of him. His feet hit the ground harder—pushing through the overgrown weeds, pausing to kick a rock into a cross-stitch of plants I couldn't name. "How do you know?"

I just did—like I know that you are only a child. Not an enemy, a dangerous threat. I said as much to Marvin, but he didn't answer and so instead I held the small, flowered swatch between scissored fingers and asked, "Why did you give me this?"

Briefly, he glanced at me. His voice as it drifted back faded out in patches. "It doesn't mean anything. It's an object, barely anything."

"So you weren't trying to give me hope?"

"I was trying to show you how little we have to go on. You can't make a real girl out of that." Some words were clear: *little, real.* Anger grew in me, that he could tell me how things were when I already knew. Like in the city, although back then I'd believed him and he'd led me into deep water when only he could swim.

"Throw it away. It'll take ten minutes to decompose."

"Like her?" I spat.

"Like anything that's only a fantasy."

If I could have, I would have gone home, left him to do the job on his own, but there were supplies we needed to try to find for Thomson, to keep him warmer through the cooler nights, the coming winter. We had work to do, items to scavenge.

"What about Shannon?" he asked. "What about her baby? Have you seen how real they are—all those bones pushing through." He paused. "She might not make it."

"Did Mr. Bobiwash say that?"

"Why do you call him that? His name's Jack."

I kicked a grey wedge of rock into the underbrush. I'd called him that since the beginning, since he appeared through the mist of our near starvation, helped us, taught us how to live. I didn't feel that we were equals, but Marvin wouldn't let it go.

"You don't call Thomson Mr. Ptacek," he said.

"That's different. It's a different relationship."

Blue chicory, sumac trees, and other plants lined the trail, tangled in ancient garbage blown around by the wind. A small cardboard box stained with red paste. White plastic bags twisted in blooming purple thistles. Even a Coke bottle, the residue of its contents turned tarry like old engine oil.

We climbed down the steep hill, the dirt hard-packed after years of use. Arms out, Marvin slid on the worn soles of his too-small work boots, catching himself in a run when he reached the bottom. *If he breaks his leg . . .*, I thought, as I often do, but I'm finished warning him. He rounded a heap of plywood and splintered two-by-fours and disappeared. I heard clanging, the grind of metal, as he pulled things apart.

I was relieved to be alone. Marvin went his way and I went mine. Once every few weeks we went to that section of the dump—more remote and not thoroughly scavenged, so we still find interesting things. Once, a camera popped to the surface. A small silver box with a cracked black screen on the back. Shannon had just had her baby and I'd yearned to take a picture of her with the infant, its damp face squeezed shut. I thought pretending with a prop would keep my memory sharper so I took it home. In the city, I had lots of photographs, mostly from when I was a kid. They were stored in a wooden crate once used to ship yellow apples from China. Those fat ones speckled with rust spots, named Fuji, after a mountain. The pictures were left behind in the apartment I'd shared with Margo. I don't know what happened to them. I don't even know what happened to her, where she ended up, how she adjusted to her new life, whether she even survived.

Plastic is easy to find, and that's what we'd come for. Hunks of heavy sheeting to fasten over cedar boughs, cut grass, whatever we can use to insulate the north wall of the living room since Thomson was sleeping there. A ragged corner was sticking out of a puzzle of mouldy tile board and drywall and I started to dig. Plaster crumbled in my hands. I refastened the scarf around my mouth to keep out the dust and mould spores and worked slowly, trying not to think about rats. When I pulled the piece clear, I saw that holes from old staples scarred the edges but those could be patched with spruce pitch. Satisfied, I stuffed it into my backpack on top of some walnuts we'd found on the walk, earlier, before the argument had bubbled up. There was a harvest there, once they were hardened by frost.

Objects tumbled as I climbed a high pile, gently setting my foot on a rusty oil tank and stepping on the side of a washing machine. I reached for a barbecue, the kind that you fill with charcoal briquettes, but the steel handle snapped off and the bottom broke away, eaten by rust. The handle, a curve of shiny steel, could be fastened to a homemade bucket or used another way so I kept it.

I dug farther, pushing past an old printer, a twisted fan, a cellphone that I pocketed to show the boys. A microwave with a tightly latching door—ideal for storing food.

Dust and sweat made a sticky paste on my face. With the long tail of the scarf that covered my mouth, I wiped my forehead. Leaving my backpack on a dried slurry of mashed paper, I walked around to the other side, to find Marvin, to tell him I was leaving. He was crouched on another pile, spinning a white bicycle tire. Small purple and pink plastic balls fell down the silver spokes. When I called his name, he looked up, squinting. The sun lit the metal spokes. He swivelled his head back and forth, trying to find me. I waved my hand in the air. "Here."

"Are you behind that fridge?"

I hadn't even noticed the fridge. A big white box. Door removed. Two shelves inside, crooked, probably bent by a bear. I climbed up, two steps, three, and pulled out one of the grill-like racks as Marvin continued taking things apart. Excavating. He tossed something to the ground and dragged another object down the side of the heap. In the corner of my eye, I saw a flash of purple tinsel.

"Come here," he shouted, and as I turned I expected the motherlode, the thing I'm always hoping for, although I'm not sure what that would be. Something impossible: a feast of calamari and pistachio ice cream. Oranges and avocados. An afternoon exploring a strange city like when Margo and I went to New York, even though things were too far along for it to be much fun. Thomson's medicine: a twenty-year supply. You, curled up, calling on us for rescue.

When I was still ten feet away, Marvin tossed a backpack to me—small, meant for a child. "You could give this to her," he said. A mermaid smiled up at me, her skin cracked, flaking off like a zombie. A rusty orange liquid stained my palms, dribbled down onto my pants. Disgusted, I dropped it, and he lifted a kid's bike into the air. From the bent wheel, one rubber tire sagged away, the inner tube flat as a ribbon. All that was left of the streamers were two sparkling tufts sticking out of white hand grips. He cupped his hand over the dented metal pole where the seat should have been. "She can ride this around the neighbourhood," he said and laid it on its side like we'd learned to do when we were kids. I'd had a bike. I'm sure he'd had several.

I wiped my hands on my pants. Marvin threw the bike and it crashed against a dented filing cabinet. As the sound faded away, we stood there, staring at each other, surrounded by debris. His eyes searched my face, waiting for me to realize he was right, as I had in the past. I stared back at him, wanting to remind him of the times he'd failed, the terrible outcomes. His voice when he spoke was gentle: "I'm just trying to show you that this idea you have of some happy family—" I lifted up the backpack and threw it at him, hard, but he jumped to the side and it slammed against a mangled plastic garden bench, splattering orange. "Sandy," he shouted as I turned and ran, my feet pounding against a skin of crushed juice boxes and disposable diapers and half-buried black bags. "It's the truth," he called after me.

His truth.

In the trees, a fish aquarium with one intact glass wall stuck out of the debris. I knew I shouldn't. I knew that the glass could be used for many things and that because of my choice the world would be a more dangerous place, but I did it anyway: swung my leg back and slammed my boot right into the centre of the pane. It shattered. Before the noise fell away, a movement flickered in the corner of my eye. I turned fast but saw only the forest, the leaves shifting in a slight breeze. A crow called and flew across my line of sight: a glossy black gap within the world.

I sank onto the corner of an old mattress, folded in half, the springs frozen with rust. Garbage all around, like the aftermath of an explosion.

I put my head in my hands and pulled them away when I realized how dirty they were: the lines on my palms darkened in orange. Marvin wouldn't look for me and that was what I wanted. To get away from him; to be free. I thought of my mother. Her stories of flying to foreign countries before she married my dad, stepping off the plane into different seasons and smells. Ecuador. India. Spain before the European Union collapsed. A round purse made of woven grass, embroidered with red and black beans, hung in the dining room. I remembered a photograph of her with a monkey on her shoulder. There were other photos too. One my father brought out to show me how I looked like my great-grandmother, same fair skin, hair the colour of spelt bread. In it, she stood on the wooden veranda, one hand around the railing, a pane of the front window broken. My baseball went through it, my father told me most times we hunched over the black pages of that album, the silver corners coming loose. That's how I remembered them—my father a series of interactions, his rough fingers fastened around my bare toes on the couch while we watched television and his voice sank into my ears, one prediction of doom after another. My mother a machinery of tasks: slicing a roast, cleaning mouldy soup from the fridge, flicking the broom over the tiny apartment floor. In motion, always, as if to deflect his words, draw them into her gears and grind them into powder so she could look up and say, *What's that, dear?*, and he'd turn again to me, speak to my still face. I missed them. Nearly two decades since we'd spoken or seen each other. But that was ancient history. Ruins under the dust of my grief.

It must be true that when people have children they start thinking differently about their own childhood because that's been happening to me. I think about you, Melissa, out there in the woods, and I realize that my parents did the best they could. If my mother felt for me as I feel for you—this agonizing pull, like our skin is attached—letting me go must have been the hardest thing she ever did. Not that she had a choice. One day, late winter, sleet streaming out of a pewter sky, I vanished, never to be seen again. As if I'd joined a cult.

Tears came. Afterwards, I rubbed the rough vines on the gold heart that I wear around my neck and wondered what my mother would have thought of you. No matter what, I had to find you. You had to be real.

Dead leaves from the previous autumn covered the forest floor. I picked one up and tore it in half, dropped it, and found another. "Demolition helps me think," Phoenix once said when we were breaking open walls to scavenge insulation. Back then we'd had a lot to think about. Now life is about survival, making it through each day, with no time to consider whether or not I'm happy. Every little break in routine means less time to put up my beets, harvest zucchini, clear away the weeds from the pumpkin patch, watch over the hens so the animals don't steal our eggs. All while Marvin is out in the boat. There is no way I could ever leave him. He is my lifeline and I am his.

It's been that way for a long time—since we got to the island and spent those first few years looking over our shoulders. Hiding. A beard disguising his face. My hair cut as short as we could with dull scissors. All three of us shell-shocked, grieving, numb. Pushing down a past that was now bubbling up. Ghosts rising to the surface, bones coming into the light, like the skulls and femurs found in the caves on the island's south shore that Mr. Bobiwash told us about. Holes in the limestone cliffs where the Ouendat found shelter from the Iroquois. They were trapped. At the turn of the last millennium, skeletons were still being found.

I stood up.

I grabbed my backpack and pushed through the woods, to the road, the scrap of fabric breaking apart in my worrying fingers. Had it come from your dress? Or another little girl's, long since taken to the mainland or dead from starvation or flu? Were you dressed in rags, your hair dirty, shorn from your scalp like the children I'd seen in the dark zone, lined up with their parents for soup. If I could see you, I'd know what you need. I'd talk to you. Understand you. Help you.

I moved quickly over the broken asphalt, down the shattered yellow line. A row of rocks lined the field, piled by a farmer who had cleared his land by hand more than a century ago. The thick cedar forest on my left seemed impenetrable. Toward the shoreline, turkey vultures circled in graceful, dipping arcs, their heads a dim, distant red, like Mars. I ran.

10 City

I hadn't been asleep very long when the springs on the sofa bed screamed from the release of Phoenix's weight. A grey light sifted through the glass door as she kneeled in front of the stove and I felt relieved. All night, I'd lain on my side, tightly curled, trying to keep warm on the thin, narrow mattress on the floor. Phoenix's olive skin turned the colour of toffee as she added a slim length of wood to the fire. I sat up, hugging myself against the air's sudden cold.

"Good morning," I whispered, and my breath steamed in front of my face. Phoenix glanced at me.

"This will take a while to get going," she said before she shut the door and stepped back to the bed. Thomson groaned a few unintelligible words before Phoenix shushed him. I lay back down, felt the heat gather slowly at the soles of my feet, and didn't wake again until the room was so hot I had to shove off the sleeping bag for relief.

It was like that down there—a constant swing to extremes. Plenty of vegetables or beans and meat for soup or none at all. When in my normal life I'd often been entertained by shows and movies stored on the Internet, we had the evening's deep silence, followed by the chaos of the soup kitchen. On those nights, about three a week, up to a hundred people could show up. Zane, whose belly hung over his suspendered pants, who lived up the road and kept to himself, let twenty in at a time through the single door while Phoenix dished out soup or assigned duties. It was hers and Thomson's project, but Phoenix oversaw it all. That became apparent pretty quickly.

That first morning, Phoenix made tea out of peppermint from their summer garden.

"I miss coffee," Thomson said as I curled my hands around the warmth of the mug. In the kitchen, Phoenix dished chunks of potatoes onto three plates and then carried them over with a jar of sprouts. As she set the food on the table, I wondered if I should have offered to help. Something bit at me, and I reached down and scratched my knee. Thomson stabbed at a potato hunk, set it down, and sliced off a rotten spot.

"These already turning bad?"

Phoenix glanced up from her food. "It's damp down here. Cold."

"We should keep them in the back room."

"Too warm and they'll sprout."

Thomson shook salt on his potatoes. "Sometimes I wish we'd stayed there. The coffee, fresh fruit, honey, heat."

"Hurricanes," Phoenix said, but Thomson didn't seem to hear her.

"Much easier to live off the land."

"We're not living off the land," said Phoenix. "Barely."

Thomson pushed the rest of the potato chunk into his mouth.

"We couldn't have known," she said.

"Known what?" I asked, lifting a pinch of sprouts to my mouth. The water in them was icy, sent shivers through my jaw. They both looked at me. Thomson's blue eyes and Phoenix's black, considering how to answer. Finally Thomson spoke.

"Everything," he said and laughed.

While we ate, Phoenix outlined the day's chores. Put on bones for broth, pick up the vegetable donations, collect wood from wherever we could find it. Thomson said he'd take me to get the day's water and Phoenix nodded like he needed her permission. Before we left, a few people came in—one of the men I'd seen at the gate and a woman with a green scarf on her head tied turban-style, like Phoenix wore hers. They hugged and I turned away, swallowing the last gulp of my tea while I wondered where Marvin was, when he would stop by, if we would be together again—but really, Melissa, what I wanted wasn't so base. It was that: those two women, standing with their hands on each other's elbows, speaking about the next steps to take. Phoenix smiled and I saw how all the complicated lines on her face relaxed.

Outside, a grey haze of smoke hung over the rooftops. Thomson cleared his throat several times and spat on the ground, barely missing my shoe. He carried two green pop bottles and I swung a blue bucket, a small jar of iodine pills rattling inside. He must have noticed me looking around.

"It's an adjustment. Think of it as waking from a dream."

I thought of Marvin's speech about the bubble bursting. "That's what Marvin says."

"Yes? What else does he say?"

"A lot."

We laughed, stepped into the road to walk around a puddle.

"I hope you're being careful with him?"

I blushed.

"He's passionate," Thomson said, and my cheeks burned hotter but Thomson didn't notice. "When I was his age I was at student demonstrations. A hundred thousand people in Wenceslas Square. Havel and his group stayed away because it was our turn." His voice was adamant, almost angry. "You know Vaclav Havel?" he asked, and I nodded, because I did, at least what Marvin had told me.

"It felt like being one of a whole, an enormous body. But it took a long time to get there. The first time I went to protest, with my girlfriend, I was beaten. The police took us a long way out of town. Four hours it took to walk home. Many students, shuffling back to Prague like zombies. My mother didn't want me to go. When I arrived home she wouldn't feed me. She threw the food in the garbage—cabbage and liver slop, something like that. She was a small woman, but she was fat and had a crazy smile, full of teeth." He touched the bottom of the bottle to his lips. "But none of that mattered. The whole damn thing was tipping and we were pushing it over."

He sounded like Marvin.

I was excited to hear the rest of the story, but he pointed suddenly at the brick row houses beside us, the same as Marvin's squat. "Built for workers. You've seen the lamp factory?"

I nodded, remembering the huge building Marvin had pointed out, that first morning.

"Founded by Charles Cobden in the 1920s. Business booming up to the '90s."

"What happened then?" I asked because I'd barely been born.

"Free trade," he said, as if those words told the entire story.

"Where were you then?"

"In the '90s? Canada. Before that, Mexico."

"Where you met Phoenix's mother?"

Thomson loudly banged the bottles together and I jumped. Two cats scattered away from the corpse of a small bird.

"Goddamn strays," he said. "They're everywhere." He was right: all over the city, animals that people couldn't afford were running loose. Dogs, cats, even exotic birds. Margo once brought home a dead parrot she'd found in a stairwell. She plucked beautiful feathers from it, as many as she could, and then laid it on our lawn. Soon the bird was a putrid rack of bones and we had cats and a few dogs milling around, waiting for the next handout.

"Do you feed them?" I asked. It seemed like something they'd do.

"Eat them, more likely."

He saw the shock on my face and grinned. Years later, I asked him about that and he told me no, they hadn't yet sunk that low. On the island we did. Anything for a meal.

We were close to the water then, and Thomson stared ahead, eyes squinting into the light off the lake as if trying to pinpoint a small detail in the waves, dark and oil-coloured, a killer whale.

"It was different then," he said. "We felt morally obligated to avoid violence. Violence would make us like them, like the regime. Now we've embodied our system. We all have to expunge it, shrug it off, even the dissenters. It's heavy and hard and causes self-hatred. Do you understand?"

"I think so," I lied. We couldn't go any farther. We were at the end of the dock. Thomson stared at the fringe of ice around the wooden footings. A flush of red prickles had spread in his cheeks, accentuating the mud-coloured troughs under his eyes, the white circle around his lips, half hidden by the stubble of beard. I held out the bucket and he took it, but he wasn't finished.

"It's better not to push for the end with violence," he said. "In the end are the seeds of the beginning and we want them to be strong and good."

What end? I wondered. I was young enough that I thought he meant me, my uncertainty at being down there, my new relationship with Marvin.

Thomson handed me the iodine pills. He went down on one knee and pushed the bucket into the lake. Both hands gripped the handle, but it was too heavy and I saw how it tugged on him, how he bent farther, fighting with it. I stepped quickly forward and helped, wrapping my fingers around the hard wire of the metal handle and pulling up on the weight until it slid onto the dock, the water slopping over, soaking our pants and sleeves. Thomson dropped an iodine tablet into each of the bottles and we watched the ochre unfurl.

"Jan Palach. You know him?"

I shook my head.

"Your age," he said. "At the end of the Prague Spring . . . After the Soviets came in 1968, he set himself on fire in Wenceslas Square."

"Why?" It astonished me that someone would do that.

"To oppose people's hopelessness, was what he said. But people were hopeless. More so, after that." He laid one hand on his chest and vibrated it there like he trying to wake himself up, bring feeling back to a numb spot.

"Be cautious of strong feeling," he told me. "Or of thinking you have no options because you don't like the ones that are there."

I didn't answer because I didn't know what to say.

Pretty quickly, back at the diner, Phoenix set me to work again. She had me scrub down the counter and all the tables, benches, and vinyl stools. She handed me a dish detergent container with BLEACH written in blue marker down the side. There were no plastic gloves so I used the scrunched-up corner of an old brown bath towel and dipped it carefully into the mixture of untreated lake water and bleach, but my hands ended up red and raw. They stung right through lunch—boiled eggs, sprouts, and raisins from the previous summer—and into the afternoon when I was on to the next thing: untangling the wires on a tarnished solar panel someone had donated. There were others there—the woman I'd seen in the morning, cutting rotten spots out of a pile of tiny hothouse peppers, and Zane, moving quickly despite the huge stone of his round belly. I watched Phoenix, waiting for her to stop or even pause, but she never did, that I saw. It was like she was stronger than everyone else, moving around with a force that compelled us to follow. When night came, and I fought to stay awake without any kind of caffeine, Zane opened the doors and people started coming in. Phoenix hovered at the end of the counter, ladling, while I did what I had done that first night: handed out bread. We launched the soup kitchen like a theatre production and I played my role, my arm moving automatically, but I was too exhausted to feel the kind of meaning or contentment I thought I'd feel. Past midnight, I was too tired to talk or think about anything, so when a pane in the front window was broken, my reaction was dulled.

We were in a booth, three or four of us, Phoenix making tea behind the counter. The doors were already locked. Thomson was talking about how salt was once used as a currency when the front window suddenly shattered and half a brick tore the brown curtain, pulled it off the nails that fastened it. From outside we heard whooping. Phoenix ran. One of the cups tipped over on the counter, the hot water dribbling down. She flung the door open and screamed after them. "Fuck off. You're wasting your fucking lives."

It happened so fast that we sat there stunned, only Thomson still moving, acting normally, lifting a mug to his mouth. He coughed once or twice but then calmed and Phoenix came back in, her face flushed plum, pulling off her sweater.

"Bastard kids," she said, and their sound still carried: raucous laughter, fading like animal noises in the woods.

That night I fell onto my thin mattress at the foot of their bed, exhausted, but for a long time I couldn't sleep, wondering if they'd come back. Afraid, until Phoenix asked me, out of the blue, so sudden I thought she must be blurting out words in her sleep:

"Are you okay?"

"Yeah," I said, and the springs creaked as she rolled over in the bed. Thomson already snoring.

The next few days were similar. One task after another, usually arranged by Phoenix. Most mornings I fetched water. Smashed apart frozen beef bones. Dropped lye down the outhouse hole. By the third or fourth day, I felt ready to collapse. It was mid-afternoon and I was gathering the courage to tell Phoenix I needed a nap, even just a short one, when Thomson appeared and asked for my help. Phoenix set down the knife she was sharpening.

"Come on," he said. "We aren't hosting a state dinner." It felt like that, as if every day we were readying for an important occasion: a dinner with royalty, a political summit.

Already I'd been to fetch another round of water and it was now nearly gone. I didn't want to go again. I moved closer to Thomson, although I didn't even know what he wanted me for. She looked at me, studied my face.

"Fine," she said, sounding annoyed, and examined the gleaming blade before setting it down to work on the next dull tool.

Outside, Thomson and I walked along the empty storefronts.

"I thought you could use a break," he said.

Gently, I slid my hands into my pockets. They hurt from the bleach. I stared down the street at the park at its end, the city beyond.

"This is how she moves forward," Thomson told me. "How she makes sense of things." When I didn't respond, he said, "She must always be giving."

I nodded, but I was thinking that it would be great to be on the receiving end. I felt like a slave. Even my paying job hadn't been so hard.

"Shouldn't people be allowed some freedom?" I said.

Thomson stopped. We stood beside a smashed-up Starbucks I hadn't noticed before.

"You came to us, remember? She isn't the enemy."

Still, I felt afraid of her, her sternness, the stubbornness of her walls. I wondered if we could ever be friends. Thomson turned the corner and I followed. My eyes filled with tears—mostly because I was exhausted, my hands hurt, I didn't know how much more I could take. I hadn't even contacted Margo. Looking back I realize that was the beginning, Melissa: my initiation, my first understanding of what adult life would be like. Things that you grew up learning: how difficult it is to exist on this earth, to survive.

But Thomson didn't give me any sympathy. "It's only been a few days," he said, and I pushed the heel of my hand against my cheekbone, wiping away the tears.

We were at the hives by then, down the laneway where I'd first knocked on their window, wanting in. Thomson pushed the last slivered ridge of snow off the white box. His knuckles were covered in scars and one fresh wound, red and scabbed over. Although the nights were warming up, it was still too cold to expose the bees, but I listened as he named each part: hive body or super. Frames, foundation, brood chamber. He laid one hand on the top of the hive and before he could speak, I said, "Home."

We didn't have enough food to host the soup kitchen that night and the freedom felt like a snow day had when I was a kid. We did have bones, though, and Phoenix set a stock to bubbling in a huge pot, mixing in carrot shreds, broccoli stalks, and a clove of garlic. The hot plate stayed on low, using a trickle of energy from the solar-charged battery pack that had been sucking up the sunlight on the springlike days we were having. The smell made my stomach growl. I was always hungry because of how hard I was working. That day, after the hives, I'd helped clean the chimney and then had gone for more water after all.

Phoenix brought tea into the back room while Thomson stayed in the kitchen. I sat up to accept a cup, leaning my back against the closet door, which pushed inward from my weight. Phoenix's cup cooled on the coffee table as she worked on mending one of Thomson's shirts.

When I was tired of the silence, I asked, "What's the plan for tomorrow?"

"More of the same."

I nodded. Tiny leaves bobbed on the tea's surface.

"Does Marvin ever come by?"

"You're still thinking about him," she said, and I pushed my shoulders up in a shrug. It was true: he ate at me, partly because I felt forgotten.

"He's good-looking," Phoenix said.

"Yeah."

"And he knows it."

"I guess you know him well," I said. She didn't answer so I took a breath, about to dive. "He told me about you, in Mexico." I nudged my head to one side. "Before."

The shirt slumped on her lap. It was blue, the kind a businessman might once have worn: a pointed collar, wide cuffs. "He's quick to share everybody's stories but his own."

"You don't like him, do you?"

She shifted. I saw the slight give in her face as she decided to answer.

"We have history."

Sounds came from the kitchen: the splash of water, the ting of hard things—fingernails, Thomson's ring—against the aluminum bowl used as a washbasin. Her eyes lifted, met mine.

"Not like that. Not sexual." She picked out a thread. "Thomson knew Marvin's mother from university. They'd been lovers, then friends. We moved in with them when we came from Mexico. We were children, like brother and sister."

I hadn't seen any sibling closeness between them, only a kind of wrestling, arguments over principles.

"I understand him," she said, "but I can't help him."

Marvin seemed like the last person who needed help, who needed anything, actually. We were silent, breathing in the scent of mint. The night had settled. She sat against the black square of the doorway, like an actress on stage.

Finally I said, "Tell me where you come from."

Candles cast drifting veils of light over her face. I watched the slow reveal of her wide forehead, cheeks, lips, as she told me about the hollow, breathy howl of jungle monkeys, her parents' stuccoed house where spiders crawled out of the cracks, how they'd run a stick around the rim of a log hive and pull out drooling honey. The story looped back, skipping over her mother's violent death, to the cold Canadian November, Marvin's mother's home, the tulip tree in the front yard with its huge pink blooms turned to frosted clumps. In the kitchen, Thomson sang in Czech. Phoenix's voice dropped so I had to lean forward to hear.

"We had to come here," she said. "At his rooming house there were used needles on the floor and everyone smoked and his . . ." she swallowed hard, sat back, and I saw her start to stiffen. "It was in the news, all about this place; how could we not help?"

Her gaze fell away. Abruptly, she stood, took my cup, and it clattered against her own.

"It's history," she said—meaning, I think, *and the rest is history*—but I didn't correct her. When she left the room, I pushed down inside my blankets and curled onto my side, a trembling vibration inside me, and brought Marvin into my mind, remembering how he'd kissed me, and more.

I slept well. The weather was warm enough that we only needed a fire in the deepest part of the night. In the morning I found Phoenix in the kitchen, scattering tarragon over the surface of the soup, white bones set aside on a plate. Thomson and Zane stood at the front of the diner, draped in bright light from a hole in the wall that had been the rest of the window.

"What happened?" I asked, and as Thomson turned my way I heard the glass crunch under his shoes. "They came back?"

"It's all right," Phoenix said but with an angry snap in her voice. *Was it Marvin?* I wondered. *Had he done this?*

All day long I tried to ask her, but she kept her distance, avoided me when I attempted to catch her eye. I focused on following instructions and did extra things like cleaning the counter without being told and washing out towels, but throughout the long morning and into the afternoon, she ignored me. The openness she'd shown me the night before had closed.

Then, shortly before the soup kitchen opened, she finally spoke to me.

I was peeling carrots, three bags of them, their caps a tangle of pale yellow roots. She came in and out of the room and finally I saw her fill a kettle with water and place it on the free burner. As I worked at the counter, she walked up to me and said, bluntly, "I think it's time to wash." Eyes on mine, she waited for me to catch her meaning. At first I thought she meant the carrots and I moved quickly to the basin of boiled, treated water, but as I dropped in the handful of orange sticks, I realized she meant myself.

"Oh," I said, tightening my arms against my sides, trapping the smell, and she left me there to answer someone's question. My face burned red. For days I'd been so caught up in the work, in answering her needs, that I hadn't bothered with the demands of my own body. Luckily, my period hadn't come.

Did I hate her then? Yes and no.

She returned, arriving in silence beside me.

"So let me help," she said and carried a silver bowl of hot water into the back, beckoning with her head for me to follow. I didn't. Not right away. Really I wanted to run away, let my humiliation lead me back to Margo and complain about this bitch with the weird name who I didn't understand. But I followed.

She put the bowl on the coffee table, a towel on the floor for me to stand on. I crossed my arms over my chest.

“I’m sorry,” she said. “You didn’t realize?” That was Phoenix. Honesty like a razor-sharp stinger. “Sandy,” she said, like I was a child. Emotion clogged my throat. I didn’t move.

She tapped a few drops from a brown bottle into the water. The scent of lavender drifted up. I did what she wanted: unfastened the buttons of Thomson’s old cardigan and pulled off the long-sleeved shirt that said OCCUPATION EARTH in cracked orange letters. I wasn’t wearing a bra. Phoenix nudged a piece of wood into the morning’s coals to start the fire again while I took my pants off and my underwear and socks. Goosebumps stood out on my skin. Did she look at me? I don’t remember.

From the restaurant, I heard Thomson cough. I must have looked nervous because she smiled and said, “It’s fine.” She rubbed soap into a cloth and ran the warm water up my spine, scrubbed behind my ears. I could have done it myself, but it felt good, her attention, the careful, tender touch she gave me that seemed so different from her fierce everyday commands.

When she left the room, I cleaned between my legs. After she came back, I kneeled on the towel and let her wash my hair.

“We should cut this. You’ll only get lice.”

“All right,” I said, soapy water running into my eyes. I reached for a towel. My fingers closed around my shirt and when I brought it to my face I found the awful smell. The door swung open. Eyes cleared, I lifted my head to see. Marvin. He looked at us. Phoenix’s hands in my hair, a half-smile on her face. A red tint to mine. I think he knew right then how I felt, even before I did, but he’s never said anything. Not once, in all the years. I understand why. To begin that discussion is a step down a path he doesn’t want to travel, a trail toward his own guilt. And perhaps more than that: grief.

My first instinct was to cover my breasts. Phoenix’s hands remained where they were, her fingers scrubbing at the roots. He closed the door and was gone.

She leaned back from the sudden force of me. I pulled the stinky shirt on, jeans with no underwear, and shook her off when she reached for my slippery fingers. I went after him, running barefoot through the restaurant. Everyone watched. The street was crowded with people waiting for the soup kitchen. I didn't see him, not even slipping around the corner toward his squat.

Returning, I plucked the shirt away from my wet nipples. No one said anything. They were all wondering, I could tell, but I kept walking, my arms wrapped around myself, shivering from the cold.

In the room, Phoenix was cleaning up. My underwear and socks kicked in a pile by the folded bedding, the towel tossed beside the washbasin. She gathered cups, including a mug containing a sticky pool of whisky. I wanted a drink.

"Find him?" I shook my head. I wanted to leave, have a night off, head over to his place . . .

"Start cutting some bread," she ordered, moving toward the door. It was too much for me.

"In a minute," I snapped, and Phoenix turned so fast I felt the wind made by her body.

"Marvin is a chicken-shit," she blurted, and I almost laughed at how her accent made the slang seem crisp and artificial. "He's scared of what he can't control." We stared at each other. "You see how he comes only when he feels like it. But you seem okay with that." She left then. I stood there, skin clean under my filthy clothes. The fire hissed. I kicked at the bowl of water, spilling it. What I didn't want to admit was how my body still hummed.

Surprises exist, Melissa. We are never everything that we think we are. Even in a single lifetime, we are capable of shifts as huge as history. But that doesn't mean that everything works out. Sometime I will tell you the story of the *Titanic*, an ocean liner they said couldn't sink and it did. Sucked more than two miles down, to the bottom of the sea.

Changed, wearing a pink top that looked like pyjamas and a pair of too-tight jeans stiff from being hung on a line, I went back. Phoenix was at the hotplate, a crowd of people around her. They pulled back, holding bits of food between their fingers, and as I got closer I saw the uncertainty on their faces. A huge frying pan spat and hissed, and Phoenix reached into a jar and dropped in another handful of squirming grasshoppers. They browned quickly.

“Want one?” she asked as I walked by, but I ignored her. Someone else was cutting the bread. I went to the chalkboard where the jobs were written out. My name was on the bottom. Sandy: Dishwashing.

It was the worst job—grease and vegetable bits and soggy bread crumbs accumulating in tepid water that could rarely be refreshed. The sting of bleach on my still raw hands. I turned to the sink and rolled up my sleeves and that was how I spent the night: staring down into dirty water, cleaning the mirror surfaces of the bowls.

11 Island

I ran home. Down the long, empty road with the huge blur of nature on either side. The backpack bounced on my shoulders. I wanted to drop it off and check on Thomson before moving up the coast to the caves. Once again, the house was empty. The chaise lounge and couch unoccupied, blankets dropped on the floor. In Thomson's room, the stripped mattress was bare. Books, with creased and torn covers, piled on the side table. I spun around and went outside. An electric hum was in the air, like the sound that streetlights used to make, and I raced up the trail, through the pines to find Thomson standing in the clearing. Both hands wrapped around the handle of his cane. The pointed tip sunk into the sand.

"You can't keep coming here," I started, but my voice faded out as I followed his gaze. A thick carpet of bees covered the face of the wooden hive. I moved to grab the smoker off the rubber bin, but Thomson stopped me. "That won't help," he said, and I remembered. So close to swarming, that was all they could think about: packing up, moving out. There wasn't time to consider enemies. The smoker hung from my hand.

"I didn't get all the queens," I said.

"No." He watched the buzzing crowd while I watched him. It took him a long time to speak. I was about to give up, grab his arm, try to force him back to the house, and leave to look for you, when he said, "We could try to kill the new queen. But they'll die defending her. We'd get a lot of stings." My head bobbed in useless agreement. We stood there watching and finally I said, "I think I know where she is."

"The queen?"

"The girl," I told him, and under my breath, because I wasn't sure I wanted him to hear: "Melissa."

He glanced at me, eyes clouded, the whites yellowed. Lifting his stick, he swung the end toward the hive. "This is what's happening," he said, without moving his gaze from the hive.

Chastised, I stood and watched. *Don't you care?* I wanted to ask. I wondered if Marvin had gotten to him, if they'd been gossiping about Sandy's delusions, if they knew something I didn't. Thomson shifted, spread his legs in a V so he could stand more solidly. He switched his walking stick to his other hand so he could curl his fingers around my forearm. I felt his weight as the bees crowded closer, their sound growing louder. Their bodies glistened like facets in a slab of quartz. We wouldn't have any more honey, not even the tiny supply we'd harvested the summer before and burned through quickly in winter. All the things the bees gave us would be gone and into my mind stormed images, things I tried not to think about: Phoenix, our past history, life a continual process of letting go. I leaned over to say that to Thomson, but he was focused on the hive, waiting for the swarm to lift. His fingers white from holding tightly to his cane. Not wanting him to tire out, I ran over to the house and returned with a chair and a blanket to spread over his knees. As I sat on the ground, the dampness seeped through the seat of my pants. Finally I pulled the lid off the blue plastic bin and sat on it. "Can you settle?" Thomson said, his voice snapping amid the buzzing drone.

"Sorry," I muttered, but the truth was I didn't want to be there. Inside me I felt the same frenetic energy as the bees, intent on going elsewhere now that I thought I knew where you were. But the longer I sat, Thomson silent in his chair, staring at the crowd of insects, the more I doubted myself, the more I thought you'd be gone, vanished, a fantasy that could no longer exist, once I climbed through the stone mouth of the cave.

I pushed myself into a squat, ready to bolt. "Thomson?" He didn't reply. The bees pressed tighter, the queen at their centre, preparing to move as one. Crowded at the hive's opening, they grew louder and Thomson reached for me. His fingers tight around my own, his eyes glowing as several thousand bees lifted in a buzzing cone and floated over to the yellow goldenrod, the forest beyond. He pushed off the chair's edge to stand. I helped him. Together we followed, our feet snapping fallen twigs, crushing pine cones. They were too fast for us. The colony drifted quickly away and finally disappeared.

Thomson smelled. I'd been neglecting him. Lost in my reveries, as Phoenix would have said and Marvin had implied at the dump. Silently, we went back to the house. Thomson slumped against me, my arm around his back. He was as narrow as one of Mr. Bobiwash's kids by then, but unlike them he had the stench of illness on him, of fever-sweat and rot. The caves would have to wait.

In the house, Thomson slept while I built a fire and set our blackened soup pot on the stove. While the water warmed, I went outside, wandered around the garden, examined smudges in the sand by the fence footings, places where the chicken wire could be pulled up and you might be able to crawl beneath. I made the gaps wider. When the pot wobbled from the force of the bubbling water, I woke Thomson and we moved slowly to the wooden chair in the kitchen. Gently, I opened the top of his robe and let it fall to his waist and pulled off his shirt. I mixed the hot water with cold, soaked the green washcloth and squeezed it out. "Okay?" I asked, rubbing hard soap made from ashes and animal fat onto the fabric. He nodded and I slipped the cloth under his arms, over his chest. I dipped it and squeezed it over and over again, dirt appearing in the water, colouring it grey. When I sponged the skin of his stomach, the meagre folds, he said, "Phoenix used to do this for me." Outside, the birds sang. A chickadee, calling into dusk. "When I was first sick."

"I remember."

He looked confused. "You don't. You weren't even there."

I didn't tell him how I'd been thinking about her, the circle of time.

The water dripped onto the linoleum, which was worn through to the floorboards beneath. I wiped it up, worried about mould setting in, the poisons brought by moisture.

"Let's talk about her," he said. "We never do."

"We do," I said, even though he was right. I handed him the cloth and turned away as he sponged his limp penis, his grey pubic hair. A lump had hardened in my throat and I squeezed it with my thumb and index finger, tried to rub it away. Through the kitchen window, I saw the clouds, coloured like limestone, a band of light stabbing through.

I helped him stand. Cleaned his back, behind his knees. He kept talking. "She comes to me sometimes. When I'm far gone. When I'm thinking that's it, I'll never make it to morning." I pushed Thomson back to sitting. By then, the water was black. I dipped the cloth in, let it steam off the heat. Thomson chuckled at a secret joke.

"You're almost done," I said, and he blinked like I'd jolted him out of a daydream.

With a blanket over his shoulders, he sat while I worked on his feet with the last of the clean water. Dirt stained the skin between his toes. The washcloth pulled out pine needles, grains of sand. Thomson's eyes stayed on the top of my head, waiting, but I couldn't talk out loud about Phoenix. Instead I wanted to think about you.

"I think she's in the caves," I said, looking up. He grunted, his eyes showing only a sliver of white. I wondered who he thought I meant but then he spoke.

"You know that caves are portals."

"To where?" I asked. It was better than talking about Phoenix.

"The Underworld."

I rubbed a froth of soap on the cloth.

"Bring an offering for the deities. That's what the Mayans do; they'd leave jadeite pendants and ceramics next to huge stalagmites." His arm lifted to emphasize the height. I rinsed his feet.

"Do you believe that?" I asked.

He shrugged. "Better safe than sorry."

Marvin came back when I was crossing the yard. "Where are you going?" he asked, lifting a turtle with both hands. The creature's webbed feet dangled heavily. I stared at him, still angry.

"A walk," I lied.

"Wait for me," he said and moved toward the house. His slow lope, not even hurrying.

"Don't wake him," I shouted. After his bath, Thomson had quickly fallen asleep.

When Marvin returned, the turtle left in the cool burrow of our cellar for me to make into soup, he said, "I saw something shiny. Up the shore."

We stared at each other. "What is it?"

"I don't know," he said, and we walked together, him in the lead, without speaking.

At the beach, the wind pushed hard off the lake like it was trying to get us to leave. Water beat against the shore, steady waves, smashing. Anything we said had to be half yelled so we didn't really speak. I wrapped my hand around the flashlight in my pocket, the wind-up one we'd taken from the dark zone, years ago, that last night. It was the only thing I had. I'd brought nothing to give to you or the ancestors or demons Thomson had warned me could be in the caves. I figured I was already sacrificing enough.

At the edge of the water, we stopped. I looked to the east where the land humps like the curved back of a sea monster. In that limestone body are the caves.

"This way," Marvin said, turning in the opposite direction. I hesitated, glancing at the dark sliver that was the mouth of the nearest cave before following. We moved closer to the lake. Riffles of water sucked at the soles of my boots. My socks grew damp and heavy.

"There," Marvin said, pointing at a metallic glint, a spot up ahead on the edge of the forest. Nausea rose in me as we approached. I felt the prickle of sweat in my armpits. I already knew what it was. We both did. A cargo box, sitting on its side. Marvin kicked it. The lid fell open. It was empty. Flour, sugar, tea, and Thomson's medicine, all washed away, swallowed by the lake.

"Some of them are sealed," Marvin said, his voice tight, as if he was holding in smoke.

I looked out at the water, searched for a shadow in the waves, wished for a sighting like you do when you can't believe something has happened. A death you refuse to take in. Looking for evidence that you're wrong.

Marvin stepped closer. I smelled fish on him—that sour, metallic stench that never goes away. The light press of his fingers was supposed to offer reassurance. I let him touch me. "It'll be okay," I said before he could. We both knew I was lying, like many times before. We didn't stay long like that. The empty box shuffled in the wind and Marvin kicked at it before we moved down the shore, looking for others.

Yellow daisies grew in thin layers of sand. The ratcheting cry of red-winged blackbirds came from an inlet that became wetland. The waves were the colour of lead. A rancid smell hung in the air. Rot, like the stench of a deer we'd found one afternoon, its belly hollowed out by coyotes and maggots. Marvin thrust his arm out, blocking my way. Too afraid to be annoyed, I stretched to look past him and he grabbed me roughly and pulled me forward. Up ahead, a man lay on the shore. Bloated, bare feet in the water. His swollen face mottled with shades of blue. Cheeks torn. One eye missing. The puckered socket rimmed with a black tar of blood.

Over the years, I've seen dead bodies. In the city and on the island. An old woman decomposing in a house we'd thought abandoned. A stillborn baby I helped Sarah bury like an expired seed. Each time is awful. My hand covered my mouth; I forced myself to keep quiet. Marvin turned away, vomiting into the underbrush, and I didn't say a word as he wiped his mouth with the sleeve of his shirt. He looked at the sky. The sun was sinking, a watery streak of orange dissolving into the lake. The trees dulled by the deepening shadows of evening. All colour turning slowly into a palate of greys. He grimaced and spat on the ground.

"We can't leave him," I said.

"We need help."

I started to laugh. A sputter I extinguished by covering my mouth. "I'll stay," I said, and without a word Marvin turned and ran, his body breaking through the forest, a deer escaping the hunter's scent.

Night came quickly as I sat with the body. Crickets called. Bats darted over the narrow, marshy inlet to the north. From my seat on a log of bleached driftwood, I stared at the blind hole where the man's eye had been. In Tibet, Thomson once told me, the people brought their dead into the mountains and let animals and vultures pick apart the corpses. A sky burial, he called it. He'd told me that at a time when we hadn't thought so much about dying. Or I hadn't. It sounded beautiful, but the body on the beach reminded me of the worst things about death. How still we become. How empty. A vessel, drifting out of range, into invisibility.

I thought about the supply ship: hitting a hidden shoal, swallowed quickly by the cold bay.

Nine years ago it first came, run by a combination of government, aid agencies, and volunteers. It gave us hope. Things would never be what they were—brightly lit supermarkets with asparagus from Peru and frozen pasta in microwave-safe plastic bowls—but the ship meant less work and more food and necessary items we could trade for like winter coats that needed new buttons or lanterns.

In the beginning Mr. Bobiwash went for us. He didn't judge us by our secrets. He never asked. And after a year or so we went ourselves, at first with our heads down, my hair cut short, Thomson's dyed with walnut juice. Hidden. The medicine took a lot of our supplies in trade, but even when we didn't have enough—smoked fish, sacks of dried herbs, baskets I'd learned to weave, salvaged copper or honey—the doctor always gave us what we needed. He was a kind man. I lowered my head, eyes shut hard. I didn't want to cry. If I started, I didn't think I'd be done by the time Marvin returned.

Would another ship come? Maybe, but not in time for Thomson.

When I looked up, my eyes settled on the dusky shore, its outline bleeding into the lake. An otter scrambled into view and

I watched as it fished a clam out of the shallows and ate it, the crunch of the shell breaking the silence. When I stood, it saw me and jabbered loudly before abandoning its meal to slip into the water, swim away. Marvin was long gone. I turned and headed up the shore.

In the cave, my light floated over the walls, revealing fossils. A honeycomb pattern of ancient sponge coral and a stone mollusk. Evidence of the shallow sea that had covered the island millions of years ago. There was a terrible smell, like chicken innards left out in the sun, and fear grew in me as I moved deeper, prodding with my flashlight. *It can't be you,* I thought. *It can't be.* But I was terrified. I wished I'd brought an offering after all: a bit of tobacco, a silver spoon.

On the dirt floor, a torn lace tablecloth lay in a heap like the last spring snow. Nearby, brown tuft from cattails. When my foot crushed a pile of eggshells, a movement rippled the damp air. Quickly, I stood, stabbing the light into the darker spaces at the back of the cave. The beam landed on another storage chest, on its side, empty. A scuffed black shoe. A naked leg, cobwebbed with veins. A black skirt twisted around a woman's thighs. Her cloudy, white eyes stared out of a collapsing face and I pulled away, lurching back, slipping on the shale. The light bounced up to the roof and down onto you. Your living face. Eyes widening. I cast you back in shadow, wrestling with the sudden shapes of words in my mouth. I crouched as if approaching a timid animal and listened for the whisper of your breath, the sound of your voice.

"Melissa," I said, and my voice filled the round, cold room. The light shook on the wall as I began my explanations. "I won't hurt you. The food on the red plates . . . The fish and greens . . ." I lifted the flashlight to my face to show you what I look like and then words gushed out of me, panicked, eager, afraid: "Come with me, Melissa."

You moved forward, feet shuffling against the gritty floor. I waited, aware of the mouth of the cave behind me. How we could walk through it, together, start a new life. My arm was burning from the extension of my hand. I lowered it slightly and from outside, Marvin shouted my name. The charge of a shotgun boomed through the air and right then you rushed past me like a frightened cat, your warm skin briefly grazing my fingers. Running hard as Marvin hollered my name a second time. I followed as you disappeared into the abyss of the night, the forest full of steep drops, sharp edges, poisons in purple and green. Outside, I clenched my middle, stuffed down the urge to shout your name out over the bay.

"There were coyotes," Marvin told me, out on the beach. He was holding the gun. I moved toward him. "Where were you?" he asked as I stepped into his light. But I said nothing about the woman's body or you. Marvin stared behind me, at the cave.

"Come on," I said and started down the shore, a lighter brown against the huge black mass of the lake. Marvin followed, but slowly, prodding the thick cedar along the shore, searching as we went. I could see another light: Mr. Bobiwash's. He was crouched in the long tendrils of water, by the dead man's side. Marvin walked farther ahead and I thought he was looking for you, that he'd seen you, a shadow he was trying to capture, to clarify. Mr. Bobiwash opened a waterlogged wallet and stared at it for a moment.

"Shit," he breathed at the same time as Marvin called out his name: "Jack!" Mr. Bobiwash and I both looked toward Marvin. The flashlight pointed down at a leg, shoe missing, sock torn. Mr. Bobiwash glanced back at the ID card glowing in his own yellow circle of light. "It's the doctor," he said, and the three of us were still.

12 City

The next morning, Phoenix was already gone when I woke. The bed empty, even Thomson's usual ridge flattened out. He was the only one in the restaurant, slowly turning the pages of a newspaper whose edges were already yellowing.

"They arrested eight squatters," he said when I shuffled in.

"Isn't that old?" I asked, moving behind the counter to dunk a mug into the pot of tea. It was nearly empty so I started to make more.

"It still happened." Thomson told me they'd been hauled out of empty houses in the suburbs not far from the place Margo and Walter and I had scoured out. I didn't know what to say so I asked what he thought, if the cops would soon be heading into the dark zone. He stared into his tea, at the shiny surface that couldn't give much of a reflection since the diner was so dark by then, with all the broken windows boarded up.

"They're following a strategy." His finger thumped against the paper. "They think those squatters were a Jump Ship cell." Probably he was looking for a reaction, but I didn't give him one. Not because I'm a great actress but because I didn't know much about Jump Ship other than the basic facts: responsible for a string of bombings, all for the same reason, to hasten the collapse. "The problem with them," Thomson said, "is they assume there's a clean ending and a fresh start, as if there is no cause and effect." The heat in his voice reminded me of my father so I automatically disengaged, snapped off the hot plate, let the boiling water sink to stillness. I reached for the herbs, scattering tiny yellow flowers and fragments of mint across the counter. As I swept the spilled bits into my palm, I heard Thomson moving behind me, the clatter of his mug on the counter.

"Where's Phoenix?" I asked as the flowers fattened in the hot water.

"They went to get donations. We've got our own duties: back to the bees."

The night before, Phoenix had hardly spoken to me. For hours I stood at the sink, hoping Marvin would come back, wanting to go find him, but I felt Thomson watching me, holding me to my commitments. I knew if I left like that, there'd be no point coming back. After we'd closed the soup kitchen, a string of firecrackers went off outside, spreading a red wash over everything. A sound like cracking bullets. In the back room, I lay down fully clothed, my hands tender and water-softened, the fingertips ridged with puckered skin, and fell asleep. I'm not sure how long I was out before they woke me, voices sliding under the bedroom door like those of my parents.

"It isn't only up to you," Phoenix said. "You don't even realize—"

Thomson cut her off, straining to whisper: "How long have you been so unhappy?"

Abruptly, they were silent. I was nearly asleep again when I realized Phoenix was speaking. She said something about moving on and Thomson laughed, a rare outburst, quickly muffled.

The wind off the lake was strong. A strangely warm breeze that stirred all the wreckage. A television antenna swayed in the strong gusts. Objects skittered and rolled down the street: a soccer ball, an aluminum lawn chair with frayed yellow webbing, the deflated skin of a giant blow-up Santa.

"Snow," Thomson said as we turned down the laneway, heading for the hives. "We should be seeing snow this time of year." I didn't answer. It had been years since February automatically meant snow. I'd had that argument over and over with my father, who seemed to take it personally, the way the seasons had changed since his childhood, the weather's chaos, how each day could bring something different than what was historically expected. As a kid of thirteen, I blamed him, his generation. "It's your fault," I yelled at him like a stupid teenager and slammed my bedroom door.

"Ever been stung?" Thomson asked, jolting me out of my memory.

"Stung?" My foot came down in the deep edge of a brown puddle. I leapt back, my shoe and sock soaked through. "Shit," I said and stood there like a crane, the broken rubber bottom of my runner dripping. It knocked everything loose. I opened my mouth and let out a trickle of thoughts: that I wasn't sure what Phoenix wanted from me, even if I could stay.

Thomson waved his hand, dismissing me. "Who's ever sure about anything? We're here; we make the bloody best of it."

Carefully I set my foot on the ground and felt the water gush against the walls of my shoe. I felt chastised, uncertain how to respond, but Thomson went on as if he hadn't gotten angry with me, like everything was normal. We'd reach the bees by then. He set a hat on my head, fitted with a net that hung down from its peak like a veil. He tucked the hem of the net into the collar of my shirt and pulled a nest of blue and pink elastics out of his pants pocket. Holding my forearm, he lowered himself onto one knee and lifted my wet foot, surprising me. I swayed and grabbed his shoulder. He was solid, like a stone ledge. He slipped an elastic around my running shoe, the sole flapping loose. "Have to glue those," he said and snapped the band in place, closing the gap of my pant leg. He did the same for my other leg, both wrists, but didn't bother with himself.

The bees were out. I stood back and watched them, crowded around the narrow slot of the hive's opening. Some lifting, floating over the fence, in search of blooms that hadn't come yet. By the brick wall, Thomson lifted the cover of a large wooden box. He pulled out a spouted tin can with a bellows attached and flicked a lighter to ignite the pine needles and wood splinters stuffed inside. Smoke leaked out the spout, and once it was burning, Thomson squeezed the bellows to release more. "They're pretty sluggish right now. But this calms them."

"How?" I asked as he squeezed smoke around the top of the hive.

"It tricks them into thinking they have to evacuate. The smoke disguises the pheromones released by the guard bees that would otherwise tell the hive to attack." When he said that last word I took a tiny step away, but Thomson had his hand on my back and he pushed me closer. He started to tell me more: how the bees gather up their stores, thinking the hive is on fire, when a sudden clanging startled us. We spun around to see a battered aluminum garbage can lid spinning down the road. "Christ," Thomson breathed and paused to recover before he placed his hands on the hive lid and said, "Ready?" I nodded.

That was the first time he showed me the internal parts of the hive—the cells, waxed over in the general pattern of a landmass on a map. "Those bees are forming," he told me. "From egg to pupa to adult worker takes twenty-one days. Complete metamorphosis."

Bees landed on Thomson's bare hands and lifted away. He handed me the smoker and I puffed, directing the grey coils over the open hive. Bees settled in his hair, on the bridge of his nose. Gently, he swept them off his face. I was amazed by him, all those earlier tensions with Phoenix and Marvin and the other complicated fringes of my world forgotten.

Thomson pulled off a clump of wax that glistened with honey and held it up to me. "Taste." I plucked it off his finger and slipped it into my mouth. Sweet and chewy. "Honey," I said, but he wasn't listening. He was gazing at another frame he'd pulled out. "The queen is in there. Issuing orders. Laying eggs. Without her they wouldn't even exist. She's their empress, their meaning in life."

His eyes were damp. He blinked back tears from the smoke that hung in our faces. I waved it away. He stepped back and I followed, watching as he held the back of his hand against his mouth and cleared his throat, hard. One hand still holding the frame, he turned away and coughed until he spat up. A splatter of mucus landed on the ground and I thought I saw speckles of black. His breath sounded hollow when he inhaled. When he finished, he lifted the frame close to his face and squinted.

"God," he said. "Mites."

He burrowed one hand under his sweater and pulled a pair of silver tweezers from his breast pocket. I watched as he knocked off a wax cap and pinched out the perfect milk-white body of a pupa and then a second one, spotted with red-black bits. His head abruptly lifted and his eyes found mind and I knew there was something wrong. We went frame by frame, peering across the surface of the cells, looking for infection.

We were quiet as we walked back to the diner. Thomson kept clearing his throat and once he paused to pinch a stinger out of a red hump on his forearm. I asked if he was okay.

"Fine," he said, but his voice sounded choked. The worry lines in his forehead were deep. The wind had calmed, but fat clouds were pushing across the lake and the air had turned colder. Still wet, my foot felt icy and it squelched against the pavement.

"Weather coming," I said, like a farmer, but Thomson's gaze was pointed straight ahead, still burrowing into the imaginary depths of his hive. "What do they do? The mites."

He glanced at me and seemed to consider whether or not to answer. I wonder now if he wasn't thinking about just giving them up. When it came his description was technical, delivered without emotion.

"They breed in the brood cells. They suck the bees' blood. They spread a virus that causes deformed wing. They're called the destructor. Ultimately, the colony will collapse."

"Can we stop them?"

Thomson shook his head, impatient with me.

"I can help."

He looked at me, gauging my intent, and when he spoke it seemed he'd decided to trust me. "I remember something about powdered sugar," he said. "If we can get some of that."

"Like cake sugar?" I asked, and he nodded. By then we were back at the diner. Phoenix and Zane were sorting through card-board boxes that sagged on the tables, their corners black and soggy. Zane laid out stunted ears of corn and shiny green peppers with coin-sized soft spots grown fuzzy with mould. Phoenix held up a potato. Sturdy white vines climbed out of its eyes. I waited for her to look at me but she didn't.

"We should plant this," she said to Thomson.

I picked up an ear of corn, tiny compared to the ones my family had grown.

"Any meat?" Thomson asked.

"Nothing we could trust," said Zane.

"Bones?"

Phoenix gestured at the pot on the glowing burner. "Already on."

"How much power is left?" Thomson asked.

"I brought the other panel outside," said Zane.

"Clouds are moving in," said Thomson, and I said, "It looks like rain."

"We can't do anything about that," Phoenix said, collapsing one of the boxes to bring in the back for the fire. "Where were you?" she asked, her gaze sliding over to me but barely connecting. I crossed my arms. Thomson slid into a booth. "The hives."

"You went too?" she asked me.

"Yeah."

"First time?" I didn't know what she meant. "Seeing inside a beehive," she said.

"We have mites," Thomson said before I could answer.

"Are they bad?" She went behind the counter and set a cutting board, knife, and vegetable peeler next to a pile of carrots.

"I don't know yet. I'll have to look again. Do you remember what we learned about the powdered sugar?"

Phoenix nodded. "I think it knocks them off."

Zane had left so the three of us sat in a triangle, me in the booth with Thomson, Phoenix on the stool, as she told us what she remembered about the technique. We sipped the remains of the tea I'd made that morning, poured into a jug to free up the pot for soup. After a little while, Thomson leaned into the corner of the booth, his head nodding into sleep, and Phoenix turned to me.

"So you've found what you're interested in?"

I paused, plucked a strange, soggy bloom from the tea off my bottom lip.

"The beekeeping?" Her hands worked the vegetable peeler; the tendons made clear ridges under her skin.

"Sure. But not just that. The soup kitchen too."

"You didn't seem so into it last night."

"I've been working my ass off."

"Huh," she said.

"What?"

"Do the bees believe in the hive's mission? Or do they act because it's in their nature?"

"What do you want from me?" I asked, angry suddenly. Thomson came to and started sputtering.

"Excuse me," he said, but it could have been *Leave her be,* and I could hear the wheeze in his lungs, that soft ticking sound as if he'd swallowed a clock. He walked quickly down the length of the diner to the back room. We heard the door slam.

"Is he okay?" I asked, but Phoenix didn't look up. The orange strips of peel curled on the counter like ribbons.

I tried again: "Shouldn't we find him a doctor?"

She continued to ignore me and I felt like one of those capped workers, locked away in a cell, silent. I couldn't stand it. "Last night . . ." I started to say, wanting only to clear the air, and Phoenix lifted her head, waiting.

I went over to her, sat on the neighbouring stool.

We were so close our knees accidentally bumped before I pulled mine away. I still had my tea, the mug set on the counter, my fingers wrapped around the handle. Slowly she reached for my hand, loosened my grip, squeezed my fingers so the knuckles crowded together. I wasn't sure what she was going to say, but I assumed it would be an apology of some sort so I tried to make it easier.

"It's okay," I said abruptly and pulled away. I stood and walked to the pile of flattened cardboard boxes on one of the tables and gathered them up to carry them into the back. Thomson was coughing hard, the sound a low drone through the walls. I turned back to her.

"Phoenix," I said, the boxes clustered in my arms like a collection of shields. She had moved on to slicing the carrots into orange rounds for the soup. She looked up from the knife in her hand. "Tell me the truth about him. Is he sick?"

"He's fine."

I told her what I thought I'd seen at the hives. What he'd spat out: that hunk of mucus, spotted with soot or blood. "Maybe we should take him to a hospital."

She stilled the blade. Her voice was hard. "He's fine," she said again. "It's a cold."

I stepped closer, all the flattened boxes shifting.

"Really? I don't think—"

"He's my father. He's my responsibility."

As if he was a child. In the distance, his hacking had ceased as if he could hear us, but then I heard him groan.

"Stepfather," I said.

She turned to stare at me. "Where's your father?" she asked. "Or Marvin, even, or anyone?"

It was decided. I dropped the boxes in a clattering slide and went to the back room to grab my stuff. Thomson was on the couch, a cloth in front of his face gathering those early stains. Our eyes met, but it was me who looked away, pinching back tears. It was none of my business. Phoenix had made that clear.

"Sandy," he said before I left the room.

I stopped, the clothes I'd worn down there that first night bunched in my arms. I knew how I appeared. My jaw hard, lips pressed together with rage. I hated her.

"Decide what you want," he said. "Be careful. Don't be distracted by those flies."

I knew what I wanted: not to have to leave him, to help with the hives, to be loved and valued and appreciated. But the thing between Phoenix and me felt too sticky and thick. I wanted to be free.

"Goodbye," I told him because I figured I'd never see him again.

I left hardly having heard him because I had no idea what he meant. All I knew was that I'd failed. Any belief that I was special, bound for bigger things like an important role down there, at the soup kitchen, melted away. And now I know how silly that sounds. From the vantage point of the island—living in the difficult wilderness, late summer approaching winter, I can see that I was tricked. Just as easily I could have been you, scratching your survival out of the earth, stolen eggs hot in your hands, but instead I still find myself looking back, thinking, *Where is my life?* It's like it existed somewhere else and I didn't find it. Like a city I've never visited—Tokyo or Paris—so I will never know that place, what it had to offer.

It was strange that Marvin and Margo showed up that day, jingling through the door just as I came out of the back dressed in my old clothes, pulling on my winter coat. Relief surged in me. I grabbed Margo, hugging her with one arm, and felt her lipstick smear against my cheek as she spoke into my ear: "Where the fuck have you been?" I almost cried.

"Let's get out of here," I said, grabbing Marvin's hand and tugging him toward the door. I knew Phoenix was watching, even with her back turned, scraping potato peels into the bin. I wanted her to see. Before I left, I swung out my arm and hit the side of the bowl of grasshoppers with the back of my hand. They flew across the counter, scattered all over the floor. The place went silent so the last thing I remember from the diner is the jingling of those bells over the front door, their delicate, tiny tinkling.

Outside, Margo spread her arms out and ran into the wind. I laughed. She wore a knee-length red trench coat and crushed velvet leggings. Black high-heeled boots. Phoenix didn't have anything on her, I thought. I grabbed Marvin's hand, slipped my fingers between his. I swung in front of him and stopped, kissing him. In the middle of the road, Margo wolf-whistled. The storm came then. The dark clouds Thomson and I had seen over the lake opened up and in a matter of seconds we were drenched. We ran, arriving at Marvin's squat breathing deeply, air burning in our throats. I felt almost hysterical, so high I could have sworn I'd been slipped a drug. If Walter had been there and handed me one of his pipes of chemicals home-brewed in the rented trailer Marvin told me he'd blown to smithereens I might have sucked on it greedily. Something in me wanted badly to be extinguished.

It was Walter who opened the door. "Welcome, wanderers," he said.

A huge fire burned in the hearth. Its heat and light mesmerizing in the damp and shadows. Water dripped through the ceiling, and we ran around finding bowls and mugs and empty paint cans. The pinging drops made a kind of music as Walter opened up a glass jar of moonshine he had, made in a still at his rooming house. He handed it to me. His blue eyes seemed to pulse as the liquid prickled in my mouth. "Get ready for Waltered States," Margo said, reaching for the jar, and it was the funniest thing I'd ever heard. I laughed until I cried.

Margo took her wet coat off and threw it in front of the fire, beside Marvin's mattress. It landed in a heap. I kicked off my shoes and stripped my socks off. The guys watched. I'd hung my own jacket on the hooks by the door like a good girl, the nice girl Phoenix had judged me as on the first night we'd met, saying it like an insult. My shirt was drenched and so I simply followed Margo's lead and took it off and within moments we were topless, the fire shining on our skin, the boys watching. A greed in their eyes without end.

13 Island

The darkness came, like the end of the day we left Phoenix and ran, ran. Bodies hauled onto stretchers made of saplings and the remains of old sails, carried, crashing, through the woods. A lantern swung from Samuel's hand. Bats dipped for bugs in our yard while I stayed with Thomson, his lungs grinding within the damp box of our house, the walls held with their internal weave of hidden wires. I could not leave even though I felt as if the thread that tied me to you was weakening. You were gone: vanished into the grainy, black world. Like static on an old television set. But still, I thought, I made myself think, I'd seen you. You were real.

I woke when Marvin moved in the bed beside me, his rough palm curving around my waist and down onto my hip. Gluey from sleep, my eyes wouldn't open.

I spoke toward his presence—"Did you find any more . . ."—but his lips silenced mine, his mouth hot in the cool night air of near autumn. The bodies were in the yard, I remembered, coming fully awake to meet Marvin's force with my own, arching into him, clasping the hard muscles of his arms. Moonlight scattered through our window like sulphur. He climbed on top of me and I opened my legs and he entered me as Thomson's choking cough started up and sputtered on like a useless engine. I tried to ignore it, but he moaned in pain below us, and I felt my grief rise. I wanted you. I wanted you. The you who Marvin refused, the child he turned his back on. I couldn't do it. I pushed him off, felt the break in his thrust, and ignored him when he said my name. He would not beg. We wanted too much from each other for that. He lay back as I set my feet on the cold wooden floor that had been painted blue in better days. Neither of us spoke as I went downstairs, trailing one of our blankets.

In the morning, sunlight blasted through the window. The door opened and closed and I sat up from my bed on the floor, in the corner of the living room. My back hurt and I twisted, trying to undo the knots. On the couch, Thomson was reading an issue of *Popular Mechanics* from the 1970s, pulling on the glued-together corners, his fingers awkward, like a child's. Mr. Bobiwash's wagon was in the yard, the mule shifting its feet as the hens scampered away, fussing with their wings. The boys and Mr. Bobiwash slid a body in the back, wrapped in a tattered sleeping bag I recognized from Thomson's old room. Marvin turned to me, his eyes set in dark hollows like he hadn't slept at all. "They found more."

I raised my eyebrows. More food, more medicine, more things that we could use?

"More bodies," said Mr. Bobiwash. "Corpses washed up on shore. And there was one in one of the caves." I covered my mouth. The smell of rot hung in the air. Mr. Bobiwash nodded toward the body, disguised by its shroud, only the feet sticking out: one splotchy and blue, the other clad in a worn black shoe with no laces.

"She baked awhile in that cave."

"Who was she?" I asked through the gaps in my fingers. I thought I saw him stiffen as he shook his head and turned away.

After the wagon lurched out of our yard, it was quiet. The men were bringing the bodies to town so I knew they'd be gone awhile. Thomson didn't want to eat, but I made him, holding slivers of fish in front of his mouth no matter how much he turned away.

"I'll sit here all day," I said, and he asked me if I'd washed my hands. "Of course," I lied, and he drew the fish from my greasy fingers with his fumbling chapped lips. When he wanted a fork, I knew he'd found his appetite so I got him one from the kitchen and asked if he'd be all right.

"You're leaving?"

"I've got a few things to do."

"Me too," he said, setting the plate on the couch. A raspberry tumbled off, adding a red smudge to the rest of the stains. "The swarm."

"They're gone," I told him, picking up the berry and pushing at the mark with the pad of my thumb.

Thomson shook his head. "The hive splits. The original community remains." Slumped into the corner of the couch, he stared at me. A brown arm, gaunt, sticking out from one rolled-up sleeve. His shirt flared open to show his chest, withered, covered with a tangle of hair, soft like fuzzy white mould. His eyelids fluttered, a reprieve from the intensity of his stare, and I knew he couldn't go anywhere. I stuck the berry in my mouth and lifted the blanket off the floor.

"I'll check on them," I said as I laid it over Thomson, helped him lengthen his body, lie down. Before I left, he grabbed my arm.

"Don't give up," he said as firmly as he could, but I wasn't sure what he meant.

I had no intention of going to the hives. No matter what Thomson said, Marvin was right. Over the years, the battle with the mites had worsened, demanding more time than we could give with all the other tasks we needed to do. In the beginning, we'd had the sugar, had brought it from the city, and scattered it into the frames so it coated the bees and caused the mites to fall off. But then we'd run out and our five hives diminished to one and it was time to give it up, despite what Thomson wanted. What I wanted was to find you—and I was willing to go hungry in the process.

I went back to the shore. I hoped I wouldn't find any more bodies as I looked for footprints in pockets of sand among the rocks. All I saw were the men's large tracks so I turned inland and pushed through the cedar bush toward the lighthouse. I stopped when I saw it: that white tower with its fading red trim. We had lived there the first spring, sleeping in an old bed below the room with the heavy glass lens. The wind off the water shook all the windows in their frames and the dampness of the lake crept in. It wasn't a good place for Thomson so we'd spent the last of our gas driving the short distance to our farmhouse, parked the car, and stayed.

Inside, my feet crushed crumbled plaster on the kitchen floor. The walls were covered with pockmarked graffiti from teenagers who once had nothing to do. Upstairs, a quilt and pillow lay on the bare mattress, ones I hadn't seen before. They smelled musty and old and I couldn't imagine them being used for a child. I lifted the blanket in my hands and saw holes made by moths, maybe the large green lunas that look like fairies as they drift over the milkweed.

In the yard, I stepped into the overgrown garden and gathered herbs—mint, roots of red baneberry, tall buttercup—to show Marvin that I was contributing and to keep the secret of my search. It was frustrating, this lack of evidence, of signs. Night after night I left out plates and in the morning they were always gone but there were no more footprints. You really were like one of Mr. Bobiwash's ancestors, the Natives who slipped into those caves and never came out again. If I hadn't seen you I might have believed you were a ghost. But now I knew exactly who you were—a shipwreck survivor, a castaway—and still it didn't help.

By the time I got home, Marvin was back, loosening tomatoes in his spidery fingers. A bowl sat in the squash vines, half full. He watched me walk to the house before standing from his crouch. I saw that he was angry so I held up the bag, a black fabric one.

"Herbs."

He gestured to the ground, to the red and yellow orbs, scattered on the earth, spotted with black. "What about all this?"

"I just did a bunch of canning."

"Then do some more."

"There are other things I want—"

"You want," he said. "Jesus Christ." He glanced into the woods, into imagined winter, and I saw it too: the forest clotted with white. Us, snowbound in the house. If we were lucky, if we'd prepared, we'd survive by opening jar after jar of green beans and pickled onions. Eating hens' eggs and salt fish and canned tomatoes and dried zucchini, rehydrated in melted ice.

"I have to get out there," he said, sweeping his arm along the horizon line of the lake. "I have to cut the fucking wood. The apples are dropping. And now there's this." The bodies, he meant. The dead like another harvest that couldn't have waited. "I can't do everything."

Then help me, I wanted to say, but instead I told him, "We're fine. We have a lot."

"We never have a lot."

"You know what I mean."

Marvin dropped the tomato into the bowl. "I'm not really sure I do."

I paused. "I want to find her."

"Is she worth dying for?"

"Were we?"

I stared at him, all that history between us. Quietly he looked away. "Get ready for town," he told me, "and help Thomson."

"Yes, sir," I said and walked into the house.

I buttoned Thomson's mustard-yellow dress shirt as he stood, balanced with his hand on the back of the couch. He stepped into his black corduroy pants, puckered at the knees from darning.

"You know you shouldn't come," I said, tying his belt. He sat down hard on the recliner. "Especially now."

"Why now?"

"With the doctor gone."

"That's why I'm going. To pay my respects. It's civilized."

He pulled his scarf from between the couch cushions. It was Phoenix's old orange one, patterned with large black stars, shot through with a silver weave that had snagged and broken over the years.

"It's worse when people just disappear," Thomson said but in such a low voice I pretended not to hear him. He didn't look at me as he tied the scarf over his mouth. I knew he meant Phoenix, how we'd just driven away afterwards, but his muffled voice said, "Like with the flu." Those times we have to bury people quickly, without ceremony. I thought, too, of Mona and Abby. How they faded away, their flesh-and-blood bodies vanishing into the mist over the lake. His eyes sank away from mine. "He was a good man," he said. "It's important to acknowledge his life."

In the kitchen, I nearly ran into Marvin. He stumbled backward so Thomson's tea sloshed over the side of the mug. I reached for the cup.

"I'll take it," he said, pushing past me.

On the porch, I ate a meal of applesauce and Solomon's seal root. The crows stood in the branches of the trees. One lifted into flight, spreading the fingers of its wings against the sky. I wondered if I would see you in town. If you would stand like a shadow on the edge of the crowd and say goodbye to the doctor and the five strangers and the woman from the cave. Were you grieving? Could I comfort you? Would you let me hold your hand and not vanish from my grasp?

In town, Mr. Bobiwash parked the wagon beside the playground and led Caesar, his donkey, to the water while Marvin, Thomson, Shannon, and I walked into the park. The baby lay in a navy blue sling, fastened against Shannon's chest, and I resisted the urge to worm my arms into that warm hollow, pull the skinny body out, and run. Eight funeral pyres were set up near the marina building, which was half sunk into the lake, a faded sign in the broken window advertising FREE INTERNET WITH COFFEE PURCHASE. The bodies were laid out on piles of white driftwood. Anil Sharma moved between the shrouded corpses, building tents of kindling on their ribcages. His father, Anthony, followed, laying bouquets of goldenrod and tiger lily and purple bog aster. I could see his lips moving, mumbling prayers to his gods, his convictions stronger than ours. Many had only come because there would be a distribution of salvaged supplies—the few containers of damp flour and clothes and other things from metal bins found on the island's rocky edge. We didn't know if all the shipwrecked supplies had been found, or all the bodies, but there were no reports of survivors. I didn't tell anyone else about you. I kept my eyes on Marvin and scanned the slim crowd. A gang of children ran around. The Bobiwash boys hadn't come or else they would have been playing, except for Samuel, who was too old for that.

Thomson hoisted his cane to wave at Albert, standing guard over the boxes of rations piled in the picnic shelter. We knew mostly everyone. About three families keep the town going, living in the empty stores along the main street that were looted years ago when the power went out and didn't come back on. They run the weekly market where Marvin trades fish when he catches more than we need. In the Stedman's store, its red sign smashed to shards, the shelves are filled with refurbished tools and other scavenged items alongside useless things like ice cube trays and DVD players and even a collection of credit cards in a pocket of aluminum foil. Meant for toys, I suppose, or artifacts. Beside Stedman's is the old library, a limestone building with a single intact stained-glass window. In the beginning, Thomson and I went there to save books fallen in heaps from the tipped-over shelves and dotted with mouse droppings. I found *Homesteading for Dummies*, several volumes of *Forest Plants of North America*, and a few issues of *Mother Earth News*, although the pages ripped when I tried to peel them apart. Thomson collected novels. One, *Fugitive Pieces*, we've read many times. In the story, a little boy hides in a hole in the dirt during a long-ago war and a man rescues him and raises him as his own. "It was a kind of rebirth," Thomson said. "Like this." He meant our coming north. I could save you like that, Melissa. I could pull you from that damp cave, that crypt.

Sarah, the midwife, was standing in the crowd. I waved and she walked over, carrying the leather satchel I'd found for her one day at the dump, the strap broken, a useless laptop still inside. It had been a few weeks since I'd seen her. Not since Shannon's baby was born and then, days after, when she came to treat a fungus on Marvin's foot. She asked about that and about me, my periods, but I didn't want to talk. Instead, I told her about Thomson, how his pills had been on the boat and were melted away in the big water by now. Red pellets fed to the fish. On her face was a stern expression, a sort-of serious helplessness. I realized that she didn't know what to say so I smiled and turned toward Thomson, his clothes hanging from him like robes, his hand gripping the back of the bench.

"Sit down," I said, and he surprised me by not arguing. I sat beside him and put my bag on the ground as Sarah wandered off.

Across the field, Anthony and his wife, Deepshikha, sang while Anil poured liquid from a green wine bottle onto the blue sleeping bag wrapped around the woman's body. Above the scarf tied over his mouth, Thomson's eyes glowed in their pronounced sockets. His fingers rubbed at the scar of a heart carved into the wooden bench. TLND. True Love Never Dies. I stilled his hand with my own. His knuckles rough and cold. I wanted to speak, but I didn't know what to say. The woman we found in the cave wasn't alone, I could have told him. The child was there. Marvin's and my child. Melissa. Something to give him hope.

Anil set fire to the dry wood. The flames jumped up, orange and yellow, green at their base. The sour smell of burning hair and flesh quickly filled the air. Blood seeped through the blackening sheets. It boiled, foamed, seethed like a lake in hell. I stared down, at my hands curled around the edge of the bench, the worn patch of dirt under our feet.

"I've missed so many funerals," Thomson said. "My parents'. Probably my sister's. The only one I remember is Maria's." Phoenix's mother.

A dozen kids were playing on the rusty, spider-shaped jungle gym and I watched them. One hung upside down from her knees, long blond hair tumbling down.

"We kept the candles burning for three days. And we couldn't sweep the floor. That's how they do things." He pointed at his face. "A jade bead in the mouth as currency for the afterlife."

I didn't speak. I felt his daughter's body between us, a hard thing of bone and muscle that might not have ever decomposed.

“Don’t do that to me,” Thomson said.

“Do what?”

He nodded toward the fires. The bodies, shrinking to sticky carbon, floating ash. “That.” And he counted off the steps on his fingers: “Take my clothes off. Put me in the ground. And tell the bees.” He cleared his throat and I braced for his choking cough but it didn’t come. “People used to do that. If someone got married, they’d bring the bees a piece of wedding cake. When a family member died, they draped a black cloth over the hive. I want you to do that for me. It’s bad luck not to.”

I thought of all the things I was supposed to say. *You’re not going to die. You’ll get well again.* Lies. My eyes stung from the smoke and I wiped at them. “All right,” I said.

He shrugged. “It’s a ritual,” he said, as if I’d asked why.

We fell into silence. I watched the crackling wood, a scene I once would never have imagined. Had that woman been your mother? Your aunt? A friend from the crossing? She’d been too decomposed for identification by anyone and didn’t have any ID. Now she was gone, as if she hadn’t even existed. It could happen so easily. You could lie down in the woods over winter and melt into the silent world. Vanish, like Phoenix had.

“There’s something else,” said Thomson.

“Yes.”

He breathed in and I heard the rattling start in his lungs. He sputtered and I waited, following his gaze to see Shannon, standing near the picnic shelter, staring at the men as they sorted through the boxes. “Feed the girl more,” Thomson said. “Give her my share.” I looked at him, saw the purple bruising under his eyes, the jagged red lines floating around his pupils. He squeezed my hand. “I don’t need so much.”

“But you do.” He needed fish soup, softened greens, berries, beets, more than he was already getting. On his good days, he polished his plate and held it out, wanting more and ended by licking it off. That hadn’t happened in a while, but how could I take from Thomson to give to you, barely more than a phantom?

"It's what I want," he said.

"I don't know," I said, but Thomson crossed his arms and, as if we were on summer vacation, spending a week at the cottage, he said, "I'm getting a bit tired of fish."

I shook my head. "You can't give up."

The fires made two tiny flares in his pupils. "I'm hoping she can help you."

"Help me?"

"Move on. Maybe even forgive."

He drew in a deep breath and I knew whatever he had to say would be important, part of his final words. "Marvin. Yourself. When I'm gone—" he started, but something caught in his throat and the scarf billowed from the force of his hacking cough. He bent forward, pushed his stick in the dirt. Gaining leverage against the violence of expulsion, his lungs working and working to push out the rot. I rubbed his back, looked around for help, and spotted Marvin and Shannon arguing by the picnic shelter. Shannon half turned away, her face red, her fingers like bars around the baby's form.

When he had finished, Thomson pulled his scarf down and spat on the ground. A clot of blood, dark like a period at the end of a long thought. A fresh slick of sweat covered his bald spot. Marvin ran over and I pushed the blood into the dirt with my shoe, burying it, making it into nothing but a smear of dark mud.

"Look at this," Marvin said. Two bottles of pills rattled in his cupped hand. I reached for them, but they vanished into the side pouch of his cargo pants. "Albert found them in a ration box. They weren't even with the doctor's stuff. We might not have even gotten them if the boat had come in like normal."

He was looking at me, his face glowing like a kid's. The medicine would keep Thomson going. Hope prickled in me, but Thomson was bent forward, elbows on knees, taking long breaths that sounded like someone filing down a rough edge. Marvin tipped one pill from each bottle into his hand. He tugged Thomson's scarf down and fed them to him, Thomson's lips working Marvin's palm like a horse.

"We should get home," I said as Shannon's voice carried across the clearing, angry, arguing:

"That medicine's for everyone."

I had an urge to run. To take the pills and leave. I'd walk home if I had to, along the south shore. I'd go into hiding. In the caves. At the lighthouse.

Shannon rushed toward us, the baby a lump, like a growth, that she ignored. She held out her hand and said, "Give them to me."

I stared at her. "They're his," I said. "Without them he'll die."

"Not the Rifadin," said Shannon. "Anyone can use that. You can keep the other."

"It won't work on its own. It'll wreck his kidneys."

Her eyes were bright green, like the deepest part of a fire. I tensed, unsure what she was capable of. The baby arched its back, its small wrinkled face blazing red, and I suddenly wondered if I could use the pills for you, to keep you healthy. Crush them into your food, into the extra rations.

"They're his," I told Shannon, with anger powered by guilt.

Shannon ran a hand through her dirty hair, pulling it off her face, forming troughs, while we waited for her next move.

"Water," Thomson said, tugging on my sleeve. I pulled a jar from my bag and handed it to him. Shannon watched as he drank, hunched over, the liquid spilling from his lips to the ground. The jar was too heavy.

"Help him," I said to Marvin at the same time as Shannon started to speak.

"He's old. He isn't the only sick one." She pulled the sling aside, tugging at the baby, and started to unbutton her blouse.

"Oh my God," I said, stepping forward but unable to stop her from pulling open her shirt, folding down the nursing bra that Sarah had made for her. A red nipple appeared, encrusted with pus. I turned away, embarrassed for her, enraged, and saw the men staring, even Thomson, the jar lowered to his knee. All of them, frozen, except for Mr. Bobiwash, who raced across the lawn toward her. The warped tattoo writhed as Shannon hoisted her breast. The baby screamed, shoved awkwardly against her mother's bony side, reaching for the available breast. The sound seemed to break the spell. Shannon tipped her chin up, smiling, proud.

"All right," said Marvin, his voice choked.

I swivelled to face him. The jar leaned precariously on Thomson's knee, about to empty down his leg. I grabbed for it as I said Marvin's name, but his hand was already slipping into his pocket. Shannon opened her fingers, the lines on her palm drawn in dirt. Marvin put the pills there as Thomson coughed again, a hard hacking. Mr. Bobiwash slid his arm around Shannon, but it was she who turned them away, moving toward the wagon.

"She can't take those," I shouted as they left. The prayer group looked over but I didn't care. Those people were already dead. I started to follow but Marvin grabbed my arm and I felt Thomson, too, fumbling for my fingers, his hand damp, clutching like a child. He held on to me as they walked away.

14 City

I woke in the bed where I'd fallen. The empty jar inches from my face, its wide mouth reeking alcohol. Reaching out, I shoved it aside, heard Margo groan from deeper in the bed as the glass clattered across the floorboards. Marvin loosened his arm from around my waist and turned over. We were crowded together and his shoulder blade jabbed into my arm. I shifted away from him as scenes from the night before sharpened into focus in my mind. A clunking noise came from the kitchen. I sat up. Steadied the boulder of my head. Found our clothes, my jeans and Marvin's, Margo's shiny silk top, all heaped together like fruit at the base of a tree, still damp.

Walter was in the kitchen, his naked ass a fat white moon as he dug around under the sink. All the cupboard doors and drawers were opened. I remembered the look on his face, that slim, doubting smile while the three of us watched Marvin standing on a chair, his leather jacket flapping open, eyes lit wildly from the wind-up flashlight shining under his chin, as he read out pieces of his manifesto—*for a long time we have walked the cliff's edge of resistance, always mindful of the steep drop a single crumbling footstep away* . . . Half naked, he'd gone on and on. Margo beside me with the tip of her finger between her teeth.

I'd felt outside myself, Melissa: like I was two people, one standing in the doorway, sandwiched between Phoenix and Thomson, watching across the room with judgment and disgust, the other raising my fist with Margo's and cheering Marvin on because what he said made sense. I thought I was on his side. But we were playing. Like birds of paradise, the male moving in a crazed dance of bright feathers to attract the duller female. And I fell for it. By the end of the next day he would have me. There was a river and I was in it and it was sweeping me along where it would. Everything happens for a reason.

I went outside and threw up. An acidic gush of moonshine and the few bits of food I'd eaten the day before. Descending the porch stairs, I tried to scalpel away the images of the four of us—Marvin and Margo, Walter's eyes on mine as he . . . I shuddered.

Margo came outside. The acrid drift of her cigarette made me retch but nothing came out. "You okay?" she called.

"Will be," I said when the nausea had passed.

She climbed down and rubbed my back and I leaned against her, feeling like she got it, like she understood, like she was soothing the ache of my shame. Hot tears filled my eyes and vanished into the soil, already dark from hours of rain. I thought of Thomson's warning about strong feelings. That urge to sink myself, to dive into every last dark corner, had brought me far the night before. A fervour like a hungry black hole. I groaned.

"Hey," she said, and I waited for her to tell me it would be all right, that I didn't need to cry. But that wasn't what she said. "Marvin has coffee!" she told me, her voice a loud whisper like she didn't want them to hear her glee. The heel of her boot crushed the cigarette butt and together we went back inside.

I sat at the kitchen island, a mug of black coffee in front of me. The others weren't nearly as hungover as I was. Head in hands, I tried to anchor myself in the moment, listening to the crinkling of Marvin's rolling paper as he made the morning's cigarettes and conversation about what to eat.

"Found these," Walter said, tapping his metal hand against the dusty surface of a sardine can, and Marvin told us that there were chickens.

He pointed with his chin. "A couple streets that way."

"I'll go," Margo said, and Marvin pulled a ten-dollar bill out of his pocket.

"Pink house. Guy's name is Chan." Walter followed her out the back door, carrying a mug in his good hand. It was only the two of us then, the scratch of Marvin's tobacco against the clean white squares of paper, the soft calls of pigeons in the upstairs rooms.

Then the flick of a lighter and smoke drifted through the room's dim light. I groaned. Marvin dunked an empty mug into a bucket of water and slid it over to me. "Drink this," he grunted, the cigarette hanging from his bottom lip. I tasted the bleach and could only swallow half of it. I supported my head on one elbow.

"You going to make it?"

"Don't know."

"You didn't seem so drunk last night."

"You did."

"Not drunk. Excited."

I pulled my fingers out of my hair, brushed a tangled bunch behind my ear.

His lips curved into a shy smirk that he wiped away with two fingers. "About the future," he said.

I didn't ask him what he meant because I didn't want to get him going. I remembered that day in the botanical garden, in what seemed like another lifetime. But Marvin didn't start any lectures. Instead, he nudged the cup of water toward me, encouraging me.

"Drink up," he said. "We've got plans."

"We do?"

"We're going to celebrate your freedom." I didn't answer. I wasn't sure I wanted to be free.

"From the tyranny of the do-gooder," Marvin said. "The prison of the plutocracy."

"It wasn't so bad."

"You didn't seem torn up about leaving."

"It's complicated."

"I saw that," Marvin said, a freeze in his voice that stopped me from speaking except to tell him that the only plan I had for the day was to find my way back to my old bed, in the apartment I'd shared with Margo. "Suit yourself." He turned away to pull a small cast-iron pan out of the compartment in the bottom of the stove. The metal and steel rattled with his movement.

Margo and Walter were laughing when they came in the back door. She was carrying a white bowl, five brown eggs inside. I swung around on the stool to face her. Abrupt, because I was ready to leave, couldn't stomach breakfast, wanted to get back to my job hunt, to an ordinary life. I asked her for the key to our place. Somewhere along the way I'd lost mine, probably under the fold-out bed at the soup kitchen.

"I'm going to head back," I said, imagining that nothing had changed. But a silence fell, like the ones that seemed to emerge whenever Marvin and I were alone. Her eyes widened with fake worry.

"You left," she said.

"What do you mean?"

"I had to make decisions."

Walter pushed into her side, his arm spreading around her shoulders. The lurch of his hip into hers tipped the edge of the bowl sideways. Two eggs tumbled out, splattering on the dirty tile floor.

"Walter! Fuck!"

We all stared at the splattered yolks, the tiny slither of a bloody umbilical.

"Well," Walter said. "You can't make an omelette without breaking some eggs." He laughed, but no one else did. Margo looked up from the mess on the floor, straight at me.

"I moved in with him," she said and clarified, as if there would be confusion: "Walter."

I paused. Remembered my room the day I'd left, the bed unmade, the digital alarm clock set for 8:00 AM, an orange sweater I'd found in a box on the street in my laundry basket to be cleaned.

"What about my stuff?"

She shrugged, her arms extending snakelike, like a Hindu goddess looking to hypnotize. My voice rose.

"What's that mean?"

"You disappeared off the face of the earth. You never even fucking called."

The men watched.

"Did you give back your keys?"

"Yeah."

"Has it been rented?"

Margo shrugged. "Probably," Walter said into the last cold pool of his coffee.

I put my hands over my face. When I removed them, I saw that Margo's eyes were dark and hard. Like Phoenix's, I thought, as I stormed past her, slammed the back door. My throat grew tight with a choking sensation I'd never felt before, not after my parents were evicted or even when I was laid off. How would I get my things, I wondered, but then quickly realized I had nowhere to put them, no place to live. No money. Very few friends.

I thought about returning to Thomson and Phoenix, begging them to take me in again, but I knew I'd burned my bridges the night before. I rubbed my forehead, clenched my arms around my chest. My stomach lurched and I leaned over the railing, let loose a hot gush of liquid. The worst of it, Melissa, was that I knew I wasn't unique. All over the country people were abandoning things—walking away from houses they could no longer afford, leaving cars, pale yellow traffic tickets ruffling under the windshield wipers like feathers—whether it was their choice or not. I was not special; my terror was not unique. Instead, I was simply joining their ranks.

No one came for me. The smell of eggs and canned fish and cigarette smoke drifted through the screen on the kitchen window, over its rotten window box filled with dried-out soil, the yellow husks of dead begonias. For nearly an hour I stayed outside, staring up at the stupid, happy faces of the couple on the billboard. Had anyone ever felt like that? Like the future, symbolized by the image of the clear, blue horizon behind them, the lilting boat, wind billowing its pure white sail, was right there for the taking? My parents, I remembered, the day that snake of oil had appeared in their field, before they'd lost everything. I sat on the top step, pulling on the roots of my hair, until I realized I had no choices. I was not free.

"She returns," Marvin said when I went back inside. Margo leaned against the counter, smoking. She'd put lipstick on without a mirror and it bled outside the boundaries of her mouth.

"I can go back, right?" I asked, and her wrinkled silk blouse rippled when she shrugged.

"It was all still there when I left."

"They might have sold it," Walter said. "That's what I wanted to do." Margo reached out and pushed at his forearm. "What?" he asked. I turned away. It was too much and I felt sweaty and grubby and wanted to get clean, brush my teeth, before I could start thinking about what options were left open.

I asked Marvin about that, if I could bring a bucket of water upstairs, if he had any soap, and he said, "I can do better than that."

He led me to a wooden shed in the backyard. A black barrel sat on the roof. Piping fed down from it and ended in a shower fixture suspended over a stall with plywood walls. A towel lay over the back of a chair. A bar of gummy, homemade soap sat on one of the wooden joists. Hooks made from bent wire hanger were hammered into the beams.

"I can't guarantee the temperature, but with how warm it's been . . ."

It was impressive. "You should make one of these for the diner."

"I did," he told me.

He stood in the doorway. "Do you want help?" He came toward me, reaching for the bottom of my shirt, but I stepped away. I didn't want to be touched. He lifted his hands, palms out, and then pointed at a nozzle above the shower head. "Just turn that open. Close it when you're done. It runs through fast."

"Marvin," I called before he walked out. "What you read from last night. Can I see it?"

"Sure," he said, and he was gone.

The water was so cold it made me hold my breath. I hunched over, letting it drop its needles on my back before I rubbed the soap hard between my hands, made beeswax-smelling lather and cleaned all the grimy crevices of my body, washed my hair as best

I could, and rinsed. When I finished, I realized how hungry I was, how thirsty. I turned the water back on and drank until the barrel emptied, which wasn't much. The clothes I had were wet still and dirty from running through the streets but when I pulled back the shower curtain, I saw that Marvin had brought me other ones. A pair of his jeans that were tight at the hips and that I had to roll up and a black T-shirt with the anarchy symbol hand-scrawled across the front in crinkled red paint. I put them on.

Suddenly I was in a different life. Mid-morning, broad daylight, the air cool enough to need jackets over long-sleeved shirts and sweaters. Marvin's hand hovered over my lower back when we turned left instead of right at the street the diner was on. We passed a derelict car, the back tires both flat, a dirty blanket stretched out on the back seat, and I glanced back as Zane came out the doorway of the diner. Two large, bleached bones in his hands. After they'd been used up for soup Phoenix sent them to the park for the stray dogs. Thomson didn't like it, but she always said that's what they did in Mexico. Zane saw us, saw me, and tentatively lifted his arm. Quickly, I turned away. Bile rose in my throat again, burning, and I thought I might throw up again but only a sour acid burp emerged. One link in that new chain, I kept walking down the road, and the four of us stepped through a gap cut in a plywood-reinforced section of the perimeter's fence on the western edge of the dark zone. Margo first, then me, then the men, into an overgrown thicket in the back corner of a city park.

On the other side, crouched under the blanketing boughs of a spruce tree, the three of them tugged their hoods up. Margo tightened and tied a bow in the turquoise strings of her hoodie, worn under her wool-lined jean jacket. Walter pulled a balaclava over his head, his blue eyes brightened by the black of it.

Marvin, his face circled by a grey hood, said, "You can't wear that."

"Why?"

"Too obvious. Too much of a *fuck you*."

"That's what I'm going for."

"They'll target you. You'll get arrested." Marvin's voice hammered, loud in the trees' close, prickly cave. I wondered where they were taking me, could already hear the din of noise, conversation and drumbeats, the loud peal of horns.

Walter took it off, flopped up the hood of his green military parka without a word. Marvin pulled a blue tube of fabric out of his pocket, like a grandfather retrieving his hankie. He handed it to me, brushed his hands over his ears in demonstration. "Cover your head."

"Why?"

"You'll see," said Margo, so I did as instructed. The material pressed my still-damp hair against my ears and my head felt cold. Like four kids entering Narnia through the back of a wardrobe we walked into the park, which was scattered with slumps of dirty snow and garbage. Beyond that: people, thousands of them. I didn't see police. We moved through the crowd as if in a maze, Marvin leading. Past protestors drumming on overturned plastic pails, under banners demanding jobs, income parity, solar energy, and a whole new world, now. He stopped when we were dead centre of the crush that pushed along the street like the muscular body of a snake. My gaze wandered, kept catching on white-haired men and women with their heads wrapped in colourful scarves, thinking I recognized Phoenix and Thomson over and over again. Would they be there or was it a regular workday for them—Zane taking the bones to the park, Phoenix stirring scattered spices into the broth, Thomson gathering water all by himself. Guilt surged in me, like I'd made them promises I hadn't kept. *Powdered sugar*, I remembered, and wished I could at least do that, leave it on their doorstep in the middle of the night, hoping no one else would take it.

"This is what democracy looks like," Marvin shouted, blasting me into the moment. The words a singsong chant, held up by a hundred voices, more. Marvin's fist jabbed into the air and I found the rhythm and followed. A kid spray-painted BOMB THE BANKS on a plate-glass window just before a rock smashed through it and he hunched down and scurried back. We turned a corner, curving west as if following the sun, and saw police spreading out from a side street to line the edge of the crowd. We surged forward, filling the open street, and I felt a hard thing thrust against my shoulder like a punch. A Plexiglas shield shoved me away from the cops' line. Through the thick plastic, I stared at the officer's wide, frightened eyes. His pulse jumped in his neck. I stopped walking, wanting I guess to explain, to tell him I was blameless, but Marvin grabbed my arm, as he had that first night, his fingers hitting the same spots where he'd bruised me when he'd told me how he saw things, the inevitable end. On the other side of the road, I saw a protestor swing from a flagpole above the doors of a hotel. He lit the flag on fire. Cheers erupted as flames ate at the fabric.

Two police on horses rounded the corner. People close to them threw down teddy bears that were crushed by the horses' hooves. Stones flew. A cloud of tear gas appeared up the street, billowing toward us, and I heard screaming, shouting. Marvin's hand closed around mine and he pulled me back but his fingers slipped loose and I lost him. He, Margo, and Walter pushed against the current, escaping just as the police line swung forward, corralling us like a herd. Another heavy shield pushed me. A man in front of me fell to the ground. Zip-ties quickly fastened around his wrists. I felt fingers grabbing at the back of my clothes and, I could have sworn, a creature's hot breath on my neck, and I ran as hard as I could, dodging between people, aiming for the sidewalk, an opening along the wall of boarded-up storefronts. Just as the tear gas hit, I saw them. Walter with his balaclava held up to his face, his arm around Margo, turning into the mouth of an alley. I tried to go to them, but a thousand sparks combusted in my eyes. I stopped. Blinded. A horse whinnied. I reached my arms out, feeling my way toward what I thought were the buildings, searching for the safe hollow of a doorway. People slammed into my arms. I lowered them, totally lost, not knowing where I was, which direction was which, how to move forward. I started to hunch, hoping to disappear, and then I smelled vinegar, a blast of it, in my face. Nausea rose in a surge and somebody pushed me, grabbed me, led me, lifted my hand to touch a wall of cold concrete. I threw up and then arms tipped me back and water gushed into my eyes, over and over. When I could see again, as if in a dream, I found Marvin. Blurry, as though I was looking through swim goggles. Like an outlaw, he had a scarf tied over his nose and mouth. One exactly like Phoenix's: red, printed with black skulls and cobwebs. Rubber bullets cracked in the air.

"Come on," he said and pulled me down an alley to the other side of the canyon wall.

We went to a bar called the Pantomime and sat in the courtyard. Garden gnomes that had lost all their paint and looked albino stood on the shore of a frozen pond. Music blared from speakers bolted to the surrounding brick walls, a driving guitar chord that agitated me and made me reach for Margo's cigarette and suck a long drag. I felt exhilarated, high, and when I saw Marvin's eyes trolling the crowd, serious, assessing, I reached out and touched his arm, brushed the hard muscle under the cold leather of his jacket, remembering how he was when he came to my rescue: his assurance, how he took charge. Marvin's mood switched, seemed to lighten, and he met my gaze and smiled.

"This is it," Margo said. "This is all there is: right fucking now."

"Live in the moment?" Walter said sarcastically.

Margo stuck her tongue out at him. Under the table, his knee jumped, making the whole table tremble. It was like being in a treehouse, susceptible to wind or freak storm. My stomach churned. I braced myself against the table's edge and he looked at me and said, "I'm guessing we busted your cherry."

I ignored him, but he kept going.

"Your first protest," Walter said against the scratch and flare of a match.

"No," I said, although it was. I'd seen them before, from a distance, staring down streets at the bloom of tear gas in a far-off intersection. Close enough, I'd always thought, uncertain what they were even trying to accomplish. I had a job. I had food. That's what I thought then. Margo made a face.

"Yes," I admitted.

"Good for you," said Walter. "A good girl like you."

"She wasn't so good last night," said Margo. I crossed my arms, slouched deeper into the seat, waved the drift of smoke away from my face. I didn't like them talking about me as if they knew exactly who I was, as if all that defined me was the swing of my moral compass.

"I do what I want," I said.

"Ooohhh," said Walter.

"And what do you want?" Marvin asked.

They were all looking at me: three sets of eyes, eager for something. Around us was a babble of conversation, voices raised over the music. Most of the people there were from the protest, their black hoods slackened, bandanas slouched around their necks. In the corner, a couple was making out.

I pulled the cigarette out of Margo's grip. Took a deep, long drag. The others relaxed into laughter.

"Are we ordering?" Margo asked.

"Get some fucking food," said Walter. The table shook as he turned to Marvin. "It's on you, right?" I wondered about my money for the salvage job, if I'd ever get it. I started to ask when Walter stood up. "Beer's on this guy," he shouted, and people cheered.

"Fuck off," Marvin said to Walter.

"You don't want to share your allowance? Donate to the grand hope of humankind."

"What's your problem?" Marvin asked.

Walter shrugged.

"Keep it the fuck down then," Marvin said in a harsh whisper.

Margo tried to placate him. "We're on the same team," she said, her hand reaching to him under the table.

"Yeah," Walter said. "Sure."

"Well, what the fuck do you want?" said Marvin.

"Get a goddamn move on. Deliver the same destruction that's been dealt."

Marvin crushed his cigarette out. "That's not what it's about."

"What's it about?" I asked quietly because I thought the question made me look stupid.

Marvin and Walter spoke at the same time. "Pushing forward," Marvin said, but Walter's voice was louder: "Tearing down."

In the silence that followed, a server approached our table and Margo ordered beer and onion rings. Marvin's eyes hovered over the waitress, wary. I glanced at her and saw she was pretty: black hair shorn on one side of her head, long and glossy on the other. *I probably look like shit,* I thought. My eyes still stung, were likely red. With my fingers, I combed out my hair, which was flattened to my skull.

When she left, Marvin twitched his head toward the patio crowd. "We all want the same thing."

"These idiots?" Walter yelled, loud enough that several people looked at us. Margo stared down at the table, her lips set in a tight, embarrassed smile. "They're not thinking end games. They're giving the cops a job; they're giving their moms and aunties something to tsk at on TV. They're having fun." His fist slammed on the table so hard that the glass ashtray jumped, landing again with a loud thump.

"We need full system overload. Re-fucking-start."

Marvin lit another cigarette, his shoulders hunched around his ears like a turtle trying to pull in its head. Walter took it from him and Marvin let him have it, hoping, I think, that it would silence him. As we sat there, waiting for the food, Walter's cigarette burned to a pillar of ash in his artificial hand. Any slight movement and it would shatter.

"Humanity's renewed through violence," he muttered after a while, but he seemed bored, reciting the phrase by rote. I remembered Marvin saying it, explaining his sudden, senseless act at the travel agency.

"Are you trying to educate her?" Marvin asked.

Walter lifted his dull eyes from the table and they flooded with a manic sparkle. "I was telling the ladies," he said, lifting his metal hand. His cigarette fell to dust. "Fuck," he said and dropped the filter on the ground.

"Ladies." Margo sneered and rolled her eyes as she reached for the beer. I stood up. "Going to powder your nose?" she asked, and I nodded, relieved when she didn't follow.

Inside the bar, I stood for a minute to let my vision adjust. When the blackness lightened to a deep, fuzzy grey, I walked past the broken pay phones covered in grubby stickers and swung through the red door marked FEMMES FATALES. For a long time I'd been ignoring what was right in front of me, but the past twenty-four hours had dragged me deep into the centre. There was no more denial. It almost made me laugh: the thought of the three of them, creeping through the night, lighting fuses, running away as the long, squiggly lines burned down like sparklers. Jump Ship.

On the toilet, I pushed my hands against my face and sat for a moment, pressing my fingers against my eyelids, watching the weird kaleidoscope of colour and pattern as I'd done as a child. I thought about our farm, the day the letter came. The teachers were on strike so I was home. My father was downtown trying to talk the Co-op into selling him seed at cost. That spring, the bank had given my parents half of what they usually got. My mother had to sign for the letter, her hands shaking. There was only one way things could have gone before she ripped the envelope open and that was millions of dollars for oil rights. Instead, it was a notice of foreclosure. For non-payment of bills, the paper said, lying on the floor where my mother let it fall.

They gave up. Packed. Pulled dusty oak chairs out of the attic. Hired an auctioneer. Antique vinyl records, my grandmother's good china, all sold to the highest bidder. After we moved into the nearby town, my mother got seasonal work sorting peanuts at a plantation. Her hands those first days so red and raw. My father stayed home, the burgundy drapes drawn in our apartment's three rooms, convinced that the government had stolen his land. He waited for derricks to appear in the fields, their steel heads bobbing. He drove past his former crops at all hours, usually with me in the passenger seat, until the bank took the truck too. He hired lawyers, one after another until he'd spent thousands we didn't have with maxed-out credit cards. My mother fought to keep things afloat, and as a teenager, I comforted him after her angry outbursts. My arm around him as we lay on the bed, tears marking his face like furrows. I loved my parents, Melissa, but there was no way I could go back to that.

I didn't have to wonder what Marvin would have done.

He wouldn't have let them take the farm. He would have chained himself to the farmhouse chimney, the one my grandfather built sixty years ago by slapping the mortar in, brick by brick.

I pulled my hands away from my face.

Jump Ship had never hurt anyone. I knew that much from the media.

They were making a point, standing up for the powerless, working to redirect the whole society. Pushing forward, as Marvin had said. And what had I been doing at the diner? Dishing out bowl after bowl of soup, unsticking and re-adhering the bandage while beneath it the wound grew septic. I tried not to think about Phoenix, how fast she held to her beliefs and more: how she must have watched me leave, slamming that bowl aside, running away from the complex currents between us.

At the sink, I washed my hands and looked at myself in the mirror. My eyes were red-rimmed, as if I'd been crying. I pushed my scraggly bangs aside, smoothed them with spit. I was brave, I told myself. I could fight for my future. Like pioneer women in the old days, I pinched my pale cheeks. I was so young then. Young enough to think that I would be safe no matter what I did, that my choices somehow carried no weight, that what mattered most were my desires. That those two things had to be linked.

On the patio, I asked, "Why are we out here? It's freezing."

The pitcher sat in the centre of the table like a lodestone. Margo poured me a glass.

“Can’t smoke inside,” said Marvin. Walter spun an onion ring around on his metal pincer and Margo laughed. I reached for one and the greasy batter melted on my tongue. Marvin rested his arm along the back of my chair. It was like we were a couple, two couples, out on a fun double date.

15 Island

On the way home from the funeral, the wagon bumped over frost heaves and potholes. The pills rattled in Shannon's hand, cupped like a thing she'd harvested. In the back, where the bodies had been, I held the baby, handed to me like an apology by Mr. Bobiwash. The wagon had been washed out twice, but the smell of the corpses remained and I buried my nose in the infant's soft, sweaty neck. A hard thing jammed in my throat like those huge vitamins my mother made me take when I was little, to give me a long life.

Beside me, Thomson nudged the baby's leg with his fingers, his nails already turning a milky shade of blue. Marvin sat across from us, staring out at the rust-coloured fields and collapsed cedar fences, one arm stretched casually along the wagon box like we were out for a Sunday drive. I wanted to kick him, hurt him, for what he'd done. His green eyes drifted over as Thomson's voice emerged from beneath the scarf tied over his mouth. "What's her name?"

The three of us looked at Shannon and Mr. Bobiwash. Neither spoke. *The baby is just* the baby, I thought, *like you are just you*. But then, you are also Melissa. I've cared enough to give you that.

She lay in my arms, barely moving. I wondered if that was why Mr. Bobiwash hadn't named her himself, because she was hardly anything more than a little bit of nature. The muscles in his arms tensed as he twitched the reins, encouraging Caesar forward. As he glanced at Shannon and gently reached over to tug the gap in her shirt closed, I thought about what he'd lost. Mona and Abby. How she told him they would come back but never did. I suppose he waited as long as he could before finding a wife to help him care for his farm, his three boys. Did he regret that? Did he wish he'd left with Mona, packed up his family, and started over? When Shannon first came I tried to be friends with her, but she was hard, had let the difficulties of life act on her like a resin. Solidified, she stood to face them, as Phoenix had done, although eventually in Phoenix I'd found the soft pitch, that pliable wax.

Thomson's weight pressed into my shoulder, pinning my arm so it had started to tingle. I pushed at him and when he shifted, I felt the sudden space but then the baby began wriggling, her arms lifted like she was wrestling with an invisible snake and the wet heat of her urine soaked through to my arm. She started crying. Shannon didn't react. Her head bobbed with the rocking wagon. Drool glistened at the corner of her mouth. I wondered if she'd already taken some of the pills. I jostled the baby, hushed her. Marvin watched and I imagined his thoughts. *See? You can't even handle her.* The tiny hand lifted and grabbed at the swing of my heart locket.

Thomson squeezed the baby's flushed toes. "What about Phoenix?" he asked, his eyes sliding from Marvin, over the back of Mr. Bobiwash's head, to me. "As a name," he clarified, his voice tight, and then he started again to cough.

At our driveway, Marvin helped him scramble to the wagon's edge and then half lifted him to the ground. I gave the baby back to Mr. Bobiwash, whose face was a storm of tension, lips tight, his eyes not meeting mine. This was the man who had saved our lives without asking any questions, had shared whatever he had with us until Shannon showed up. I waited for him to act, to take back the pills from Shannon, to do what was right. But she slipped the bright bottle into her jacket pocket and that final rattle shook us loose. I stepped back. Mr Bobiwash snapped the reins with one hand and they quickly drove away: the clomping hooves, the creak of the wooden wheels, the baby's sudden scream, swallowed by the day.

Along the laneway, the forest pushes in—maple and oak saplings spreading onto the dirt drive, raspberry canes I'd picked clean a few days earlier. Thomson's coughing eased and Marvin and I helped him walk, each supporting an elbow, until he shook us off, his thin arms lifting like a fledgling bird. But he was weak and slumped forward, palms wrapped around the rocks of his knees. Marvin and I waited, ready to catch him if he fell. "I don't want any damn pity," he said. "This is how things are." When he straightened, his eyes were on mine.

"But they don't have to be." Thomson smiled. His laugh lines appeared first and then the dark stains on his teeth when he pulled the scarf down.

"Sandy . . ." I couldn't wait any longer. My finger jabbed toward Marvin.

"He condemned you."

"Don't be stupid. Those pills might keep that baby alive."

It was true what he said, but I was angry. I looked at them: Marvin standing behind Thomson's shoulder as if they were a team. I wanted to remind him of what Marvin had done, the path of destruction that had sucked us all in. *He also condemned me,* I could have said, but I didn't. Instead, I asked, "So you want to die?"

It was an accusation but Thomson didn't answer. Around us, the forest shifted and snapped and I thought again of Phoenix's last moments, how we'd told Thomson, how he'd held on to her body like he was trying to catch up to her.

I turned away. "What next?" Thomson caught my fingers and squeezed, but I didn't respond. I couldn't look at him.

"Work," Marvin said. "And for you, rest." He meant Thomson. There was no rest for either Marvin or me, even though we'd been up most of the night. Marvin's voice was light, like a hospital nurse's. When I turned back, I saw his hand clamped on Thomson's shoulder. He kept it there as the three of us walked, a weight Thomson had to carry. I held his elbow, the thin branch of his arm.

Halfway up the drive, we heard a loud buzzing and stopped. Marvin moved through the long grass beside the car. When he pointed, we followed his finger to a cone of bees hanging from a branch on the oak tree. I turned to Thomson, saw an old light ignite in his face. "Look at that," he said. "They're staying close to home."

I waited until Thomson fell asleep before I went to find Marvin. He was at the boat, spreading pitch on the keel using a hardened paintbrush.

"Did you get all the tomatoes?" he asked as I approached.

"That wasn't your decision," I said.

"What wasn't?"

"The pills."

"No. It was Thomson's."

"He couldn't even speak!"

Marvin's voice was cool: "I knew what he wanted."

"He told you?"

"He thinks differently about death than you—"

"You have no idea how I think. And when I tell you, you deny me over and over. All you do is tell me how I must be wrong."

Like honey, the sap drooled from the brush in Marvin's hand, making shiny worms in the dirt. "It's always been like that," I said. "Your superiority. Didn't you learn anything—"

"What was I supposed to learn?" he shouted, surprising me. We stood, the whole deep past dug out between us, a cold and dangerous crevice. Marvin stared at me and I felt like he was daring me: to climb down, find whatever lesson it was that was waiting, pull out the rusty artifacts.

"You can't keep killing people," I said. "Thomson. The girl." Marvin shook his head, smiling the all-knowing smirk I hated.

"This isn't about them," he said and waited—calmly spinning the brush, gathering the sap, building a golden spiral.

"They need us," I said.

"Or you need them?"

"What's the difference?" I asked, but he had already turned back to the boat.

I let the tomatoes rot. Left the too-big zucchinis sitting on the earth, hollowed out by worms. On the couch, I held Thomson's feet in my lap while he slept, his breath buzzing against the corduroy upholstery. The darned holes in his socks were rough under the pad of my thumb. The second bottle of pills—useless without the ones Shannon had stolen—sat on the coffee table and I stared at them, thinking about what Thomson had said on the bench, at the funerals, about giving you his food. It was a hard choice, an impossible one, to decide between you and that infant and Thomson, who I'd known for nearly half my life, who I loved like a father. Did I even have the choice? Was it mine? When tears came, I didn't fight them. They slid down my face as I curled myself around Thomson's smelly feet and closed my eyes, just for a minute. All went dark again.

"Sandy," Marvin hissed. My eyes opened. He took my hand and pulled.

"Just a minute." I shimmied around Thomson's feet and Marvin led me into the kitchen, to the pantry. The light was dim, but I could still see that half our food was gone. Most of the mystery cans without labels that we'd found in other houses, a few of the newly filled jars of tomatoes, green beans, pickled beets.

"Oh shit," I said as Marvin slumped against the door frame, his arms crossed, accusing. I knew what he was thinking.

"It wasn't her."

"Who else?"

"Why would she? I feed her every night."

"You think she'd stop at that?" He turned away and I caught his smell, the musky odour that I used to like. I moved toward the door, following him.

"It's not a lot," I said. "If I work harder, we can get by—"

"It's ours."

I stopped. "The pills were ours too."

He didn't answer me. By then he was in the yard, crossing into the night.

"Where are you going?" I shouted.

"To find our food," he called back.

When he was gone, the house grew still. Outside, I sat on the porch steps and watched the pale bark of the birch trees grow lighter, illuminated by the rising moon.

"Melissa?" I said out loud. The quiet pressed on me. Every rustle drew my eyes into the woods. This was what it would be like once Thomson passed away. This silence. Marvin and me, travelling our interlocking orbits until we died. I wanted more. Like I had back then, in the city, motivated by fantasy, Phoenix had said, but wasn't that how we survived? By imagining better days, working toward those images in our minds. That was the real danger of Jump Ship. Without hope, you just drowned.

I glanced in at Thomson, asleep on the couch, slipped on my shoes, and left.

16 City

I had nowhere to go. I hoped Marvin would bring me home, like a lost puppy, so when he said he knew a place I could stay I didn't really question him or make a decision. I just followed, like the other times, the times to come.

Outside the Pantomime, I took his hand. He stiffened at first, still annoyed, I think, at Walter's outburst, but his fingers pushed through the gaps between mine. Margo and Walter left, saying they'd see me later. They were heading to our old apartment to talk to the landlord about my things—a promise I'd managed to pull out of Margo.

The oak trees were reddening with early buds on the street where Marvin took me. It was lined with three-storey brick houses with peaked roofs and bars on the lower windows. We turned up a narrow cement pathway leading to a wooden gate painted a scuffed, glossy black. The hinges shrieked and Marvin stopped, waited for the sound to fall away, and then pushed it open quickly like pulling a bandage off. We went through a door and then down a steep flight of concrete stairs. Marvin snapped a light on and led me into a narrow room. The walls were the rock of the building's foundation. The ceiling was so low he had to stoop. A long velvet couch stood across from wooden stairs that led to another level, and I heard feet moving across the floor over our heads. I sneezed three times, and Marvin watched me from an opening in the wall at the other end of the couch. His arm swung into its dark hole.

"Bedroom, unless you want to sleep on the couch." He walked past me and I turned, realizing there was a kitchen. Marvin opened the fridge and I saw a can of apple juice and a couple potatoes.

"Food," he said. "No reason to go out." He pointed past the

counter. "Bathroom's there. If you need anything, slide a note under the door at the top of the stairs."

"Who's up there?"

Marvin smiled, a small motion of his closed lips. "Trust me," he said.

"I can't go out?"

"It's better if you lay low."

"I'm just supposed to stay here?"

"Start with a couple days. Who knows, maybe you'll love it." He pushed off the counter. "I have to go."

"Now? You can't stay?" I knew I sounded needy, but I couldn't help it. I wanted more of him, had already imagined the two of us there, forgetting time in the room without windows.

"Entertain yourself," he said, walking toward the door. "Do some studying." Above the couch, a shelf bowed from the weight of books. I saw titles: *Wretched of the Earth*, *Our Ancient Future*, *Life After Debt*, and a pile of Archie comics, their spines whitened, wording barely legible.

"Wait," I said and scrambled up the rough-edged stairs to press my mouth against his. It was a hard kiss but I felt him soften, and we stumbled against the wall, my elbow grazing an edge of granite so it would bleed.

That first night I slept in the tiny bedroom. It was hardly bigger than one of the booths at the diner and on the wall was a rusted iron hatch, bolted shut. The old coal chute, I knew, because we'd had one at the farm that I used to send my dolls down, entertaining myself, dirtying their long blond hair.

At some point that night, I woke, feeling restless, my lungs constricted. Overwhelmed with anxiety, I lay in the blackness. There was no clock. The only window in the place was in the shower stall, in the bathroom on the apartment's other end, and it looked into a hollow of dirt. Deep breathing calmed me. Marvin would be back, I told myself. I'd figure it out. Everything would be all right. Despite the dank mustiness of the place and the terrible feeling of being underground, it was a refuge, a break from constantly thinking about what came next, what to say, how to impress Thomson and Phoenix. I gave in, let myself be there, decided to trust him.

When I woke again, I heard the door to the upper floor closing. I located the switch to the room's single light. A teal plate sat on the top stair, three boiled eggs wobbling in place.

That happened every morning and in the afternoon, other food showed up: a bowl of watery chicken soup, half a bottle of homemade wine, hard cookies that were barely sweet.

The people upstairs were noisy. I heard the low rumble of their voices, feet confidently crossing floors, the strumming of a guitar. They came and went from the house without a rhythm.

It was like that for days. Days he left me down there and I stayed, stupidly waiting. I had no clock so I figured out the time of day by climbing out into the backyard. Often it was night and I breathed in the cold, fresh air as I looked up at the stars. The third time that happened, after I'd read all of the Archies and skimmed through some of the heavier books just so I could tell Marvin I'd read them, I decided to go for a walk. I wanted to go to the Empire. I wanted to talk to Margo and find out what had happened with my stuff. I wanted to find Marvin and find out why he had abandoned me.

The neighbourhood had fallen into a deep hush so I knew it was likely only a few hours till dawn. But halfway down the street, I started thinking about Marvin, how he'd said that it was better if I hid, how he'd asked me to trust him. I stopped walking. I stood there, staring down the street to the nearest intersection, and then I turned around.

When I got back to my basement, I snapped on the room's single light and the bulb popped, glass shattering in a miniature explosion.

I know you understand darkness. That cave. Night in the forest when the moon isn't full. But I had never been in such complete, sudden blackness before. I lifted my hand in front of my face and saw nothing no matter how hard I pushed my eyes. It was like I didn't exist.

It gave me something to do. A mission. I slept for a few hours and when I woke I felt my way to the stairs. At the top, my toes hit the plate and it crashed down, boiled eggs and ceramic shattering. I knocked, but no one came. No sound. The door wasn't locked. Daylight poured through two large windows on the far side of the kitchen. I paused, blinking, and when my eyes adjusted, I saw dishes drying on a towel beside the sink. Bright yellow flowers on the old-fashioned wallpaper.

I didn't want them to find me. I didn't know who they were. I moved quickly, searching under the sink for a lightbulb but found nothing but chemical glass cleaner, a container of dishwasher detergent, a plastic compost bucket with coffee grounds on top. More coffee. I stood and looked around. An old-fashioned phone was fastened to one end of the cupboards. I stared at it for a minute and then went to it, lifted it, and quickly punched in my parents' number. As it rang and rang, my fingers clutched the spiralling cord, working it around my palm and loose again. When voicemail picked up, I left a quick message: *Everything's fine, I'll try you soon, I love you*. Almost all lies.

After I hung up, I swallowed the sting in my throat and kept looking for lightbulbs.

There was a pantry. The walk-in kind, like a closet. The shelves were full of canned food, giant brown bags full of rice and red lentils. Four huge jugs of water on the floor. And baking supplies: brown and white flour, jars of yeast, baking soda, and a plastic bag of powdered sugar, already opened and wrapped in red elastics. My hand closed around it. It was rock hard, but I lifted it anyway, knocked it softly on the edge of the shelf, and felt the contents shift and loosen. I didn't know how I would get it to Thomson, but I took it; it felt like it was mine. When I turned to leave, something glittered through a curtain of aprons on the back of the door. I parted the draped fabric and saw it: red, gold, and silver stars shining on a map of the city. My finger hovered over each.

I left the house that day. There was nothing I needed from the basement so I didn't even bother going back down although as I walked I regretted not grabbing the toothbrush that had been left for me when I moved in. I didn't think I'd be going back. At first I wasn't quite sure where I was, but it didn't take me long to get my bearings and I walked by the New Covenant Church where the sisters handed out warm lemon tea during power outages and turned west at a corner with an empty newspaper box covered in faded stickers advertising their website. I was headed for the Empire. I wanted to talk to Marvin if he was there, Margo and Walter if he wasn't, and try to get some answers. At the Pantomime they'd made it seem like it was only them, a small operation, not the storm of stars I'd seen on the map on the back of the pantry door. I held the hard bag of sugar against my chest like a child. Part of me wished I could simply return to the diner, but I cringed with shame at those last days. Naked in the room with Phoenix, back-handing the bowl of grasshoppers in her face. Not to mention her hard cruelty and what had happened afterwards at Marvin's. Who was I? Somehow I'd get the sugar delivered to Thomson for his hives, but that was all I could do. Instead, I needed to find Marvin and get answers: how big was Jump Ship and which part of the boat was I on?

Upstairs at the Empire, the reek of mildew from the burgundy carpet made me dizzy. When I knocked on Walter's door no one answered. I tried again and then pushed open the unlocked door. Twisted sheets on an unmade bed. Empty beer bottles clustered on the bedside table. One-quarter of the wall was taken up by a life-sized poster of a woman in a stars-and-stripes bikini, straddling a motorcycle. A fringe of black mould ran along the loose wallpaper at the edge of the windows. A stack of books with broken spines on the sill. *You're living here?* I asked Margo in my head, but then thought of my own circumstances. I turned to leave, unsure where to go—back to the basement, down to Marvin's place in the dark zone, or just downstairs to the bar to wait without any money to even buy a beer—and found Margo standing in the doorway. "You shouldn't be here," she said and pushed me back into the room.

"Because Marvin says?"

"Yeah. Partly."

"Well, I am."

She studied me. "What's that?" she asked, touching the bag of sugar. I shook my head. It would take too long to explain. She walked past me to pull three home-brewed beers out of a box in the corner.

"Shit," she said. "Come on."

We went down a back stairway at the end of the hall, one I supposed the servants had used when the run-down building was a home for a single wealthy family. The steps were covered in linoleum that was so dirty I couldn't make out the pattern. In the basement, we walked along a narrow hallway with walls of stacked stone, cemented in. I thought of the catacombs in Paris, another place my mother had been—that time with my father, on their honeymoon. A postcard pasted into the back of their wedding scrapbook. As a kid I'd looked at that picture a lot, flipping past the bright photos of my parents as young people grinning in the yard at the farm.

Margo pushed open a wooden door and the first thing we saw was Walter, his face squinting in surprise. His steel hand shone violently under an exposed bulb. "Knock," he shouted.

"Who else would it be?"

"Let's see," said Walter, lifting a finger to his chin. "The cops?"

Marvin looked at me. "What's she doing here?"

"Ask her," Margo said as she handed out the beers and sat next to Walter on a futon shoved against the wall. Marvin waited.

"They're Jump Ship?" I asked, and told them about the map in the pantry, stars shining all the way to the suburbs. Walter and Margo were listening but Marvin cut me off. "What were you doing upstairs?"

"I needed a lightbulb."

"I told you to put a note under the door."

"It was pitch-black! Nobody was home."

"What's that?" Marvin asked, jabbing his chin toward the sugar.

"Can't I ask any questions?"

"No. You can't." I stared at him. "That was the point. I was keeping you out of things so you don't know more than you need to."

"I want to know."

"Why?"

Why? I wanted in, wanted a home, a family. Like I wanted to know about Thomson's illness, about you. That's me: burrowing until everything caves in. But what I said was: "Because I'm part of this."

He took a slug of beer and leaned against a work table that held a pair of rusty pliers, a Styrofoam cup half full of mouldy coffee, a book with its insides cut out. "You're here now. Sit down."

"I'm fine." I'd been sitting for days.

Marvin rustled through a plastic bag and pulled out an old-fashioned cellphone, silver, with a flip-top. "Untraceable," he said and tossed it to Walter, who caught it with his good hand. "Our next target—" Marvin said.

"Drum roll, please," said Walter, his hand pinging against the metal futon frame.

Marvin counted off the reasons on his fingers, starting with his nicotine-stained pointer finger. "They have no security. They sell to the same airlines as wealthy agencies. It's an easier neighbourhood to negotiate. Dark. No cameras."

"What is it?" asked Margo.

"Phantasy Travel."

The place where Marvin had broken the window, the night we'd first slept together. Like a clue. I looked down at the dirty floor, covered in snips of coloured wire.

"They specialize in last-chance tourism. Trips to doomed places. Create tonnes more carbon so you can see the last little bit of the Great Barrier Reef that's being destroyed by carbon. That sort of thing."

Walter set his empty bottle down and lit a cigarette. "When?" Margo asked.

"Sunday. 9:00 PM."

"They'll be closed," said Walter.

"Yeah."

"That's bullshit."

I wondered if Marvin was placating me, planning something less dangerous. But it was how Jump Ship had always operated: no one hurt, only properties destroyed. Walter pressed his wrist against the centre of his chest. "Let me do it. I'll walk in there in the middle of the fucking day."

"Like a suicide thing?" said Margo, her voice too loud.

"I'll fucking do it." Margo moved abruptly forward, planted her feet on the floor. She lit a cigarette. The room was already full of smoke. I switched the sugar to my other arm, wishing I could take it down to Thomson, help him scatter it over the bees to knock the small, tarry mites off their sweetened bodies.

"That's what I've decided," Marvin said.

"And we don't get a say?"

"You were in the army," Marvin said. "You know how it works." Walter glared at him, twisting the cigarette in his steel pincer. Marvin's fingers pinched the edge of the work table. He seemed still and powerful while Walter sank, slouching on the couch, dropping ash onto the knee of his filthy jeans. "What about the gardens?"

I lifted my head. Palms. Banana trees. Orchids that lived on air.

Marvin and Walter stared at each other until Walter finally spoke. "Shithead," he said, his voice a kind of hiss, and he settled his gaze on a patch of crumbling mortar as he smoked, one puff after the other, like something mechanical, a train pushing hard down the track.

"Sunday," Marvin repeated, and when Walter opened his mouth again, Marvin held up his hand, palm out, silencing him. "It's decided."

We left then. I followed Marvin out to the street, where a light snow was falling like ash. Marvin slid along the sidewalk on the gripless soles of his combat boots and shoved his hands in the pockets of his jacket. We headed north. "Can't we just go to your place?" I asked.

"That's not the plan."

"I don't get what the big deal is. I hate that place."

"It's only a few days."

He meant until the bombing.

"I'm not sure," I said.

He smirked. "You want to slow down?" When I didn't answer, he said, "It's only property."

"It's their business."

"I'm sure they have insurance."

I wasn't sure what to say.

"It isn't personal. It's a tactic."

"How is it not personal?"

"We're not attacking them, we're attacking what they represent."

He threw his half-burned cigarette to the ground. There was already enough fire in him—a heat that was contagious. I found myself nodding, knowing my father would have agreed with him, even added his own support. At the house, Marvin came into the basement. Inside the door, he pulled me against him and I dug through his clothes like some sort of tick, trying to attach myself to him irrevocably. That night was the best sex I ever had, like the lovemaking in a movie about apocalypse where the lone survivors find respite under the rubble of a collapsed overpass. I tingled. I felt the rush, the force of something I mistook for meaning. Afterwards, I told him I loved him. The words erupted out of me. Elemental, a current of water or flame. He didn't speak, and I lay there for a while hoping he hadn't heard me, that he'd fallen asleep.

"What's with the sugar?" he said into the dark.

"It's for Thomson. His hives." I didn't tell him that I'd stolen it.

"You're planning on going back there?"

"No," I said, hoping he'd offer to take it for me but he didn't. When we woke, the eggs at the top of the stairs were cold. We ate and then Marvin left, swallowed by the mouth of light that was the doorway to the outer world.

He disappeared after that. I couldn't help thinking it was because I'd confessed my feelings to him, feelings I wasn't even sure about once his powerful presence had dissipated.

I felt uncomfortable that we'd left it at that, but I somehow settled into a routine in the tiny basement. Three or four days passed and then a knock sounded on the door. I looked up from my ham sandwich, a book bent open in my greasy fingers. It was Margo, her arms wrapped around a cardboard box.

"This is all I could get."

Inside, I dug out my things—an old orange coat that was warmer than the one I had, a pair of jeans, socks and underwear, a few books. Margo wandered through the apartment, sticking her head in the dark coal bin, glancing up the flight of stairs that led to my keepers.

"What about the rest?" I asked as I pulled out a change of clothes.

She shrugged. Like the money from the salvage job, I'd never see my stuff again.

In the bathroom, I left the underwear I'd been wearing for days in the sink to wash out later. When I came back out, Margo was picking at the edge of my sandwich, putting bits of crust into her mouth.

"Marvin's coming tomorrow," she told me. "He wants you to plant it."

You would think that during those long, empty days I would have come to my senses. But until Margo passed on Marvin's command, I hadn't really been thinking about Jump Ship at all. Only in moments, in the middle of what I thought was the night but was sometimes midday, when I'd wake, worrying, waiting for the future to unfold. There were sleeping pills in the bathroom cabinet and I took them in fragments, breaking the tiny discs into dusty quarters that I pressed into the bowl of my tongue. Mostly I thought about Marvin, what he was doing: Where was he? When would he come back?

"Me?" I said to Margo.

"That's what he wants."

"Where is he?"

She lifted the top slice of bread to look into my sandwich. A smear of yellow mustard over the fatty ham.

"Have it," I said, annoyed.

Like a little kid, she picked it up with both hands. "Around," she said, with her mouth full.

Arms crossed, I leaned against the counter.

"You don't want to do it?"

I looked at her.

"I already told him I'd be a better choice, but he says he wants it to be you." I heard the tinge of jealousy in her voice. She turned away, walked to the couch. The doorway to the bedroom I never slept in was a solid black rectangle. I imagined Marvin in there, hiding, listening to my answers. Like this was a test.

"What's involved?"

Margo told me how it would play out, the acting I needed to do.

"I have to talk to the people?"

She sat on the couch. "You can't stay here all your life."

I thought about Phoenix and Thomson. What they would have said. But I already knew. They had nothing to worry about, in their safe, snug home, only the grasshoppers scratching to get out. Margo curled her feet under her, her shoes still on. She wrinkled her nose. "Smells in here."

"Would you do it?"

She raised her eyebrows. "What makes you think I haven't?"

17 Island

We were all out that night—me, Marvin, Mr. Bobiwash, even Shannon and the boys. The only person who stayed home, sunk under the cold surface of his illness, was Thomson, asleep on the couch. Just starting to wane, the moon spread an amber wash on the lake, so I made my way easily up the shoreline even though I'd left the wind-up flashlight at home. All afternoon the wind had pushed west so I could still smell the bodies and the acidic stench of the ashes they'd raked into the beach sand after the cremations. We hadn't stayed for that, only for the lottery of supplies, only until Mr. Bobiwash gestured us over to the wagon and we gathered without speaking or making eye contact. Shannon the last to arrive.

The waves slapped against the stone. Thick roots of cedars gripped the corners of the rock. I scrambled over boulders and jumped over puddles, thinking about what Albert had said in town: that the wind would blow in the rest of the boat's floating timbers and any buoyant trunks. We all knew that more than eight people were on the ship, so there was that too. More bodies, like in those strange seasons when the carp or the pickerel die off and the shore is cluttered with puffy rotting bodies, glossy as candle wax. I didn't want to see that. I couldn't take much more. I moved as fast as I could to find you, hoping you wouldn't run. That instead you'd call out: *Help me. I'm here.*

I didn't know where I was going. I wandered the shoreline, over limestone beaches, through forest, in fields. For a long time not really looking but only thinking: about my past, my parents, the story I've been slowly telling you. *There are no happy endings*, my mother often said to me shortly after I ran away from home to go to the city. And when we came to the island, I told that to Thomson, as if he needed to hear it from me. But he listened. He nodded and said, "Yes, that's true. Life goes on and on."

At the western end of the island, the cliffs are steep. I climbed up, inland, into the evergreens and pushed through prickly boughs of blue spruce. When I reached the thicker cedars I had to crouch, nearly crawling, sharp needles digging into my palms. In the clearing, water boomed into crevices carved in the limestone wall. Several feet from the edge stood the lighthouse. One window lit with a weak flicker. I pulled back, crouched in the cool, dark forest, and watched. The yellow light leapt and danced, reminding me of the movement of the bees. From far away, a coyote started howling and then the candle flashed its final light and sputtered out. It was dark, but the building glowed in the moonlight. I didn't know what to do. There were no noises except for the animals. Were you sleeping inside? For a long time I sat there, until the memory of the candle started to fade and lose its form and I wondered if I had imagined it. My eyes ached with exhaustion and I closed them for one second, let the weight of my muscles relax, and the next thing I knew I was waking up, the musty smell of last autumn's leaves in my nose, their dry prickle scratching my cheek. I sat up. Thomson, home alone. The moon had arced farther, casting the lighthouse into shadow. I walked carefully like Mr. Bobiwash had taught me, consciously lifting my feet. When I reached the road, I turned east, toward home.

I heard Shannon before I saw her. Grunting from exertion; glass smashing. The baby was screaming inside the house. I jogged up their short driveway to see Shannon lift her arm like a baseball pitcher. An object flew out, hit their garage door, and shattered into shiny fragments. I expected food to slop out: my tomatoes and strawberries, mushy white slabs of zucchini, but as I got closer I heard wood snapping and nearly tripped over a pewter frame. Shannon pulled another picture out of a box beside her. The boys were in the yard, Eric with his hands over his ears, Graham relentlessly spinning.

"What are you doing?" I called as Shannon hurled the second picture. The glass smashed, the pink frame split at all its corners, the photo curled out.

"Cleaning house," Shannon said as I walked closer. I saw that the picture was an image of Mona, baby Abby on her lap.

"Let's go inside."

"Mind your own beeswax."

"Where's Mr. Bobiwash?"

She crossed her arms, still dressed in the plaid shirt she'd unbuttoned at the funerals, the white gridded lines showing like slim edges of glass. Her eyes slid across the hem of trees at the end of their field. The coyote called again, and Graham moaned but Shannon didn't notice.

"Jack," she said. "Fucking call him Jack."

"Come on," I told her, losing patience. I was surprised when she did. We left the mess she'd made for morning: the photos spread on the ground like frost.

Eric calmed the baby while I made tea. Peppermint, the last of the bag that I'd brought days earlier. Their supplies were very limited and I wondered if they were being stolen from as well. It chilled me because of the mouths they had to feed: three boys and the baby. I wondered how much you could eat.

"Did he go to the lighthouse?" I asked as I carried two mugs to the table. Shannon sat with her feet apart, boots still on. The pills were there, the single bottle they'd taken. I could steal them, I realized, easily slide them out from under Shannon's dull gaze. But when I looked back she was staring at me.

"God knows. He was gone when I woke up."

"Has the baby fed?"

She nodded absently, and I didn't know if she was telling the truth.

We sipped in silence. The tea was tepid because I'd shut the stove off early, saving power, so I swallowed as quickly as I could, mindful of getting home. There were no lights on, no candles or kerosene lanterns. If they were like us, they'd be conserving the kerosene because the boat brought it.

After a few minutes I said, "Maybe you should see Sarah."

Shannon stared at me. I leaned forward. "She has herbs: St. John's wort, valerian."

She smiled, a hard, disbelieving grin. "And that'll help with the children?" The door clicked open. I pushed my chair back and looked through the doorway. Samuel held a finger to his lips and slipped upstairs. When I turned back, Shannon said, "You can't understand. You've never been a mother."

I felt angry and then embarrassed, and then a strange absence of emotion. The way she'd said it was matter-of-fact, telling a truth. She put the tea down and pushed it away like she didn't want it anymore.

"It's like this. They need you. Like parasites. You're the host."

Her eyes focused on mine, seeking sympathy. And it was then that I told her about you, partly to show her that I did understand, that I had a child to care for and feed. She listened carefully as I called you Melissa, as I described you as my own.

Back home, Thomson lay on the couch, damp and quaking, his fever back. My fingers jumped away from the heat on his forehead. Marvin came in from the kitchen as I was peeling the covers off to change him into dry clothes. Thomson pulled at the torn satin hem of the pink blanket, fighting me. I felt panicky. My fault, my fault, and my guilt came out in a blast of anger.

"Help me," I shouted at Marvin. Together we stripped off the damp cotton of Thomson's T-shirt, peeled off his sticky pants.

When he was settled again, I twisted open the bottle of pills and fed him one. The doctor had told us to use only the two medications together. I remembered that day—the boat bobbing up and down, fastened to the cement pier with fat yellow ropes wound around iron cleats. The vertical line in the doctor's forehead had deepened as he spoke. "We're working with a limited supply," he'd said. "We're back to the Stone Age." But I hadn't wanted to hear.

In the kitchen, I crumpled stained pages from an old news magazine and piled them in the cookstove under a tepee of kindling. When bubbles filled the bottom of the pot of water, I made tea as I had at Shannon's, but this one out of a mixture of mullein and thyme and mint, ingredients we still had. Marvin pulled Thomson up, one large flat hand holding his back while he put a pillow under his head with the other.

"Does he really need *tea* right now?" he asked sarcastically, but I ignored him. Kneeling, I spooned the tepid, green brew into Thomson's mouth. When he tried to speak, it dribbled onto his neck.

"Alive," he said, and I shushed him. Marvin stood back, watching like a new father, unsure what to do. Thomson laid his hand on my forearm, those long, slender digits, fingernails dirty because I didn't clean them enough. "Who has time for a manicure?" he'd joked with me the other week when I came in from snapping the suckers on the tomato plants, trying to get all the fruit we could, only days before you'd showed up. Thomson tried again. His eyes swam over mine, trying to focus. Like a drunk, he carefully enunciated.

"The hives."

"I know," I told him and wiped the wetness from his lips with my sleeve. The sound of the swarm came back to me: that insistent hum as they held their formation without any walls, no neatly structured home.

How did they do that? I had never asked and now Thomson was beyond such conversations, opening his mouth for the spoon like an infant. When the cup was half done, I set it down, and he slumped back but then opened his eyes again, surprising me. I readied another spoonful.

"I see her," he mumbled, rippling the surface of the tea.

"Who?" I asked as Marvin walked over and turned the lock on the door. Had you been there while we were out?

When Thomson was asleep, Marvin told me he hadn't found the food.

"Where did you look?"

"The caves, the lighthouse."

"When were you at the lighthouse?"

"Why?"

"I was there. I saw a candle."

"When?"

"Tonight." I waved my hand. "Earlier."

He glanced at Thomson and I knew what he was thinking. *You left him?*

"I didn't go in," I said.

"Probably Sam," Marvin told me. "Maybe he meets a girl there."

I didn't believe that. "We'll keep looking," I said, but Marvin shook his head.

"It's long gone."

I curled a fist against my mouth. Seeing the slender supplies at the Bobiwash house had scared me. How would we get by, keep Thomson alive through the winter? Was it you? And why, when I was already sharing with you, inviting you into our family, our home? For the first time in many years, I felt like Marvin and I were on the same side: you had betrayed me.

It was dawn, the first fragile light like the inside iridescence of a shell. We'd been up all night.

"Bed," Marvin said.

"You go," I told him, drinking the rest of Thomson's tea. He looked at me with suspicion, but I saw the heaviness in him and he hoisted himself up the stairs. I sat in the armchair, watching Thomson sleep. A couple hours later I woke as Marvin clomped across the floorboards to go fishing. Later in our bed, I dreamt there was a flood. We rushed to the attic to keep from drowning, and through the window, I saw Phoenix. She was naked and hugely pregnant, her bellybutton popped out. Her face and swollen body were illuminated by angles of light slicing down through the water. She looked happy. I struggled to open the window, but it had been painted shut and then she was just gone, swallowed by deep green at the edge of the sea.

18 City

The day after Margo visited me Marvin took me for a late lunch. It was our first real date. When he came to get me I went into the bathroom and put on the lipstick Margo had brought with my things. He didn't notice. His eyes flicked around the place, moving from the nest of blankets on the couch to the jug of milk sitting out on the counter. We stood awkwardly in the kitchen, trying to find words because the connection between us had changed. After the Empire Tavern, I'd told him how I thought I felt and I couldn't take the words back. I felt vulnerable and he was all business—slipping the milk back in the fridge, crackling with his unspoken expectations of me. I admit it was exciting to have him there, especially after the deadening, lonely blur of basement living, but as he leaned against the table, watching me, there were gaps between us, like the spaces between those Russian dolls. He hadn't kissed me. I wasn't sure how we fit or what he wanted or how we'd ever get around to speaking about the bomb.

On the way to the restaurant—a glossy place with a patio full of steel and glass bistro tables—we talked about how warm it was. The crocuses were already beginning to bloom, their purple heads hovering over the dirty remains of the snow. The weather would be good for Phoenix and Thomson, I thought, remembering the pots of herbs they grew outside the back glass door. The hives.

It had been a long time since I'd eaten a good meal. I had to intentionally slow down, stop myself from stuffing the fresh baked rosemary bread in my mouth, sucking the marrow from the chicken bones. When we finished, I dipped my fingers in the bowl of warm lemony water the waiter delivered and watched as Marvin fished three bills out of an envelope full of money.

"Where'd you get that?" I asked, reckless, and wasn't surprised when he ignored me. It was from his mother, I know now, a psychotherapist who lived near one of the city's ravines. The house he grew up in was built in the 1920s and had stained-glass windows and the tulip trees in the yard that Phoenix had told me about. Marvin only told me about his family that first winter, when the three of us filled the cold nights with bits of our stories, thinking we weren't going to survive.

After lunch, Marvin led me down a side street and turned west along an alley. We popped out at a quiet intersection and crossed diagonally to a coffee shop called Galaxies. He wasn't talking and his silence seemed purposeful, as if it was carefully aimed. As soon as I saw Walter, I knew.

"Now?" I hissed, but Marvin only smiled. He hadn't prepared me or even asked me, only dragged me into his trap. The place was crowded. I couldn't say anything. In the back, we found a table near Walter but pretended not to know him. I watched him, reading one of the community papers. He rubbed the side of his nose, and I noticed the slant to it and wondered how it had been broken. We sat there a long time, nearly an hour, until the three of us faded into the background and no one noticed us anymore. All the while, Marvin played with my hand, rubbing my wrist, whispering praise like a doctor doing an examination—*just relax, you're doing great, don't look around too much, that's right.* Any resistance I had, he softened it, and when Walter finally downed the last of his drink and walked out, I moved with Marvin to his table. Marvin read while I chewed on the straw in my lemonade. And when he smiled at me, I stood with him, and he pulled a black backpack out of a shadow under the table where Walter had left it.

Down the street, we stopped and he slid it on my shoulders. My arms thrust back and through the straps. Breath held. A weight I didn't know how to refuse. If I put it down, where would I have gone? A question that is simple to answer in retrospect: to my parents, despite their deep imperfections, or somewhere, anywhere, else.

We walked a long way, passing through the city's silver high-rises to get to the poorer side of town. I wanted to ask questions, but Marvin had started talking a lot, lecturing me about people he knew, friends of his mother's, who paid small fortunes to escape the hard winter, burning barrels of oil for one fun week in the sun.

"They feel nothing. There's no moral obligation. No concern for the future."

I wondered how he knew that.

"Your children," he said. "Mine." I heard the division there, and because, for those last few moments, those final city blocks, I was still a young, naive girl, I thought I knew what he was trying to tell me. *We're not together; there's no future here.* I felt angry. My eyes scanned the details of the street: the doorways that opened as we walked by, a blond woman carrying her shopping bags, a store window that displayed fake white furs and recycled red leather shoes. Eventually I blurted out a question.

"What happened with you and Margo?"

"Christ, Sandy. Really?"

"Yeah." I shifted the backpack, gently, like a baby.

"What are you? Fifteen?"

"Were you ever with Phoenix?"

He pulled a hand-rolled cigarette out of his pocket and stopped walking to light it. I regretted bringing her up, but all he said was, "What do you think?"

Under the tight strap, I shrugged. I didn't meet his eye; instead my gaze followed a woman in a belted fuchsia dress on the other side of the street. People were happy in that neighbourhood, I realized. It was a part of the world that seemed intact, without worries, apart from the security guards standing in the shop doorways, the cameras perched over us that Marvin had told me to ignore. It was wealthy.

"She's like my sister," he said, and when I didn't reply he nudged my shoulder with his own. "Relax," he breathed, exhaling a thin stream of smoke. That wasn't possible. My limbs moved stiffly, my back tensed under a backpack weighted down with a pipe bomb attached to a modified cellphone, hidden in a resin-hardened book.

At the travel agency, the window Marvin had broken was boarded up. They'd stapled a poster of a beach onto the plywood. Tall palm trees, like the ones we'd seen at the botanical gardens, arched over white sand. I had wanted that. I'd grown up wanting that, listening to my mother tell stories about stepping out into the gasoline smell of a foreign summer, her regular winter life left far behind. I was like the people Marvin talked about who would have done that: ignored the future, answered my own desires.

"Go in," Marvin said and rushed by without slowing, leaving me standing, stunned, at the door.

"Wait," I said, but he didn't.

I hesitated only briefly before I pushed through the door. Bells sounded, a deeper tong than the jingly ones at the diner. There were a couple desks on each side of the space. All empty, except one. An older woman looked up from her computer. Silvery hair pulled back in a messy bun, lips outlined in dark red pencil, the inner colour faded. When she stood, she knocked over a picture on her desk of a black dog.

"Hello," she said, righting the photograph. "Isn't it a beautiful day?"

I didn't trust my voice so instead I stretched my mouth into what felt like a grimace but was meant as a smile. Sweat trickled down my spine. Carefully, I hitched the backpack more securely onto my shoulder and turned away from her, to look at a shelf of promotional materials. Marvin had told me what to do. Walter and Margo were up the street. Marvin watching from the doorway of a pawnshop across the road. I picked up a handout about Macedonia, a place I'd never heard of.

"Don't speak with her," Marvin had told me. "Don't engage. Keep your head down."

But she walked up to me, her head tipped to one side, interested in what I wanted, which places in the world I hoped to see. She gestured to the glossy page pinched between my fingers. "Have you been?" I shook my head. "Beautiful," she said again, the second time in only a few minutes. "So historic."

I looked again at the sheet: red tile roofs, a green domed church with golden crosses, the snow-crested mountains.

She pulled a flyer about New York City off the shelf. "Our more local destinations are popular."

My hands were clammy. I cleared my throat.

"Last year," I said. "I went with a friend." Without meaning to, I gestured to the window where Margo would soon appear and flinched. I shifted the backpack. The book Walter had chosen to hide the bomb in was called *Manufactured Landscapes,* and on its cover a toxic red river snaked through a black wasteland.

The other night in his workshop I'd asked them where that was but none of them knew. It was hard to believe it was on earth, our earth, the same planet that held tropical beaches and coral reefs and the mountain trails of this place called Macedonia.

"Where is this?" I asked, disregarding Marvin's rules.

"Europe," she said, stepping forward at the exact moment that Margo slammed against the window, laughing.

She kissed the glass, leaving a bright pink lipstick stain. Walter, behind her, licked the window like the maniac he was, and as the woman stared at them, startled, I did my job. The one Marvin assigned me. The one that meant my future. I opened the backpack and slid the book behind the shelf. The cackle of Margo's fake laugh trailed down the street and the woman stumbled backward and leaned against a desk.

My heart banged against the wall of my chest.

The backpack felt conspicuously empty, slouching on my shoulder, the opening gaping. "Leave," Marvin had said. "Right away."

The woman wiped at her eyes, leaving delicate, spidery streaks of mascara. I noticed the wobble of flesh on her neck. "Are you all right?" I asked.

"This violence," she said. "First the window, now . . ." Her gaze settled on the wide, blurry smear of greasy pink and spittle. Through it, I saw Marvin crossing the road.

"Jenny," he said when he pushed through the door. A made-up name, a made-up story. I stepped toward him, relieved to be told what to do, to get away, but as we walked out the door, I glanced back, wanting already to make amends, to say sorry. *It's only property*, they had said, and Marvin praised me as we walked south, his arm around my shoulders. It was dusk, and the sky was turning pink. Thin streaks like crepe paper tangled in the crumbling chimneys. The end of a party, its quiet aftermath.

We went back at night to watch. Marvin told me to wear dark colours, but the temperature had suddenly dropped and the only winter jacket I had was bright orange, a style several years old.

"God," he said when he saw me. "You're a flare."

Margo laughed as she pinched a joint out of Walter's claw.

Across the street from the travel agency, they tucked me in a doorway and stood in front like a fence. The streetlights were out in that section of town and car alarms screamed in the night. Nothing moved. I smelled the stale alcohol on Walter's breath. Marvin pulled a cellphone out of his pocket and stepped back into the hollow with me.

"Ready?"

I wasn't. I was afraid. But I'd come too far to stop it so I only watched as Marvin dialled. The second before he hit the last digit, Margo said, "There's a light." We all saw. A sudden pulse of yellow from deep inside the building. But it was too late. Marvin's thumb dropped onto the number pad and the building exploded, pushing all of us back into the same burrow like a family of rats.

"Fuck," Walter breathed, and a tremor seized my insides and what I wanted was to run from the sudden throbbing silence into which the rubble clattered relentlessly down.

What we did then we hadn't even discussed. Marvin and I ran south and Walter and Margo went north. There was no time to talk. We wove through the streets, down alleys, reaching the dark zone by the time the sirens started from a long way away. On the other side of the fence, in the first layer of the area's darkness, Marvin and I turned around and saw it: a pillar of smoke stained orange.

Even in the dimmest light, his face caught some of its glow, and I saw the wildness in his eyes. We followed a route I didn't know, along roads that smelled of urine and rot. He swept his penlight over broken glass, a mash of papers, the torn cover of a book. In the mess I spotted a couple of dark zone dollars. His voice drifted back to me—snippets of confusion about what had happened, why the black window had suddenly lit, how it must have been a sensor—but I couldn't follow his words. I was cold, trembling hard, dressed only in a forest-green hoodie because Marvin had taken my orange coat and tossed it behind the cement footing of the overpass. The big meal I'd had for lunch lurched in my stomach. I focused on moving forward, making a plan to stumble onto a slushy patch of lawn if I had to throw up. "It'll be all right," he said as we turned up the walkway of his house, but I already knew that was a lie. Dread had rooted in me like an impregnation, something you can't reverse.

When we got to Marvin's squat, he held out his hand at the end of the walkway, stopping me. A sliver of light showed through the boards that covered the front window. A thread of smoke wound out of the chimney. We smelled it.

"Someone's here," I whispered as if he didn't already know. I won't forget that moment, ever. The sudden shape of Phoenix inside the open door.

At first I thought they must have known, that she and Thomson were there because of what we'd done. Marvin's map was still pinned to the wall and the red stars glowed like spots of shiny blood. I tried not to look at them. Casually, Marvin stepped across the room to the fire that they'd built. I stood with my hood still up, hiding my face, my chest heaving as I tried to catch my breath.

"Go to the fire," Thomson said from his spot in a chair. "Get warm."

Phoenix leaned on the kitchen door frame as if ready to disappear. She didn't look at me and I felt relieved, that the state I was in could be excused as anxiety over seeing her. I moved to the flames, turned my back to them.

"What are you doing here?" Marvin asked, once I was beside him.

After a beat of silence, Phoenix and Thomson started speaking at the same time, unintelligible, but then Phoenix's shrill voice fell away. "Mob of kids," Thomson said. "They got in, destroyed everything." He didn't say anything else.

"That's it?" Marvin said.

"We tried to stop them. What do you want me to say?"

Marvin kicked at a piece of wood that was rolling out of the hearth. "Who were they?"

"We don't know," said Phoenix. "Those same kids."

"Little fucking bastards," Thomson said.

"Where are the others?"

"Zane went to a shelter, I think," Phoenix said. "They all ran. They're scared."

"And you're not?" I asked. I still hadn't turned around.

"I didn't say that."

"They're brought up thinking they can have whatever they want and now they're just taking it," said Thomson.

"That's not how I grew up," said Marvin.

I backed up, lowered myself onto the edge of the mattress. My legs felt like jelly. How could he say that after what we'd done? I put my hands between my knees and pressed tight to stop the shaking, trying not to think about what we might have done. I wanted to lie down, black out, sink into deep sleep, disappear.

"They wrecked the hives," Phoenix said. "The bees are gone."

I glanced back. Her eyes darted away from me.

"They could have swarmed," said Thomson. "Gone to find a safe place. It's been warm enough, at least during the day . . ." His voice rose in pitch and faded away, like an old faucet squeezing shut.

"Can we find them if they swarmed?" Thomson didn't seem to hear me. He opened and closed one fist as if making sure his hand still worked. Marvin started rolling a cigarette, scattering tobacco into the paper's curve.

"We didn't want to come here," said Phoenix.

"You can come here," Marvin said, sharply looking up. I heard the snap in his voice. "Where else would you have gone?"

"There are places," Phoenix said. "We'll figure something out. We don't want to get in the way." She pushed off the door frame and walked over to Thomson, sinking onto the floor beside him. "We'll clean up and start over again."

I could see her more clearly, her face was lit by the flames. Bluish skin stained the bags under her eyes. Her face was drawn. I wondered if that was what she wanted. Marvin lit his cigarette and dropped the black curl of the match onto the hearth.

"Yes," Thomson said, pulling out a hanky. He spat into it before speaking. "The drones will sacrifice themselves to try to keep the queen warm. They'll cluster around her." He stared off into a corner of the room. "But there isn't much for food."

"We'll make do," said Marvin.

"The bees!" Thomson shouted.

The fire popped in the sudden silence.

"It's an early spring," I said.

"Freakishly early," said Thomson. "A frost could still come."

Phoenix put her head in her hands. I felt sick still so I stood and walked through the kitchen to go outside. In the yard, I leaned against Marvin's showering shed and thought about the woman. The manifesto, Marvin's doctrine, was programmed to e-mail at midnight and I hadn't even read it.

The moon was almost full, and the giant faces on the billboard stared out in a morbid kind of glee. When the back door of the house opened I expected to see Marvin, but it was Phoenix. She leaned against the porch railing and I stayed in the yard, unseen, as I imagine you doing, hidden in the forest, watching me with my troubles with Thomson, while Marvin and I argue about you.

Phoenix wiped her nose on the tail of the scarf tied around her head. She was above the spot where I'd thrown up, days earlier. I stepped forward, stood at the bottom of the porch stairs.

"Are you crying?"

"Fuck off," she said and wiped her eyes like she was angry at them.

It frightened me, seeing her vulnerable like that, so displaced. I thought of the church where she'd been buried and had dug herself free, crawling over the dead bodies with the instincts of an animal. I climbed the stairs. She crossed her arms over her chest. I was afraid, but I reached out and my fingers brushed her upper arm, the slightest contact, barely anything. It was all I could do. She rubbed her nose with the back of her hand. A gleam of snot shone on her skin as she stared out at the moon, the shimmer it made on the water.

We needed another mattress, and Phoenix said she knew where we could get one.

"The diner?" I asked, but she shook her head

"I know another place," she said. "At least there's no shortage of stuff in this world."

When I told Marvin I was going with Phoenix, he didn't say anything but his jaw tightened and I could tell that he didn't want me to leave. We were safe there, hidden in the farthest house from the gate, and maybe it was more than that. Maybe it was about her. His jacket hung on a hook by the door, and I pulled it on over my hoodie before Phoenix led me out to the street.

We passed house after house in silence, walking quickly, and I breathed heavily as I tried to keep up. Phoenix hadn't turned the flashlight on. It hung from her hand like a wand, and when we rounded the corner at the end of the street she pointed it toward a column of orange smoke, billowing skyward.

"What the hell is that?"

"A fire. We saw it on the way down."

"Big one."

"Mmmm," I mumbled.

Of course I didn't like lying to her. I knew she'd eventually find out. As soon as she heard the news about Jump Ship's latest hit she would know how far my connection with Marvin had gone. My whole body tightened against the night's dampness and the dread, and I felt like a stupid, lost kid in Marvin's large leather coat.

"What did Thomson mean about the bees?"

She told me, explaining how they swarm.

"Should we look for them?"

"We'd hear them," she said, glancing into a garage with the door ripped off. We kept walking and I started listening. I heard the crackle of the sidewalk's debris under our feet. Distant sirens. A baby crying and the occasional sound of a person scurrying through the streets like a rat, exactly the same as we must have sounded. In my mind, the swarming bees formed a golden column, a sacred thing, a thing that shouldn't die. I don't know why I would have thought that, when I'd faced that living woman and heedlessly laid a bomb at her feet. By the time Phoenix turned up the walkway of the apartment building, I'd forgotten what it was we were doing.

"You think they'll be in there?" I asked, meaning the bees.

"Who?"

"Never mind."

It smelled like mould inside. My nose instantly started to run. The lobby was full of the wreckage of ripped-apart furniture. Chunks of yellow foam like the remains of a hail storm. Rusting springs. Phoenix stopped so she could wind up the flashlight and the sound rattled down the long hallway. We followed the light to a door that she unlocked. In the shifting glow I saw black spots polka-dotting the walls and ceiling where water had come through. Cans of food were spread on the kitchen counter.

"They're all opened," Phoenix told me. In the living room, the walls were covered with newspaper articles. We stood together, reading about old crimes: the collapse of an oil rig off the Falklands, the violent demonstrations against the tar sands, groundwater contaminated by fracking. Phoenix pressed a finger against one article, securing its floppy corner. It was a story about Jump Ship's first action, an explosion at a debit machine. I moved. I stepped to the side and focused on a map tacked onto the wall.

"I used to live here," she said. "In this apartment, with my boyfriend."

"Your boyfriend?"

She nodded.

"Where is he?"

The flashlight beam made a lemon-coloured circle on the floor.

When she looked up, her face was shadowy and I couldn't make out the expression in her eyes. "There is a right and a wrong, Sandy. You know that?"

"Of course," I said, but the truth was that, no, I wasn't so sure about that. I thought morality was malleable, that you could be convinced of either side, that it only depended where you stood. After all, we lived in an age of moral ambiguity. The TV heroes I'd grown up with were drug dealers, vampires, serial killers.

Phoenix pushed a tack into the loose corner of the newspaper clipping. The illustration showed a blasted-out hole where the bank machine had been. "Because this isn't the way," she said in a way that made my stomach drop.

"I didn't mean . . ." I blurted out, but she walked away before I could finish, leaving me with my guilt, a huge rationalization stuck in my throat. I didn't mean what? To fall for Marvin? To become a kind of terrorist?

I looked at the map. It was bigger than just the city. There were no gleaming stars stuck to it. The red roads all led out of the city. Chest tight, I unpinned the four corners, folded the large paper into a small square, and stuffed it in the pocket of Marvin's coat.

Phoenix was in the bedroom. Nervously, I watched her, waiting for what she would say. Did she know? She stared down at the mattress, stained with a rust-coloured circle.

"I'm okay with that," she said, and we tipped the bed on its edge and carried it awkwardly out of the apartment building. Phoenix in front and me trailing, shuffling up the street to Marvin's squat, my latest home.

19 Island

When we arrived on the island, it was the first week of March. The ides, Thomson called it. Everything behind us, the whole long drive, had happened in the dark. I'd never been in a car so long or travelled so far. After we crossed the bridge, Marvin drove us along the island's stony length, a limestone ridge rising in the middle like a spinal column, before we came to the flat lands where it is possible to farm. At the lighthouse, we found food in the kitchen cupboards. A can of beef ravioli that Marvin tapped open with a bent nail and a rock because the only opener was electric. Underneath the sounds of greedy eating and the constant crash of water lay a bedrock of silence. It felt like we were waiting for someone to tell us what to do and that someone turned out to be Mr. Bobiwash.

Without him, we would have either died or never stayed. We might have tried to leave, walked for a month with our fugitive faces somehow hidden, to get back to that dangerous city. A journey like my mother told me my great-great-great-grandmother made when she was separated from her husband in the 1800s. Travelling through winter forests still as tableaux, threading the edge of the Niagara River. How would we have done that? Needing to stay secret, with no food, no knowledge of what edible plants grew in the ground? Drifting, as if only air could keep us alive.

The morning after the funerals, it was white outside. A mist spread over the bay like icing. Thick enough that I knew Marvin would either be home soon or buried inside it, lost until it cleared. Thomson's fever continued to burn so I changed him again. Tossed his shirt into the pile with the clothing from the night before. There was laundry to do, vegetables to be plucked off the damp ground, raspberries rolled off their cotton-white posts. My eyes burned from sleeplessness, but I went about my chores: setting a fire in the cookstove to boil water for tea and warm the oven. I had to make bread before weevils crept into the last of our flour.

When Thomson murmured into wakefulness, I brought him a bowl of Solomon's seal root and oats from the southern farm fields. We had no milk. I spooned the mush into his mouth, but half the time he didn't want it, pushed me away, stuck out his tongue so mushy gobs tumbled out. Scraping the food off the bony table of his chest, I plugged his nose so he had to open up and then stuck the spoon in. The steel clattered against his teeth. It was force-feeding and I hated it. When the knock came it was a relief, even though I knew who it would be.

Mr. Bobiwash stood on the porch, staring into the yard. Hands in his pockets, back turned. His hair, light brown, streaked with grey, pulled into a ponytail held with a rubber band. Mona used to cut it short but after she left he stopped bothering. He turned around and our eyes touched and bounced away like opposing magnets. The mist was cold on my face and hands. My lips felt stiff with anger. He looked over my shoulder and nodded toward the couch.

"How is he?"

"Not good. Not good at all."

I crossed my arms against an urge to cry. Mr. Bobiwash held out a jam jar, the lid glinting like a gold ring, and I almost started to laugh. *Thomson's life traded for blueberry preserves,* I thought, but he opened his fingers and showed me the clear glass. Pills inside, dark red like blood. That was how he'd brought us seeds, in the beginning. Tiny white flakes that became tomato plants. The larger, spotted beans.

"Thomson knows he's old." I didn't know if that was an excuse for Shannon's actions or the reason he was there, helping us.

"But what gives her the right—"

"It seems we're living more by natural laws now."

"So there are winners and losers."

He said nothing. It reminded me of Marvin, years ago, telling me the bombing wasn't personal. Mr. Bobiwash held out the jar, and as I reached for it I felt the wet mist on my bare arm. I stepped back from the door, gestured for him to come inside.

With Thomson in the middle of the room, unconscious on the couch, we talked around things. The weather, Marvin's whereabouts. That's how it's done. I remembered my aunt, my father's sister, dying of breast cancer, planning a trip until she passed away, her new hair a downy mess. How my mother helped with her denial, bringing her glossy catalogues for Alaskan cruises and bus tours in the Orient, right up to the end. Stifling a yawn, I went into the kitchen. The bread was rising on the stove. I pulled a drowned daddy longlegs out of the water bucket and filled a cup.

In the living room, I rattled Thomson's pills into my palm—a red one that Mr. Bobiwash had brought and one of the others. I pushed them between Thomson's lips one at a time while Mr. Bobiwash watched. He drank sloppily from the water I tipped into his mouth. As I mopped his chin with my sleeve, I asked more about Shannon.

"Is she taking the pills?"

"I don't know."

"They won't do her any good."

He shrugged. "She thinks they will."

"I don't know what will help her," I said, and I told him about seeing her the night before smashing all the photos in their yard. I wanted to ask him where he'd been, to say that maybe if he was home more and helped her out—but I didn't. He sat down in a chair across from Thomson. "How's the baby?"

He paused. "It's hard to tell."

"The pills might hurt her," I said, but he didn't answer. We couldn't look it up on the Internet or ask a pharmacist.

I saw the concern in his face. The skin around his mouth sagged; there were crow's feet at the corners of his eyes. He looked a lot older than when we'd first arrived, fifteen or so years earlier, and I started to speak, to offer to ask Sarah for help, to bring her to Shannon, but his gaze shifted over to Thomson and he said, "Feverfew. Do you have some?"

You'd taken it: a full jar of mixed crumpled herbs, Thomson's fever tea.

"No," I said. "We hardly have anything. There's hardly anything left."

I thought to tell him about our stolen food, about you, but I didn't want him heading out there, pushing through the damp, waxen world to haul you out of it. Not that I thought he'd hurt you. I wasn't sure what he'd do. He'd set traps the other day, at the Sharmas'. Big enough for a child?

Together we looked at Thomson. His face the colour of cold ashes, hollow triangles sunk in his cheeks. He stirred and groaned something about diameter or Demeter.

"He wants us to tell the bees," I told Mr. Bobiwash, but he didn't respond. I wondered if he already knew, if he already understood. "He's almost gone," I said, and then I said a whole lot more. The whole story gurgled up in my mouth, thick like excess saliva. I told Mr. Bobiwash about Phoenix, about most of it, except you. I talked and talked and cried and swallowed some of the sticky mass down and said, "People died." Mr. Bobiwash held up his hand. It hovered between us. Long fingers, a wide palm full of lines like the map of an estuary. Thomson had settled into a calm sleep, on his stomach, his knuckles resting on the floor. The story hung in the air like an eclipse. I felt his eyes on me, dark and intense like Phoenix's, but when I glanced over I saw that he was actually watching Thomson: his pale cheeks, the flutter of his straw-coloured eyelashes. Nervously, for something to do, I went into the kitchen and built up the fire again, dunked a mug into the tea. The porcelain cup hit the aluminum pot and the clanging sound broke the stillness, startled me. Mr. Bobiwash drank it at the window, looking out at the last opaque heaviness in the air.

"Then you came here?"

"And you saved our lives," I added. He glanced over and his face gave nothing away, but I realized there was nothing he could give. No forgiveness or condemnation. I was alone with my story. I dropped my eyes to the floor, to Thomson's hand jerking against the rough boards. Gently, I lifted his arm, turned his body over, heard his breath widen like a wind running from forest to roof, the fine whistle. Mr. Bobiwash watched me.

"You know my name's Jack," he said, and when I smiled, I felt the crust of the tears I'd shed crack open on my skin.

We went outside and as Jack stepped down into the yard, Marvin came out of the trees. I saw him look at Jack, then me, and his gait slowed and then sped up. He lifted his hand to show four large fish hanging off a stringer, their tails glistening.

"Lake trout," Jack said. "They must have been deep."

"The fog brought them up," Marvin said. "Hold on."

He went into the kitchen and wrapped one of the fish in the pencil-stained pages of a child's math workbook. I stood on the porch, watching the yellow finches flutter bright as crayons around the trees. I felt awkward, uncertain what to say after my morning's confession and I wished I'd said more, not kept you a secret but let it all out, opened the walls that were secured around Marvin and me. Jack took the fish and started to leave, and I opened my mouth to tell Marvin about the pills but he went away from me. The two men moved together down the lane. Halfway to the road, beside the wreck of the car, Marvin lifted his hand, laid it on Jack's shoulder. They faced each other, Marvin's mouth moving, and I knew he was talking about you.

"You told him?" I asked when Marvin came back into the house. I'd started making bread and my hands threw ingredients around: a yellow scattering of yeast like bee pollen, white explosions of flour on the floor.

"Be careful," Marvin said.

"You didn't even ask me!"

"You don't own her. She's taken half our food. It's time to do something."

"And I'm not the person for the job."

"Apparently not."

"Asshole."

"You should get some sleep. You look like hell." His own face was reddened by the wind; his hair pulled back into a greasy, greying ponytail. "I'll watch him," he said.

But I wasn't ready to let it go.

"And what's the plan? Give her to Shannon?" Marvin didn't answer. He'd gone to the door. He was looking into the living room. My fingers were covered in flour and I held them out from my sides. "I'm sure she'll do a great job."

Thomson started coughing and then he choked, sucked in a long breath and held it, and we ran into the living room. His lips puckered as he tried to find air. Marvin pulled him into his arms and Thomson's breath rushed out and he coughed hard, his mouth filling. "A cloth," Marvin shouted and I grabbed a T-shirt from the heap on the ground. A smell of rot rose to my nose and I jerked my head away as the shirt filled with grey mucus, spots of black blood against the white smears of flour from my hands.

20 City

Marvin left in the morning. The mattress shifted as he got up, but I didn't open my eyes until the front door closed with a quiet click. I knew where he was going—to find out what had happened at the travel agency, to learn what people were saying about us—and I was glad he'd gone. Talking to him would have brought it all back when I wanted to pretend that the night before had happened to someone else, that other people were responsible. Going to sleep I'd tried to still my mind by focusing on the hiss of wet wood as it burned in the hearth, the sturdy presence of Thomson and Phoenix on the other side of the gap between our beds, Marvin's body held in the arc of my own. I knew I was cornered, but I was convincing myself that I could make that corner comfortable: wallpaper it, drag in a comfy chair, feed the fire, have friends over. Like I still had choices.

I pushed off the slippery sleeping bag Marvin and I had tugged between us the whole night and sat up. Only Thomson was there, sleeping on his side. The thin skin of his eyelids tinted yellow like old paper. His mouth had fallen open, and even from a few feet away I could smell the sourness of his breath. I stood up, pulled on my hoodie, and went outside.

It was cold. A crust of frost shone on the green grass growing around the billboard posts. In the outhouse, I hurried, rubbing my hands against my naked thighs, thinking about what I'd do that day. I hoped Phoenix had a plan, that she'd set me to work so I could move on autopilot, shut down my brain.

Thomson was still sleeping when I went back to the living room so I tried to be quiet as I built a fire. I made a teepee out of kindling, but the paper basket was empty. Walter had burned the rest of the pirate novel the last time I'd been there. He'd burned a lot, even slid delicate prints of red and white roses from the upstairs bedroom into the flames. They were pretty and I'd felt an urge to stop him, but we were all too far gone by then so I'd just watched the petals turn to black with the rest of them.

Near the front door, the map I'd found lay on the floor, fallen from Marvin's jacket pocket. I wondered if he'd seen it as I tore a strip off the western edge, the area I'd grown up in. The ripping sound woke Thomson. He came to blinking, saw what I was doing, and told me to stop.

"I don't care about shitty novels that never should have been written, but maps?"

It was too late. I'd tucked the single strip—a ribbon of small towns and cornfields—into the wooden tent and set it ablaze.

"Let me see." I carried over the rest of the map and he spread it across the bumpy blankets. Lying on my stomach, I showed him the blank spot where I'd grown up, wishing I hadn't burned it. His finger followed a road from the city, through the land's nearly blank interior to arrive at an island, shaped like a leaf, floating on the edge of a huge bay.

"I know this place. In another life, I visited there." He described the empty farmhouses of the original pioneers, how they stand in fields all over the island, falling down.

"With Phoenix?" I asked.

He nodded, still staring down at the map.

"We should go there," I said. "All of us." It was easy to imagine: the four of us moving into a place where we could plant a huge garden, buy chickens from a local farmer, eat eggs and fresh meat. I thought of the perfume of blooming apple trees, the crackle of cornstalks in the fall. Phoenix and I braiding garlic. Catching fish on sparkling lines. Babies. Beautiful things that seemed a long way away but possible.

Thomson straightened and his back cracked. "Do you know about the Crusaders?"

I shook my head.

"They left France and other places to fight in the Holy Land, but when the Muslims forced them out they couldn't find their way back to their towns and villages, their families. They just wandered until they died because they had no way of knowing where they were." He handed the map back to me, the whole unruly sheet. I struggled to fold it, creasing it incorrectly so I had to start again. Thomson turned away, went onto one knee like he was proposing. I tried to help him stand, but he pushed me back, one hand sweeping through the air.

Phoenix wasn't in the kitchen. Thomson went outside, and as I followed him with my eyes I saw her, walking across the clearing with two bottles cradled in her arms. She wore a jean jacket, a bright pink hood casting her face in shadow. Behind her, a bank of grey clouds stood in the west like a landmass. The faces on the billboard stared down like gods as she passed underneath them.

"Good morning," I said when she came in the door. She didn't answer, only smiled, that same thin smile that was like a branch snapping back in the woods. I didn't let the sting stop me. "How did you sleep?" She set the bottles on the counter and pushed the hood off her head with the heel of her hand. She didn't have a scarf on and I saw that her hair was growing in, a slick of black against her skull like a seal's skin. From outside I heard Thomson peeing off the porch.

"Not well," she said. "But I don't. You?"

I shrugged. "Okay." She turned away, poured water into a pot, and put it on Marvin's cookstove to boil. The burning gas roared and it was too loud for us to talk. I watched as she searched through Marvin's things for teabags and cups. A final blue flame puffed when she shut off the stove. Thomson came into the room, standing in sock feet, his belt undone, the buckle clattering as he moved forward to claim a cup of tea. Phoenix pushed his hand away. She was using a single teabag for all three cups and hadn't finished.

"What happens today?" Thomson asked.

Phoenix turned to me. "Can you look for something to eat?"

I nodded and assessed the kitchen—a useless green refrigerator, the closed cupboards. In one, I found two cans of sardines and an old apple, its skin tightening into wrinkles. Marvin's food. I wasn't sure about eating it, but decided we had no choice. I didn't say anything about the cellar preserves Margo and I had found, covered with dust in the stone-lined basement and dated. They were decades old. Walter had thrown a few jars into the street, making a mess of corn relish and crab apples, since washed away by the rain.

I set the items I'd found on the kitchen island. Phoenix sliced the withered apple into wedges and I opened one of the cans of sardines and started on the second but she told me to save it. "The hive back at work," Thomson said while I looked for a fork.

"You know the worker bees are all female. The males impregnate the queen before they're driven out of the hive. The queen lays her eggs and the nursery bees care for them."

Phoenix bit an apple slice in half. She watched Thomson without reaction, her dark eyes almost cold. She already knew about the bees. I stood to the side, listening, somehow hidden. She slid the sardines over to him, but he ignored them. He pulled out a handkerchief and wiped his lips. I saw the weakness in him and recalled that he'd been coughing in the night, a sound that had drifted into my dreams, became the strange call of a giant bird.

"It takes a mass of thousands to build the hive society and one or two humans to destroy it," Thomson said, and his eyes found mine. I dropped my gaze, uncomfortable. "But then they begin again."

"Hopefully smarter," Phoenix said, flaking apart the tiny silver fish with the tines of her fork. She lifted a bite to his lips. He looked at her like he was wondering if she'd given him the right answer and then opened his mouth, chewed slowly, and took the fork from her to dig into the tin for more.

After breakfast I went with them to the diner. We moved through the quiet streets, down the same road I had travelled many times to gather water. It was strange being there without the busy structure of the soup kitchen, an agenda, a list of things to do. Without Phoenix bossing me around. Instead, she moved slowly, like we were passing through the humid, sticky centre of a heat wave. Thomson and I matched her pace. At the restaurant, the plywood Zane had installed over the front window lay scattered like a giant deck of cards. Phoenix climbed through the opening while Thomson and I used the door. Inside, fragments of shattered dishes covered the checkerboard flooring. I felt the crush and slide under the soles of my shoes along with the sticky remains of the soup. Spinach and mushy carrot chunks were smeared over the walls and counter. Potato chunks stuccoed the walls.

"They weren't hungry?" I said. Neither spoke. "What a waste," I mumbled, thinking of all the people we'd fed with one pot of that soup.

In the back room, the grasshoppers were mashed into the carpet. A few beat helplessly against the glass walls of the terrarium and Phoenix fished them out. We followed Thomson through the open sliding door to the toppled hives. Phoenix opened her cupped hands to let the grasshoppers go and they sprang down onto the sofa bed mattress that had been dragged outside and burned. Hive frames were scattered, the honeycomb loosened. Thomson picked up a piece and looked into its empty octagons. Honey drooled down, the remainder of their winter stores. He caught some with his finger and sucked it off, staring down the back alley that led to the street. It was the first time I saw him like that, his face clenched in anger. I thought that I might cry and I kicked the corner of the mattress, watched the carbon scatter into black dust. I couldn't understand this kind of destruction—personal and pointless, a violent reordering for no apparent reason. I wondered what Marvin would say, but I could already hear his argument in my head: something about people finally getting angry at stop-gap measures, ripping off bandages. *As long as we have these voluntary supports, governments don't have to face the truth of widespread poverty . . .* Blah, blah, blah. To him it wouldn't be personal. I shook my head to clear it and noticed Phoenix watching me. But when she spoke it was to Thomson.

"Maybe the bees got their revenge."

"Bees don't understand battle."

Her voice was quiet: "Of course."

"It's still possible they found a new home," he said. A few buzzed around our heads, but there were hardly any, only three or four, and we watched their stumbling flight and knew that they'd soon die.

I helped them pack. Phoenix found a used garbage bag and we filled it with their towels, sheets, and clothing. Thomson gathered torn books and found the Buddha candle, scarred but intact. I dug through a drawer in the kitchen, pulling out tiny plastic bags full of herbs and spices, while he talked to us about the Roman Empire, how modern scientists had defined its vastness by the amount of recovered objects. Clay vessels used for shipping olive oil and wine discovered on the ocean floor in heaps, so many that the archaeologists stopped bothering to bring them all up. Useful things, he said, and with anxiety I thought of my own lost items, left behind at Margo's and my old apartment, never retrieved. If I'd known that they were meant to last me the rest of my life, I would have tried to go back. I would have collected the items I cared most about: my grandmother's aluminum applesauce maker, the curtains with the embroidered blue birds, books from my childhood like *The Secret Garden* and *Harry Potter*. Stories I could have read to you.

It was difficult to leave. The restaurant seemed like an empty shell, its fragile inner life killed off. Phoenix moved with her face and body hardened and Thomson seemed to grow even older as we went out the front door and left the soup kitchen behind, another place joining the general destruction. As we walked south, Thomson peered up at attic windows with panes popped out. I knew what he was looking for: the swarm. I wasn't sure if he wanted to talk, but I asked him anyway:

"Where did you learn about bees?"

"Long story." He paused and I thought for a second he wasn't going to tell me. "In Chiapas, in Mexico, I lived with a family named Luna. My friend Ignacio kept bees the way they do, a traditional way, in a log hive. That's a method we couldn't use back here, in the city, so I had to learn the Langstroth hives, the box hives that you know." He waved his hand as if physically scattering the distraction. When he spoke again his voice was quieter. "Ignacio taught me about the bees and how they fit in. Ah Muzen Cab . . ."

"Ah Muzen," said Phoenix, correcting his pronunciation.

"Ah Muzen Cab," Thomson repeated. "The god of bees and honey. His image is carved into the temple in Tulum."

His voice faded away. "Was that your father?" I asked Phoenix.

"Grandfather."

Thomson reached for Phoenix's hand, squeezed her fingers and held.

"When he died we buried part of the hive with him and then I married his daughter."

Phoenix stared straight ahead as if alert for danger. Over the lake, the clouds had thickened. An antique armchair lay on its side, surrounded by loose stuffing that scudded down the sidewalk as the wind picked up. All around us lay this ruined wasteland that I was fitting myself so snugly inside. *Be careful what you wish for,* my mother used to say, and when I thought of her I felt an ache of pain and guilt layered on top of all the other sadness. My throat burned. I blinked back the heat in my eyes, trying to cool it but I couldn't. My vision blurred and I stopped walking, staring down at the sidewalk, at the long grass working its way through the cracks. Phoenix looked back at me. Thomson turned around. Both of them were staring at me and I waited but they didn't speak.

"What happens now?" I asked, struggling not to cry.

"What do you mean?" Phoenix said.

I gestured behind us. "Will we rebuild?"

It was what I was holding on to: a montage of clips, like in the movies, the four of us working together, making something meaningful. Scrubbing floors. Hammering walls into place. Gathering the bees. Dropping into bed at night, exhausted but content. A family. A solid footing that didn't require impossible demands.

"We?" Phoenix said, but Thomson gripped her arm.

"Of course," he said brightly, but by the stiffness in Phoenix's face I could tell that it was probably over, that part of her life, the last viable option I thought I had. The heavy garbage bag pulled my right arm down. With my left hand I covered my face. The explosion reverberated again in my brain and I realized I couldn't stop it, that it had already happened, was real. Everything in me ached to go back to the beginning. I wanted to have stayed with Phoenix and Thomson, to have made my amends with her, broken up with Marvin, returned to my old apartment, relived it all and done it right. Called my parents. Held on to my things. Not planted the bomb.

Phoenix pulled a scarf out of her coat pocket. I pressed it against my face. The fabric smelled sour, like milk gone off. I could tell that was all she was going to give me. No protection, advice, a tampon compassionately handed over in an emergency: the things women expect from each other. But Thomson was there and as I blubbered, drooled snot into Phoenix's scarf, I told him how much I wanted a home.

"Everyone does," said Thomson. His voice was tender, worn from the earlier effort of talking about hard things. He curved his hands around my upper arms. "We'll make one together."

I looked at Phoenix, but she was staring over my shoulder. I glanced back and saw people, three or four of them, walking through the intersection. A man dragging a pipe that clattered hollowly over the broken asphalt. I wondered what we looked like, what I did. I hadn't seen my reflection since the day before when I'd fussed with my hair in the bathroom of that basement place before Marvin picked me up for the bombing, as if it had been a date.

"Come on," Phoenix said. We hurried to Marvin's squat. There was no more time for tears.

By the time we got back it was raining. We hurried around the side of the row house, our feet appearing as watery reflections in the cellar windows. The kitchen was silent and cold and I wasn't surprised that Marvin hadn't returned. I was used to him disappearing for days. I dreaded what he might tell me when he returned so part of me wanted him to stay away.

For lunch we split the second can of sardines and a box of half-crushed crackers Phoenix had found. The food supplies we'd retrieved from the diner would keep us going for a couple days—half a large bag of red lentils, potatoes that needed their vines cut away, seven or eight carrots. After we ate, we went into the living room, all of us wondering what to do, I think. It reminded me of those boring summer days when I was a kid and my dad would bring my mom and me to his high-school buddy's trailer on the manmade lake near our farm. How I rode my bike around in endless circles on the narrow, gritty roads, walked as far as I could into tepid water, dove down to clutch at the bottom. My mother, on a blanket, stroking the dry grass, reading through dark glasses.

Thomson took the chair while Phoenix sat on the edge of their mattress. Over her head I could see the Jump Ship map and my fingers itched to take it down, use it as a fire-starter. Neither of them had said anything about it and I kept waiting for them to notice, step closer, peer into the sparkle of the stars and innocently ask, "What's this?"

We made up jobs that day. Thomson thought the walls of the house were insulated, that we could pull yellow or pink fibres loose and use them to blanket the windows on either side of the hearth. They weren't doing any good. "They're just holes in the walls, sucking out the fire's heat."

It was a project for us.

Upstairs, in a bedroom at the front of the house, Phoenix and I broke open a wall. Scarves tied over our mouths, we used the iron poker from the fireplace to smash apart the plaster while Thomson watched. We found a tangle of yellowed newspapers, and the three of us sat on the dusty floor reading articles about an expedition to Antarctica and severe job losses after the Wall Street crash. Thomson pulled the papers apart like he was plucking feathers from a bird, delicately and with great care. He pointed out advertisements for automobiles, silent movies, kit houses, and syrups claiming to cure a wide range of ailments.

"Everything and nothing has changed," he said.

We never did find insulation.

Like a mom, Phoenix asked me to set the table across the room from the fireplace. I used a hodgepodge of dishes from Marvin's cupboards and spoons we brought back from the diner. Thomson even put his Buddha candle into the centre. He'd had it for years. Dust was caked in the crease of its belly, the wick frayed on top. With ceremony, he lit it.

"Impermanence," he said as we ate the soup Phoenix had made for supper. We watched the fat, smiling face melt away. With the change in the weather and the damage we'd seen at the diner, we all knew the bees were gone. That was their funeral, I think.

After we ate, Thomson stayed at the table reading. Phoenix and I went to the mattress. The three of us solid within the shifting orange light of the fire. Phoenix pulled items out of her backpack, stuffed full from the diner. She sat beside me, and when she moved, I felt the springs give, the press of her leg against mine. Smelled her: sweat and a faint treacle of perfume, a different kind, one I hadn't noticed before. She ripped apart a torn flannel shirt of Thomson's, blue with black stains on the cuffs, brown spots freckled across the front, to show me how to make pads for when my period came. I felt embarrassed with Thomson there, but he didn't seem to care. He was deep inside another book, although he hadn't finished *Black Robe*. We'd seen it outside the diner, the cover torn off, pages trampled into the mud. I resolved to find him another copy but never have. Instead, over the years, we've talked the story through, drawing it to various conclusions—some happy, others terribly tragic. It doesn't help that it was based on historical fact, with an ending already written.

Phoenix pulled out a pair of partially rusted scissors and a tiny sewing kit in a red plastic box. She asked me when my period would come and I told her that I didn't really know.

"Maybe another week," I said as she cut into Thomson's shirt.

She showed me how to sew the pieces together. My silver needle slipped through the fabric, weaving a line of bright red thread. We worked awhile in a deep throb of silence, until Phoenix looked over and reached for the fabric in my hands.

"Your stitches are too loose. Pull them out and make them smaller." She picked at the threads with her short fingernails before handing back my work. "Didn't your mother teach you to sew?"

"Not really." But I'd learned other things: how to plant corn, cook, care for men.

"Where are your parents?" Phoenix asked.

I felt a stab of grief. Remembered the phone, how it rang and rang before I'd left my last message.

I must have looked sad, staring down at my sewing, plucking out the tiny strands, because Phoenix said, "Are they dead?"

"No," I said, surprised. The fire was burning down. I got up and laid a split length of door trim across the flames. When I sat down, she asked: "Do you want your own children?"

"Someday."

"Not with Marvin?"

I smiled. I couldn't imagine Marvin as a father.

Phoenix kept sewing, her stitches quick and close. I adjusted my arm to avoid the lift and fall of her elbow. "I don't hate him, you know."

"I thought you hated me."

She paused with her arms resting on her knees. "I wasn't sure what you wanted."

"And now you are?"

She shrugged. "You're searching. You moved here, didn't you?"

I thought she meant Marvin's. I wasn't sure how that showed anything positive.

"From that small town," she clarified.

Leaving home hadn't seemed like a choice. That night my father hadn't let me sleep. Even as I gathered all the items from my purse—loose sticks of pink gum, crumpled receipts, a comb woven with my long hair—he'd kept at me, telling me how things were, would be, everything in the world I had to be afraid of. I still felt it, the sickness in my belly, the bruises left from his voice.

When he finally went to bed, I stayed up with my mother arguing about the life I wanted. Over and over she asked me what I thought I could have. Did I imagine something spectacular? That was the word she used, gesturing at the curtained window, spit flying from the sharp consonants.

"I guess," I said to Phoenix.

"It takes courage to leave, to try something new." Her eyes drifted over to Thomson, who was watching us, the book flat on his lap, pages bright like wings. He shook his head. "No."

"There's nothing left here," Phoenix said.

"There are still people who need us."

"The ones who drove us out?"

Thomson stood up. "We talked about this. We rest and then we start again."

Phoenix lowered her hands to her lap. The needle caught the light and shone like a delicate thorn. "How do we start again? Where?"

"It's what I want," Thomson said, lifting his book. From where we were sitting, it seemed to cover his face. Phoenix jabbed at the flannel, steadily working. Her face had hardened. We stopped talking and I focused on my task, squinting at the binding thread. After a while, Thomson said, "It isn't just us anymore. We aren't alone." His gaze shifted from Phoenix's downturned face to mine. Our eyes met and moved away and soon we settled back into our tasks. It was complicated, but it was love, the tender green beginnings, pushing hard through all the dirt.

21 Island

Supper as usual, but not enough for all of us. Thomson too sick to eat and I opted not to, nauseous with hunger as I made a plate for you in the kitchen. The jars you had stolen were enough to last awhile, but what if it wasn't you? All I knew was that you'd been eating the meals I set out, that this link had been built, a bridge between your wild self and me. I had decided I would maintain it, despite Marvin, my sense of betrayal. No matter what.

Fried bulrush root, the last hunk of the trout we'd had for lunch. Half a tomato, the seeds gone black. I dug them out. I covered it all with a cloth, the ancient plastic wrap used up, and left it on the porch like a stubborn message.

Marvin carried the food back inside. The round, red plate hovering between us. "Why are you doing this?"

"Do you need to understand?"

He pointed at the fish. "I caught that. I slave over that. My fingers bleed from the nets."

Thomson coughed. We turned to the sound, braced, shifted back to face each other.

"You want to be like an animal. Snarling over what's yours?"

"If it comes to that."

I waited, but he didn't say anything else. "We can't pretend she doesn't exist."

"I'm not pretending," he said. He swung his hand up to gesture at the emptied pantry. "She's made herself very clear."

"She's a child," I said slowly, loudly, as if talking to someone who was deaf or didn't understand the language.

"We don't have the luxury of feeding every lost waif. How much wood do you think we've got left on the island? How many fish in the bay?" He rifled violently through the gold discs piled on the counter. Two fell to the floor. "How many usable tops for canning?"

His face had tightened like the hatch of our root cellar. No light showing through. My stomach growled, but I laid my hand on its concavity. I turned away, walked into the dining room, and headed for the stairs to our bedroom. Marvin followed me.

"I don't understand what you're doing," he shouted up at me. The present tense was startling, as if you were the thing that demanded analysis, not the choices I'd made early on with him. What about that? The story I was trying to tell.

The next morning, after Marvin had left, the food was gone. I chose to believe that you took it, that you'd eaten your share.

Thomson rallied.

"I thought I was a goner," he said as he looked around the room. Purple spots the size of plums dotted both cheeks, although the whites of his eyes were still yellow. Both of the pill containers sat on the scarred table, next to the cup I put down. I wondered if Marvin had given them to him the night before but didn't bother asking. Thomson wouldn't remember.

"So did we," I said, my voice catching. I cleared my throat and his gaze swung over to me. If he thought I was getting sick neither of us admitted it. For a while, in the beginning, I'd tied a scarf over my mouth but it got in the way. *My nightingale*, he called me then, when he wasn't in remission, his voice thick with delirium.

Thomson's legs, knotted in the coiled blanket, swung off the couch as he sat up. We rearranged the bedding, put a pillow behind his upper back, and I helped him hold the tea. Four hands lifting it to his mouth. His Adam's apple bobbed sluggishly in his skinny throat. He looked slowly around the room like he was a visitor who had just arrived. When his eyes reached the coffee table, he pulled away from the mug. The thin green liquid dribbled down his chin, spotted his shirt. "What are those doing here?"

The pills. Bright red dots in the clear glass jar. Only six left.

"Mr. Bobiwash," I said. "Jack." His name a new motion in my mouth. "Brought them. For you."

Thomson shook his head, a constant swing, even as he spoke.

"They're not mine. They're not meant for me. I don't want them." He coughed, hunched forward. I laid a hand on the back of his neck.

"It's only a few—" I started to say. A few days. A few days of life.

But Thomson shrugged my hand off, pushed me away. His voice was gruff. "I don't want them."

My bottom lip trembled. A burn of sorrow behind my nose, in the centre of my head. Thomson touched my arm.

"I'm more curious than afraid," he said.

Tears threatened, but I held them back with a quaking wall, eyes closed until the footings took.

"I keep wondering if I'll see her."

I didn't need to ask who. I wrapped my hands around his tea, keeping it warm.

"Phoenix. Imagine that." Thomson didn't really believe in an afterlife, in anything past death, but I didn't argue with him. "Like your little girl," he said. "Slipping out of the shadows."

"Melissa is real."

"Phoenix is too."

I straightened. "You've seen her?"

He glanced at me and his head shifted slightly. "You know what I mean."

Not flesh and blood. Not anymore. My eyes searched the ceiling's corners, cobwebs I'd missed with my infrequent cleaning, hanging in swaying lines. I remembered how you looked in the cave, that sudden flash of your face. I froze the moment in my mind, saw you there, stilled, and pulled you out of the horror of that place like cutting a rose from a thorny bush. If only it were that easy.

Thomson made me leave him. Insisted I return the pills. I thought about holding on to them in secret, pressing them into his mouth when he was delirious and couldn't tell the difference. But he was right and I knew it. The medicine would do more good for the baby, might mean the difference between her life and death. Might help Shannon. I thought of Jack, bent over in our living room, a great burden balanced on his spine. Up the laneway and onto the road, the pills rattled in the glass jar. I hurried because I needed to get home, didn't feel right about leaving Thomson alone. It felt like a long way, and as I went I sang a few songs I'd made up over the years, a way to dispel boredom. But my voice grew quiet as I neared their house and saw the wagon moving toward the road, Jack in the driver's seat. I lifted my hand to wave, expecting him to turn toward me, headed for our house, and past us, into town. Instead he swung right, leaning to the edge of the wagon seat, the inner rein pulled hard in his hand. I stopped. In minutes all that remained was a faint cloud of dust rising off the road.

I followed. At the end of the main road, a narrow dirt trail led into the forest. I kept to its edge, moved through the thick hem of trees, until the white building appeared through the branches like pieces of a puzzle. Mr. Bobiwash, Jack, moved in the scene, crossing from his wagon to the lighthouse, the shotgun leaning on his shoulder. Before he went inside, he turned and looked behind himself. I tucked myself behind the wide trunk of a beech tree. When he pushed through the door into the kitchen, I crept closer. Through the window where I'd seen that glowing yellow light, watched until it went out, I thought I saw the small curve of a face, a body turning away, but when I squinted to see, it vanished. The glass obscured by the oily sheen of the morning sun and the twitching reflections of flickering leaves. If you were inside, you were silent and still, almost invisible. I waited. Pushed my palms against my ankles to keep away the bugs. Sat there for what felt like hours, until worry about Thomson overtook me and then I quietly backed up the trail and walked home uncertain what I'd seen. At the Bobiwashes', I slid the jar of pills into the mailbox without a note or any mention of why we were returning his gift.

22 City

Phoenix nudged me awake with the cold steel barrel of a gun.

"Up, up, lazybones," she said as I rubbed my eyes. They opened painfully, stung by the smoke that was always around, that gathered in my face when I bent to blow smouldering kindling into flame.

"What's with that?" I asked.

"It's a gun."

"I know that."

The corners of her closed lips nudged upward; a rare smile. "Hunting."

"For what?"

She stirred my sleeping bag with the iron tip. "Whatever we find."

It made me nervous, but I got up. Through the small windows beside the fireplace, the light glowed purple. A bruiselike smudge of dawn in the sky.

"What time is it?" I asked, an old habit. The only clock they'd owned had been smashed into a mess of black numbers and white plastic gears at the diner.

"Early," said Phoenix, standing there while I put on my shoes. There was no reason to dress because I'd slept in my clothes as we all had, as we did every night. Together we looked at Thomson, curled on his side, asleep on the original mattress, where I'd first slept with Marvin. I wondered where he was, if he had gotten into trouble. If I'd ever see him again or should be afraid and go deeper into hiding. It was crude how we'd done things, how Marvin had used me, put me in harm's way because I was innocent, he later explained, a new face, and I wouldn't have been suspected. But all was quiet in the dark zone, apart from nighttime when we'd lock ourselves in, listening to the shouting that echoed through the fenced-in neighbourhood.

"Should we wake him?" I asked.

“Let him sleep,” Phoenix said, and we left through the kitchen door.

Phoenix led me through the clearing behind the house. The earth was scraped and piled into patches where we'd been breaking it up, preparing for a garden. I'd shown them how to save seeds, digging into cucumbers with dented skins and withered hothouse peppers spotted dark purple. We laid the tiny fragments out to dry in the sun hoping that, when the time came, they'd sprout.

We passed the hulking box of the lamp factory. With Marvin, that first morning, I'd turned left to meet up with the fence, but Phoenix brought me along the lakeshore to an inlet that fed into a sluggish, muddy river. The shore was clotted with willow trees, their branches draping down, stirring the brown surface. We walked along the water's edge into a park I'd never been to before. Close to a huge oak tree Phoenix stopped and held her hand out for me to do the same. She lifted the gun and peered down the barrel. It cracked. A black squirrel fell from a fat branch, landing with a crunch onto a puddle that had frozen in the night. Phoenix ran. She picked the dead animal up by the back leg and I saw how her face glowed like lit copper. Like a happy kid. I had never killed anything, not like that, but by the time she handed the small body over to me, I was smiling too.

She shot two more and then lined them up on the ground. I watched as she pulled a jackknife from her pocket and crouched over them. Their blood sank quickly into the snow and pink innards gathered in the melted hollow. Her hands worked confidently—skinning, slicing, gutting—and her face stayed focused on the task. I thought by then that I knew her but realized that I didn't. There were angles to her, facets I hadn't seen yet.

On the way back, I carried the meat, wrapped in a plastic bag we'd pulled out of a clutch of frozen reeds.

“Where did you learn that?”

“We took a course. Hunting and skinning small animals.”

“You and Thomson?”

"Me and my boyfriend." I glanced at her. "My ex. And Marvin too. It was a wilderness survival thing."

I had a lot of questions, but I knew that Phoenix only talked when she wanted to. I held up the small package of meat and started to say something about the meal we would have, but she interrupted me, her words rushing out.

"Marvin had this huge energy."

I wondered what was coming—something about the two of them, how they'd been together, deeply in love. I looked at the red wall of the factory, coloured brilliantly with hundreds of graffiti tags. People marking their places. I had the feeling that whatever she was going to tell me would send me away, would kill another idea of home.

"We talked a lot about changing the world. At the Pantomime. Drinking. Smoking." A smile appeared on her face, slight, marked by past injury, it seemed. "We had this idea that everything needed to be broken down in order to be built again."

I stopped walking.

"Let the ship go down," she said. "Stop bailing."

"Jump Ship."

She nodded.

"What happened?"

"You know. We blew things up."

She looked down, at the bag, blood in its pinched corners. I wanted to stop her. I felt like I was being shut inside a box. The truth a close compartment when all along I had assumed it was wide open. The six of us rammed against one another, circling around the same fate, when I thought there'd been space between us, that we were individuals, that Phoenix could take me away from the madness of Marvin and the others. Save me. Show me something new. "I met Walter through Marvin. They were in a class together."

"Walter?"

"Dialogues of Dissent, Modern Imperialism." She waved a hand. "Something like that."

"You met him—"

"He's my ex."

"Walter?" My voice shrill with surprise.

"You know him?"

I paused. "No." Then, "Yes."

Phoenix laughed. A small explosion of sound.

"He's—"

"Crazy?"

"So you left," I said, wanting her to nod and smile and avoid all the middle part. She didn't know about the travel agency. Did we need to learn these things about each other?

"No," she said. "Not right away."

She looked past me, out at the choppy lake. I saw it reflected in her eyes, the chaos of light and motion and sound, unstoppable. "I know, Sandy," she said. "I know what happens when people insist on how right they are . . ."

I waited.

"You know that first explosion?"

The bank machine. It had happened before I left home. Phoenix's face was flushed, a sudden brightness in her eyes. "It was thrilling. How right we felt we were. The power. Watching that sudden shattering. We were this force." She kicked her foot against a drifting bit of garbage, a hunk of oily Styrofoam. "You must feel that."

I couldn't find any words.

"With Marvin," she said.

When I didn't answer, she kept going. "But then the next one. The car dealership, where Walter lost his hand."

My mouth opened. Quickly I closed it, stared at the ground as she described it all: the panicked race through dark streets, Walter's gushing hand.

"Marvin and I took off our shirts to staunch it. There was blood—"

She swallowed, glanced at me. My face pale, I'm sure, watching our four shoes. "One of the guys at the Empire was a medic from the war and he helped us and then asked a lot of questions and then said he wanted in. Other cells started up."

The house I'd stayed at. The basement. The Jump Ship map.

"I got out. I argued for something else, something like what Vaclav Havel would . . ."

Her voice faded to silence. She paused for a long time. I thought she was finished.

"You know the rest. Thomson was in that awful rooming house." Her hand went to her chest, laid there, flat. I thought she was going to cry. "We came here. We started the soup kitchen. For a long time I could believe in that, but now . . ."

I wanted to tell her. To confess. Explain about the bomb, that mysterious throb of light, Marvin. I wanted to move closer to her, curl in the hollow under her breasts, lay my head on her belly, and tell her how we were the same. But I didn't. I stood very still and said, "It's sad" because I didn't know what other words to use.

She took my hand, as if we were linked, sisters or something else, but I still felt a betrayal. When I let go, I saw smudges of blood on her fingers and how they had transferred to mine.

I couldn't fit it all in my head. The relationships between everyone had shifted and spun. I remembered Margo's nasty words about Phoenix, Walter talking about her in the car, all the lies about Walter's hand. At home, Thomson studied me. He could tell something was wrong, but he didn't say anything, didn't ask any questions. Phoenix went outside to set up a spit for the squirrels, and I slid the sleeping bag off the mattress and dragged it up the rotting stairs.

"Careful your feet don't go through," Thomson called after me.

I lay on the hard floor. The window looked out onto sky, a wide emptiness without obstacles that felt like a relief. I fell asleep and in my dream I was home, not in my parents' apartment but at the farm, banging a nail into the wall to hang a painting of white stone ruins. The nail kept wobbling, bending, as if it wasn't solid. I couldn't get it in right. The plaster smashed into a white powder that fell to my feet. My father stood in the doorway, a dark shape giving directions, but I couldn't understand what he was saying. Phoenix came through the back door, the one that looked out over my mother's large vegetable garden and the cornfields beyond. A scarf of thick black lace tied tightly around her head. She took the hammer and laid it on the table. The painting leaned against the wall and I remember how she smiled at me, gleeful, innocent, like she looked when she'd killed the squirrel, and she swung her boot back and kicked in the glass. *What are you doing?* I asked and then I realized we were somewhere else, in a greenhouse my mother used to bring me to where I learned to rub the leaves between my fingers and take away the scents. Lemon verbena, chocolate mint, licorice, lavender. I woke to her arm wrapped around my middle, the fire a dying red throb in the hearth, but it was just another layer of the dream. When I really came to, it was still day. Phoenix stood in the corner of the room. I started when I saw her, as if she was a ghost.

"You were making noises," she said.

I told her about my dream—the black scarf, the broken glass—and that's how I'm able to remember it, all these years later.

"What do you suppose that means?" The sun glowed on her face, cast her half in shadow, so it looked like she was partly made of gold. I shrugged. She smiled and looked around the room, at the walls covered in a print of pink roses climbing wooden trellises. Long ribbons of wallpaper hung off the damp plaster. "Look at this place," she said, touching one of the roses, a closed bud. "It must have been nice."

I nodded.

"Did you just need a break? Is that why you're up here?"

"I guess so." I ran a hand through my greasy hair. It was getting time to cut it. Phoenix came closer. I pulled the sleeping bag into my lap, piling it, bunching it with my fist.

"I shocked you," she said. "About Walter. All that."

"A little."

But of course it was more than that—it was Marvin lying to me, not halting even after blood and injury. It was whatever I'd stumbled into. Calculated, clearly thought-out actions that felt to me as accidental as tripping and skinning my palms on the pavement. I let the slippery fabric go and crossed my arms.

Phoenix sank to the floor beside me, sat on the edge of her hip with her legs curled to the side.

"I didn't know what I wanted, who I was." Her dark eyes were on mine, so deep I couldn't meet them, could only occupy the edges, glance carefully inside. "I wasn't even Phoenix then."

"Who were you?"

"Nelli," she said and lifted two of my fingers with her own. Her hand was warm. A current swirled in me, but something hard clenched shut in my throat, damming the flow. I pulled my hand back.

"I'm not like that," I said and flinched because the words were harder than I wanted, more convinced. I didn't actually know what I was like, who I really was.

She laid a palm on the floor. "Right," she said and pushed herself up. "How stupid of me."

Her words stung, and when she left the room, I wanted to call her back. It took until she was halfway down the stairs and then I shouted out her name. Her footsteps paused. I felt the shudder in the floor as she came back up.

"I don't know," I said. I was starting to cry, my eyes hot puddles.

"It's all right," she said and touched my dirty hair, ran her fingers down the side of my face, stroked my bottom lip so lightly I had to scrape away the tingling with my teeth. When she crouched down and kissed me I could hardly kiss her back. We spent an hour like that, cautiously touching, twin blooms stirred by strong wind.

Marvin came back that afternoon. After Thomson had called upstairs to Phoenix and me, reminded us of the work that had to be done. I was pinning a wet shirt to the rope line strung between the porch and the outhouse when I saw him loping across the clearing. He held his heavy coat over his shoulder because the day had grown warm. Part of me was glad to see him, relieved that he was okay, but I also felt a raft of other emotions. A thrilling confusion over what was happening with Phoenix. Anger at what he'd held back, the whole history Phoenix had shared. He'd only told me the good things, to get me interested. *No one gets hurt,* I remembered them saying, with Walter right there. Did Margo even know what had happened?

Marvin's face was pale and there were circles the colour of charcoal smudge under his eyes. He looked older, even though it had only been five or six days since I'd seen him. I left the clothes in a heap in the basket and glanced back at the door, the empty porch, the closed kitchen window.

Quietly, I said, "Why didn't you tell me about her?"

"Phoenix?"

I nodded.

"Which part?"

"Walter," I said coldly. "What's with all the fucking secrets?"

He sighed and shook his hand like he was waving away smoke. When he said my name and stepped closer, I knew he had bad news. I braced myself. The silence was marked by the soft patter of the wet clothes, not wrung out enough, dripping on the dry earth.

"What? What is it?"

I was still waiting when Phoenix came outside, carrying a shovel to dig a fire pit under the spit. She moved down the porch stairs and I turned around, blocking her view of Marvin. I wanted to push her back, stand between them, pry the two worlds apart. But I think she saw the guilt on our faces.

"What are you talking about?" she asked as Thomson appeared, holding a dresser drawer to turn into kindling. The door slammed shut behind him, closing on our snug, private home. I flinched at the blast of noise.

Marvin stood apart from us and told them about the bombing. His voice a monotone, speaking in a way that meant it didn't matter anymore because it had already happened. It was fact. Nothing could change that. I wrapped my arms around myself, unable to stop him. Thomson and Phoenix listened, and when Marvin finished, Thomson threw the drawer onto the floorboards of the porch. The rectangle shifted into a diamond shape.

"Are you incapable of change?" he called down to Marvin as if from the deck of a ship.

"This isn't about you," Marvin said. "You had your time; you did things your way."

"You think my complaint is about ego?" Thomson yelled.

Marvin held his hands up, palms turned outward, giving up. Phoenix stared at me.

"This morning . . ." she said.

"I was going to tell you."

"The fire, the night you came down." Her mouth moved into a half-smile. "Shit," she said, and she crossed her arms around the handle of the shovel. I saw the walls that had so recently dissolved between us reset themselves. Thomson's cheeks seemed to collapse, as if a sinkhole had opened inside him. He was shaking his head, his mouth the worm of a scowl.

"Thomson," I said.

"There's something else," Marvin said loudly, staring straight at me.

"The travel agent?"

The others watched. Marvin shook his head, staring down at the ground. "She's fine," he said and lifted his eyes to look at us. "It's Margo."

A shivering terror went through me, like that feeling in a nightmare when you realize the bad guys are right behind you, ready to crawl up your spine.

"That night." He sighed and ran his fingers through his hair, tugging at the tangles as he tried to find the words.

I was already ahead of him. I breathed his name: "Walter."

Phoenix looked at me, then back at Marvin.

"They took off, but he wanted to go back."

"He always got too close," Phoenix whispered.

"They hid out across the road, but then she went in and the ceiling caved in on her. They got her out in time, the paramedics, when they finally got there, but it seems . . ." His head tipped forward, hard, like his neck had suddenly stopped working.

"What?"

His hand lifted, a finger tapped the hard bone around his eye. "She's blind."

He had stepped closer so by then we were almost within arm's reach. I wasn't sure how I'd ever touch him again, how I'd ever find my way back to any life like the one I'd had. Suddenly I was looking around, realizing I recognized nothing. No landmarks. No familiar features.

"Why did she go inside?" I asked. Only Margo. Stupid, risk-taking Margo.

Marvin shook his head. "I don't know."

Phoenix's shovel clanged against the wooden porch. "You have to do something. Call the police."

"What will that do?" Marvin said. "They'll arrest her. And us."

"And him," she nearly shouted.

I looked past Marvin, toward the lake. The water like steel under the bright sun. When I shifted my eyes, transparent yellow spots hung over everything. Marvin had come right up beside me without my noticing. I started to shake and he touched my arm.

"Christ," Phoenix said, turning away. I heard the door slam from a vast distance. He asked if I was all right and I told him that I was but I knew I never would be. I would carry those circumstances like the heavy lead X-ray robes they used to make you wear, back when doctors could take pictures of your bones, see everything inside you.

Thomson cooked the squirrels on a spit in the backyard, and the four of us ate supper quietly, as if after a funeral. Marvin's fingers held tightly to the tiny bones. I hadn't seen him like that before, like a small boy. My reflection was a blur in the metal fork, and I kept sneaking glances at Phoenix but she wouldn't look at me. I saw the hardening of her jaw when Marvin started to talk.

"We've made a difference," he said. "You should see what's happening up there."

"Haven't we seen enough?" said Thomson.

Marvin acted like he hadn't heard him. "This group threw buckets of blood into seven banks across the city."

"Whose blood?" Phoenix asked.

"Chaos," Thomson said. "And casualties."

"Walter says that," said Marvin.

"Thomson doesn't mean it in a good way," Phoenix said.

"And Walter does? His fucking girlfriend's blind. Look what he's lost."

I pushed a pile of tiny ribs around on my plate.

"You're not hungry?" Thomson asked me, and I shook my head.

Phoenix's knife shrieked against her plate. Marvin looked up at her. "He's committed to what he stands for."

"Where's Margo?" I asked, but Thomson talked over me, squinting at the front door like he was waiting for someone to come in. "'Ideology gives people the illusion of behaving morally and having an identity while making it easier for them to give those things up.' Vaclav Havel."

Marvin stared at him. "Is that how you felt, when you were revolting?"

"Those were different times."

"Yes, you had a whole world waiting, that blissful reality on the other side of the wall."

"A different jail cell."

"All we know about what's next is collapse and whatever hard world comes after that." His words were clear, but I heard a softness in his voice, like his foundation had grown punky, holed by soft rot. "But the band keeps playing as the ship goes down."

Phoenix interrupted: "So it's okay if people die."

"No one's died yet," Thomson said, like he could see Marvin's side.

Marvin stood and his chair fell back, booming against the hardwood floor. I stared down at a shiny island of grease on my plate as his boots pounded upstairs. He went to the room Phoenix and I had been in earlier that afternoon, where the pigeons lived and the other creatures that came through the broken windows, the gaps in the eaves.

23 Island

Thomson was crossing the yard when I returned. Consciously planting one foot in front of the other, his robe swishing around him like the rough-edged feathers of a crow. As if he really was a bird, I approached slowly, not wanting to startle him. I caught his arm but this time there was no chastisement. I did not try to stop him. I knew where he was going, where he wanted to be. We walked through the forest, to the bees that had been left behind.

The remaining hive was toppled. Thomson pulled on me as he rushed into the centre of the clearing. That was it: both sides of the colony were gone.

"Who did this?" he hollered, and his voice sputtered into a cough. He grabbed the back of the chair I'd brought out days earlier. My hand hovered around his elbow, waiting to help him. When he finished, he wiped his mouth with the back of his hand, watery blood smearing across the grey stubble on his chin, and said, "Your kid."

I started to defend you, but he swung toward me, the robe filling with air like the whirling dervishes he'd told me about a long time ago. "This is your fault."

"I didn't do this."

"Your neglect did this. Wandering all over looking for what you want." He poked his finger at me, word by word. *Want* echoed in the clearing before his left food lifted and slammed down, crushing an angular chunk of honeycomb. I didn't know how he'd found the energy. "This is where you are, Sandy. Stop looking for ways out."

"She's not a way out. She's a person."

"An obsession."

I didn't answer.

"A reverie, a fantasy." He reached for the chair and hung there, his back curved, body starting to sag. "You go blindly into things. You don't consider the consequences."

Phoenix, he meant. I knew he meant her. Grief rose in me like something loosened from the lake bottom, bobbing to the surface. Thomson reached out and his fingers felt bone dry, already skeletal. When he said my name, I leaned awkwardly against his thin arm and cried as he stroked my hair, his long fingers tangling in the knotted ends. Snot bubbled in my nose. Angrily, I wiped it away.

"I meant the girl."

"I've considered the consequences. Her dying alone in the woods. You would help her—or you would have."

"I wouldn't keep her a secret. I wouldn't try to do it alone."

Thomson's gaze wandered to the broken box of the hive, clobbered into splintered boards. He pushed away from the chair and bent to pick up part of a frame, the honeycomb splitting off it, the whole thing covered in honey. When he stood, he spread his legs to regain his balance. The kimono rustled, flapping open so I saw his skinny, naked thighs, a flash of more. I looked away and he glanced down, realizing, and moved quickly to redo the tie. When he stumbled, I reached for his arm and he dropped the frame and half-tied belt and the robe opened wider.

"Oh, fuck."

"Stand still," I said and secured the belt with a hard knot.

"Now I won't be able to undo it. You'll have to cut it off me. All for fucking Christian modesty." The last he said loudly, head back, barking into the sky. When he dropped his face to mine, I noticed the brighter blush in his cheeks. His eyes shining like mercury. He stood close enough that I hung upside down in his pupil, a tiny doll.

"You know, I've never seen you naked."

"Thomson," I scolded, and he blinked, bent his head, and then looked up again, and around, as if confused.

"I love you," he said, on the verge of begging.

"I love you too."

"Despite everything. Despite what you took from me. Despite your lack of sorrow."

"I feel sorrow!"

"But it was you." He was yelling again. "You left the soup kitchen, you joined Jump Ship, you planted the bomb, you watched it all happen, and never said no."

"Please stop," I said. I didn't know how he knew everything because I had never told him. I pressed my hands against the sides of my head, stared down at the wreckage of the hives without really seeing it. The silence throbbed in my ears. I couldn't believe he knew it all. I couldn't believe he had never said anything. That we had simply gone on, the whole mess shoved deep inside each of us like the contents of a sunken ship. You, a diver, prodding the weakening hold.

"Make amends," said Thomson. "And then choose the prison you occupy."

"What about Marvin?"

"We're not talking about him."

By then he was tired. He struggled to breathe as he gripped my arm. He seemed like he was about to fall over, land in a gangly heap in the sand and tall weeds, so I steered him toward the trail. "Didn't anyone ever tell you to make the best of things?" he asked as we moved slowly up the narrow path. I stared down at the ground. We were obliterating our own footprints as we walked back to the house.

Halfway there, he paused, leaning hard against me and said, "If she hasn't come by now . . ." and for a brief insane moment I thought he meant Phoenix. "You need to let her go," he finished, and I realized he meant you, my phantom, floating through the dark woods.

"She'll come," I told him with conviction.

"What do you want from her?" Thomson asked, and if I'd had a chance to answer, I would have said, simply, *love*. A fantasy of you painting eggs at Easter while the television rattled on, of taking you shopping for your first training bra. The things I had. A second chance. But I didn't have the opportunity. His breath sputtered out in a barking cough and he kept coughing. Between the demolished hive and home, he laid a trail of oily blood. I helped him onto the chaise on the porch and said, "Hold on, hold on," sobbing as he clutched at me, his eyes wide, flashing panic. His lips and chin covered in blood. I tipped his face into a dirty towel, rocking him back and forth. "Thomson, Thomson, stay, please stay." When he died, it felt like all the air left the world, sucked out as his body sank back, like a boulder, like a felled tree, into that other, unknown place. His soul, like a bee, drifting upward. Invisible.

Time passed. An hour. Two. The light, the forest, the birds moving around me. Thomson so still. Twitching at first for what seemed a long, desperate time, his body expelling its air, the blood settling in his lungs, a sediment he couldn't choke on anymore. When I was able, I lifted myself up. I went into the house and pulled a plastic bucket out from under the sink. At the lake, the walk long and quiet, I filled it. Carried it back to the porch, lathered soap onto a cloth and washed his face. Rusty swirls floated in the water. I pulled off his robe, tugged his T-shirt over his head. Threw them in a pile to be burned. I cleaned him. Under his arms. Behind his knees. Each slender finger. Everywhere. An intimacy with his body he hadn't had with mine, or anyone's for many, many years. I remembered him and Phoenix sleeping together, how odd I'd found it, the two of them sharing the same, square nest. But I couldn't judge because I barely knew them then. In total, I had known Phoenix much less than a month.

I pulled the sheets off Marvin's and my bed and carried them to the porch. I rolled Thomson's body to one side and shoved the edge under him, tipped him back, and did the same on the other side. An imperfect job. Once I was done, I realized I'd forgotten to close his eyes so I pulled the fabric off his face and found him, staring upward at the sky, still looking terrified from that final, hard journey. I wondered what he saw now, where he was, and started crying again as I closed his eyelids and again covered his face. Out in the dirt yard, the boughs of the Jack pine nodded in the breeze, bobbing over the flaking shingles on Marvin's shed. The chickens squawked so I stepped down into the yard and scattered the last of the feed. Soon we'd have to let them fend for themselves on green weeds and random seeds, or eat them. I walked away, up the drive. I heard a tinny, echoing drone and followed the sound to the car. Bees were drifting around the windshield. They slipped in and out through the narrow gap of the hood. I paused, turned to tell Thomson that they'd settled in the engine block, and remembered with a lurch that he was gone. The resetting of reality over and over again: *he's gone, is gone, is gone.* Aimless, I wandered down the trail to the shore. The boat still out. Marvin a small spot on the lake. My footsteps crunched and cracked against the silence, and I thought of Thomson's stories: about the last member of a tribe from an island off the California coast who survived on his own for almost twenty years, a woman in the 1800s cast off from her captain father's ship with the crewman who had impregnated her. For an entire winter, he'd told us, she lived on a sliver of water-bound rock, her lover and baby both dead. "How'd she get food?" I'd asked. He shrugged. "Gull eggs, plankton, whatever was close at hand."

"But I'm not alone," I reminded myself out loud, my voice a strange vibration in my throat. The water stretched before me, unresponsive. I walked back home. To Thomson, lying there, the sheets freshly stained from his body.

Marvin's shed was locked, with the shovel inside. I wanted to dig, to tuck Thomson safely into the soil and let him leave. That's what he'd asked of me: *Don't burn me. I want to feed the flowers, not drift off into ether.* Uselessly, I tugged on the padlock and then looked around. A pile of bricks stood stacked against the wall. I picked one up and slammed it against the old steel until the lock popped open. The smashing sound boomed through the silence. My ears rang and inside Marvin's shed the sudden darkness blinded me. I blinked and blinked again until the details came clear: a pile of unravelling yellow ropes, a coffee can of bent nails waiting to be straightened, a stack of magazines on the plywood desk. I flipped through old copies of

National Geographic and *Mother Earth News* that we'd taken from the library. Near the bottom of the pile, a wrinkled paper stuck out. I lifted the magazines to reveal the Jump Ship manifesto, stained with spilled tea and age, the first part taken from the declaration of the Zapatistas, the rebels Phoenix had known as a child: *We were born of the night. We live in it. We will die in it. But tomorrow there will be light for those now crying in the night, for those to whom day is denied, to whom death is a gift, to whom life is forbidden.* I thought of you. I thought of all the nights you'd had to spend out in the darkness, alone. My eyes jumped down the page: *We are the peasants in the king's streets. He and his guests watch from their narrow castle windows, in between the entree and the dessert course.* And farther: *The wealthy live for what they can get in the current moment while we are focused on the questions of the future. How to improve life for our children? What is necessary is to hasten the collapse for all so that we find ourselves on an equal playing field. Only then, once we jump ship and swim for new shore, can we begin to rebuild . . .* The word repelled me: sanctimonious and even untrue. Marvin didn't care about that anymore—children, rebuilding, creating a better life. All we worked for was survival, subsistence, hand to mouth. The kind of existence Phoenix had known as a child.

A movement through the dirty four-paned window caught my eye. A vulture's talons touched down in the yard. Dust clouded around it. It folded its wings back onto its body like tucking away a cape and turned toward Thomson. I ran outside and threw nails until it spread its huge brown-black wings and lifted into a pine. Its pebble eyes stared from the wrinkled red head. Another one landed in the branches. And they watched. Waiting. In the shed, I found the shovel hanging from a nail hammered into the back wall. As I lifted it off with one hand, my gaze fell behind a gashed water barrel, into the dusty corner, onto a stack of red paper plates.

Five of them. Licked clean. My sacrifice, my offering, stolen by Marvin. I stumbled back, the heavy shovel dropping. My free hand fumbled for the corner of the desk. All his arguments against feeding you flooded my mind. The way he positioned his body as he tried to convince me, leaning in, aggressive. And all the time, he was taking it, eating it, his lips greasy with his own greed. The food I had meant for you. Another betrayal. Another death because of him. My chest felt thick. The shed smelled of mould and autumn rot, the dirt in the cellar under our house. The door had closed behind me so I shoved it open, climbed out into the fresh air off the lake. With the shovel blade stabbed into the earth between my feet, I sat on the porch steps. My emotions swung from searing grief to rage as the vultures dropped from the tree, arriving like guests at a wake. I let them. They came closer and I called to them. Thomson behind me, clumsily shrouded in the flowered sheets.

"Try it," I enticed. "Try it and I'll kill you. I'll feed you to Marvin."

Suppertime had come and gone.

My anger woke the savagery inside me and I had stopped thinking of you at all. Except as something else I'd lost.

The birds were still there when Marvin returned. Coming out of the woods, he saw us—them, me, Thomson. The pile of plates on the step like a buoy marking a treacherous rock. His eyes swung from them to Thomson and he released the long yardage of green net. It fell to the ground as he ran to the body, rushing around me like I wasn't even there. The plates scattered as he raced past. I watched them go, fluttering to the ground, flipped over, their undersides bright white.

Marvin pulled the sheet away from Thomson's face. He lifted his hands, moved them around, uncertain where to touch. Finally he knelt and leaned against the solid shelf of Thomson's ribcage, laid his arms around his waist and wept.

I had never seen Marvin cry. Not after Phoenix or anything else. His tough, tanned face collapsed at all the wind-carved lines, and I let him have his moment. The vultures shuffled at the edge of the yard as if made uncomfortable by Marvin's grief. When they got too close, I waved the shovel, waited, but Marvin kept crying until I couldn't take it anymore. The birds watched as I walked up the trail to where the hives had been, carrying the paper plates. There, I started to dig.

Into that hole I put my anger, my guilt, my wasted life. I put the hope I'd felt for you, destroyed by Marvin, and my love for Phoenix and Thomson. The world had come unglued—all the pieces of my life drifting without connection—and that hole seemed to be the only central point. My arm ached from a torn muscle that had never properly healed, but I dug, throwing dirt, faces flickering in my mind. The travel agent, mascara clumped around her curious eyes. Phoenix. I remembered our garden. The first one we would have had. The seeds Phoenix and I had planted in the city. Tomato and cucumber that hadn't even had time to sprout. When we left they were just pots of soil in a tiny greenhouse Phoenix built using the plastic sheeting that had covered the diner's glass door. Her memory itself was like a softening seed, its walls cracking open, uncurling inside me. My lungs had to shift, my liver, my heart. It hurt, all that movement of things long fixed. I jabbed hard at the packed earth and the shovel broke and I sat on the edge of the grave with the wood handle in one hand, the iron blade in the other. Tears came, sputtering up like the poison in Thomson's lungs. What would I do without him, without you? Without her?

With my wrist, I pushed away the wet on my face, smearing grit over my skin. Marvin came down the trail, dragging another shovel, scoop-shaped, meant for snow. He inched out of the woods and stood at one of the forest's many openings. More and more the woods seemed like a maze. This one room—where the hives had been, where Thomson's grave would be—could have been the labyrinth's centre.

"What you did . . ." I said, lifting up the plates. I threw them and they scattered, polka-dotting the ground. Startled, the birds lifted from the trees into their safer arcs. They looked down, dipping lower, assessing. Did he even realize what he'd done, how he'd pushed you into exile, probably sentenced you to death? "Do you believe in anything anymore? Do you even have a conscience?"

"There's no more room for ideology," he said, his voice cold. "Do what thou wilt shall be the whole of the law."

"That isn't what that means. It isn't so base."

"Not like stealing food from a child."

He banged a fist against his chest. "I'm real, Sandy. I'm taking care of us." He came closer to me and I hardened, knowing I'd do whatever it took to keep him away.

"And what is she? A ghost?"

"Every day I go out on that boat, that tiny leaking prison cell, and bail like mad to keep from sinking. Fish and fish and fucking fish. I stink of it." He glanced off at the open trail, the criss-cross of drooping goldenrod in full yellow bloom. "But I can't stop because the whole house of cards is built on my back. And then you take it all and start giving it away like it comes from nowhere, like it's this fucking magical bounty." He was breathing hard by the time he finished.

"You think I'm home watching television?"

"Protein. That's the hard part."

I paused. "So you went ahead and ate it."

"I tried to stop you, but you wouldn't stop."

"You condemned her, like you did him." I jabbed at the shallow trough where Thomson would soon be lain out. In the silence, unspoken truths drifted between us: the others who had lost their lives because of Marvin. The forest shifted like the switching of a set.

"And me," I said quietly. Her name hung between us. Finally I said it out loud: "Phoenix." My eyes burned, dangerously hot.

"You came willingly," he said. "You both did."

"I didn't know what I was doing."

"So it's my fault? You're a victim? An innocent?"

"You used me. I was a tool to you. Somebody to do your dirty work."

He leaned toward me, his hands bunched around the shovel's handle, like cedar roots. "You were a grown-up, Sandy. You made choices."

He looked like a stranger, like someone I'd never really known. I shook my head, broke a hard clump of dirt into powder under the heel of my hand. A blue jay screamed its accusations. My head was full of the image of him in his shed, acting in secret, like he had in the city. He and Walter, who had long turned to ash and that one claw of metal that had been his hand. Twisting wires, taping together explosive pipe. I thought about Thomson's words about forgiving him, making amends, and wondered how that would ever be possible.

"I know you wish it was me and not her. As if the three of you could have survived." He laughed: a dry outburst of air.

"We were doing fine."

"Right. I shouldn't have bothered coming back."

"Do you want praise for that?"

I didn't want to delve into history, think about what might have happened if Marvin hadn't returned to the dark zone that last night. Looking back with him was like a dangerous crossing on a rickety bridge.

"The girl," I said, my voice strained. *She could have been mine*, I wanted to say but couldn't. That pain was a hole I couldn't show him. Behind me the tall, straight pines creaked like the sound of someone crossing an old wooden floor.

"She's fine," Marvin said.

My eyes jumped to his face. "How do you know?"

"There are things I know. There are things you can trust me with."

"Tell me."

He looked away. Anger roared up in me. I sucked in my breath and hollered into the woods: "All your fucking secrets. You're allowed to have them but I'm not."

He didn't speak.

"I can't do this anymore."

Marvin scraped the shovel along the rectangle of dirt I'd outlined for Thomson's grave, loosening another layer. "Really? Where would you go?"

"I don't know. Town. I could go to Mr. Bobiwash. Jack."

Marvin considered me. "Jack," he said. He bent over and picked up the smoker, its side caved in. "And Shannon?"

I shrugged, staring at the sunset, bleeding red through the trees.

"You have two choices, Sandy. Stay or leave. Decide."

He started shovelling, tossing dirt at the base of the pines. I knew what he meant: *live or die*. There was once a time when we could have had it all, gambled for the chance at something better like I'd done by leaving my parents—setting out for greener pastures. But Marvin supported me, fed me, kept me warm and alive, and I him. Long ago, in that fire-lit city, my fate had been determined. It was how things were in my great-grandmother's time. It's how they were again. Still what I wanted more than anything right then was to leave, seek out that other life I was always supposed to have. Marvin stopped, the shovel blade half buried in a heap of earth.

"You know you can't lay everything on me. You still think there's some magic doorway."

"And to you it's all doom and gloom. Shatter the illusion until we have nothing left."

"That's not what I mean."

"It is what you meant. Wasn't that why we did what we did?"

"That's not what I mean now," Marvin said more gently. "Things are what they are." He kicked at the ground. "Life."

"How very Buddhist of you."

He glanced away, toward the house, the few birds spiralling like sparks from a fire.

"Thomson would say, *Look at how the birds are trying to eat me*."

"Don't," I said, flinching. "He wasn't just meat."

"I fucking know that, Sandy. Christ."

He pushed the snow shovel back in, awkwardly breaking away the inches. I shoved in the metal blade, loosening the soil's hard weave. When Marvin stopped, his forehead gleamed with sweat.

"But you know there are some tribes that eat their loved ones after they die. It's a sign of respect, of the great circle."

I stared at him. His eyes shone. The low sun lit the waxy skin of his cheeks. I noticed the sharp point of his elbow, the skinny trunks of his legs. He grabbed at the taut skin of his stomach. "And if you're hungry enough," he said. "If you're fucking hungry enough."

I saw, finally, that he wasn't far from that, but when I spoke, my voice was hard.

"She was hungry like that too." He blinked once. His gaze slid off into the bone forest.

"I know," he said as I left him on the edge of the grave.

Eric and Graham were standing in the yard. Clumped together, staring at Thomson's body on the porch. The birds gathered at the peripherals, lifting their wings as if they'd been invited to supper and made to wait. I rushed over to the boys.

"It's all right," I said as I slid my arm around Eric's narrow shoulders and tried to pull him against me. He tugged away from me and ran off, around the side of the house. Branches cracked as he entered the forest. My thought was that he'd scare you away. But then I remembered that you were not here. You never had been. The plate, the offerings of food, taken by Marvin and gobbled up in the shadows of his shed. Like a burrow for an animal.

"Eric," I shouted after him. Graham went to Marvin's shed, scaring the vultures away. He leaned against the corner, staring. I covered my mouth with my hand, trying to contain my grief. That morning came back. How I'd asked Thomson to stay, to hold on, instead of helping him leave, saying goodbye. It had been chaos, like it was with Phoenix, not a desirable parting.

Eric walked out of the woods, staring sideways at Thomson's body, afraid. He came to me and I put my arm around him again. Graham stomped on loose nails, slivers of shale that had worked their way up from the water. Those boys had seen so much. I pushed tears into the skin of my cheeks as I led them through the kitchen door to find something to eat. We should have been laughing around the table like family, friends. Not retrieving corpses and burning them. But death was everywhere.

Inside, I used the last of the water to wash my hands.

"You know he was very sick," I told the boys. "He's in a better place now." The words came automatically, like I remembered my own mother talking about my aunt, others who had passed away.

"Can we see him?" Eric said, surprising me.

We walked through the house to the front door. Dusk shadows filled the front porch, but we approached Thomson together and I let them look, uncertain what to say. After a minute or so I tugged the sheet off, briefly, so they could squint at his pale face, the mouth slack. I was glad I'd cleaned him. Marvin came out of the woods then, the front of his shirt stuck in the waist of his pants, the back trailing like a tail. Eric looked at him.

"Dad sent us," he said.

"Everything okay?" Marvin asked.

"Shannon—" Eric started, but Graham interrupted him.

"Hungry," he said, one hand flat against his belly, palm cupped over the knot of the blue rope that held up his pants.

"What about Shannon?" I asked.

"She's crazy," Eric said, his eyes large, and Graham laughed, a high-pitched, half-mad little giggle that usually made me smile. Marvin gestured at the flies landing on Thomson's face and I waved them away and replaced the sheet. *The bees*, I remembered then, and told the boys how they had made a new home in the car engine as I led them back inside. Marvin grabbed a pickaxe and went back to finish digging the hole as night came on. Inside, the boys and I made what we could for a late supper. We didn't have a lot, but we cored a few apples and stuffed them with the last of our beet sugar and I had Eric light a fire in the cookstove. While we worked, I told them about you, the shadow girl who moved through the woods. I made it sound like a story, but when I finished, I asked them if they'd seen you, if they knew about you, and they both said no. I wanted to ask more—what was going on with Shannon, if they knew why Jack had been at the lighthouse—but it was Thomson's funeral so I decided to wait. At least until we were sitting down, our stomach rumbles quieted by supper, or until I tucked Eric into bed, if they stayed.

When Marvin came back, his hands and neck were smeared with dirt and his armpits wet from sweat. "We're ready," he said as he went to wash his hands and discovered that the water bucket was empty. I didn't look at him; I didn't care what he needed or wanted. The apples were wrinkled and steaming on top of the stove. Graham whimpered. When Marvin got back from the lake, the four of us went outside and circled Thomson. I fought not to cry.

"Can you carry him?" I asked Marvin.

"We all can."

"The boys shouldn't have to," I said, but Eric stepped forward, tugging Graham's sleeve. Marvin lifted Thomson's shoulders and I supported his middle while the boys carried his legs. Clouds covered the half-moon so we moved slowly, creeping along the trail to the hives and the hole at its end. The flashlight, tied to Marvin's belt, scattered bits of diminishing light. I wished we could have waited until morning but that wasn't what Thomson had wanted. *Right away*, he'd said. *Plant me like a hungry seed.*

"Slow down," Marvin said, and I heard him skid his foot over the ground, searching for the hole. When he found it, we manoeuvred ourselves around the grave, the body hanging between us.

"Okay," Marvin said, and as I kneeled to lower Thomson in, the boys let go and Thomson's shoulders slipped out of Marvin's grasp. The sudden weight pulled me down and I fell in the grave, tangled with Thomson, my arm pinned under his waist. I felt his body beneath mine, his hip joints poking into my thighs. My stomach pressed against his. Thomson's last lesson: Sooner or later, this is where we all end up.

Dirt tumbled in on me. Dry clods falling on my arms and legs as I lay there. My face was close to his, but there was no breath coming out of his mouth. His body felt fragile beneath mine, like a rotted floor that could easily give. He had been my teacher, my friend, the father I'd hardly had, but he wasn't anything now except a memory, a form that would be gone by spring. The sobbing came like coughing, an expulsion I couldn't control. Part of me wanted to be buried with him, but I pushed off his chest and saw their three faces staring down.

"I'm okay," I said, wiping my wet face on my sleeve.

Marvin's flashlight illuminated the arteries of cedar roots in the soil surrounding me. When his hand came down, fishing for me, I grabbed on to it. My fingers were slippery from tears, but our grip held and he pulled me from the grave.

At the table, we ate as if in ceremony, a special family dinner. The boys split open the soft yellow flesh of the baked apples with tarnished dessert spoons. I pushed an underdone potato, dug up early, around on my plate. We had half a smoked fish, split in four. The flesh of it like cold metal on my tongue. The only sounds were the boys' smacking mouths and Marvin's knife blade scraping against the ceramic plate and Graham humming a rhythmless song while he ate. My eyes avoided the empty couch. Marvin and I were silent, but I kept thinking about the story he'd told over Thomson's grave, one I'd never heard before, about Thomson taking him and Phoenix to the city zoo. "He showed us the elephants," he'd said. "And told us how they work together, even grieve for their dead, visit the graveyards of their ancestors' bones. But we were teenagers. We thought we were too cool for that." I felt the boys, listening hard, and thought about all that had come after that, for Marvin and for me. "Elephants," I heard Eric mutter, and Graham's clammy hand had fumbled for mine in the dark. It hurt me to sit at the table, thinking, buried in the same heavy fog that had lived between Marvin and me for years. I wanted to leave, like we'd left the city that night, our pasts falling away in a mess of glass and blood and bombed-out wreckage. Or so I'd thought. I hadn't realized the wreckage had stayed, still intact, like a bee colony's abandoned home. I laid down my fork and looked up.

"There's something I have to do."

In the bedroom that I'd first claimed as my own, before Marvin and I began occupying the same one, I opened the closet and pulled Marvin's backpack off the shelf. The words were still there, written on the outside flap. Inside were the few things I had gathered in my final minutes in the dark zone. Over the years I'd taken items out, like spices and books, but others I'd left as mementoes. The bottle of lavender oil. Phoenix's scarf, the skulls and cobwebs marked with a black-edged burn hole and stained with her blood. Throat hardening, I pulled it all out, everything, piece by piece.

24 City

I don't know what time it was when I went after Marvin. The others were asleep and I had been too, all three of us under the same blankets.

A nightmare woke me, a dream about driving into light so bright I couldn't open my eyes and stumbled the car into a forest fire. I lay there awhile with my arm around Phoenix's skinny body, leaning into the lavender smell from the scented oil she smeared in her armpits, thinking. After supper I'd gone into the kitchen to talk with her while she and Thomson did the dishes, but I hadn't really known what to say or how to explain the choice to go along, bring the bomb inside that building, stand there as it detonated. She'd done it too, so she might have understood, but I knew she was angry at me for not telling her about it, not fully opening up to her even though we had been together. I felt the hardness in her that I had known from the diner, heard it in how she banged the dishes around, her back turned to me.

I didn't know what I would say to him, but I got up and went upstairs. Marvin was awake, smoking by the light of a candle pressed into a pool of wax on the floorboards. He reached out and pulled me toward him and I let him kiss me. It was different from Phoenix. With him, it was like the quick, close gathering of heat before a fire ignites. We were bound by what we had done so it felt natural to make love again, with all of that history already between us. Although I felt guilty. I didn't know how I'd tell her, how I'd reveal this other self.

Afterwards, we lay in the cold dark and I watched the ember of his cigarette lift and fall. The smoke hung over us like a gloomy fog.

"The travel agent," he said. "I'm sorry. She died."

I pushed myself up on one elbow. The sleeping bag slipped away and the cold air stung my bare skin. A sound came out of my throat as I realized what he'd said. How he'd lied. Her face appeared in my mind, but I couldn't do it, couldn't remember, couldn't look at her. It was too much so I shoved her down like a weight dropped into deep ocean. I squinted at him through the sudden wet blur in my eyes.

"I was protecting you. If you didn't know, it could be like you weren't even there."

"But I was there," I said, too loud. His excuse was bullshit. He'd lied because Thomson and Phoenix were there when he came home, watching him, waiting to judge. He didn't answer. Rain tapped on the roof like a countdown. I got out of bed. In the bathroom down the hall, I threw up in the toilet before remembering that it wouldn't flush.

I sat on the floor of that bathroom for as long as I could stand it. Breathing the smell of my vomit and the residue of strangers' waste. I thought I was nothing. I didn't know how I could escape what I'd turned into. It was like all my wrong choices ended in that bathroom—I didn't know that the worst was still to come. After a while I stood up, stared into the split seams of my face in the broken mirror, and went back to Marvin because there was nowhere else to go.

"You okay?"

I nodded, although I wasn't. He slipped his hand in his pocket and drew out a golden thread. A heart dangled, opened up, pictures inside. The locket.

"Margo wanted you to have this." I took it from him. The grandfather with his bushy moustache, the quiet wife.

"What happened?" I asked, and Marvin told me the truth.

"She heard cries for help. Walter tried to stop her, but she went in anyway."

I closed my fingers around the necklace, sealed it in my fist.

"Thanks," I said, but I meant it for Margo, who I would never see again, who had been far braver than me.

When morning came, Marvin wrapped an arm around my waist and pulled me to him. I felt his erection against the small of my back. As the faded flowered wallpaper came into focus, I remembered what he'd told me. She was dead. I had killed someone. And Margo . . . Dread flooded through me. I coiled like a small thing, waiting to be crushed or carried to safety.

We lay like that for a long time, hours it felt like, before Marvin said, "We should leave. Right now."

"And go where?"

"Away."

I thought of Thomson's island. But it seemed impossible: the idea of starting again, as if we were innocent. I told him about the map I'd found, how Phoenix wanted to leave the dark zone, what Thomson had said about the Crusaders. As I talked, the cold seemed to pool in my stomach. My body ached from lying on the hard floor. I knew that there was no going back.

Marvin scratched his cigarette out, leaving a soot-black streak on the floorboard. He turned away. I thought he was angry at me, and to be honest, I felt almost relieved, ready to be on my own, to figure things out for myself, but then he spoke. The words sounded automatic, like a recording.

"There's a rally at the botanical gardens today. Walter's planning an action."

"An action?"

"You know."

I stared at the ceiling, at the grey patches where plaster had fallen away in amoebalike shapes.

"I'm serious," he said. "We should just fucking go." His voice broke at the end. He covered his mouth with his fingers. I stood on shaky legs. "Shit," Marvin said under the narrow tent of his hand.

Outside the window, the rain had turned to snow. Fat clumps drifting down. I pressed my hand against the rough bark of the flaking sill, a weird calm inside me. From up there I could see all the way to the lamp factory and past that to wide water. The whole empty horizon. The clouds in the distance a blur of grey and white.

Behind me, Marvin sat cross-legged on the hard floor, the sleeping bag over his knees like a pelt. With his head in his hands, he sank deeper, as if gravity had strengthened its hold. Downstairs, I heard shuffling, the low tones of Phoenix and Thomson talking. The crack of wood. The night's chill in the house had sunk into me. I thought I'd never be rid of it.

We were like that for a little while. A frozen vignette. The lake in winter when you look out at it, expecting it to move, but it doesn't. Its skin is a solid mass. What changes is the light around it, the currents underneath. Finally, I spoke.

"What's his plan?"

"Simple. Blow it up. I think he's ventured far."

Like a traveller, I thought and remembered Margo's story of him in Afghanistan. Had he ever even been?

"How many people?"

"Hundreds." He reached for his boots. I heard the heel clattering against the floor as he pulled one on. I turned back into the room. "What are you doing?"

He stopped. "I don't know."

He opened his tin and pulled out a bent cigarette. I saw the tremor in his hand as he straightened it. After the match flared orange, he inhaled, blew the smoke toward the cracked window. His shoulders hunched like he was carrying his pack, fully loaded.

"It was our idea. Right from the beginning. Our grand fucking finale."

I thought of the maps—on the wall downstairs and the one I'd seen on the door of the pantry at my basement hideaway. Both with the gardens in the centre of the sparkling stars.

"To kill people?" I asked because I couldn't believe it. How far had I come?

Marvin shook his head, an adamant swing from left to right. "But Walter," he said, and when he spoke again he sounded ashamed. "He's taken over. He heard about the rally and . . ."

I got up. I needed a break. When I moved toward the door, Marvin asked urgently: "Where are you going?"

"To get some water." My throat felt raw and when I swallowed, I thought I tasted blood: the cold, coppery flavour of it filling the back of my mouth. The floor creaked underfoot as I moved to the top of the stairs. Beneath me, Phoenix and Thomson's voices rumbled, reassuring at first, until I heard the hardness in them. Halfway down the stairs, I stopped. Light from the fire flickered through the room. It was blazing, the air warm. They didn't see me so I lowered myself onto the step and peeked through the banister. Phoenix sat on the edge of their mattress, wearing only a pair of underpants and a sea-green T-shirt, the collar cut into a ragged V. One arm held across her chest, holding her breasts. Thomson in the bed, propped up by pillows, facing her so all I saw was the top of his head.

"We're running out of time," she said, her voice so low it was almost a whisper.

"It's the coward's way."

"Will we serve people better in jail?"

"Lots of people have gone to jail," Thomson said, scratching at the roots of his hair. "Many good people. Dissidents."

"I don't want that. For me or for you."

"We didn't have any part in this."

"The police won't make that distinction. If we pack now, if we go to Marvin's mom."

Thomson was shaking his head steadily, like a switch had been flicked.

"She won't blame you," Phoenix said, her voice getting louder.

"I haven't been able to stop him."

"No one has!"

"But he wasn't your responsibility."

She stood up. I realized she was wearing a pair of denim shorts, white strands hanging from the frayed edge. "Forget it," she said. "We'll figure out another way."

One half of her face grew dark as she turned away from the fire. I thought she might see me so I sank lower, tucked my chin to my chest. My heartbeat thumped in the cage of my ribs.

"Stay," Thomson said. Phoenix looked at the ground. "Stay with me."

"They'll think I'm just like him. They won't understand the difference. I have that history."

By then she was facing me, full on, only her eyes turned away, set on Thomson's face. Her body, the curve of her waist, clear through the thin fabric of the T-shirt. My neck prickled and I glanced back, up at the landing, but it was empty, the door exactly how I'd left it, slightly ajar.

"We have to stop it," I told Marvin, afraid of what would happen to us all if Walter's plan went ahead. Marvin was Jump Ship; Margo, me, and Phoenix. But he already had his boots on. His face tightened in on itself in a way I hadn't seen before. Determined. When we got to the bottom of the stairs, Phoenix and Thomson stopped talking. She was standing with her back to the fire, a blanket draped over her shoulders, a mug in her hand. Her bare toes squeezed the edge of the brick hearth. Thomson sat in a chair, his sock feet on the mattress. They both looked at us, expectant, but Phoenix's eyes quickly slid away from mine. She took a gulp of her tea. I felt far from her, as if our stories had come together only to break apart. Two separate entities. I wanted her to be free. She had already made her decision about what road to follow.

In that moment, I was pushing again toward some sort of happy ending. I thought Marvin and I could be heroes, stop Walter's plan, return and convince Thomson and Phoenix to leave. Maybe Marvin would come with us, maybe he wouldn't. Either way, this was my family now. I remember feeling that, Melissa, and feeling brave. I thought it would be easy.

"We're going out," I said, pulling on my green hoodie. When Phoenix spoke, I barely heard her through the soft, linty dark.

"Where?"

I told an effortless lie. "Marvin heard about this dumpster full of frozen food. He saw it last night. It'll still be good."

"Really," she said. "And how will we keep it cold?"

"We won't. We'll cook it all and eat it."

She paused. "Do you need help?"

Marvin shook his head. "We got it," he said, lighting another cigarette. Chain-smoking.

She pursed her lips, considering. I felt her analysis. It was my turn to look away. Marvin reached for my hand, but I shoved mine in my pockets. Phoenix saw and her eyes were warm when they met mine and I knew we'd be together again. A bloom opened in my throat. I couldn't stop the smile.

"Get ready," I said as I pulled on the doorknob. "We'll have a feast." The damp outside air burst in, pushing aside the heat from the fire. When Thomson cleared his throat, I anticipated coughing, but he just said my name and I stood there like I was waiting for someone, welcoming them in.

"Be careful," he said without looking at either one of us.

As we left I remembered the Rumi quote. *Flies gather on a wound*. I had to wave them away, live with what I'd done, accept the consequences. Act.

Halfway up the street, I looked back and saw Phoenix standing in the doorway, a slender pillar in the ruins all around.

25 Island

I walked to the door, carrying Phoenix's scarf. The boys watched me go, but Marvin didn't even look. Graham shifted, his right leg moving out from under the table to follow, but Marvin laid a hand beside his plate and said, "Stay here."

It was dark out, but I knew the way. I walked along the stone and sand of our laneway, my eyes slowly opening to the world. The forest lightened to grey and I thought of Phoenix turning off her flashlight as we walked to that apartment—Walter's old place, I realized later—to pick up the mattress. The dread in me that night, and fear. The fire from the bomb I'd planted burning not far away. The secret a new sliver inside me as my eyes hunted every hollow for Thomson's missing bees. I ached for her to be there, walking with me toward the trees. How my life would have been different, how it could have been. Regret burned in me as I reached the car and carefully opened the front passenger door. The hinges screamed. I shimmied over to the driver's seat and listened to the bees' loud buzzing as I draped the red scarf over the steering wheel. I didn't have the smoker, but I didn't care if I got stung. I felt tough as a beech tree, my skin a thick, smooth bark. Grief a running sap inside me.

"We had Thomson's funeral," I said out loud and then: "because he died." I adjusted the folds of the scarf, pulled it flat to reveal a skull, the wide black eye sockets, the crooked teeth. Stupidly, I expected something to happen—the bees to pause—but the night went on. The oak leaves rustling above me. The chorus of frogs and crickets. A stone formed in my throat, a hard thing defining the open, yawning absence. Thomson felt close by, like he was watching me, like he still existed. I had felt that about Phoenix too, those first few days afterwards on the island, and a terror that we'd left her behind. Fingering the hem of her scarf, I hoped that they had found each other, in the heavenlike afterlife Thomson didn't believe in. That dream seemed ridiculous to me, a reverie, and I remembered Phoenix calling me on the fantasy I'd created out of the dark zone. How young I must have been to imagine that place as a kind of retreat, somewhere that would serve me. Although I had been happy in the last days, before Marvin returned and laid the outcome of our actions at my feet. An innocent, Marvin had called me, and that's how I'd felt—new, only just learning who I was. He'd taken all that possibility away from me . . . A few bees drifted in from under the steering wheel and rose in a lazy flight. One landed on my wrist, crawled through the fine, brown hairs on my forearm, and then lifted, buzzing around my face, near my eyes. Thomson? *Choose your prison*, he'd said.

My nose burned. Sobs pushed out of my lungs. I wept. Of course it had been my fault, my choices, each step a mistake taken only by me. Those long days living in darkness while I waited for Marvin to tell me what to do and then did it. I lifted my hands to cover my face as the bee flew away. Pain poured out of me, long held under the weight of blame. Tears soaking Phoenix's scarf, brightening to red the dull brown stains of her blood.

I did get stung. A sharp pinch after I'd cried for half an hour. I took it to be Thomson, telling me enough was enough: *Get on with it! There's life to be lived.*

When I climbed out of the car, I don't know what I expected. More of the same, I suppose. Silence. The continuing toil of the everyday life that Marvin and I knew. Smoking fish, gardening, going to town. Shannon occasionally opening the door so I could check on her children. There would be more grieving, I knew. For Thomson, all the others—even my parents, who I'd pushed down deeper than anyone. On my way down the laneway, I swallowed a resurgence of tears and thought of what I would tell them, if I was able, if I hadn't let them go so carelessly—*I'm all right, I've come full circle, my hands know what to do in the dirt.*

I was almost at the house when the crack of a gunshot broke the night's silence. It sounded to the west of us, in the direction of the lighthouse.

I turned around.

Another shot popped through the quiet woods. Marvin jogged up behind me, a beam of light jumping in his hand.

"Wait here," he said as he rushed past, but I knew that wasn't possible.

The boys reached me—Eric's eyes big in his head, Graham holding two fists in front of his chest. I didn't want them to be hurt, but I knew something important was happening so we followed Marvin, walking carefully but quickly, our eyes on the distant cone of light spreading from his hand. Graham's fingers tightened around mine and then Eric let go of me and raced ahead. Where the road curved north, we heard another blast coming from the lighthouse and the sound of Jack shouting. The baby crying, screaming into the night. A relief to hear her, lungs functioning, alive. My heart pounded. We cut through the woods.

"Come on, Graham," I coaxed as we picked our way through the thin branches that snap back like whips. Through the trees I saw light glowing in the windows of the lighthouse as if it were a fully functioning home. We broke into the clearing, Graham and me, tripping over the remains of a wire fence at the edge of the yard.

"Sandy," Marvin shouted, and when I looked up my gaze met the hollow eye of a shotgun, pointed at my head.

"You and the retard," said Shannon, her hair a wild cloud around her face.

I felt my bladder weaken, but I held it. From behind, Graham clutched at me, his hands picking at my waistband. I reached one hand back to still him. The gun came closer. My voice stuck in my throat as I tried to force her name out.

"Shannon."

The gun still stared.

"Put it down," said Marvin from across the clearing.

I swallowed, felt the barbs of my fear. "We can help."

Shannon laughed. "How can you help?" she said and laughed again. A cold chortle, cracking like the ice breakup in the spring. Graham started to wail. A soft mewling that grew gradually louder.

I squeezed his elbow, held on. The gun hovered, then shifted toward the lighthouse and came back. Like a creature, a heron, searching the water for fish. My mind worked to think of something to say, to try to stop her. I imagined all of us dead, her suicide. The season changing. Our bodies buried in snow, thawed out, finally discovered, and the townspeople gathering to take what had been ours.

"Where's your baby?" Shannon turned to the lighthouse. Through the window, I saw the recycling bin they used as a crib set on the table and next to it, the infant lying on a quilt. Bending over her, a girl. You. All that I wanted. Right there.

"See," Shannon said and aimed the gun at the window, at you. My hands lifted to my face, horrified, at the same time as Jack lunged across the bullet's path. A shot. The glass shattered. A girl's scream. Jack on the ground. It felt like minutes passed, stretched into hours, before my mouth opened and I screamed Shannon's name. The gun swivelled my way. Regret roared in me and a buzz of yearning—*I do not want to die*—and then she was down. Marvin sprawled over her, pinning her to the ground. My own legs collapsed. The sting of gravel on the heels of my hands. Eric and Samuel ran to their father. Graham turned in circles, his hands over his ears. I grabbed his leg, pulled him down, and held him. Marvin pried the gun out of Shannon's arms. She lay on her side, her knees to her chest like she was in pain. Dressed in black jeans and a dark red sweater, she reminded me of a leech, undulating back to the deep after feeding.

"Are you all right?" Marvin asked, crouching beside me. I nodded and nodded and finally said, "Yes," realizing he couldn't see me in the dark. He handed me the gun and left to help Jack. The light from his flashlight revealed a slow seep of blood. Marvin kneeled, pressing both hands hard on Jack's left leg.

"Get the first aid kit," he shouted, and Samuel broke away from us, running down the weedy laneway, heading for their house and the kit we'd each received from the supply ship.

"Is he dead?" Shannon asked me, but I didn't answer, and her voice rose into a trembling wail.

I spent a long time with Shannon while Marvin tended to Jack and Eric went inside to help with you and the baby. I wanted to see you, to go to you, but I didn't know what to say so I stayed, sitting cross-legged on the ground. Shannon lay beside me, curled like a closed shell, calmed after a while by my hand stroking her hair. The gun was on my lap and I suppose I felt it gave me power, the ability to say whatever I wanted, because I started talking. I told Shannon everything I've told you, Melissa. First I said that Thomson was dead and then moved backward into the whole entire story of my first meeting with Marvin. I told her about the people who had died, the travel agent, even Walter. Margo's life forever altered. I wasn't sure if she was listening until I saw a glint where her eyes were and took it to mean she was crying. And then I told her about Phoenix, who I'd loved.

When I finished, the baby was screaming again and I looked up to see you through the shattered window. You wore a red plaid shirt I'd seen before on Shannon. Patches on the elbows. Jeans, rolled up at the ankles. Dirty white shoes. Fear on your small face.

"You see," Shannon hissed. "You see how she took everything."

"She's a girl," I said as I stood. "She's just a little girl."

Samuel held the flashlight while Marvin worked on Jack's wound, searching for the scattered bits of shot as small and black as mites. At the soft edge of the light, Eric comforted Graham. You stood just inside the lighthouse door, the baby crying in your arms, a red flag flapping wildly. Finally, I crossed the yard.

On the kitchen counter, Marvin's and my preserves stood in a neat row. Candlelight gleamed on the walls of the jars. Your small face looked stunned, in shock, as your eyes followed mine. It all bubbled out in a blur of words I didn't understand, like you were speaking another language. I stepped forward. Beside the cupboards, your tangled hair crackling in the uneven light, I held you. The baby between us. Your body stronger, older than I'd imagined.

When you calmed, I stepped back and said, "My name is Sandy."

When you didn't answer, I said, "Melissa," and you looked up at me. Tears hung on your eyelashes.

"Is that her name?" you asked, lifting the infant. Your first intelligible words to me, spoken with the tiny fingers curled around one of your own. I didn't answer. I slipped an arm around your slender shoulders and together we looked down at the baby's face, half covered with the marking of that wide-open wing.

26 City

Phoenix did not have a burial. This story is her only tombstone. She can't disappear, like one of those frightened Natives, driven from their home, still hidden in the caves. So I will tell you what happened next. Marvin and I left the dark zone. We went through the fence single file, threading past the sharp ends of the cut chain-link. It was cold so I pulled my hands into my sleeves, burrowed them into my pockets. We walked quickly, moving through the litter of sagging tents and soggy piles of ash in the empty field between the dark zone and the city's edge. We moved under the highway overpass and into the maze of tall buildings, down alleys, heading east. Wet snowflakes stung my cheeks.

"After this is over," I said and started to tell him that I thought we should leave, the four of us. Find our way across the map's green width and settle against an edge of blue. But he didn't respond. He marched like we were military, moving steadily toward the smoke drifting up from the occupied parkland that surrounded the shiny glass dome. And I followed.

We heard the drums from a mile away. A constant, hollow beat. The sound filled my head, stirring my anxiety, and I hated it. Since I'd been there last, the shantytown had expanded. Blue tarps were strung between tree branches. People hunched in circles around fires built in rusty tire rims. Snow piled gradually on the roof of a collapsing screen tent. Ahead of us, the dome of the botanical garden was fogged, like an eye overgrown with cataracts.

We worked our way through the crowd, weaving past a knot of people passing a joint. I read some of the banners, held by people and nailed onto trees: FREE ENCAMPMENT, PRIVATE LAND FOR PUBLIC USE, PEOPLE BEFORE PROFIT. Marvin told me about the park, how the police were threatening to evict the squatters who had been there for years, acting on the request of the bank that owned the gardens.

A few people waved at Marvin as we walked but he ignored them, sharply swivelling his face away. He gave them a wide berth and I followed suit, tugging on my hood to more fully hide my face. A woman who looked like Margo—blond hair, dressed in tight jeans and a denim jacket—stood on the other side of the road. I gave her a second glance before remembering where Margo really was—in the hospital, her world gone blank. I wondered what would happen to her. As we got closer to the gardens, the crowd thickened and Marvin reached his arm back. I grabbed his hand.

Four guards stood in front of the main entrance, cradling their rifles. The crowd leaned toward them, shouting to be let in. Marvin led me around the side of the building where a rectangular greenhouse jutted out. A tall hedge ran along its edge. He looked to see if anyone was watching and then pushed into the space between the structure and the thick cedar and I followed. Our cheeks slid against the cold glass as we worked our way through the narrow space. As we went, hidden from view by the thick bushes, I heard hooves clomping, horses whinnying, the sound of an arriving force. Marvin moved faster, grunting as he held back the branches with his forearms. Eventually, we came to a blocked-off door. Marvin wrapped his coat around his elbow and smashed the pane, and we slipped inside, listening for an alarm but none came. We had scratches on our hands and faces, thin lines of blood like the written beginnings of the story that the day would come to be.

There was no one inside. "All the security guards are out there," Marvin said as we moved past the case of epiphytes. The trail led past the pond and into the palm room. The windows were blurred by a fog of condensation. We stood under an arch of fronds.

"What do we do now?" I asked.

"Sandy," I heard. The harsh whisper of my name from behind us. Marvin and I stared at each other, scared, until I turned and saw Phoenix standing on the other side of the jungle.

"What are you doing here?"

She came to me, her hand out. "You don't have to do this. It's not your fight."

"We do," Marvin said.

"Don't speak for her," she snapped. An ivy vine snaked over her shoulder and she pushed it off.

"Because you will?"

"Stop," I said. "Go," I told Marvin as I grabbed Phoenix's arm. I told her what was happening, Walter's plan, that we were there to search for the bomb. She listened, arms crossed, as Marvin moved in the distance, shoving foliage aside, an urgent rustle.

"This was Marvin's plan," she said, her eyes climbing up to the greying glass dome. It was nearly dusk. "The final show. He always said it was selfish, this place. All for the sake of beauty. No function, only form." She plucked a dead yellow leaf off an African violet. "He doesn't understand ecology. He sees himself as separate."

"We don't have time," I told her and led her deeper into the gardens. Together we dug into the underbrush, beating aside palm leaves and other plants. Any second the whole place could go up, Walter dialling in from outside. Sweat tingled under my arms, slid down my back. When Marvin shouted out for us, I jumped. We followed his voice to the desert room. A fat coffee-table book called *Civilizations* lay on the low stone retaining wall that held a garden of sandy soil and cactus plants, some blooming papery yellow flowers and others stubbled with short thorns. Marvin slid a blade out of his jackknife and looked at us once like a diver stepping off a boat.

From outside, I could still hear the drums. A constant rhythm dulled by distance and the green world between. Like a child, I put my fingers in my ears. Phoenix stood close to me, her arm pressing against my elbow, while Marvin carved the resin-sealed book open and worked his fingers into a nest of wires. Carefully, he detached the cellphone and held it up with a look I hadn't seen before. Victorious. Admitting his ravenous attachment to life.

He threw the phone and it landed softly in the sand. Split open, emptied, the book sat beside the globe of a barrel cactus. Phoenix bent over, pressed her hands against her thighs.

"Shit," Marvin breathed, kneeling in the dry sand. Phoenix sat on the stone ledge. I realized my armpits were wet with sweat so I took off my coat and sat beside her. Her palm was clammy when I picked it up and I understood how scared she'd been.

Right then we should have left.

We should have hurried south to our safe home.

Instead we stayed. Like sightseers, we wandered down pathways, giddy in that glassed-in island of spring and summer where red and orange tulips were blooming. Phoenix touched everything: the rubbery leaves and tree trunks, a white flower she lifted with gentle fingers to show us.

"My grandmother grew these," she said, and both Marvin and I leaned in and smelled the perfume that mixed with the lavender scent of Phoenix herself. Together we moved through the succulents, where the loamy soil was spotted with fuchsia and scarlet petals. We pushed up the sleeves of our sweaters, carried our heavy load of coats. Outside, the crowd grew louder, batons smashing against plastic shields. I heard the hot neighing of a horse, imagined steam snorting out of its nose. A booming voice shouted, "Get back, get back, get back."

Marvin looked at the front doors, listening. I waited to see what he'd do, expecting to see him burst out from inside, break into the centre of the action. But he came with us as we walked back toward the secret door.

At the pond, our faces rippled across the water's surface. Copper pennies shimmered on the reflections of our lips. A stone smashed through the roof, then another, their shapes pounding into the soil around us, the glass a weird sparkling rain. We hunched over and ran and when we reached the back door, Walter was there. "I knew you'd pussy out," he said to Marvin. I turned around, but Marvin looked only at Walter. I felt tired: one more lie, piled on the rest.

But Marvin defended himself. "These people are on our side," he said, his arm sweeping backward to the blur through the windows. "They want what we—"

"All they want is an easy life."

"So we kill them?" Phoenix asked.

Walter turned to her, as if he'd just noticed she was there.

"Your highness," he said and pretended to curtsy. His lips stretched into a sneer that suddenly vanished so he was glaring at all of us. He taunted us when he spoke, like a cruel teacher explaining elemental things to confused students.

"This is metamorphosis. The old is destroyed to make way for the new. You don't pick and choose."

None of us knew what to say.

"It's simple. You don't have the balls for what has to be done." He stepped closer to Phoenix, his voice vicious. "You're alone. You only care about yourself."

I was afraid. I could see how far gone he was; how his pupils had turned into fat black stones.

"Walter," Phoenix said and lifted her hands as if to show him that they were empty.

"Passive resistance," Walter mocked as he slung his backpack around and unzipped it. I could barely breathe as we waited to see what he'd pull out. A plastic water bottle. Insanely, I felt relief, thinking he was just thirsty. But then he screwed it open with his good hand and flicked it toward Phoenix. The liquid splattered at her feet.

Gasoline. Behind me, Marvin lifted his hands like a conductor about to cue the show. "What the fuck are you—"

Walter interrupted. "You get the last word, buddy. E-mail's set to go at midnight. Signed and sealed with all our names." Like a wizard's wand, his metal hand swept over all of us, stopping at Phoenix. "Even yours, although you don't fucking deserve it."

He didn't move right away. He stood there, the point of a triangle, Phoenix and Marvin each a corner of its base. Me, an incidental object, detached. All of us uncertain what was happening so we were surprised when Walter upended the bottle over himself, drenching his shirt and pants, the liquid darkening the colour of his clothing. Simple clothes. A pair of khaki pants, a faded red polo shirt. The vapours stung my eyes and sent sharp pains darting through my head. I tried to speak, but all I could say was what the others had begun shouting—*No, Don't, Stop*—a rush of urgent denial even as Walter bowed his head almost elegantly and ignited himself, turning rapidly into a flaming pillar that flew toward the front window and crashed through the glass.

Outside, the crowd slumped into silence. Like a weapon, he quieted them. Then he started to scream. I remember that, with a horror I can't describe, can't put words to, won't.

Marvin followed Walter. He jumped through the window's jagged hole and then reached back for me. I stepped over the ragged edge of glass on the sill. Phoenix was slower, her eyes scanning the crowd outside with Walter on its edge. Spinning flames. She seemed frozen, hugging herself with both arms.

"Come on," Marvin shouted at me, and I reached back for her. I put my arm through the empty window, bunched the sleeve of her shirt in my fist, and hauled her out of the jungle. She stumbled on the sharp edge, straddled it. I heard her cry out, but I assumed it was fear and I pulled her harder, doing what I thought was right. Trying to get her to safety.

We shoved through the circling crowd. No one knew what to do. As we left, I saw the mass split open, police breaking through, riot shields drawn up to push Walter to the ground. But then we were gone, slipping into the dark streets. The snow cold and blunt against our bare skin. Whenever I moved my head, glass fell from my hair, made a tinkling sound in my ears. I looked at my hand and my fingers were red. Phoenix leaned crookedly as we ran. We headed south, toward the dark zone, that block of blackness where we knew we could hide. I saw the broken yellow pawnshop sign. THE SALVATION ARMY SHELTER. The soot-black travel agency, its insides dug out. The street smelled of wet ash and garbage. My throat burned from running. Strangely bent, Phoenix hung between Marvin and me. She grabbed at our elbows, shoulders, upper arms, like a climber looking for a handhold.

"I'm all right," she kept saying as we tried to keep moving, even thought we weren't asking. We could still hear the sounds of the protest behind us, shouts and screams and glass breaking. People ran by us, their feet slapping down the centre of the street. Phoenix was too slow so Marvin stopped and like a fireman, he slung her over his shoulder as if he'd pulled her from a burning building. Blood ran down her leg. Coming quickly, coming so fast.

"Wait," I said as I looked back and saw the trail of it, fat, red spots marking our escape. "Put her down." My voice shrill, scared, but he ignored me and we moved under the overpass, across the clearing, until we reached the chain-link fence. Smoke trickled out of the barrel, but the fire had gone out.

Beside the overturned steel sink, Marvin laid her on the ground.

"Phoenix," I said. Over and over.

As I'd seen on TV, I asked her questions: how many fingers am I holding up, do you know where you are, what's your name, what's your real name, where were you born. She didn't answer them. She struggled to sit up, pulling at the clothing around her waist, her fingers fumbling on the button of her jeans. Marvin laid his hand on her chest to push her down. I could tell she wanted to look, to see what had happened, so I tugged up on her long black sweater. Marvin fished his cigarette tin out of his pocket and tried to light a match. His hands were shaking. The third one took and we saw. We saw.

A shard of glass stuck through her pants, into her upper thigh. Not large, maybe the size of a pencil worn to a usable stub. Marvin reached for it.

"Don't," I said, lifting one hand to stop him but I couldn't. Like a stinger, it came out easily. Then, black like oil, the widest tide of blood.

I bent over her, held on, my arms around her shoulders. She pushed me back and then lifted her hand to awkwardly touch my face. There was blood over everything so her finger slipped into my wet nostril and we actually giggled before I spoke, sobbing, saying only her name and *I love you. I love you. I love you.* The words in my mouth like a last hard sliver of candy, about to disappear.

"Oh, Jesus Christ," Thomson said as Marvin and I carried her inside. My hand was under the hem of her sweater, sliding on the blood-wet skin of her waist. We laid her on the mattress. Thomson stared at her, covered his face with his hands, lowered them. Turned away, turned back, as reality grabbed hold.

I didn't notice when Marvin left but some time later, an hour, maybe less, maybe more, he blasted through the front door. Our heads swivelled his way. I stifled a laugh. Hysterical.

He went into the kitchen and came back carrying his backpack. "Sandy," he said. "Sandy." His eyes wouldn't look at Phoenix. Thomson stared at him. "We have to go."

Phoenix was laid out, her hands layered on her belly, set there by Thomson. He sat beside her, his palm cupping her fingers' hard bones.

"No," he said.

"Sandy," Marvin said. "Get up."

I didn't move. I sat cross-legged at the end of the other mattress, my gaze glued to Phoenix, as if magnetized. Thomson kept talking to her, telling her good things, guiding her spirit to whatever came next, when all I could do was cry and cry.

"Thomson," Marvin said. "Thomson."

Thomson stopped talking. After a moment, he looked at Marvin.

"Do you want this for Sandy? Or for me? As soon as Walter's e-mail goes . . ."

"I don't care what happens to you," Thomson said.

Marvin flinched. A brief hardening of his face. He gestured to me. "Well, what about her?"

Thomson glanced at me. My face a blotchy mess, eyes blunted

from what I'd seen. I made a noise in my throat that was supposed to be words but didn't sound like anything.

"We have to go," Marvin said, rattling the map in his hand.

I gathered some things—Phoenix's scarves, her lavender oil, a few books. All shoved in Marvin's backpack. We took the wind-up flashlight, blankets, and what food we could find: plastic bags of cumin and cayenne stolen from the restaurants where Phoenix had once worked, lentils, dented cans of ham. Thomson wanted to bring Phoenix's body with us, but Marvin said no. Before we left, he set fire to the patchwork on the walls, the edge of the Jump Ship map, but it didn't take, kept extinguishing into acrid smoke. In the end we left her there, like something too expensive to keep.

We used money from Marvin's mother to fill the gas tank of the stolen car. For hours, we drove north. On that journey, Marvin hardened up, cast in his seat like bronze.

Thomson sat up front, bent forward, the seat belt wrapped twice around his still-bloodied hand. From behind, I laid my hands on his shoulders, rested the side of my face on the seat back, held in my own sorrow. The three of us were silent for a long, long time.

After a while, we reached a place of absolute darkness. The only light came from the car, pointing into a tunnel of snow.

Thomson navigated, following the flashlight's yellow circle on the map I'd taken from Walter's old apartment. He gave Marvin instructions. At the turn-off to the island, Thomson pointed left and Marvin swung onto the narrow street and the car slid over a patch of ice. He pumped the brakes until we came to a stop, sideways on the empty road.

"Are you sure about this?" he asked, and all Thomson said was "Go."

We wove through strange white mountains lit by the first pink of dawn. The forest on either side so thick it looked like walls. The car scraped over frost heaves and lurched through potholes and any town we went through seemed empty. Thomson turned to check on me in the back seat. I was holding on to Phoenix's red headscarf, the one printed with skulls and cobwebs, wet with tears I couldn't remember crying. He reached back and squeezed my arm with his thin fingers, a grip so hard it hurt.

We drove for hours more. Until we reached the other end of the island, until we found the lighthouse, until we couldn't go any farther unless we dropped off the limestone cliff, into the deep, cold lake. The water was silver in the daylight, shiny as a skyscraper. I had never seen such a beautiful place. So beautiful that even in the midst of all that pain, I felt it take my breath away and stir my shattered heart.

27 Island

That is the story, laid bare to you, Melissa. My own. Who I was and who I am. You, I have realized, never existed except as a shallow trough in the earth, a footprint that started this journey. I kicked it in. Obliterated the toe-marks, the heel. A burial.

Of course, there was grief in that for me. A letting-go. A new understanding of aloneness. But then Marvin called out for me, at the lighthouse, that night. He gestured with his bloody fingers to Samuel's hand shakily manning the flashlight. I left the girl and the baby and steadied the trembling beam by wrapping my hand around the boy's wrist, holding it still.

"Don't look," I whispered to him while Marvin pierced his father's skin with the curved needle, running the black thread through.

Melissa was the girl I thought I was feeding. The phantom.

But the one who exists, who I saw in the cave, flesh and fiery blood, gave me her name that night, in the lighthouse.

"I'm Abby."

She watched. Standing in the doorway, awkwardly moving her baby sister from one skinny hip to the other. Her gaze followed Marvin's fingers and occasionally jumped up to her father's face. Jack bit down on a towel. The fingers of his right hand dug into the dirt.

Eric and Graham drifted off to the steep edge of the shore. They stared at the black nothing of the lake, stretching out into the rest of a world that they would probably never see. Abby had seen some of it. I wondered what had happened to her after she'd left the island, a sleeping, sick toddler carried by her mother. Where had she gone? I thought of her in that cave, the dead woman decaying in the heat, and I realized that must have been Mona. Mona, my old friend. Abby's mom. "Hold it steady," Marvin said, and all eyes looked at me as I blinked back tears.

We stayed at the lighthouse that night. Jack couldn't walk so Marvin and the boys and I carried him inside. We laid him on the kitchen floor, and Marvin gave him one of the precious penicillin pills from the first aid kit. Abby pulled a blanket off the bed upstairs and folded a sweater for him to use as a pillow. She lay there with him while the boys watched her. As the night deepened, Eric and Graham gathered closer to their stranger sister. By dawn they were sleeping in a clump, like kittens.

I didn't sleep. I stayed outside with Shannon. She had refused to go in. Not with any words but only by lying there, like a slab of soundless rock, millions of years old. In the yard, I watched the bats swoop around us. When it got late and they slid into their hollows, I looked at the reflections of stars in the waves. My mind kept turning to you and then remembering and then seeing the emptiness that was there. I thought of Thomson and Phoenix. I thought of the travel agent and wondered who she'd left behind, what lives I'd played my part in damaging. More tears dropped on the knot of my hands. As if on a widow's walk, I stared out at the water although I felt I wasn't searching anymore.

Dawn came, deep streaks of red in the east. The eight of us started walking home. Shannon trailed behind like a squid's defensive ink. The boys and Abby closed around Jack. Marvin carried the gun. At the laneway to their farm we all stopped, except for Shannon, who rushed by and went into their house. The baby sputtered in Eric's arms.

"Abby shouldn't be here," said Jack.

"Should any of you?" Marvin asked.

Jack shrugged. "We'll see."

"Abby can stay with us," I said. Marvin looked at the ground. Another mouth would take Thomson's place and for now it would be all right.

"Wash that out," Marvin said, pointing at Jack's leg, the skin exposed under the large rip in his pants. Jack nodded. It was him who'd taught us: use water boiled with a small bit of cedar bark as antiseptic.

Abby's face looked even paler in the morning light. Stricken white. Dark circles like blotches of soot under her eyes. She stared at the distant door that Shannon had slammed shut. Jack put his arm around her and whispered into her ear. Graham kissed her on the cheek. The four of them started up the laneway, and I stood by her but she didn't acknowledge me. When my hand cupped her shoulder, she turned like a startled cat. I expected her to bolt, run off into the woods again, but she didn't. Fear vibrated through her body so I started speaking to her, telling her everything would be all right.

"You'll see your father every day," I said, but she still cried as we set off to walk the couple miles to our house. I didn't know what to do. I was not her mother. I had never been a mother. After a while, I gave up trying to soothe with words and just laid my hand on her back, between her shoulder blades, and kept it there as we walked. I felt the movement of her small body, the resistance, and the stubborn pushing forward, and felt proud of her. All she'd been through and still more to come. Really, we were strangers. She didn't know us: we were only people she stole from who had then tried to keep her away.

On our way up the laneway, I felt her start to pull away again. I took her hand, but she tugged against me, leaning toward the woods. She recognized the garden, I saw it in her face. *Those tiny footprints,* I remembered and looked down at her feet, dressed in a pair of dirty sneakers without any laces. She would never go back to living wild, I promised myself. There would always be food for her, no matter what. Marvin went ahead of us and opened our front door and waited. We offered her fish and potatoes, the leftover baked apples still sitting on the table, a warm bed to sleep in. Stories to be told. After a little while we went forward. Up the stairs, across the porch marked with Thomson's blood, inside.

"You knew," I said to Marvin the next night. I had opened a precious bottle of dandelion wine, wishing we'd had a drink or two with Thomson in those last days.

He twirled the golden liquid around in his glass. The night was cold so we'd lit a small fire in the living room hearth. Abby, upstairs, in bed. A sliver of contentment pierced the grief in me. I had hope.

Marvin nodded.

"When?"

"Not until that night. After the funerals."

"When our food was gone."

"Yes."

He sat on the brick hearth, feeding the fire with pickets we had harvested from a collapsed fence. He looked so much like he had—his young self costumed with the greying beard, the salt and pepper in his hair, the lines worn into his face from the weather. It was eerie, like seeing a ghost.

"Jack didn't know until that night either," he said. "All I knew was I found our food at the lighthouse and there were other things: clothes adjusted to fit, a pair of little kid shoes."

He cleared his throat. The words, the confession, came slowly.

"And I saw her. One eye peeking around the door frame, lost in its socket." He lifted his gaze to mine. "I couldn't take from that."

"That?"

"Her," he said. "Her."

"But our food?"

"Jack said he'd replace it."

"But you didn't want to tell me?"

He shook his head. "Couldn't."

"You don't trust me."

"You would have been over there, kidnapping her."

"No," I said, but perhaps he was right.

I picked up my wine.

"Do you trust me?" he asked.

"I don't know," I said. Twice our story had been told; three times, if you count this writing. I wondered if I could let it go, bury it, let it finally rot. Forgive.

"And the plates? The food I left out for her?"

"I ate it," he said. Eyes on the floor, he held his glass loosely. I watched the liquid tip like the whisky had so many years ago on my first night with Phoenix and Thomson, when I stayed there, when I tried to establish a new life. Marvin finally spoke and his voice was tight.

"I'm sorry," he said, and the regret moved in him like a rock-slide. I listened until the rumbling stopped and all was quiet again.

Epilogue

Abby stayed with us for several weeks. She helped us salt and smoke the fish and turn the rampant crop of zucchini into jars of relish. When I decided to trap the swarm and re-establish the hive, she helped with that too, pumping Thomson's smoker to sedate the bees. Marvin rebuilt the box hive and we stood it in the clearing, over Thomson's grave. He had argued against it, saying the mites were a losing battle, but I had decided that you didn't throw a bounty away because of the problems it presented, the required hard work.

Two weeks later, Shannon died of an overdose of Thomson's pills.

We buried her at the edge of the trees in the field that once grew hectares of wheat when Jack's grandmother was still alive. Samuel pounded a crude cross into the ground. I spoke about watching her give birth and about how brave she was. Tears were shed, which was good. No one spoke about relief.

That autumn, the boys and Abby worked hard to bring in their harvest of squash and corn and Marvin and I helped when we could. I continued tending to our own garden and looked after the baby, who Jack named Melissa after all. I found a woman in town whose baby had died and she lived at the Bobiwashes' house as a wet nurse until Melissa was weaned. She was pale and slow, shell-shocked by what had happened to her, and her hands only lifted the baby, fed her, set her down with the same kind of detachment Shannon had. It was up to us to give Melissa love. Sarah gave me tinctures and Melissa grew stronger. As she grew older, she was over so often she was practically our child. She would always be sickly, but you wouldn't know it by the way she flashed through the forest with her brothers, playing games in the summer.

"You spoil her," Marvin said often. Each time, I asked him how he thought that was possible. In the way that we lived, with so little, to be spoiled meant getting a second helping of rhubarb and honey or finding a bounty of raspberries in the woods. As she grew, her birthmark slowly faded, and I told her about her mother in the kindest way I could.

A few years later, Samuel married Albert's granddaughter and brought her home.

In October of that same year, Abby turned sixteen. For her birthday, I gave her the locket that Margo, Walter, and I had stolen. I told her that the pictures inside were my grandparents because I wanted to pass something on, even if it was a fictional lineage, even if we weren't blood. She fastened it around her neck and the chain glinted under her deep brown hair. At first I missed it, the embossed surface that I was used to worrying with my fingertips, but after a while my hands became still.

The supply ship came just before ice-in, two months after Thomson died. When Marvin saw it moving across the bay like a shadow from another time, he rowed along the shore to the pier to meet it. He came home with flour, aspirin, and news of the world. As he talked to me about swaths of suburbs taken by fire and a religious order moving into empty big-box stores, I remembered Thomson's story of a place he'd seen in Israel, where stone pillars had stood for centuries before an earthquake covered the city in dirt. Thousands of years later, it was unearthed by a man digging up his sewer system. Archaeologists excavated and there were the ancient buildings, the shops, the amphitheatre with seating for a thousand that had been filled in with silt. Thomson had walked the streets, stepping over grooves worn inches deep by the wheels of Roman chariots, thinking about the people who had lived there long ago.

Other ships have also started coming—lowering their sails to drop anchor in the bay and rowing to shore with items to trade. Oranges came one spring. Marvin and I traded several jars of honey for two and brought them to the Bobiwashes'. We split them into segments and watched Melissa, Abby, Graham, and Eric suck the sweet juice from the pulp. I told them stories about how it had been for us, when we were their age and the bright grocery stores were full of everything you could imagine: clothing, cat food, greeting cards, oranges, avocados, papaya full of clotted brown seeds like fish eggs. Fingers busy, they listened, wishing, I could tell, for that world, for all that was behind us. "Who wouldn't?" I said to Marvin when we left, and it was like what I'd said in the botanical gardens, a hundred-odd years earlier, but this time he listened and I could feel in him the regret and I felt it too. I reached for his hand and we walked like that, a rare and comforting thing.

When Abby was nineteen, she fell in love with a boy from town whose parents ran the new general store. Their wedding was held on a warm afternoon in late August, a decade almost to the day that she'd come back home as a castaway, a feral child. The sky glowed bright blue. I helped her get ready in her bedroom at the Bobiwash house and then we walked outside, into the field that stretched behind her father's home. The turkey vultures tipped their dark bodies over us, temporarily disappointed, the tops of their wings burnished amber by the sun.

In the evening, after the ceremony, Marvin and I walked home along the wide dirt path that ran alongside the impassable asphalt road. We passed the wreck of the old Toyota where the bees had once settled their swarm. Inside, Phoenix's red scarf lay rotting on the steering wheel. A rosy dusk hung all around us, above the branches of the ancient oak, over our house, the wide lake beyond. We looked at the dark orange ribbons in the sky.

"Hopefully we get some rain tomorrow," Marvin said as we walked down the path to the hives.

In the clearing, Marvin rolled a cigarette out of our homegrown tobacco. I used his match to light the half-burnt sumac stuffed in the tin smoker. I wanted to harvest a piece of honeycomb to give to Abby, for good luck, for fertility.

Before pumping smoke into the drift of insects, I laid a piece of peppermint cake on the nearest hive.

"There was a wedding today," I said as the bees floated up and around.

Whenever I talk to the bees, I feel Thomson. He's there, underneath us, in the earth. Over the years, I've stopped missing him so much. Phoenix too. They're always with me. And you are also. Not Abby, but whoever I thought you were. A shadow. A band of sunlight that breaks through the clouds. A ghost. It doesn't matter so much anymore because I have stopped looking for the things that I don't have. Each year, as the seasons change, as the days grow longer or incrementally shorter, losing fragments of their light, I concede. To the paths that are drawn. To the places my feet fall. To life.

Acknowledgments

The University of Guelph Creative Writing MFA program helped me immensely in honing my craft: thank you to profs and colleagues for enriching dialogue and specific feedback on early scenes. I'm deeply thankful to Susan Swan, who provided creative support, encouragement, and generosity with her mentorship over several months of this novel's growth. My agent, Samantha Haywood, has been an unfailing supporter, and I am truly grateful for her tireless work on my behalf. Editors Jane Warren and Anita Chong offered thoughts that certainly enriched the book. I'm especially thankful to Ruth Linka at Brindle & Glass and my editor, Lee Shedden, whose suggestions and astute observations helped polish those last rough spots.

Huge appreciation for my mother, Laura Carter, who read every single draft, offering thoughts, suggestions, and a listening ear as I wrestled with things. Nancy Jo Cullen provided perceptive notes, which I greatly appreciate. Thanks also to my stepfather, Ulrich Kretschmar, for corrections on bees and geology. I am blessed with incredible support from family and friends and am deeply grateful for my husband, Jason Mills, whose love and unending support (and kick in the behind when needed) mean the world to me.

Many resources inspired and assisted in the creation of this world and its characters, including *The Long Emergency* by James Howard Kunstler; *Why Your World Is About to Get A Whole Lot Smaller* by Jeff Rubin; *The Life of the Bee* by Maurice Maeterlinck; *Bee* by Claire Preston; *The Weather Underground*, directed by Sam Green and Bill Siegel; *The Power of the Powerless*, directed by Cory Taylor; and *A Place Called Chiapas*, directed by Nettie Wild. I am also indebted to the beekeepers I interviewed for various magazine articles, including Allan Sinton and Adi Stoer and especially Tom

Morrisey of Lavender Hills Farm, who gave me a face-to-face tour of his hives. Any mistakes are my own.

The excerpt from the Zapatista writings comes from the Fourth Declaration of the Lacandon Jungle, written by Subcomandante Marcos in 1996. "Do what thou wilt shall be the whole of the law" comes from Aleister Crowley. Vaclav Havel's quote about ideology that Thomson paraphrases is from Havel's essay "The Power of the Powerless," while the details of underwater Roman amphora are from an episode of *The Cousteau Odyssey*. The stories of lone survivors of collapsed civilizations are from *Collapse: How Societies Choose to Fail or Succeed* by Jared Diamond. Island history is drawn from *Exploring Manitoulin* by Shelley J. Pearen, on which my island is roughly based.

LAUREN CARTER has published in several literary journals and been nominated for the Journey Prize. *Lichen Bright*, her first collection of poetry, was long-listed for the ReLit Award. Her non-fiction articles have appeared in a variety of publications, including *National Geographic Traveler*, *This Magazine*, *The Georgia Straight*, *First Nations Drum*, *The Writer*, and *Adbusters*. A transplanted Ontarian, she currently lives in The Pas, Manitoba. *Swarm* is her first novel.